Top Ten bestseller Louise Bagshawe is the author of twelve novels, published in more than eight languages, most recently the massive *Sunday Times* bestseller *Glamour*. She is married with three children and lives in Northamptonshire.

Praise for Louise Bagshawe

'Juicy and compelling' *Heat*

'Jam-packed with edgy, sophisticated women and sexy, powerful men, you'll be hooked by the racy, romantic intrigues, and the twists and turns of the plot' *Woman*

'A page-turning novel of power, money, lust and greed' *Daily Express*

'Witty, inspirational and unputdownable' *Company*

'Intelligent and lively' *Mirror*

'A gloriously glossy blend of glitzy women, handsome men and the power of friendship' *Living Edge*

'A fiery read that's impossible to put down' *Now*

'Bagshawe has the classic blockbuster formula at her fingertips and she's not afraid to use it' *Daily Mail*

Also by Louise Bagshawe

Career Girls
The Movie
Tall Poppies
Venus Envy
A Kept Woman
When She Was Bad . . .
The Devil You Know
Monday's Child
Tuesday's Child
Sparkles
Glamour

Louise
Bagshawe

headline
review

Copyright © 2008 Louise Bagshawe

The right of Louise Bagshawe to be identified as the Author of
the Work has been asserted by her in accordance with the
Copyright, Designs and Patents Act 1988.

First published in 2008 by HEADLINE REVIEW
An imprint of HEADLINE PUBLISHING GROUP

First published in paperback in 2008 by HEADLINE REVIEW
An imprint of HEADLINE PUBLISHING GROUP

1

Apart from any use permitted under UK copyright law, this publication
may only be reproduced, stored, or transmitted, in any form, or by any
means, with prior permission in writing of the publishers or, in the case
of reprographic production, in accordance with the terms of licences
issued by the Copyright Licensing Agency.

All characters in this publication are fictitious and any resemblance
to real persons, living or dead, is purely coincidental.

Cataloguing in Publication Data is available from the British Library

978 0 7553 3606 7 (A-format)
978 0 7553 3607 4 (B-format)

Typeset in Meridien Roman by Avon DataSet Ltd,
Bidford-on-Avon, Warwickshire

Printed and bound in Great Britain by
Clays Ltd, St Ives plc

Headline's policy is to use papers that are natural, renewable and
recyclable products and made from wood grown in sustainable forests.
The logging and manufacturing processes are expected to conform to the
environmental regulations of the country of origin.

HEADLINE PUBLISHING GROUP
An Hachette Livre UK Company
338 Euston Road
London NW1 3BH

www.headline.co.uk
www.hachettelivre.co.uk

This book is dedicated to Tills

Acknowledgements

I'd like to acknowledge the heroic patience of my editor, Harrie Evans, who bore with me during my third pregnancy and as a new mother, juggling family and politics. Few writers are as lucky. As ever, her clear notes dramatically improved this book. Michael Sissons remains the best agent in London. He broke me as a novelist and I could not be more grateful for this career. Growing with Headline is a fantastic experience – I know I'm insanely lucky. Thanks to everybody in the firm, especially Kerr MacRae (can I have another Trump lunch please, Kerr?) and Jane Morpeth. Debbie Clement at Head Design did an amazing job with the look of the novel. Emily Furniss is a PR magician; Lucy Le Poidevin markets me brilliantly. The Sales force continually lift the books to new success all round the world. I am particularly grateful to Peter Newsom, James Horobin, Barbara Ronan, Katherine Rhodes, Diane Griffith, Sophie Hopkin, and Paul Erdpresser. And special thanks to Celine Kelly for putting up with me and saving my bacon on those reviews!

Prologue

It was a terrible thing, the old man thought, to be so rich, and to be so bored.

Clement Chambers sat, stretched out on a veranda chair, on the terrace of his mansion in the Seychelles, looking down over the cliffs, across a verdant hillside towards the sea.

His estate had a spectacular view of the azure waters of the Indian Ocean. They lapped against the fine powdery sands of his five-mile-long private beach, a facility he had visited a total of once in the last year. It took up the whole of the rocky inlet viewable from this angle; Clement loathed trespassers on his privacy.

The estate, the Palms, was a fortress. Oh, its walls were concealed, and it was heavily landscaped, but it backed into the sheer rock of the mountain and was surrounded on all sides by discreet and deadly soldiers.

Clement had enemies. You did not get to where he was without them.

He ensured he was safe. Safe from assassins, and kidnappers. He enjoyed the warm weather, the blue skies, the splendid isolation of the tropics. When you were worth several billion dollars, anything you needed in life came to you.

His security firms vetted all his staff. And all his lovers. Every one of them understood the sovereign importance of complete secrecy. Money, and fear, had kept it that way. Not a whisper of scandal ever reached the outside world.

He watched the waves lap his beach. And his brilliant mind started to plan.

Clement Chambers had a reputation. He was a gentleman, and that mattered immensely to him. He had a coat of arms. Inherited when . . . well, on his brother's death. Even though he had spent three decades in the tropics, surrounded only by lackeys, he was careful to live his life as an Englishman abroad. Rather like Noël Coward. Clement admired Noël Coward. He wore white linen suits and Panama hats. His apparel was designed in St James's and Savile Row. His wine cellar was unsurpassed, his house was hung with glorious English masterpieces including a Stubbs and a Constable. He donated large sums of money to the right charities, and he was a member of London clubs he never set foot in; White's and the Travellers.

For most of his life he had cared about money, and through money, power. Now that the Chambers Corporation was a gargantuan global firm, his pristine reputation mattered more to Clement than anything else. The great museums of the world had wings named after him. As did many of the most prestigious hospitals. Sloane-Kettering, in New York, was the latest beneficiary. And if a disgruntled employee, or the loser in some deal, were to complain, or dare to write or broadcast something bad about Clement Chambers, then his overpaid contingent of libel lawyers sprang into action.

He received good press these days.

Nothing but good press.

It was all about protecting that great reputation, Clement thought. But now he was safe, now he was impregnable, he was bored, very bored. It was time to inject a little fun into his life.

Clement Chambers was about to shake things up.

He smiled gently at the prospect. Yes; she would do. She was interesting, so pliant, but so sharp. A tigress.

And he always enjoyed setting the cat amongst the pigeons.

Chapter One

It was *GLITZ* magazine's hottest cover of the year.

A sensational scoop. Never before had they agreed to be photographed together. The women London was obsessed with. The girls every working woman wanted to be.

The fabulous Chambers cousins.

They were living the dream. While the city's career girls stumbled out of bed, snatched breakfast and clambered on to the Tube and buses, ready for another tough day at the office, the Chambers girls were lying in bed, idly preparing themselves for their massages, their shopping sprees, or another celebrity-crammed party. They had the best addresses, the hottest wardrobes, the sharpest haircuts. They were attractive.

And they didn't do one damn thing to earn it.

The public didn't know whether to love them or hate them. But British girls all secretly yearned to *be* them.

The magazine flew off the shelves. On the cover, the Chambers girls posed, styled in long white gowns with gold necklaces and armlets, like the classical goddesses they were named for.

Juno. Tall and statuesque, a gold circlet in her long dark hair, wound into a plait and worn like a crown. Ever insistent on her dignity, a pure cloak of ivory wool fell around her shoulders, to cover her arms. Not as beautiful as the others, but still striking; handsome, perhaps, with cool blue eyes and pale skin. Queen of the gods; queen of London's snobby social circuit. Her soirées were legendary, her contacts book read like a copy of *Debrett's*. Safely married, Juno was a favourite with society mavens from Sloane Square to Eaton Square, from Ascot to Glyndebourne.

Athena, her little sister. Her scruffy, private identity hidden in the photo shoot, brilliant academic Athena Chambers had the mind – and she had the money. Styled for the fantasy of worker bees everywhere, Athena was unrecognisable; her hair tumbling down her back, professionally made up, her feet forced into unfamiliar heels. The looks she couldn't be bothered about were on display for all to see. Toned arms and an athletic body, an oval face, high cheekbones, and the same luminous gaze as her sister.

Athena was one of her generation's brightest historical scholars. Her pamphlets and essays received wide acclaim. She lived in Oxford in a glorious townhouse, and had no doubt she would become a tenured professor. But not for her the honourable poverty of the brilliant teacher. Her cleverness was buttressed with cash. Athena ate caviar, drank champagne, and had a collection of antiques that could grace a museum.

Across from these two were their cousins. Diana Chambers, her slender arms posing, holding up a golden goblet of wine. Caramel hair, cut into a sharp flame, flowed over her shoulders, complementing her snowy dress. A little more curvy than Athena, Diana was London's latest greatest 'It Girl'; she had no more intention of working than her cousin Juno, but stuffy high society bored her to death. Diana Chambers meant *style*. She attended every hot play, every great film premiere. She was seen at impossible-to-get-into exhibitions by London's hottest artists. If she was photographed wearing a new designer, sales would soar. And her parties were stuffed with the funkiest novelists, musicians, photographers, and models. Diana Chambers had made partying an art form. She was the Victoria Beckham of the cognoscenti – if she touched something, it was in style. First-year film students, the backstage crowd at London Fashion Week, the journalists on the glossy magazines – they all wanted to be like Diana. She was the new Chloë Sevigny. And everybody knew that Diana Chambers, someday soon, would simply select a billionaire of her own and marry him. It was just a matter of time.

And right in the front – of course – Venus. Staring brazenly into the camera, her thousand-watt smile seducing millions of readers. A shimmering, pearlescent robe did little to conceal her golden skin and curvy breasts. Wasp-waisted, Venus had expensively dyed flaxen-blond hair. The Chambers diamonds, a family heirloom, glittered brilliantly around her throat and on her lobes. She was eight and a half stone of gorgeous, and she absolutely adored the camera.

Venus Chambers was a little slice of Hollywood in Notting Hill. As toned, tanned and blonde as any airhead model on the Sunset Strip, she was perfectly groomed and perfectly gorgeous. She was an actress, and didn't you know it. Even if Venus was far more famous for being one of the Chambers girls than for any acting she'd ever done. You took one look at the confident, flirty butterfly on the cover of *GLITZ* and you felt it couldn't be long. Venus's big break as a film star would be along any minute. Because that was how life worked when you were a Chambers girl.

You lived in paradise. Where nothing ever went wrong.

Inside the glossy covers, there were more pictures of the girls, their jewels, their fast cars, their stylish homes. Less of Athena, who didn't present herself well. But the other three posed in depth, and the mag got a stylish silhouette shot of Athena, her wild hair blowing around her on a blustery Oxford day, walking into the Bodleian Library. There was a long puff piece about their likes and dislikes, and their close cousinly relationship. But the magazine really sold on its daring. *GLITZ* actually published photos of the Seychelles. The crystal-blue waters, the white sands and palm trees, and the lush forests on the hills. That generic shit was as close as they would get to the source of all the girls' wealth . . .

Clement Chambers. Their uncle. Multi-billionaire. Reclusive genius. Head of the Chambers Corporation, a multinational with interests from diamond mines to oil wells, mobile phones to construction. Clement Chambers, respected across the world as a man of substance. Somebody not to be messed with. Unmarried, childless and elderly, he guarded his privacy as fiercely as armed soldiers guarded his vast estate on the tropical island. The Chambers girls were his nieces.

And they were well looked after.

Their glamorous lifestyles were funded entirely by him. Half a million a year, every year, to burn through as they wished. The magic of their uncle's name. And the prospect that between them, these four women would one day inherit his colossal fortune. A sum that made their trust fund look like peanuts.

It was a fairytale. Four upper-class girls with little money to their name. Venus and Diana were orphans, Juno and Athena the children of impoverished professors. And one day, when they were in their teens, their rich, reclusive uncle appears and announces he will take care of his nieces' finances.

Every January, the money poured into the four bank accounts. Every December, it was exhausted. But why worry? the article pointed out gaily. Plenty more where that came from!

The fabulous Chambers girls were the only people allowed into their uncle's compound, other than his staff. The private Mr Chambers, the journalist wrote breathlessly, summoned them every 15 December. They stayed for Christmas, and left after Boxing Day. That was the only contact they had with their uncle, all year round.

Right now they were rich.

One day they'd be tycoons.

And all for doing nothing.

Thousands of secretaries, teachers, florists, nurses and bankers picked up their copies of *GLITZ*, flipped the pages, and sighed with longing.

Trust-fund princess. Nice work if you could get it.

Chapter Two

'Telegram, madam.'

Diana looked up from the pile of gold-edged heavy cream cards that she was sorting into lots. Seating plans. They were the work of the devil. She'd been at this chart for hours, and it still wasn't perfect.

'What do you mean, telegram?' She smiled up at her butler, Ferris, an old dear she'd inherited when she bought the flat. It was such fun to have a proper butler. Nobody else her age had any staff other than a nanny, or possibly a life coach. But Diana Chambers knew how to do style.

She shrugged, a little slither of cream silk and palest peach cashmere, delicate mother-of-pearl bangles jangling on her tanned skin. 'Nobody sends telegrams any more. Unless it's a wedding.'

'I believe it comes from the Seychelles, madam,' said Ferris, his wrinkled face inscrutable.

'Of course,' Diana said at once. 'Uncle Clem. He would, I suppose.'

A light frown crossed her pretty face. They had only

just finished the Christmas celebrations. She wasn't due back for a year.

What could Clement want?

'I hope he's not ill,' Diana said with genuine concern, taking the brown envelope from the silver tray. 'Thank you, Ferris.'

She ripped it open.

Dear Diana,

I require your presence back at the Palms. In fact, I will need to see you and all the girls here at once. Pack a suitcase and take the next plane out. This afternoon, from Stansted. It's a family matter. Don't bother calling — I prefer to tell you all face to face.

Yours ever,

Uncle Clem

Diana jumped up from her Mies van der Rohe sofa, architecturally tilted backwards at just the right angle on metal poles. Adrenalin pumped through her. She looked all around her, drinking the place in, as though she might lose it. After two years of work, Diana's duplex flat was absolutely perfect; two thousand square feet of prime Kensington terrace, brilliantly redecorated to her own design. She had personally selected every-thing, from the reclaimed Victorian fireplace to the Carrera marble in the wetroom, skilfully mixing classical pieces with the best of modern design. She'd wanted all her glitterati friends to be jealous, and it had worked. They were.

And not just of her impeccable taste and packed parties. Diana was single and very good-looking, with the money and flair to work it to the full. But unlike most of the girls on the circuit, she didn't have to marry some crusty old financier or weak-chinned landed aristocrat to bag her place in moneyed society.

Diana Chambers had the best of everything.

And a very rich uncle to pay for it.

So much better, she reminded herself, than interfering old parents who might try to keep tabs on her life, her alcohol consumption, or worse still, her shoe budget.

Rupert and Hester Chambers were dead. Diana knew them only through photographs; a handsome young couple, he tall and blond, she slender and dark but with an attractive touch of baby fat still around her face. Hester smiled a lot and had retained her dimples. They beamed at her, in their ugly sixties wedding outfits, from the steps of the Brompton Oratory. Rupert had loved fast cars, and his dodgy second-hand Aston Martin had skidded and killed them both on an icy road in Gloucestershire on New Year's Day, when Diana was just two and a half years old. They had been coming back from the pub. She didn't remember that day, but she'd always resented that part of the story; the suggestion always was that Daddy had taken a couple of drinks. Careless. Selfish. When he killed them, he left a hole in their lives.

That betrayal placed her and Venus first in the sole care of their crotchety maternal grandmother, and then at boarding school.

Just as well. Elspeth Heckles, their grandmother, who found it hard to cope with the loss of her daughter and the arrival of two young toddlers, was permanently exhausted and cross. The sisters struggled along in her small rented house on the edge of the New Forest, their modest inheritance saved by Elspeth with great discipline so that they might attend a good school. She did her duty, and two months after Venus began to board, at the age of eleven, Elspeth died, leaving the girls little but her personal effects.

School provided structure, and a succession of parent substitutes, none of them much good. Diana and Venus learned to take care of themselves. But they were in separate years, and as they grew older, they grew further apart. When you're a teenager, two years is a world of difference.

The executors of their parents' will arranged for the sisters to stay at school during the holidays, where a skeleton staff looked after the various stragglers still in the building; the forlorn daughters of diplomats posted to dangerous hotspots, girls who needed remedial holiday coaching, and the daughters of some of the teachers who lived on site. Diana and Venus, unlike all their friends, dreaded the school holidays. They hung together at those times as best they could, but longed for a return to normality.

People. Light. Noise. Diana hated abandonment, she liked to be in a crowd. And Venus dealt with life even more simply: she flashed her beautiful smile, dyed her long hair blond and flirted with the entire world. If you couldn't get love, Diana thought with pity, adulation was an acceptable substitute.

But when she was fifteen, the telegram came. The telegram that changed their lives.

Uncle Clem.

Diana flashed back on that moment now, as she held this opened telegram in her lap. She'd forgotten. Of course. Telegrams were Clem's choice of communication, his style; no emails or faxes from him, at least not to family.

Venus had come running up to her after lunch, as the girls streamed out of the refectory. Thirteen years old now, to Diana's fifteen, and turning into a real beauty.

'Di, Di!'

'Hiya.' She had been feeling down that day, and slipped an arm around her little sister's shoulders, giving her a hug. 'What's going on?'

'Did you get that telegram?'

Diana blinked. 'What?'

'That brown envelope,' Venus said. She tugged impatiently at Diana's arm. 'Come on, come to the pigeon-holes. I got one, tell me if it's fake, go on.'

Only mildly curious – her sister was always exuberant – Diana trotted along to the wall of pigeonholes, marked out for each girl by surname. Venus's was empty, but Diana noted there was a slim brown envelope in hers. She took it out, examined it. It actually was a telegram. She'd heard them read out at weddings, back when Granny dragged her along to them. But who used them in real life?

'Open it,' Venus pleaded. 'It *says* it's from Uncle Clem.'

Now she had her sister's complete attention.

Diana froze. 'Uncle Clem?'

Elspeth had talked about him, once or twice, and not in approving terms. Their distant, long-lost relation. Their father's elder brother, who had made a fortune, cut off his family, and left England to live on some tropical island. Nobody heard from him, not even a card at Christmas.

Excitedly, she ripped the envelope open. The telegram was printed in pale grey letters, on that particular kind of paper. She read it aloud.

Dear Diana and Venus,
Now that your cousin Juno, the eldest of my nieces, is sixteen years old, I am establishing a trust fund for the welfare of the four of you. The money will be administered in your minority by my solicitors and will pay for staff and housing. Upon your eighteenth birthdays, you will come into an annual allowance of half a million pounds a year

'My God!' Diana said. She gripped Venus's arm.

'Is it true, Di?' Venus was breathless with excitement. 'Do you think it's true?'

Diana didn't answer; she read on.

which you will then be able to spend as you like. From this summer, you and Venus will live in my house in Eaton Square in London, with some of my permanent staff to attend you. Treat them as staff. I do not encourage familiarity.

'I – it sounds like he means it,' Diana said. Her head was spinning, and she felt sick with nerves, as though she wanted to vomit. 'Oh God, Venus!'

I intend to take charge of family arrangements. Your cousins Juno and Athena Chambers will be joining you at your school.

Venus pulled a face. 'Don't like them much.'

You are to remember at all times that you carry my name and will now be associated with me. I shall remain in the Seychelles but will be keeping a weather eye on your progress; you will not contact me. If I wish, I will contact you. I rarely make requests, but when I do, I expect to have them granted.

Yours ever,
Clement Chambers

Diana leaned her shoulder against the wooden boxes of the pigeonholes.

'London,' she said. 'Our own house. London parties. *Half a million a year.*'

'If it's true, we'll never have to get a job!' Venus was ecstatic. 'Never! Oh Di, stuff my bloody geography homework, I'm not doing it. Who cares? I don't have to do anything I don't want to!'

'No, no.' Diana hurried to put her straight. 'He said we reflect him. You have to go on as before, nothing wild.'

'If it's true, I *love* Uncle Clem,' Venus said happily. 'I'm going to write and tell him I love him and tell him thank you. What do you think he's like? Do you think he looks like Dad?'

Diana watched her eager little sister's young face glowing and felt sad.

'No, darling, read it again. Uncle Clem doesn't want us to contact him.'

'But why?'

Diana shrugged. Why had her father got drunk and then got into his car? Why had he done it, left her and Venus alone? The ache that never went away.

'You remember what Granny used to say. That's just how he is. I think we'd better go along with it.'

And they had. All of it. The large house, where they didn't fraternise with the servants, but did meet their friends. They even looked forward to holidays. Life got easier. Diana noticed the impact of money right away.

Noticed how everybody started sucking up to them . . . And then they had to deal with the arrival of their cousins. Scruffy, bookish Athena and withdrawn Juno, boasting two living parents.

In deference to Uncle Clem's wishes, the four girls socialised. But they were all in different years, so there was a merciful gap. The cousins were courteous, but not particularly close. Diana and Venus envied Juno and Athena their parents, and Juno and Athena, in turn, envied their cousins their independence.

Clem's money sometimes seemed the strongest bond they had. Even at fifteen, and not receiving any of it actually in her pocket, Diana knew better than to jeopardise that cash. She and Venus may have been a little arrogant, and indolent, but they *always* did just as Uncle Clem wanted.

They had never met the man. But he was the most powerful influence in their lives.

It was only on her eighteenth birthday that things changed for good. Diana was summoned to London to be shown her new bank account, with its starting balance for the year.

Just as promised. Five hundred thousand pounds.

And with it, the need to actually go and see Uncle Clem – every Christmas. The telegram came to inform the cousins that in future they'd be spending two weeks every December, every Christmas, in the tropics. No other relatives invited.

Diana was not sentimental – how could she be? Christmas in the Seychelles was a chance to get out of cold, wet London.

It was also a chance to avoid the annual lull in the social scene. Christmas and New Year, a tortuous, inevitable break in the London party circuit. An almost vicious reminder of the fragility of friendship, how when the chips were down, it always came second; Diana's girlfriends and drinking buddies all dispersed like seeds from a dandelion clock, drifting back to estates in Gloucestershire, houses in Sussex, farms in Yorkshire, apartments in Manhattan – wherever the parents, or in-laws, lived. Friends didn't matter a bit when family – parents, children, grannies, fiancés – pressed their prior claim.

Christmas and New Year were the worst times for Diana Chambers, growing up. Venus said she didn't care, but how could that be true? Their cousins had them to stay every year. Diana had to endure it; watching Juno and Athena laugh with their mummy and daddy, pretending to like the lame presents that were all the professors could afford, and feeling guilty because she knew perfectly well that everybody meant to be kind. The loss of her mum and dad coloured every second, every moment of Diana's life.

But when Clement called them for Christmas, Diana was on an equal footing with Athena and Juno. And if they rubbed each other the wrong way, well, so what? At least now she was in the sun, and the four cousins were equals – all just Clement's nieces. However domineering and grouchy he was, Diana was grateful for that.

Uncle Clem's money protected Diana's whole life. The thought of anything changing that prickled the hairs on the back of her neck. Her stomach churned anxiously.

Screw the party. She had to go.

Athena, Juno, and Venus would all have received their own telegrams; Uncle Clem was *such* an old drama queen.

Diana sighed. Her schedule was jam-packed. And the press were supposed to be coming to the soirée tomorrow. She'd harangued, pleaded and bribed them into showing up; there would be a healthy sprinkling of society columnists and photographers. Diana was just starting to get some column inches, after much work and toil and rivers of champagne. Staying London's top It Girl took a lot of work. It wasn't enough to be rich; she also wanted to be famous. Not, like Venus, famous for being an actress or a model. Diana wanted to be famous just for being Diana. That was one role she'd never lose.

The party was supposed to go a long way towards her social ascent. Lots of juicy coverage and society-page pics. The *GLITZ* cover was a milestone. Diana wanted to follow it up.

But Uncle Clem had called.

There was nothing else for it.

'Ferris!' Diana called lightly.

He was with her in a second.

'Yes, madam?'

'Cancel the party at Cho's, would you?'

Behind the laconic request lay a solid morning's work. It would mean hundreds of calls, irate suppliers, and explanations to journalists and paparazzi. But the rich young woman paid well, and her butler's expression never flickered.

'Very good, madam.'

'Family emergency. Tell them that. I have to be on a plane.' Diana glanced apologetically at her thick pile of cards. 'Sorry for the bother, Ferris, but you understand, don't you?'

Indeed he did. For Diana Chambers didn't have a bean. Uncle Clement's cash paid for everything.

For Diana. For her beautiful, untalented sister Venus. For the cousins, scruffy Athena and snobby Juno. Each rolling in money, not a penny of it their own.

When Uncle Clement called, they came.

Diana picked up the phone. Time to call her cousins.

Chapter Three

Athena Chambers looked up at the professors.

The sedate tick-tock of the fine grandfather clock was unsettling her. Heavy brass hands moved around its aged face, the pendulum under the oak with its walnut inlay swinging loudly back and forth.

It was because there was no other sound in the room.

Tick-tock. Tick-tock.

In front of her, on the raised dais, sitting on their carved chairs, the senior dons of the faculty were shuffling their papers. They pushed glasses up their noses, lowered their heads and whispered intently to each other.

Athena Chambers sat below them, on the floor of the college hall, and tried to remain calm.

They couldn't deny her this post. Could they?

She was one of Oriel's best performers, with an outstanding first in an unpopular subject. Particularly gifted in Old Norse. Where else were they going to find their next generation of dons?

She had so many advantages. For one thing, she was

rich. There would be no begging for pay rises, no pushing for digs in college property. Athena lived in a splendid townhouse on Walton Street, close to the Randolph Hotel, and she drove a vintage racing-green Aston Martin. She was young, and had an unblemished academic record. Money had allowed her to concentrate, free of worry. She had seized that chance. She had a fine body of work. And she liked to think she was funky – relatively, at least.

Of course, that wasn't saying much. Relative to *this* lot, Camilla Parker Bowles was funky. The men on the stage glowered at her in their crumpled suits.

Athena was slim and pretty. Unkempt, perhaps, but so were most professors. She never made any attempt to make herself up or colour her hair. It curled around her shoulders in a soft mousy brown. For Athena, 'grooming' was remembering to brush her teeth. She wore dowdy, ill-fitting clothes from high-street shops – Jaeger mostly – and no jewellery other than her beloved signet ring. A gift from her beloved father. An academic. Athena desperately wanted to follow in his footsteps.

She crossed her long legs, hidden in their baggy trousers, and waited.

'Miss Chambers.'

Professor Mellon, the head of the panel, addressed her. Athena sat up straighter. Mellon was a brilliant philologist and a fellow of All Souls, something she desperately wanted to be. That was the scholars' equivalent of an

Oscar. He'd taught her back in her second year as an undergrad and come on to her. Ridiculous: he was married with two kids. Not to mention older than Methuselah.

But then most dons hit on Athena once or twice. She didn't hold it against them.

'Thank you for coming in to see us,' he said coolly. 'Your work is certainly impressive.'

'Thank you.' Athena smiled.

'But the panel doesn't feel you have quite the right qualifications for this particular post.'

'What?' Athena exclaimed. 'I have a starred first. I have distinctions in every paper!'

'You've certainly done well.' Dr Finkel, a thin, ferret-like man in a pink shirt, chimed in. 'But sometimes these things are a matter of temperament.'

'The panel feel you would suit a further period of research. Some publications . . .'

'Perhaps abroad – Harvard or Yale have excellent pro-grammes for women scholars,' added Professor Richards. He was the youngest, and wore a thin, cheap suit. His gaze on her now was full of hostility.

'They call it affirmative action,' Dr Finkel explained, as though to a child.

'I know what they call it,' Athena snapped. 'I don't need it.'

'The panel has decided to award the fellowship else-where, but thank you for coming in.' Professor Mellon snapped his folder shut and pushed back his chair.

The interview was over.

'Just one second. Who is the lucky applicant?'

They looked at each other reluctantly. That information would be a matter of public record. They had to tell her.

'Mike Cross,' Professor Richards said flatly.

Athena exploded. 'Mike got an *upper second*. I have better results than him—'

'He's also a rowing blue and takes part in social occasions. Some of this has to do with how we expect a research fellow to contribute to university life,' Professor Mellon said.

'And his work shows flashes of brilliant *original* thought,' Dr Finkel added.

Like hell – Mike Cross was a big, lumbering sack of potatoes. His last original thought was where to find Oxford's cheapest beer.

'Mike Cross is—'

'Our choice,' Professor Richards interrupted.

'You don't want to come across as *catty*,' Dr Finkel sneered. 'You know that's a perception problem with some of our lady academics. If I were you I'd congratulate the winning candidate. Maybe look for a postgraduate course to do.'

'But . . .' Athena nearly exploded with frustration.

'Really, Miss Chambers,' Professor Mellon said with elegant disdain. 'It's over.'

*

26

Athena stomped back up the High Street towards Carfax, hands jammed in her pockets, her long hair blowing about in the January breeze. Miserably humiliated. Bastards!

She had the brains, she knew it.

She'd done the work.

But bottom line – they hated her.

Mike Cross she couldn't be angry at. He was a nice enough bloke. Big and burly, with a knocked-up girlfriend and a respectable, second-class mind. But he knew how to charm the crusty old dons out of the trees. He'd hang around, talking about rugby and cricket, getting slightly drunk on expensive claret. Gossiping, like men did. Talking dirty about women . . .

Maybe even about her. *Probably* about her.

Plus there was the money. The dons all lived in rented college houses, or if they'd miraculously fluked on to the housing ladder, in tiny one-bedroom flats. Housing cost money up here; Oxford was the new London. The dons drove old bangers and wore their shoes until they developed holes. Athena didn't need to get on the brain-drain bandwagon and teach in America for respectable cash. She just had to sit in Walton Street and collect Uncle Clement's cheque.

She knew they were jealous. They loathed it, the fact that she never wanted for anything, and never checked a price. She would eat regularly at Le Manoir aux Quat' Saisons and hadn't bothered learning to cook, and if she

27

felt like studying an original Norse text she would fly out first class to Iceland and stay in a boutique hotel, ignoring the outrageous Scandinavian prices, and look at it herself.

Why did she need a job? Athena could feel them thinking that, the eyes on her, ignoring her cheap clothes, going straight to her Chanel bag or her hand-made shoes.

Marie Antoinette. Rich bitch. Stuck-up single woman.

Athena had the grades, the pedigree and the results. But this was her fourth interview for a research fellowship this year. And the old-boy network didn't want to know.

She reached her house and unlocked the door. Time for a shower, maybe a brisk run around Christ Church meadows. Get the aggression out. Think, for goodness' sake.

What the hell was she going to do next?

The phone in the hall rang. Maybe they'd changed their minds.

'Athena Chambers.'

'Hi, darling.' The low, affected drawl instantly set Athena's teeth on edge. Oh yes, her bubble-headed cousin Diana. Athena had had more than enough of her ditzy socialite act over Christmas.

'What is it, Diana?'

'Have you got your telegram yet?'

'Telegram?'

She looked behind her on to the seagrass carpet. Yes, there was a marked brown envelope.

'It's Uncle Clem,' Diana was saying into her ear. 'He wants to see us.'

Uncle Clem. *The money.* A shiver ran down Athena's spine.

'Lower,' Venus murmured, her mouth hidden in the crook of her arm.

'How's that?'

She gave a lazy 'mmm'. Pure contentment.

The Palladian was the smartest new beauty salon in London, so chic it was almost off the radar. All the hot magazines had been here last week, though, and she expected a storm of features to break in a month or so.

Most of them would report the presence of luscious Venus Chambers. It mattered for an actress to be seen in the right places at the right time. That ahead-of-the-curve flavour. She cultivated it assiduously.

The masseuse, a real Swede, kneaded her impeccably tanned flesh with long, smooth strokes. Venus could feel all the kinks of the day working themselves out. When the girl grabbed her feet, sore from a day of walking around in teetering Manolos, and pressed her thumbs into the high arches, Venus gasped in pleasure.

She was lying on a soft massage table, stripped down to her La Perla knickers, coppery lace to match her glowing skin. Long, silky, expensively blond hair, brushed away from the nape of her neck, fell in a smooth stream towards the floor. They were on the limestone deck of the swimming pool, mounted on the hotel's spectacular roof garden. The shadows from the azure water danced on the marble ceiling, sending dappled light all around the room. Towering walls of glass surrounded the heated pool, and Venus looked out through half-closed lids at the great sweep of London, sparkling in the crisp autumn sun.

Fabulous. She half-heartedly tried to stay awake. She didn't want to miss the sensations of her massage. Ulrika was the best in the business.

Besides, it was all good for the image. And image was vital . . .

Venus let her mind wander.

Tonight there was that important meeting with the producer at the Groucho Club. The Austrian, Hans Tersch. He had a hot script, *Maud*, about the civil war between Stephen and Matilda. Brave knights, white stallions, swords and cloth of gold . . . it was a dream picture. Venus was desperate for an audition. She'd been working out with one of Chelsea's top personal trainers, Rafael, and her arms and stomach were gracefully toned; not too muscled, but beautifully strong. She was at her slimmest and loveliest. Perfect for the part. The last three movies she'd been up for hadn't come off, and her most recent role was in a BA commercial, relaxing elegantly on a first-class bed.

Typecasting.

She got work, sure. Small parts in indie films. Occasionally a speaking role in TV drama. At least Venus could be choosy; she didn't do any of the really bad stuff: extra work, walk-ons, cheesy presenting jobs on satellite channels flogging holidays. There no question of that.

She hardly needed the money.

Her agent, Lucy, was always reminding her that she already had more press than most of the top Briterati – certainly as much as Jude and Kate, for example. Why bother trying to kill yourself chasing big parts that never came? Venus could cash in on her It Girl clout. Especially if she agreed to do anything with her cousins. Gorgeous siblings always sold well, but four upper-class cousins, named for Greek and Roman goddesses? It was gold. They could build on that *GLITZ* cover . . .

But Venus refused to go for the Paris Hilton angle. She loved movies. They said glamour to her, beauty, and fame. So she already had wealth; so what? she thought sleepily, as those sure fingers prodded and stroked her towards bliss. That was only the first step on the road . . .

After this massage, Venus would pop down to the beauty parlour. Get her nails reburnished and her toes buffed and whitened, then her hair washed and blow-dried. After that, a seaweed facial and full make-up application by Celine, who was truly an enchantress. And then it was all a question of selecting just the right bag and shoes for her Alexander McQueen satin halter-neck dress . . .

Venus Chambers would be dazzling. British, aristocratic, perfectly dressed, and all over a buff, tanned, blonde and white-toothed body that could belong to any starlet in LA.

Venus smiled. She was arrogantly sure she'd get this part. And if she had to flirt with the producer, then so what? She'd done plenty of that in her time. Idly, Venus wondered about her mother and father. Would Daddy have disapproved? But he had drunk himself and Mummy dead, hadn't he? So he wasn't around to veto her outfits. Or choice of career.

There was a soft sound of padding feet. Venus half opened one eye to see a receptionist, in the muted beige DKNY shift dress the girls all wore, approaching her with a small envelope on a tray.

'A telegram for you, madam,' she said.

'What?' Venus sat bolt upright, her languor forgotten. 'A telegram?' she snapped.

'Yes, ma'am.'

Who the hell would be sending her a telegram? Venus had a bad feeling about this . . .

The receptionist was still waiting, a bit nervously. Venus shook herself; image, Venus, image.

'Thank you.'

She favoured the girl with a dazzling smile, and ripped open the envelope.

Oh hell, she thought.

Venus pulled the towel up around her breasts and sat up straight.

'I have to go.' All the fog of pleasure had disappeared from her voice. 'Hand me my gown,' she said. 'I'm getting dressed.'

Juno Chambers Darling ignored her husband. Such a decision, what to do in Cannes. Some of his friends just weren't the right sort of people.

'So that's all right for the thirtieth? You'll throw the party?'

Jack was insistent. His rich Scottish burr cut through her musing.

'I'll think about it,' she said. Honestly, why couldn't Jack just accept his good fortune? All this messing about with business, and it never went anywhere. Cooking. Was that a proper occupation for a man?

When they married, Juno had been sure she could tame Jack Darling. He was sexy, no doubt about that, with his rugby-player body and his dark eyelashes. Very different from the chinless wonders her parents had introduced her to. Jack was a rough diamond, and all she had to do was polish him.

Juno was the eldest of the Chambers cousins. Her father had named her for the queen of the gods. She was the plainest, but she lived up to her name: she was used to having things just as she wanted them. She'd wanted

Jack, and now she'd got him. Yet she also demanded that Jack behave the way she thought a husband should.

But things hadn't worked out that way. Jack was stubbornly resistant to going along with Juno's plans to turn him into a trophy husband. Although she'd forced refinements on him – the bespoke suits, the John Lobb shoes, the memberships of the good clubs – he remained, frustratingly, Jack.

He had adapted poorly to her social life, and her desire to get established in the new expensive London townhouse. Instead of enjoying the Season and being seen at the right events, he insisted on setting up a branch of his little sandwich deli in west London. He worked late into the night and came home smelling of food. And he refused to take a penny from her.

They rowed. Frequently. These days, he was less and less willing to shower and come out as her escort. Even his handsomeness, his great asset, was diminishing as lack of sleep made him irritable and pasty-faced.

Seven-year itch? Seven months more like. Juno was starting to wonder if she hadn't made a horrible mistake.

'It's for my backers,' Jack said coldly. 'Business. The investors from France and Italy for the restaurant. We *need* to throw that party.' He softened a little. 'You know you're brilliant at it.'

Juno smiled bleakly. 'I'll see what I can do . . .'

She had no intention of putting together some ugly little soirée for greasy Continental cooks, all Lambrusco and plates of olives and salami. There was a winter ball at the Connaught in aid of Cancer Research. All her friends were going, even her cousin Diana. The press would be there, and Juno wanted to put together a table, a table of major London socialites, not the cheap, common little celebrities Diana was so addicted to. Really, Jack should come along. Escorting her. Showing that Juno, a striking woman but the least attractive of the Chambers girls, was snapped up – married.

None of *them* were! And that was something.

She loved to display her social prominence. Wealth like Juno Chambers's was still rare. Mostly it belonged to men, to husbands, who kept their wives on allowances and controlled the credit accounts. Juno spent for herself, and she never let anybody forget it.

'And I'm sure you'll do fine.' Jack Darling came up to his wife and ran his fingers down her spine. His touch still had the power to make her shiver. She tensed a little, in anticipation. Juno could never quite let go with Jack, at least not until halfway through their coupling, when the fires he stoked so patiently refused to be dampened, and she lost herself in his arms. It was a little frightening, to be so out of control. And she despised herself for her neediness, her greed for his lovemaking. It was so animalistic. Even now, when she was angry, her skin warmed to his touch.

'Let's go upstairs,' he suggested.

Bed. She'd just spent half an hour fussing around that

bedroom. Missy Hamilton, the new Countess of Cork, was coming for lunch and Juno desperately wanted to show her an immaculate house; chic, with every antique clock burnished and gleaming, her Liberty cushions just so, her Persian rugs free of every speck of dust. She was hoping to get Missy along to one of her lunches, or possibly a tea party. Juno was always glad to leave the island after Christmas. Behaving herself perfectly for Uncle Clem was a strain, and once she got back to England she could get on with her life. Juno was deadly serious about her place in society, and spending money well was an art.

She wasn't a big one for books, but sometimes she did enjoy Jane Austen, where women were expected to keep a fine home and throw dances and evenings of bridge and music. A more civilised age. The rat race was for people who had to take part in it. If you'd got your ticket out, Juno thought, glancing up at Jack again, it was positively *ungrateful* to work. There was a better, older way to live.

'I don't know . . . Are you going to be messy?' She bit her lip.

He grinned, devilishly. 'Very.'

Juno stiffened. Jack liked to take his time. What if she couldn't get the place perfect again before lunch?

'I've got a bit of a headache . . .' she attempted.

'That's handy.' He reached down and lightly lifted her to her feet, passing his hand across the front of her dress. 'I've got the cure.'

Juno shoved him away petulantly. 'Maybe later, Jack.'

His eyebrows lifted and his gaze darkened.

'We're married. In case you've forgotten. I can't get it elsewhere.'

'Is that a threat?' Her eyes flashed dangerously.

'No, this is.' Jack strode furiously towards the window, his strong hands gripping the sill. He refused to look at her as he spoke. 'I expect more than a cold fish who just puts up with me. You used to be hot, Juno. Eager.' He turned around. 'Insatiable. I have no idea what happened, but I don't like it. And if you plan on being like this for the rest of our lives, now is the time to tell me. Because I'll not stand for it.'

Juno opened her mouth to reply. Furious, but chilled at the same time. Walk out on *her*? Walk out? She, Juno, was the great prize, the rich, generous wife. All her thoughts had been about when she might – or might not – break it off with her handsome bit of rough. But *Jack* threatening divorce? She immediately clammed up inside; she wanted to clutch things to her.

'Don't throw a tantrum, please, Jack,' she said frigidly.

His face darkened with fury, and Juno crossed her arms, stiff with resentment.

There was a knock on the door. Thank God, Juno thought. One of the servants.

'Excuse me, Mrs Darling. There's a telegram for you.'

'A telegram!' Juno said brightly, false cheerfulness in her voice. 'How exciting. Bring it here, please, Wilkinson.'

The maid approached with the envelope on a silver tray. Juno took it, and lifting a pearl-handled letter-opener from her mahogany side table, deftly sliced it open.

It wasn't from Millie. The colour drained from Juno's face.

'My God, what's happened?' Jack said, moving to steady her. 'Has somebody died?'

'Oh, don't be so melodramatic,' Juno snapped. She breathed in deeply; her head was swimming, and it took her a second to recover herself. All her thoughts of soirées and lunch parties instantly vanished.

'Wilkinson. Pack two suitcases for the Seychelles. My best clothes, please.' She held up a hand. 'No – forget that; I'll take care of it.' She bit down nervously on her lower lip. 'I'll be leaving right away. Cancel everything.'

'Very good, Mrs Darling. I'll just go and call Lady Cork.'

'No!' Was the woman a moron? Why was everybody so *stupid*? Anger at the world boiled up in her. 'It's too late for that. I'll have to see her; I'll leave this afternoon. Arrange my driver for three, would you?'

'Yes, ma'am.' Linda Wilkinson scurried off. Juno scowled at the pretty maid as she left.

'I'm not going to the bloody tropics,' Jack said. His dark eyes swept over her thin body, encased in its classic Chanel suit; buttercup-yellow and cream checks, with her matching sunflower leather Dior court shoes. A string of South Sea pearls from House Massot gleamed against the pale hollows of her throat. Juno knew he wanted to peel them all off her. She clammed up with resentment.

'Nobody asked *you*,' she said, a block of ice. 'Uncle Clem wants to see me. Just me. And the other girls.'

Jack Darling shrugged. 'Trouble in paradise?' he asked bitterly. 'You're nothing without that money, Juno Chambers. Remember that. If you want me, I'll be in the pub.'

And as she stared in dismay, he walked out.

Chapter Four

The four-thirty flight was not scheduled on any airport announcement board. In Stansted Airport, the four girls were sequestered away from the other first-class passengers, huddling together by a large window, impatiently counting the minutes until they could board their private jet.

The Louis Vuitton luggage was in the hold; only Juno used anything else: she had her suitcases specially made by a firm of tanners in Wiltshire, and she and her maid had packed every silk shirt and satin gown between crisp layers of acid-free tissue paper.

Now they were ensconced in a private lounge, their hand luggage resting neatly by their feet. Venus and Diana had both opted for Prada carry-ons; Juno had an antique 1930s valise, and Athena a neat Gucci case.

They looked at each other uncomfortably.

'He said it was family news,' Diana reminded them.

'Then why all the secrecy? Why not call?' Athena asked of her cousin. She rubbed her hands nervously on her trousers. 'He's never done this before.'

'We'll take dear Uncle Clem at his word, shall we? He wanted to see us in person,' Juno Darling said, snapping her ivory-inlay powder compact shut. 'It's too vulgar to make a production out of this.'

'Give over, Juno.' Venus looked up from her nails, annoyed. 'How quickly did you pack? I bet you were terrified, just like the rest of us. Save the snobbishness for your Stepford Wife friends, can't you?'

The four young women glowered at each other.

Right now, not one of them wanted to be anywhere near her relations. But there was no help for it. They were all stuck, all in this together. The money that greased every facet of their lives was under threat. And not a single one of them could do anything other than panic.

'Let's not fight,' Athena Chambers said, picking up on her sister's stiffening back. 'You know how Uncle Clem hates that sort of thing.'

'He also hates women who are improperly dressed,' snapped Juno, embarrassed by Athena's ensemble. Cheap black trousers and a nondescript apricot shirt. 'You look like my housekeeper. On a *bad* day.'

Athena flushed. 'I rushed to get dressed. Everything was in the wash . . .'

'Where *did* you pick that up?' Diana drawled.

Athena blushed. 'Well, BHS was open and it was on the way to the station, so . . .'

'I despair,' Juno said furiously, disgusted that Athena

41

was making a show of herself in front of their two cousins. The further Juno rose up the social ladder, the faster Athena scrambled down it. While Diana and Venus, in their individual styles, were very chic. Not in classic society terms, but hipper, fresher. And Juno was glad they'd chosen to use Uncle Clem's wealth in a different way. She certainly could not compete with them on looks . . .

They weren't twins, but they could almost have been. Two tanned, willowy beauties, with long glossy hair. Venus's, as befitted an actress, was dyed blond, a tone-on-tone melt of shiny buttercup and platinum. Her eyebrows were thinner, her teeth pearly white, and she had noticeably defined muscles under her brown skin. Juno looked suspiciously at the swell of her cousin's breasts. She had a full cup size on Diana, maybe two. Plastic surgery? Juno wouldn't put it past her. She looked at them, then back at her sister, and softened. She had to admit they made quite a quartet.

Venus dressed sexy. Rich sexy, but conventionally female. Today she was wearing a Pucci halter-necked dress in patterned silk, teetering Manolos in flesh-coloured leather – strappy sandals that laced halfway up her toned calves – and a glittering necklace of pave diamonds and white gold. A peek-a-boo keyhole at the front of her dress revealed the tops of her firm breasts. Over it all, a crisp tailored coat by Joseph, snow white, picked out her tanned blondeness. And her bag was

Hermès, a Kelly. Perennially stylish. Chanel sunglasses balanced on top of her head.

Diana, the It Girl, was slightly less obvious. Prada handbag, to match her carry-on. Both in chestnut leather. Versace dress and jacket in tailored cream cotton with a daisy detail – again, the paleness of the outfit highlighting her tan. She was a darker blonde, deep honey and caramel tones, with chopped strands in buttery yellow just framing her face. Her shoes were chestnut, too, Christian Louboutin with the sassy red soles. And she wore a necklace of polished wood and sea pebbles with a gold 'D', the rich, orange colour of twenty-four carat, set in the middle. Juno could not place the piece, but it was obviously cutting-edge and highly expensive.

She herself had not gone that route; she wore a seashell-pink dress and coat by Robinson Valentine, sedate YSL pumps in black leather, and carried a neat little Kate Spade handbag, black with jet and pink crystal detailing. Her hair, coloured a ladylike shade of light brown, like demerara sugar, was swept up into a neat plaited bun, and she wore her best South Sea pearls around her neck, with a large pair of Dior sunglasses perched on her forehead. Juno was confident her look would have been appropriate in any ambassador's garden party from Rio to Hong Kong.

But Athena! Mousy-brown hair, untouched by stylists – maybe scarfed through once with a Mason Pearson. Low-budget clothing. Ray-Bans, for heaven's sake. A necklace of crystals. At least she appeared to be wearing some decent Jimmy Choo flats, and her handbag was Gucci. But Juno's baby sister was a tousled, tumbled mess.

'You look like you're trying to make a statement,' Juno said coldly. 'And it isn't "I care about you, Uncle Clem".'

'Don't bug me, Ju. I've had a bad day.' Athena made a face.

'Once we got those telegrams, I think we all had a pretty bad day,' Venus said.

The girls sighed in unison.

'I hate not knowing.' Diana spoke for them all.

Venus chewed on her lip. 'I just wish you hadn't worn white, Diana. I mean, I'm in white.'

'You hardly own the colour,' Diana replied.

Athena chimed in. 'Well, frankly, I couldn't give a damn what any of you think of my clothes. Uncle Clem will be pleased to see me.'

'Are you sure about that? He does have certain standards,' Juno snapped.

Athena glared. 'It's all sexist rot.'

'Don't be stupid. He dresses for dinner himself,' Venus reminded her. Her voice tightened. Hell, she wanted a cigarette. She'd given it up in November, in an attempt to gain back the glowing skin she'd had as a teenager. Plus it stained your nails and gave you wrinkles. And bad teeth. The LA producers hated it.

But right now, stuck here again with Diana and the cousins, it set her teeth on edge. Venus was angry with Uncle Clem, angry with her cousin Athena, angry with the world. She ached for nicotine. A lovely long drag on a Marlboro Light. That'd calm her down.

It was going to be a long flight.

'Mrs Darling and the Misses Chambers?'

The stewardess came up to them wearing the crisp plum-and-silver uniform of all Uncle Clem's domestics, bowing slightly at the waist.

Juno was pleased to be first. So like dear Uncle Clem to insist on those old, old lines of precedence: married women before single. Her mind briefly flicked back to Jack, storming out of the house, and she shivered.

'Yes,' she replied.

'If you'll come this way, ladies. Your jet is waiting.'

'Thank you,' Diana said, and as one the four young women stood and pushed their sunglasses down over their eyes.

As they walked, high heels clip-clipping through the first-class lounge, male heads turned to stare at them.

Rich bitches.

Spoiled, petty, and absolutely gorgeous.

'Can I get you some champagne?'

Another stewardess hovered with a tray of drinks. They were at cruising altitude now. London was already a distant grey splurge in the muddy green countryside, and the plane was heading inexorably south, to the crystal-blue waters of the Pacific.

'I have Pol Roger, vintage Krug, Veuve Grande Dame . . .'

'I'd love a Bellini,' Venus said. 'If you have fresh peach juice?'

'Of course, Miss Chambers.'

A second hovering attendant rushed off to make it.

'Just water,' Juno said, wary of anything that might dull her complexion. As the oldest cousin, she took extraordinary care to keep it from showing.

Diana asked for vintage Krug. Athena shook her head grumpily. The humiliation by Professor Mellon kept replaying itself in her head.

'I want a proper drink. A chocolate martini.'

Juno set her lips tightly until the stewardess had vanished.

'I'm warning you, do not arrive drunk.'

'One drink,' Athena said. 'Then it's water and fresh fruit the whole way.' She stretched luxuriantly; under the thin cotton shirt, she had an amazing body. 'I'm exhausted. I want to get to bed anyway. After a massage.'

Athena did not want to be here. Ever since that telegram had come, she'd been worried. Very worried. What if the money dried up? She'd had plans for it this year. She was going to stop buying pricey antiques and invest in some stocks and shares. She needed money of her own, to go down to her parents in Sussex and offer to buy their house. Boswell House was her childhood home. It mattered to Athena in a way it never had to Juno. She loved it passionately. But if the money dried up, she would have to split it with Juno, and then, God forbid, Juno might want to sell it . . .

No – Athena needed that trust fund. And right now, she was so stressed that she needed a drink.

'Very well.' Juno was scheming as to what to dress Athena in before they arrived. She had packed an entire spare outfit in her hand luggage, so as to be absolutely fresh for their chauffeur-driven ride up to Uncle Clem's private villa complex; a crush-free dress in palest mink jersey by Nina Ricci with a matching long lace cardigan. The shoes were Christian Lacroix, white satin but dyed to match and embroidered in real gold thread. Athena's feet were smaller than Juno's, but these were mules, so she could just wing it.

Her make-up box would help, too. Juno had a Victorian marquetry box filled with the essentials; La Prairie skin caviar moisturiser, Chanel lipsticks and eye shadows, scent by Hermès, foundation by Kanebo. She never bothered with mascara, considering it slightly tarty. Since she could never be a flashy cod-American pin-up like Venus, or a chic fashionista like Diana, Juno had developed her own brand: elegant, ladylike, and formal. She was always impeccable. And, by extension, she was determined that her own sister should not let her down.

'Here you are, ladies.'

A handsome, effete steward with icy-blond hair had arrived with their drinks. He solemnly handed over each one, as a hostess set out some snacks on the table: glossy black olives, bowls of fragrant strawberries with chopped mint, golden ripe peaches, spiced roast walnuts, prosciutto and figs, tiny *boules* of herbed goat's cheese. It was all laid out decoratively on Spode China Rose plates, with Lalique crystal pitchers of iced spring water. The cutlery was antique silver, marked with the Chambers family crest. Uncle Clem did not believe in artificial, poisonous airline food, and scorned the sort of commercial arrangement where business-class 'luxury' consisted of Häagen-Dazs and helping yourself to a glacé cherry.

'Thank you.' Diana winked at the steward, causing him to blush; all of the girls wondered if he was another of Uncle Clem's little follies.

Uncle Clem was a confirmed bachelor.

And somehow sexless. Every year since they were eighteen, the Chambers cousins had been travelling to the Seychelles. Never once had they seen an 'escort', or 'special friend'. No companions of any kind. The female staff were older, elegant, sometimes crusty women, and the men invariably decorative. Uncle Clem apparently had an eye for muscular Scandinavians. But none of the staff ever seemed to climb up the ladder.

Uncle Clem was old-fashioned to the point of prissiness. The girls collectively believed he would rather pull out his own fingernails than discuss something as vulgar as sex.

No. His concern was the girls' future, and behaviour. Everybody in Uncle Clem's orbit had to have the best of everything. Particularly his heiresses. And he was fusty about mannerisms and charm. Just like a colonial ex-pat in the days of Empire, insisting that everything had to be more British than the British. The girls must take their tea from a cup, not a mug. They must not slouch. They must dress for dinner. They must be modest and well presented. He didn't object to a little modern chic, so long as it fitted these patterns. Diana and Venus instinctively toned things down; Athena was always a problem; only Juno fitted his mould perfectly.

The other three suspected she would inherit more money than they did.

But nobody ever asked. Uncle Clem wouldn't like that. If it was infra dig to discuss sex, how much worse to talk about money!

And what would be the point? Money flowed all about them, wrapping them in its soft caress like a hand-woven pure cashmere blanket.

'Mmm. Gorgeous.' Athena sipped her crystal-clear chocolate martini. It was icy cold, with the perfume of cocoa liquor, and the relaxing hit of the alcohol instantly softened her frustrations and annoyances. She reached out for a small bone-handled fruit knife and sliced up a golden, juicy peach, popping one slice into her mouth. It tasted of distilled sunshine, perfectly ripe, as though it had been plucked from the orchard that morning.

She pictured Professor Mellon's darned jacket and the pinched look of envy and spite on his face.

'You know,' Athena said, saying aloud what they were all thinking, 'it's so good to be rich.'

They were awakened with tisanes of passionflower and jasmine just before landing. The private airstrip on the island of Mahe, tucked away on a natural shelf carved out of Mount Mahons, glowed green and white in the early afternoon sun; clouds of frangipani blossom and gleaming broad-leafed coconut trees were everywhere. It looked much as it had done at Christmas, but this time their hearts were filled with anxiety.

They were *never* summoned back.

To be coming without presents, Advent calendars, stockings, and the blown-glass decorations Uncle Clem commanded they bring with them just seemed so *wrong*.

'He didn't say it was something bad,' Venus remarked doubtfully.

'Let's not talk about it,' Juno decided. The other three looked at her meekly. The closer they got to the compound, the more Juno was in her element. 'We'll just tell Uncle Clem our news.'

'What news?' Diana asked innocently. Wasn't the point about the Chambers girls that they never had any news?

'We'll just tell him about our lives. Same as we always do. And that we're glad to see him. Everything will be just the same as usual,' Juno insisted.

The others nodded. Change was disturbing. They determined to put a brave face on it.

The limousine was waiting; perfectly air-conditioned against the baking tropical heat, which hit them in the face as they stepped from the private jet. The saluting chauffeur opened the door as their luggage and carry-ons were whisked into the boot; inside, the girls leaned back comfortably against the buttery leather seats.

'Perfect,' Juno said, smiling firmly.

The other girls ignored her. It wasn't perfect. Something was up.

The gates of Uncle Clem's complex loomed over them, white marble pillars veined with pink gleaming in the sunset against the dark green vegetation. The wrought iron, cunningly carved with fantastic beasts and flowers, swung aside automatically, and they were back – back in the familiar grounds of the Palms. Close-cropped lawns and lushly planted beds of flowers, lupins and roses imported from England, surrounded them; Uncle Clem was also fond of box hedging and antique garden statuary.

They pulled up outside the guest villa. Servants in their plum-and-silver livery rushed up to open the doors and whisk the suitcases into their rooms. Uncle Clem liked them to stay together; it suited his idea of family. Close-knit family.

But Christmas at the Palms was as close as they ever got to that. And sharing the villa always chafed.

Mrs Foxworth, the chief housekeeper, was waiting to meet them; her brisk eye swept approvingly over Juno, neutrally over Diana and Venus, and settled disapprovingly on Athena. Juno had forced her sister into the change of outfit, but since the clothes were not her own, they hung unflatteringly from her slim frame, the dress gaping a little at the breast and revealing a plain cotton bra, slightly grey from the wash.

Bright red spots of embarrassment landed on Juno's cheek. She glared at her younger sister. Hell! Why was Athena such a little brat? She acted like a bloody pauper. Juno's white hands silently balled into fists. Underneath her tautly calm exterior she was in full-blown panic. Athena was going to ruin it for all of them!

'Athena and I were just going to freshen up, Mrs Foxworth,' she said appeasingly. 'After a shower and a change . . .'

Juno did not want her uncle angered further. Whatever was going to happen, Athena needed to be presentable!

'If that could wait, madam? Mr Chambers is in the drawing room in the main house. He's expecting you all. Shall I take you in?'

'Expecting us . . . now?' Venus's voice quavered.

'Yes, ma'am. At once. Would you kindly follow me?'

The girls exchanged glances. They *always* freshened up.

What the hell was going on?

Juno took the lead, reasserting herself.

'Certainly, Mrs Foxworth. Do take us to *dear* Uncle Clem.'

Diana looked at her cousin with dislike. Juno, bloody Juno, she thought. Always his favourite.

Venus shook her shoulders and smoothed out her sleek blond hair. She unconsciously thrust forward her surgically enhanced tits, drew herself tall, and put a little slither into her walk. Gay or straight, she was convinced she could charm any man. Especially her dear old uncle. After all, who was the actress here?

Athena, aware of the glares of her sister and the contemptuous head-tosses that Diana was shooting her way, didn't really care. She was tired, she told herself mulishly. And make-up was so shallow and silly. Honestly, all Uncle Clem wanted of them was family loyalty, right?

Unable to help herself, she smothered a yawn.

All three of the other girls scowled. But nobody said anything. Mrs Foxworth was walking, the soft sound of her canvas shoes crunching on the fine gravel. Twilight had streaked the golden sky with blue, and a servant had lit the glowing torches scattered throughout the gardens.

Already tiny white moths were fluttering towards them. Two huge torchères carved of solid brass flanked the limestone portico of the main mansion; soaring orange flames flickered shadows on the white steps, dancing across the four young women as they followed inside.

The interior of the house, classic colonial, was as familiar to them as their own bedrooms. A crisply polished black-and-white-check tiled floor. Leaded-light windows. Genuine Greek and Roman busts that would have done credit to the Metropolitan Museum in New York. Clouds of calla lilies and green roses scented the air from large gilt vases, and here and there a maid or a butler could be seen, in uniform, polishing or straightening quietly in the compulsory soft shoes.

Mrs Foxworth knocked gently on a large oak door.

'Come in,' Uncle Clem's quavering voice called.

The formal parlour inside was lined with mahogany panels; a glorious grandfather clock dominated one end of the room, and various chesterfields, high-backed burgundy leather chairs and chaise longues were placed artfully around the room, standing on an exquisite Chinese carpet in creams and golds. In the vast stone fireplace a fire had been laid, ready to burn late into the night, set around with aromatic woods and spices. But it was a little early for that. The evening was still hot, and between them, they were nervous and sweating.

'Mrs Darling, Miss Chambers, Miss Venus Chambers and Miss Athena Chambers, sir,' the housekeeper said.

'Thank you, Foxworth. That'll be all.'

The door closed behind them, and the four girls stepped forward into the room. Standing on the edge of the rug. Trying not to stare.

Uncle Clem, in one of his typically tight, rather prissy white suits, a small rattan fan laid beside him on the deep blue velvet chaise longue he favoured, looked much the same as usual. His typical silver salver of drinks and crystal tumblers was laid before him – part of their welcome ritual every year.

But something was very different.

A woman.

A woman sat beside him. Not in the uniform of a servant, either. A petite, olive-skinned, dark-haired girl, no more than thirty years old, if that. She was wearing a clinging dress of palest ivory silk, a necklace in a thick collar of gold, delicate strappy cream sandals, her toenails neatly styled with a French pedicure. She wore what was evidently long, lush hair curled up on the top of her head in formal braids, set with white feathers, seed pearls and diamonds. Her lips were streaked fire-engine red, like a forties film star, and her nails, long and sharp, matched.

And so did the enormous blood-red solitaire glinting on the slender fourth finger of her left hand.

'Darlings! Will you have a drink?'

'No thank you, Uncle Clem,' they chorused. Unable to tear their eyes off the tiny brunette sitting next to him.

Her hand resting possessively on his knee. Large,

almond-shaped Oriental eyes regarding them steadily. Full of challenge.

'It's so lovely to see you,' he said, in a voice cracking with age. 'And now you know why I couldn't tell you over the phone. Far too important for that! You are all good to come so quickly.'

They murmured their assent.

Juno exchanged a glance with Diana. All of a sudden she had a very bad feeling about this. A very bad feeling indeed.

'Well, I promised you good news,' he said heartily. 'And here it is! This is Bai-Ling.' Uncle Clem turned his leonine head and gave her a whiskery kiss on her smooth cheek. 'We're engaged to be married!'

Chapter Five

'I am so glad you could all come,' Bai-Ling purred at the girls as their chairs were pulled out for supper. 'And such a long way, too! It's good to see that devotion to your uncle.'

The beeswax candles were lit in the antique candelabras; outside, the noise of the fountains splashing into their basins mingled with the chirping of insects. But despite the soft, dancing light, the tension on the four beautiful faces was clear as day.

Bai-Ling looked at them all smugly.

'Will you have some wine?'

'Champagne,' Athena said defiantly, and nobody so much as tried to stop her.

A waiter glided over and filled her glass with her favourite; Moët Brut Imperial, a light demi-sec.

'Uncle Clem.' Juno cleared her throat, and her cousins held themselves taut. 'What a delight . . . and you never said anything.'

'We have been dating for more than one year now,' Bai-Ling jumped in, her smooth olive arm laid possessively on Uncle Clem's shirt sleeve. Her eyes danced a warning to Juno. Back off.

'And where did you meet?' Diana chimed in. She shook out her dark hair and smiled at her old uncle encouragingly.

'Jakarta,' Uncle Clem said heartily. 'I went to look at another shipment of sapphires. Bai-Ling was born in Thailand.'

His wealth had been built on jewels and gold; treasure the old-fashioned way: a couple of gold mines in Samarkand, then a diamond strike in Siberia, one of the first, and finally expert bulk trading of coloured goods around the world: Brazilian emeralds, Thai sapphires, Indian rubies. Jewel-buying trips were some of the few he still made outside the complex, perhaps once a year.

'A beautiful country,' Venus said. 'Although I hear it has a terrible problem with prostitution.'

'Oh,' said Bai-Ling, smiling demurely, her dark eyes flashing with contempt. 'Really? In my circles ladies don't talk about such matters.'

'What circles are they?' asked Venus.

'My father is a jewellery dealer in Phuket. As soon as I met Clement, I felt so protected.' She turned to him adoringly. 'You looked after me, my darling.'

'I lost my heart,' Uncle Clem agreed.

His nieces toyed with their food. This couldn't be happening. Uncle Clem couldn't be getting *married*!

'It's a beautiful ring,' Athena said, slugging down a hearty gulp of ice-cold bubbly. She was tired, and feeling loose-lipped. 'Is it a ruby?'

'A ruby!' Bai-Ling's slash of a red mouth curled upwards disdainfully. 'No, darling, it's a diamond.'

'A *red diamond*?' Juno was shocked. She knew something about gems. 'How lovely, may I see?'

Bai-Ling extended her willow-thin wrist towards the older woman. Yes, the stone glittered with a fire no pigeon's-blood ruby could possess. The facets sparkled in the candlelight, the colour was clear and true, like a strawberry, and Juno was quite sure there were almost no internal flaws . . . it had to be twelve carats, maybe more. A perfect, huge *red* diamond. The world's most expensive stone.

'Very pretty,' she said coldly, damning with faint praise. 'Just like you.'

'I never expected to find such love in the autumn of my life,' Uncle Clem said, his high-pitched voice squeaking with enthusiasm. 'But Bai-Ling has opened my eyes to new vistas . . .'

New vistas? He'd been stuck in this house, a semi-recluse, for thirty years!

The cousins glanced at each other.

'I feel young again!' he exclaimed.

'We're all delighted for you both,' lied Diana. She couldn't wait to wolf down her expensive meal and get back to the guest villa. She had to think.

'I knew you would be. My precious girls.' He beamed at them proudly, and the four young women gazed back with real affection. For all his quirky, eccentric ways, Uncle Clem had given them respect and approval.

And money, of course; lots and lots of money.

'When's the wedding?' Diana asked.

Ah, yes. The four-billion-dollar question.

Venus, Athena, and Juno stiffened beside her. Three mother-of-pearl spoons paused, hovering over their individual mounds of caviar.

'Well,' Uncle Clem leaned forward too. The air crackled. Here it comes, Diana thought. She saw the way the rheumy old eyes narrowed. You could forget, with Uncle Clem's peculiarities, just how brilliant he was. You didn't make hundreds of millions by being dumb.

'We're thinking of getting married at Christmas,' he announced.

The four women stifled little sighs of relief. Christmas! Almost a whole year away.

'It's a long time.' Bai-Ling faced them down, her almond-shaped eyes steady on the four girls. 'But we need it to plan the wedding. It will be the wedding of the century!'

'And we also need the time for you to adjust,' Uncle Clem said gently.

'Adjust? We couldn't be more thrilled,' Athena said, forcing a smile.

'I can see how you are all very excited,' Bai-Ling agreed. She smiled slightly.

Uncle Clem coughed, and his eyes danced across the four of them.

'Well, girls, I meant adjust financially. After all, once Bai-Ling and I are married, we will want to start a family right away. Our children will be our heirs. And she and I have discussed things; it's not healthy to have the estate drained away from the family. My wife will need a certain style to manage her new life . . .'

Juno felt an icy fear grip her heart, like a cold fist squeezing in her chest.

'We decided that the trust fund winds up on December the first,' Bai-Ling confirmed. Her gleaming white teeth bared in a cruel smile. 'That should give all you ladies plenty of time to settle your affairs.'

'But . . . Uncle Clem.' Her worst fears realised, Juno couldn't stop herself blurting it out. 'We *need* that money. We're used to it . . . What will we do?'

'Oh, come along, poppet.' Her uncle's voice registered surprise and disapproval, and the coldness of his tone blew across them like a chill wind from the sea. 'You didn't always have this money. You used to be perfectly fine. You're bright girls and I'm sure you'll be able to stand on your own two feet. I wanted to stop the draft this month, but Bai-Ling persuaded me otherwise.'

'Very kind,' Diana managed through clenched teeth.

'We don't want any hint of disagreeable things,' Bai-Ling replied condescendingly. 'All my future nieces now have plenty of time. And after all,' she leaned forward, bony elbows propped up on Uncle Clem's antique Bali table, 'you have had much money from the pot. Millions. I am sure you have saved money and are all set for life. Clement is a most, most generous man,' she purred, draping her left hand purposefully under her chin. So that the light flew from the stone that was worth more than all of them put together.

'Stand on our own two feet.' Athena laughed wildly. 'That'll be a change. At least I have a job.'

'A teaching position at Oxford. Paying you twenty thousand a year,' Venus sneered.

'Which is about nineteen thousand more than your acting career brings in,' Athena snapped back.

Venus tossed her head. She thought bitterly of the producer she'd stood up to come here. All that money on grooming – wasted.

Juno, biting her lip furiously, battled for control. She wasn't going to let this skinny bitch ruin her life. Disgusted with herself for cracking in public, she breathed in deeply and turned her eyes, doe-like, towards her uncle.

'Well I think it's a good thing,' she lied shamelessly. 'We're all indebted to your past kindness, Uncle Clem, and the *important* thing is to concentrate on getting ready for your wedding.' She shot a silky look at her young aunt-to-be. 'I'd like to be involved in that,' she added with a bright smile. 'Bai-Ling has never been to England,

and she'll need showing the ropes of English society.'

Venus lifted her head, like a deer sniffing the wind, and looked gratefully at her cousin. Yes, yes, very clever. They knew so little about Uncle Clem, but one thing was absolutely clear – he cared about his image. Bai-Ling was an exotic foreigner, she was way too young. If they could use that, drive some sort of wedge . . .

Juno was smiling at Uncle Clem. 'Let me help Bai-Ling for you.'

Bai-Ling shifted angrily in her seat.

'Your uncle already show me ropes,' she hissed.

'*Has* shown me *the* ropes, dear,' Juno said sweetly, the glory of battle singing in her veins. 'You see, Uncle Clem? Anything we can do for you and your future bride will be a pleasure.'

'Oh I do think that's a splendid idea,' Uncle Clem agreed, his voice a little warmer. 'You see, Bai-Ling? I told you they would take it well.'

Despite their exhaustion, the cousins met up in the villa. There was no big announcement; they all simply proceeded, as one, to Athena's bedroom. It was the smallest of the four, and located in the middle of the building, with a skylight instead of a window casement that might hide a prying servant's ears.

'But I thought he was . . .' Venus began.

Diana shrugged. 'Evidently not. And it's as old as the hills. Infirm billionaire, grasping gold-digger.'

'She must be forty years younger than he is,' Juno hissed. 'Little tramp.'

'I'd say fifty,' Venus replied. 'She hasn't had any work, except maybe the tits.'

'Don't be vulgar,' Juno responded.

Venus laughed shortly. 'Or what? Uncle Clem will get mad? Disinherit me? Face it, Juno, it's time to pull that stick out of your ass.'

'Don't talk to my sister like that,' Athena said.

'Why not? You always do.'

They glared at each other.

'This isn't helping.' Diana jumped in. 'Look – look. We're all tired. Let's just calm down. We need to think.'

Venus nodded.

'Very well,' Juno said.

Diana sat down on one of the chesterfield leather chairs and pressed her hand to her forehead. Then she looked at Venus and her cousins.

'Have you noticed something, girls? It's like this every bloody Christmas. I know you feel the same way I do. We get on the plane, we're nervous, we want to impress him. Within a few minutes we're rubbing each other up the wrong way. Juno wants Athena to be groomed, I want Venus to tone down the sexiness. And we both side with our sisters against the cousins. It's just horrible. All the while putting on a sort of fake cheerfulness. By the time we land at Heathrow, we'd all be glad to not see each other again for six months. Admit it.'

Astonished, Juno actually laughed.

'You're a brave girl to say that.'

'You know it's true,' Diana said.

'It is. It totally is,' Athena agreed. 'You ask me, we're less like family on this island than we ever are at home. You know Juno and I feel guilty every time, too, because we don't dare to say no to Uncle Clem. We really should have Christmas with Mum and Dad.'

'I wish I was back in London right now.' Venus yawned. 'In bed.'

'Yes, but we're here.' Diana shrugged. 'And we're under a lot more bloody pressure than usual. What happens? We're at each other's throats. Girls, we have *got* to pull together, if only to stop this insane idea of a wedding.'

'You're right, Di.' Her sister nodded.

'Yes, you are.' Juno sighed. 'I apologise for snapping at everyone. Now let's try to think of practical things we can do.'

'Maybe we could have Uncle Clem sectioned,' Venus suggested brightly. 'And if he dies we can challenge the will . . .'

'Based on what? He's perfectly compos mentis.' Athena shook her head. 'That's what happened when Anna Nicole Smith inherited. The children challenged. She'd had him make a video with his lawyers declaring his competency to sign a will. She died a very rich woman. And I'm sure Bai-Ling will have thought of all that. Besides, if Uncle Clem thinks we're just after his money . . .'

They fell silent. Nobody wanted their uncle as an enemy.

'But it's so *selfish*, though.' Venus wailed what they were all thinking. 'To go and get *married* to some teenager. *Now*, when he's this old . . .'

'Medical science is amazing these days,' Athena said gloomily.

They were silent. Each one of them looking into the abyss. No money meant no life. It was simply the end of everything worth having.

'Here's what I suggest,' Juno said. The other three looked hopeful; she was Uncle Clem's favourite, she'd know what to do. 'Let's spend tomorrow making a great fuss of Uncle Clem and Bai-Ling. Then let's go home and take stock. We have to work together. *We have to stop this wedding.*'

'Stop the wedding,' Diana breathed. 'Do you think we can?'

'We have no choice,' Juno stated flatly. 'When the money's gone, what will we have left to show for it?' She knew what parties cost. And plastic surgery, chauffeurs and the best coats. 'Do you have any capital reserves left, Diana?'

'No.'

'Nor me,' Venus admitted, cheered by the fact that someone else didn't either. Half a million a year could go *very* quickly in London – if you knew where to shop. A single first-class flight to LA could be ten grand. It was a pittance, really. She hardly knew how she'd scraped by.

'Athena?'

Athena blushed. She could see what they were thinking. *Let's ask Athena, she buys her clothes at jumble sales.*

'I don't have any cash either. Apart from the house – I've got that.'

'So what did it go on? Drugs?'

'I don't do drugs.' Athena looked reproachfully at her big sister. 'But I do collect antiques . . . and paintings.'

'Any of them worth anything?'

'Some of the antiques. The paintings . . .' Her voice trailed off. An art assessor had told her she had common taste. Her pictures were realistic images, not the conceptual art that had taken off since the sixties.

'I see.' Juno tried to sound disapproving, but there was no conviction. She, after all, didn't even own her house. There was a fifty per cent mortgage on it. Her spectacular wardrobe, her jewels, her Napoleonic entertainments . . . her small but hugely expensive wedding . . . 'Well, we still have until the end of the year.' She stiffened herself. 'We simply must stop Bai-Ling marrying him.'

'And getting pregnant,' Diana pointed out glumly. 'I bet she's already trying. Once you've got the kid, you get a slice for life. I can't see Uncle Clem disinheriting his child even if he *did* dump her.'

They shuddered. Their golden future was tarnished and crumbling all around them.

'We'll go back to London.' Juno was firm. 'And we'll finish Bai-Ling.'

Venus shrugged. 'We'll all have to work together.'

Juno smiled. 'I'm afraid we will.'

Chapter Six

Athena walked up the gravel path to the house, tugging her Husky around her. It was bitterly cold, the bare branches of the apple trees dancing blackly against the white sky. The dull winter's day could not ruin the sight of the Georgian rectory, though: honey-coloured stone, with its formal eighteenth-century face, large sash windows, and doves perching atop the roof. A thin wisp of smoke twirled up into the pale sky. Good – there was a fire lit in the drawing room. What she really wanted was a hot buttered crumpet, perhaps with Marmite. They always had that at home – it was something of a tradition.

She was so looking forward to seeing her parents again. Distant, self-absorbed, remote academics, they neither knew nor cared about the worries with Uncle Clem's trust. And in this house, neither did Athena.

But they would soon have to care. For years, Athena and Juno had been satisfied their parents were happy. For a long time, at the start of every year, their daughters offered to send them a portion of the trust fund. Marcus and Emily lived in genteel poverty; Athena would have sent them half of her money and not thought twice about it, and she was sure Juno would have done the same.

But they were stubborn. Her father especially. Marcus refused to touch one penny of his elder brother's cash, funnelled through Athena or not. Whenever she raised the matter, his normally calm face darkened, his lips tightened, and Athena saw the anger dancing beneath the surface.

'I do not want to depend on Clement, darling, thank you.' Marcus's dark brows drew together. 'Your mother and I are fine. Please don't ask me again.'

Eventually, she hadn't. The Professors Chambers demanded respect. Athena knew that if anything went wrong, she and Juno were a safety net, there if needed. Now that safety net had been torn away.

'Hello,' she called out, pushing the heavy front door open. It was rarely locked; there had never been a burglary here in thirty years. The house was located in Sussex, on the edge of the Pevensey Levels, and on a good day you could look out to sea. A fringe of oaks shielded it from the road, and the entrance to the drive looked like a dirt track in a forest.

'Hello! Darling, Athena's here.' Her mother, her hands covered in flour, came out of the front door and gave her a kiss. 'I've made seed cake for tea.'

The dogs came bounding up in a tumble of russet fur;

Bonzo and Fido, their red setters. They jumped enthusiastically all over Athena, tearing at her Jaeger coat in welcome. Like they saw her just yesterday.

'Darling, hi.' Her father, Professor Marcus Chambers, lumbered over towards her from his library, spectacles pushed halfway up his nose. His eyes, small behind the thick lenses, sparkled with pleasure. 'Good to see you, Athena. I hope you're hungry, your mother's been cooking all day.'

'Starving,' Athena said honestly.

She looked around the house. It was beautiful still, but it was falling apart. Her keen eye could see dust and holes; woodworm in the panelling. There was a suspicious stain on the wall, under the oil painting of her grandfather, that looked like damp; the paint was peeling everywhere, and she saw patches of mould on the ceiling. The old Afghan rugs laid out on the limestone floors were threadbare from generations of moths.

Boswell House needed a lot of work.

She had always planned to do it herself. She adored this house, and its four acres of garden, with the pear orchard and the lavender walks and the clipped yews by the duckpond. Juno wasn't interested; it was miles away from London, the Henley Regatta or Ascot. Athena had always seen herself settling here, with a brilliant husband (an academic shortlisted for the Nobel, perhaps, or a fellow of the Royal Society or All Souls – a scientist, so he would never compete in her own discipline) and a bunch of ruddy-cheeked children, healthy, beautiful, scarily bright.

But it would cost to buy out Juno's share. And she was starting to think it would cost a hell of a lot – hundreds of thousands. More to keep it up.

Since her parents wouldn't let her use Clem's money, Athena had planned to invest in stocks and use her own profits. But somehow she'd just never got around to it.

'Come into the drawing room,' her father insisted. 'Tell us all the news. We've finished lunch, but the kettle's just boiled.'

'I'll bring the tea,' Emily Chambers said. 'Have you eaten? It's still a long time till supper.' She brushed her floury hands absent-mindedly against her gardening trousers. 'We didn't expect you so soon.'

'I know. I had to come early.' Athena shivered. 'I've been a bit restless. You know, Mum, I'd love a crumpet. With Marmite.'

'Absolutely.' Emily smiled, pleased her daughter was eating. With her long legs and her wild, unkempt hair, Athena was sometimes a bit gaunt. Like Marcus, she could get so absorbed in a book she'd forget her supper. She was gangly, a bit like a daddy-long-legs, with dark circles under her large brown eyes with the smoky black lashes. A gorgeous face, but mousy hair. And being tall and thin made her flat-chested. The lack of boyfriends worried Emily too. Athena had been a boisterous, tomboyish girl, but as she grew into her brains she had withdrawn more and more towards books.

Juno, who had a determined streak, was single-minded; she was married now. Emily had to admit she found it easy to forget about her elder daughter. Terrible to say, but Athena had been their favourite: a beautiful child, and with that spark of intelligence that two dons required, a first-class brain to carry on their legacy; a better-looking slice of themselves.

Emily patted her daughter's arm.

'You need fattening up. Go and sit with Daddy.'

The fire was indeed lit in the old drawing room hearth, a big stone inglenook fireplace with a copper grate, and Athena plopped down into the old red cotton chair, sighing with pleasure. Her father was surprisingly good at a couple of practical things: laying fires and fishing. The room was warm, and she basked in the heat, stretching out her feet in their soft, high boots; stylish chestnut leather from Dior, but not very practical. As her toes warmed, she looked out of the lead-paned windows down to the pond; a heron flew disconsolately away from it, all the carp having long since been eaten.

'So I heard you were turned down for tenure.' Marcus looked owlishly at his daughter. 'Have you kept up your publishing schedule?'

'Yes.' Athena sighed. 'They just don't like me.'

Marcus frowned, then shrugged.

'Well, you must keep at it. Apply to Cambridge, perhaps.'

'That's next on my list.'

She smiled as her mother brought through a tray of tea and started to serve everybody; the same chipped old mugs they'd used for years. Athena remembered being sent on a mug hunt throughout the house. Without the girls around (Juno was brilliant at finding hers), there were probably several rotting away in the bathrooms, or under beds, thick with bluish mould.

'I actually came to talk about something else,' she said, blushingly accepting a crumpet. It was toasted just right, buttery and salty. 'The money.'

'What money?' Her mother poured out the tea and offered Athena a mug; her fingers, still cold, curled around it, letting the warmth spread through them.

'Uncle Clem. He's getting married – I told you.'

'How nice,' Emily said vaguely.

'Clem will do exactly as he likes,' her father said, and his eyes were cold. 'Always has. I wouldn't try to get in his way, Athena.'

'But Daddy.' She was aware it sounded like a wail. 'He's telling us he's going to cut off the trust fund. At the end of this year it runs out for good!'

Her father's reaction surprised her. Athena watched Marcus slump back in his chair, stunned; but the look on his face, as he glanced at her mother, was one of utter relief.

'I see.' When he spoke, his voice was calm. 'Athena, you're an intelligent woman. As is Juno. I'm glad that Clement has decided to look elsewhere.'

'But we're his family.'

She didn't understand the gaze that passed between her parents.

'Clement is a semi-recluse,' Marcus said. 'He has had no contact with the family, not even when Rupert was killed. And one day, out of the blue, he decides to fix it by pumping obscene amounts of cash at four young children. Athena – it is unhealthy. Your mother and I would never stand in the way of your prospects. But I am pleased, if he's decided to stop playing games.'

Playing games? Athena swallowed some tea to hide her expression. Didn't they get it? The trust fund was deadly bloody serious!

'I believe you're better off without that money, darling,' Emily Chambers agreed. 'It made you all behave a little oddly. And what's life without a challenge?'

Easy, Athena thought, mulishly. Pleasant. Smooth.

'Do you mind my asking . . . do *we* have any money?'

'We? Your mother and I?'

Athena nodded.

'Oh good Lord, girl.' Marcus hooted with laughter. 'Don't be so ridiculous. We're academics. Mummy inherited this house. It's all that's kept us together over the years.'

'I see,' Athena said glumly. She'd half hoped that Uncle Clem wasn't the only rich eccentric, that her parents might have their own secret stash.

'And of course we don't own the house.' Athena had

polished off her Marmite crumpet, and Emily cut her a slice of seed cake; it was dark and delicious. 'That was sold years ago, when the school bills for you and Juno got too difficult.'

Athena brushed the crumbs away from her mouth, half choking.

'What? Sold Boswell House?'

'That's right.'

'But you still live here,' she said, panicked.

'It was one of those new deals,' Marcus said. 'You sell it to an estate firm, and then you can live in it until you die and they give you some money every month. Reversing the mortgage. But we don't own it any more.'

'Very useful to have that cheque,' Emily said brightly.

Athena felt tendrils of anxiety loop around her heart. She had forgotten just how much she loved her childhood home.

'But you never said anything . . .'

'We didn't want to worry you.' Marcus brushed her concern aside. 'The arrangement means your mother and I have no financial worries, and after all, when we die you can easily buy the house back from the developers.'

Athena felt a rush of loss close around her, like a winter fog from the marshes.

'But Daddy, you know I would have given you *anything* you needed. Bought Boswell from you, even.'

'Not with my brother's money, darling,' Marcus

responded. He was quiet, but she knew he was absolutely firm. 'And you have no money of your own, after all. No, this way seemed best.'

'What do they plan to do with the place?' She tried to keep her tone casual. Outside the old windows, a skein of geese flew cackling, black across the white January sky.

'Flats, I think. They're going to develop it.'

'But there's no parking.'

'They're going to use the garden for that,' Marcus said.

Athena set the seed cake carefully down on her mother's pretty China Rose plate. Suddenly she had completely lost her appetite.

Chapter Seven

Venus crossed her legs and stared Marcia Trope down. They were sitting in the main office of a very private letting agent in the heart of Mayfair, all wood panelling and marble busts; discreet and elegant. Venus wore her favourite ivory wool wide-leg trousers by Dior; a snowy chiffon halter-necked top by Armani and a subtle silk beige mac by Chanel. The pearl-bead and platinum Tiffany watch finished it off. More than usual, she wanted to project wealth today. Because they were conducting different business than usual.

'But Ms Chambers.' The estate agent seemed perplexed. 'The redecoration in the second bathroom was done exactly to your taste. The pink Carrera marble was sourced specially . . .'

'I don't care.' Venus was nervous, and it made her icy cold. 'I'm ending my lease and that's all there is to it.'

'Technically,' said the older woman gingerly, 'you *are* obliged to stay the full twelve months . . .'

Venus shrugged, a little slither of cappuccino lace and silk.

'The Contessa is welcome to sue me . . . if she wants certain facts to come out in public.'

'To come out . . .'

'Tell her she forgot to clean out the larger wardrobe in the second bedroom.' Venus held the agent's eyes coolly. 'And I am *very* well connected in the press. As is my sister Diana.'

Marcia Trope had no intention of telling her client any such thing. The Contessa owned nine premium properties in Venice, and she did not like the bearers of bad news.

'I'm sure I can find another tenant.'

'That would be best.'

'Then let me show you some of our newer places, Ms Chambers. Perfect for the artist. There's a sweet little mews in Notting Hill Gate at three thousand a week, or a Park Street townhouse for three and a half . . . no garden, but an adorable scrap of roof terrace.'

Three thousand a week. Three and a half . . . When had that started to sound like serious money? Before last Thursday, Venus wouldn't even have heard the figures. She had paid no more attention to the cost of her Eaton Square duplex than she did to the prices on a menu.

'Actually, I'm thinking of Paris,' she extemporised.

'No problem.' Marcia beamed. 'We have an office right on the Rive Gauche.'

'Perhaps next week,' Venus replied. 'I have a packed schedule. Projects . . .'

'You're doing some charity work?'

'Acting projects,' Venus said coldly. 'I have some things in the pipeline.'

'Really?' Marcia's kohl-rimmed eyes widened, and she smiled sharply. 'How exciting. Films? TV shows?'

'I can't discuss them,' Venus demurred. She was starting to feel uncomfortable. 'I must be off – got to pop to Harvey Nicks before lunch.'

'We have some cheaper properties,' Marcia said suddenly as Venus stood up. 'Not on the same level of luxury, smaller, of course, but still smart postcodes. I have a studio flat in Walgrave Road, just off Earls Court . . .'

Venus flushed to the roots of her ears.

'And why on earth would I be interested in that?' she demanded. 'I'm not looking for somewhere for my chauffeur.'

Well, well, Marcia thought, as Venus stalked out of her office, half slamming the door. Trouble?

She picked up the phone and dialled her friend Griselda, a personal shopper from Berlin who'd landed a prime spot at Harrods. Griselda was known to be the best in town, and often picked out clothes for the fabulously sexy Chambers sisters.

'Hi, sweetie. Marcia at Gardenia Properties. Tell me, does Venus Chambers still buy from you on account?'

Venus dropped her bag in the cloakroom at the Groucho Club, and immediately raced downstairs to the Ladies. It was imperative to check appearance at the last minute.

She was a perfectionist, and one dropped lash could smear your cheek with mascara, or your lipstick might have bled slightly – an hour's worth of careful making up absolutely ruined.

Hans Tersch liked the ladies, that was the rumour. She was damned lucky he was still considering her for his new movie, *Maud*. She wanted it so badly, she could taste it, metallic in the back of her mouth. She could just see herself, all Anglo-Saxon blondness and rosy cheeks, her slim figure wrapped in a cloak of pure white wool, mounting bravely onto an ivory palfrey as she galloped away from Oxford, camouflaged against the snowy fields . . .

Nothing could be allowed to spoil that. It would give her the recognition she craved. Venus was destined for great things, she could feel that in her bones. Why the hell hadn't it happened yet? After all, she was very beautiful – wasn't she?

The mirror reassured her on that point.

Angular cheekbones. Pouting, full lips – possibly thinning just a bit with age, but still hot enough – dark hazel eyes broadened and softened with an expert application of Chanel, her skin artificially tight and perfectly clean, from once-a-week Kanebo facials, and her teeth gleaming from the porcelain veneers she had so wisely invested in.

Venus found herself pathetically grateful she'd gone for the veneers, and that mini-lift, in October. If she'd waited until today, she might have put it off. As it was, she was still gorgeous – stunning, in fact. And she thought that in a soft light she could pass for twenty-nine.

Hans was waiting for her at his table upstairs. Venus was pleased to see he'd already ordered a good bottle of champagne that said to her he was in a mood to make a deal. Alcohol put everybody in a good mood.

She was uncharacteristically nervous. Pity she couldn't have had a little coke to loosen her up, give her that zing of confidence. But the club was very strict about drugs, and Venus had no intention of getting banned. She wanted to show she was responsible. Nothing must threaten getting this part.

'Darling.' He stood, beaming at her; a short, stocky man, bald, muscular, in a well-cut suit and with a commanding sexual presence. His eyes swept over her, lingering appreciatively on her gently swollen (carefully constructed) breasts and the wasp-like trim of her waist. 'It's so good to see you.'

'And you.' Venus's nerves unknotted, just a little, and a new kind of fluttering replaced them. Damn, he was attractive. One of the most successful indie producers since Harvey Weinstein. Houses in LA, Cannes and Gstaad, she had heard. And recently divorced from wife number three. They had only met for a few minutes at a party on the Croisette last spring. But he still remembered her!

Her mind drifted briefly into a steamy casting-couch fantasy. That would be fine with her. She could sleep with him *and* get the part. Fame, fortune and status all in one go . . .

Venus kissed him on the cheek, and felt a surge of lust ripple through her as her soft lips met his stubble.

'Have you ordered?' He nodded, and she beckoned to a waitress. 'I'll just take a mineral water and a large salad with grilled chicken. No dressing.' It wasn't on the menu, but Venus was used to having her whims obeyed.

The waitress looked at Hans for approval and he shrugged.

'Right away,' she said, grinning.

Venus chose to ignore her. 'So, *Maud* is an incredible script.'

He nodded. 'Not my usual thing, but Denise Meyer, the writer, does fantastic epics. I have money already. Let's face it, *Bad Boys III* isn't going to bring me the Palme d'Or. This one might. Call it a vanity project, but I want my damn Oscar.'

Oscar! Venus's eyes lit up.

'And so you're thinking of using fresh talent?'

'Well.' Hans shrugged. 'Epics are big budget below the line. I don't want to gamble away everything. Above the line, I want to keep costs low. I'm looking to cast total unknowns.'

Hmm. That stung. Venus hadn't had her big break yet, it was true, but there had been small parts in British

TV series, and after all, her *name* was well known in all the right places; she'd brought Spielberg and his wife to one of Diana's parties a few years back, and Tom Cruise had shown up to that party on the yacht at St Tropez . . .

'But you're still talking to me,' she said, laughing lightly.

Hans gave her an odd look.

'Quote for this is scale.'

Scale! The Screen Actors Guild scale? Minimum wage? She could barely pay for a month's worth of Crème de la Mer with that.

Disappointment clouded her face, and Venus saw it mirrored by incredulity in Hans's.

'Maybe this isn't for you, babe,' he said. 'There will be no perks on set. No trailers, no gofers. Sandwiches for lunch. I want to keep costs at an absolute basic level.' Hans shrugged. 'Like I said, vanity project.'

The food arrived. Venus pushed a few leaves gingerly around her plate as Hans tucked into his thick-cut Chateaubriand and switched over to claret. Hell! It wasn't her week. No house, no meal ticket.

But she suddenly knew she desperately wanted the part. Maud. Brave warrior woman. Facing down the English barons. Possibly wielding a gleaming sword. The script went heavy on the queen's sensual nature. Venus liked the idea of herself as the new Elizabeth Hurley, from hot young thing to superstar in the space of a single film.

'Look,' she said gently, when Hans paused to sip his wine. 'I want the part. I'll audition . . .'

'Of course,' he laughed. 'I'm only talking about auditions. You are a total unknown. But I liked your look in that chicken cube commercial. You were funny.'

Venus flushed with suppressed rage. That bloody Oxo commercial! Why had she agreed to do it? She'd been teased by Diana for months. She, Venus Chambers, sexy young actress, dressing up as some tired old housewife! She was convinced it had set her career back years and years.

'Glad you liked it,' she said stiffly.

Hans didn't notice.

'So, I think I will give you a shot. Come to the auditions tomorrow. Our offices in Walpole Street.'

'I know where they are. How many other girls are you seeing?'

'Around twenty,' Hans said easily.

Twenty girls. Twenty damn girls! It was practically a cattle call. She was going to bust herself open fighting for a part that paid scale?

'You can thank me properly later.' Clearly he took her confusion for gratitude. 'There's a little party at my house tonight.'

'You have a place in London?' Venus was glad to change the subject.

He winked at her, and it was very sexy. 'I have a place everywhere. Alma Terrace, Kensington.' He handed her a card. 'Dress sexy. Everybody else will.'

'Don't I always?' Venus purred.

She was a little happier now. After all, not all of those twenty chicks would be coming to the producer's party. She needed to look hotter than hell, because this was the *real* audition.

'Hans Tersch,' Diana said thoughtfully. Venus could almost see her sister flicking through her mental Rolodex. 'Mmm, yes. Very big hitter. Fabulous yacht, the *Brunhilda*. Fifty-footer. Taken a lot of his Hollywood cash and sunk it into developments in San Francisco. Rolling in it.' She raised an eyebrow. 'Come to think of it, can I tag along?'

Venus frowned lightly. She was obviously much prettier than Diana with her funky clothes and boring hair, but still – she loved her sister, but she didn't really want the competition. On the other hand, having junked in her place in Eaton Square, she was now doomed to share a flat with Diana. Already Venus saw it was going to cramp her style.

'OK,' she said reluctantly. 'But Hans is mine. You can bag one of his rich friends.'

Diana smiled maddeningly. Venus was her guest and she was damned if she was going to be limited in her choices.

'We'll see,' she said. 'I wonder what I should wear. I have a fantastic Alexander McQueen, new collection, absolutely tiny waist. Definitely Louboutin shoes. It'll be very forties. Elegant.'

'Sounds perfect.' Sounds dull. Venus instantly resolved to go in her own Chloe halter-neck dress, a plunging froth of nothing with a micro-skirt that needed tape to stop it sliding off her artificially perky nipples. Let Diana do 1940s; Venus would go for all-out blonde bombshell. Tanned, toned flesh and lots of it. Make Hans *want* to be on set with her for three solid months.

'What are you going to wear?'

'Something a bit LA,' Venus said vaguely.

Diana wasn't fooled. 'I do wish you wouldn't dress trashy. You're too old for it, you know.'

Venus tightened. 'Too old? I'm in my early thirties.'

'You're thirty-four. Who do you think you're talking to?'

'Somebody two years older than me,' Venus snapped.

Diana paused. 'Well, we've both kept extremely well.'

But she wished she hadn't brought it up. The wives and girlfriends on the circuit got younger and younger. Diana told herself she liked her freedom, liked having a succession of fashionable beaux. For one thing, it helped with column inches. Was it her fault she enjoyed being recognised, worshipped and adored? She was rich – there was no need to settle down too soon. Diana had an innate horror of pregnancy and children. Just *imagine* getting that fat and bloated, and afterwards, well! Your style would be cramped for simply *years*. You couldn't go to nightclubs, and if you did, the men gossiped about you. The world was still a very sexist place.

Diana had always assumed that she would settle down one day – when her beauty was on the cusp of fading, when last-minute ski parties in Chamonix and cruises down the Nile lost their appeal. She'd marry some divorced banker or oil mogul, who already had children with his ex and didn't want any more. After all, nobody could call her a gold-digger. Diana Chambers was a modern hostess, and she had all the confidence of a girl about town with her own money.

Not any more, though.

The thought of it terrified her. Ever since they'd come back from Uncle Clem's, Diana had woken at night with the sweats.

Despite her brave words, Juno hadn't been in touch with any of them yet about solving the Bai-Ling problem. Maybe she was out of ideas. Trying to detach a foolish old man from a grasping sex kitten would be extremely tough.

And Diana was anxious. The bills for her cancelled party had to be paid. When would she be able to throw another one? Her bashes cost thirty grand a time and up. It was simply impossible to downscale. Everybody would know. They'd be like sharks in the water.

Her timetable had moved up. Diana needed to find a man. And fast. Her competitors were younger and hotter. She hated to think of that. And she was worried that the rich guys could smell her desperation. From her previous lofty perch, she had laughed at the gold-diggers whenever they packed into a room.

There was no way Venus was going to Hans's party by herself. From now on, the Chambers sisters were going to be professional guests. At every blasted A-list bash from now until Christmas!

Diana wanted to be married. She'd never seen what it was like first hand, not when Daddy had selfishly taken that chance from her. Uncle Marcus seemed happy enough. But for Diana, marriage was a necessary social status. And she'd thought she'd had time enough to achieve it. Get a family, be a mother to her own children, although Venus and she had never enjoyed that luxury. She wouldn't panic. The money was still coming, at least until Christmas. Enough for maintenance. Diana had a wardrobe, after all, stuffed with couture. It was just time to use it.

'I think we should make a big entrance,' she mused. 'Definitely get out the rocks.'

The Chambers diamonds. They belonged to Clement, but they were a family heirloom; he had inherited them before any of the girls were born. And he allowed his nieces to wear them. They were kept in a safe at the bank.

Venus smiled. 'Why not?'

'Are you unpacked?'

Venus nodded. 'If you're really sure I have to have that broom closet.'

'It's a perfectly good double bedroom.' Diana prickled with annoyance. 'You can go rent somewhere else if you prefer, darling.'

'We have to save our pennies,' Venus replied loftily. She scowled at her sister. When she was a big movie star, she wouldn't forget how unhelpful Di was being right now. Anyway, they were practically the same size. Even though Diana was a bit low-key compared to her, she did have a few things worth borrowing. Hermès bags and teetering shoes . . . McQueen dresses were sometimes hot, a few vintage Alaias . . . Venus would just show her how to wear them, that was all.

'Yes.' That miserable thought took the fight right out of Diana. She hated dwelling on it. 'I suppose we do.'

'Let's get ready for the party, darling,' Venus suggested. 'You pop to the bank and get the rocks. Bags I dibs on the choker.'

'My house, my bedroom, *my* choker,' Diana said crisply. 'You can have the brooch and the earrings.'

Venus sulked. But having Diana out of the house would give her a chance to go through her wardrobe.

'All right,' she agreed, reluctantly.

Chapter Eight

Alma Terrace was tucked away at the end of Allen Street, a little oasis off Kensington High Street. It was easy to spot Hans's house: number 40 was lit up, with a procession of couples thronging outside the front door; blacked-out SUVs were circling the block.

Venus let Diana jump out of the taxi first. Her sister certainly looked good, she thought with some misgivings. A chic little dress in grey with pale silver piping, cygnet-grey polished leather shoes with those unmistakable red soles. She looked put together, a sort of silent film siren. At her throat glittered the slim but lovely Chambers diamond choker, a delicate web of leaves and branches in eighteen carat and crisp white stones.

Venus hoped her own outfit would eclipse her sister's. The cream silk of her halter-neck slithered sexily over her surgically enhanced curves, with tape protecting her nipples. Just as well, or they'd be bolt upright in this freezing cold night. She had selected a magnificent fox-fur coat, its rich reds setting off the long chandelier earrings that glittered at her lobes. She had secured the brooch, a fan of icy diamonds, right at the place where the halter met, so that eyes would be drawn down to her ample cleavage. Her shoes, with a four-inch heel, teetered under her skirt, throwing her taut little butt outwards and upwards. A good pair of heels could take two pounds off you, and Venus owned nothing but good pairs. Underneath it all she wore La Perla knickers, a sexy little scrap of barely there white lace. Toys for girls, toys to make her feel good.

Venus offered Diana her arm, and they walked together up to the door.

'Venus and Diana Chambers.'

The security guard flipped through his guest list.

'I'm sorry, I don't have a Diana Chambers . . .'

Diana flushed.

'Reichardt, it's fine.' Hans had appeared. He stood in the doorway with a martini in his hand, an iced glass containing a fat olive. His dark eyes swept across the girls, gleaming with pleasure. Venus saw him skim over her dress, pure white against her golden skin, and then settle on Diana, elegant, silvery-grey, her caramel hair carefully coiffed.

Venus felt a snake of jealousy coil around her belly.

'You're very kind to let my sister tag along,' she said sweetly, and lifted up her shoulders, shrugging off the fox fur in a deliciously rich slither. That left her exposed in almost nothing but a long white silk shift, sky-high heels and diamonds.

It worked. Hans turned his head for a better look, and she saw his pupils dilate a little.

'I'm sure she doesn't tag along anywhere,' he said politely.

Diana smiled like a crocodile, silently enraged at Venus, standing there in her tarty dress.

'I think you know my friend Jude,' Diana offered, dragging Hans's gaze back to herself.

'Jude Law?' She nodded, and the producer grinned.

'And the Epsteins . . . and maybe Barbara Schott.' Casually Diana threw out the names of some major players in British film finance.

Hans was charmed. 'Of course. I asked Barbara tonight, actually, but she was tied up in Monaco.'

'Pity.' Diana smiled softly up at him. 'Now I won't know a soul.'

'You'll know me,' he said. 'Come inside, ladies. Somebody will fetch you a drink.'

Venus glowered at Diana as a waiter pressed a chilled kir royale into her hand. The place was thick with billionaires. Why did Diana have to aim her barrels at the one guy Venus needed to impress? But then again, she'd been like that since they were sharing a nursery together. Always had to have the coolest toys. Only wanted what Venus had. The red-headed Barbie. And that miniature Donkey Kong game on a keyring . . .

Hans had been chatting to Diana for eight minutes

now. Venus had counted, watching them together by the exquisitely real-looking designer gas fireplace set against Hans's fabric-covered walls. The townhouse was exquisite, in fact: damask wallpaper, Georgian silver candlesticks, elegant Regency furniture, and a huge oil painting of the Black Forest, hung right on top of the mantelpiece. Obviously an Old Master by someone or other.

It was surprisingly old-money for a Hollywood bad boy, even one from Europe. Who had decorated for him? she wondered idly. She must get the number.

Two younger women were standing together in one corner. Gaily Venus swooped down towards them, knowing that any movement would make her sinfully thin silk dress ripple like water against her curves. No way was she going to chase Hans Tersch. Instead she'd hook up with these bimbos, put the wives at their ease. Venus Chambers was never at a loss. In fact, after a minute of socialising with other women – a smart diversionary ploy – she told herself she'd find the richest single man in the entire place and hook up with him. Candy. Baby.

'Hey there,' she said breezily, extending one manicured hand. Her nails were done by Celine, the latest whiz from the Bliss Spa, with tiny crystals set in a French polish, so they glittered and sparkled like the diamonds dangling from her lobes. 'I'm Venus Chambers. Good to meet you.'

The girls were about twenty-one, twenty-two, and obviously dressed in their prettiest frocks. But strictly B-list. Ghost, and Pied à Terre shoes. Funky necklaces of driftwood in one case and cheap-as-chips citrine in the other. They had short-ish bobs, always a mistake; rich men liked long hair, something to grab on to in bed. Good glossy sheen, though, Venus mused; one was raven black, like Louise Brooks, and the other a stunning auburn. The redhead had striking blue eyes and milky-white skin, very smooth. Venus could see her in a commercial for Scottish smoked salmon. Or Scotch whisky.

'The actress?' asked the brunette.

'We loved you in *Mrs Micawber*,' said the redhead. 'I'm Lilly Bruin.'

'And I'm Claire Downes.'

Venus smiled her most superior smile. Fans! *Mrs Micawber* had been her first movie; she'd had a small part and got critical raves. That was five years ago, back when anything had seemed possible.

'How do you know Hans?' she asked, taking a sip of her champagne.

'I'm dating a friend of his,' Claire said. She pointed to the corner of the room.

'Ollie Foster?' Venus asked.

'Yes – he's a lot of fun.' The hazel-eyed brunette tossed her head. Venus's stomach knotted. Ollie Foster was about forty-eight, and a petrochemical billionaire. Last she'd heard he was just starting divorce proceedings. He had steel-grey hair, and his Savile Row suit couldn't disguise his paunch.

And he was dating this . . . this teenager? Venus would have thought he was prime target territory for somebody like *her*. Not Claire Downes, whoever the hell she was. It terrified her to think that men were looking for women that much younger. What was her dating range, then? Some sad old sack in his sixties? Ugh.

'I bet.'

'And I'm here to talk about one of Hans's movies. *Maud*. I'm an actress – he wanted to see me before auditions tomorrow.'

Venus wondered for which part. There was Molly, the Saxon wench who was Henry Plantagenet's lover. Probably that.

'How nice. Could be a big break for you.'

'And you?' Lilly asked politely. Already her blue eyes were scanning the throng just past Venus's shoulders. Venus didn't take offence; no girl in her right mind wanted to be stuck at a party with a bunch of women.

'It's just social. Hans is an old friend,' Venus lied. No way was she telling this little chit she'd agreed to audition. Far too shaming. In cream silk and diamonds, all high class t&a, she knew she looked like a movie star. And you had to act *as if* until you were one.

'Maybe you could put in a good word for me,' Lilly said. There was a note of pleading in her voice.

'Sure.' Venus winked at her, although she had no intention of doing so. The kid could sink or swim on her own. 'Excuse me now,' she said brightly, and glided away before one of the younger women could break up the group first.

Perfect. There was Harry Delacourt. Venus had met him at something or other. Old Etonian, big pig farm in Devon, gambling debts, small flat in Chelsea, coke habit. Definitely nowhere close to big enough, but affable and charming. She could use him for introductions. Harry's great gift was to be connected. Venus pounced.

'Harry,' she purred. One delicate hand on his arm; his eyes lit up as he looked at her, and Venus kissed him gently on both cheeks, giving him a dazzling smile. 'How are you? So good to see you.'

'Very well,' he said. 'How are you? I heard you popped over to Mahe with the girls.'

Venus's face froze. 'From where?'

'I have spies,' he said. 'All well with your uncle? No trouble in paradise, I hope?'

'No,' Venus insisted, determined to get off the subject instantly. 'None at all! Harry, introduce me to your friends . . .'

'This is Akihito Tomura. Works for Lazard.'

Venus bowed slightly, not liking the way Tomura leered at her boobs. No class.

'And this is Karl Roden. Karl owns the Victrix Hotel Group.'

Venus immediately turned towards him like a sunflower raising its head. *Mmm*, she thought. He's something special . . .

The Victrix Group. Simply the best, most exclusive hotels in the world. There was one in every major city, and they were the *dernier cri* in luxury – with a price tag to match. Venus always booked in, at least when she could get a room. And preferably if one of her even richer friends was paying.

Karl himself was fifty, she guessed, but a good fifty. Salt-and-pepper hair, lean, muscular body, a hungry look in eyes framed by thick black lashes. A sensuous, slightly cruel mouth. Venus's eyes cast down for a wedding ring, but his hands were bare.

'Delighted,' he said, looking her over. Approvingly.

'So what are you doing in town? Going to give us another Victrix London?'

'Venus,' purred a voice behind her. 'Always talking shop.'

Venus closed her mouth. Her sister had arrived.

'I'm Diana, Venus's sister,' she said.

'Karl Roden and Akihito Tomura,' Venus snapped, infuriated.

Karl took one of Diana's hands, raised it to his mouth and kissed it. It was all Venus could do not to bristle. Bloody hell! Diana had totally *forced* her way into this party and now she was blocking Venus's every move. Maybe she should go back to Marcia after all. Living with her sister was going to be a nightmare . . . like Christmas at Uncle Clem's, but lasting for months.

'Charmed,' he said softly.

Venus knew that look. You could tell in an instant who was into whom. Karl liked her, but he liked Diana better. She wasn't going to humiliate herself by trying to compete.

Her glance took in the scene. The young girl, Lilly, had managed to get herself next to Hans. The body language said it all, giggling and flirting. And he didn't seem disinterested; the powerful Austrian body bent closer to her . . .

That was too much. Venus Chambers was not going to be pushed aside by some teenager in a high-street dress. She sashayed over to Hans, drawing her shoulders backwards so her breasts thrust out a little.

'Excuse me for interrupting,' she said, ignoring Lilly's instant scowl, 'but I forgot to tell you, Hans, my cousin Juno is having a little party on Sunday for Polly Sheffield—'

'Who?' Lilly asked rudely.

Venus favoured her with a sweet smile. 'The Duchess of Sheffield,' she said. Rumour had it that Hans Tersch was a snob; he collected the best of everything, from paintings to aristocrats. 'Jemima might pop in. Are you free?'

'Unfortunately not. I'll be back in LA.' But it had worked. Hans turned towards her. 'We'll talk a little more tomorrow,' he said to Lilly.

'Sure,' Lilly said, smiling furiously, and stomped off.

'That was cruel,' Hans said.

'I don't know what you mean.' Venus pouted.

He grinned. 'Oh, I think you do.'

She smiled, unable to keep it up. 'Sorry. I got annoyed, she was monopolising you. And I wanted to talk about the script.'

He slipped an arm behind her unobtrusively, and ran a thick, callused finger lightly down her bare back, caressing her spine. Venus, to her amazement, instantly dissolved in a pool of lust. There was something about the total power of the gesture, the possessiveness of it, that turned her on. Men were dazzled by her beauty, and usually wooed her, desperately, with expensive gifts and bouquets of flowers.

Not this one. Under her dress, her flesh stiffened, and tendrils of wanting curled snake-like in her belly.

'No business at the dinner table,' he said lightly. His eyes on her, his gaze steady. Telling her he could feel her reaction. His hand went lower, and his thumb brushed across the small of her back.

Wanting to stop her body's reaction, Venus moved away. He was smiling at her still, and it made her feel exposed and vulnerable. Man, he was hot. Not her usual type, not at all. Venus half-heartedly dated bankers and property moguls, men with neat bodies and good suits. None of them had ever really struck a chord. Her true love was an idea – Venus Chambers, movie star – and everything else faded into insignificance in comparison with that dazzling vision.

But Hans Tersch was direct, rude, thickly muscled. Confident to the point of boorishness. Her eyes flickered over the strong pecs and biceps she could see under his shirt.

'You will sit next to me at dinner,' he said.

'No – Janey Epstein is next to you. And Melissa Meyer.' Venus had looked over the table setting.

'I will move Janey,' Hans said, his guttural accent low. 'I'm sure you will be much better company.'

Diana picked up her salad fork again and pushed a few glistening leaves around her plate. Dripping with olive oil, and that was far too many calories for anyone. She watched her figure constantly, and had acquired a delightfully small appetite. Salads came undressed, chicken was grilled with lemon juice, pepper, and no skin. She took a long pull on her mineral water; hydration kept the skin plump.

'That's a beautiful necklace,' Claire Downes said. She was seated opposite Diana, and her large eyes were even wider in the candlelight. Next to Claire was Ollie Foster. He kept resting one hand on her knee. 'Is it from Butler and Wilson?'

'No.' Diana tilted her head, amused. 'Garrard's. Made for the family in the twenties. Venus is wearing the matching earrings.' Ollie Foster smirked, and Diana made sure to reward him with a wink. 'Thank you, though.'

Claire's eyes flashed. 'It must be nice to have some family things you can wear. Especially if – you know – you don't have a man buying them for you.'

'Oh, I wouldn't expect a man to support me,' Diana drawled. 'Men loathe it when you see them as a walking credit card.'

That hit home. The men sitting around her, big hitters, the lot of them, were beaming amusedly. Diana did a quick head check of their marital status and net worth. She was seated next to Jock McPherson, the sadly married stud-farm owner, on her right, but on her left was Karl Roden. Hooray for that. Ollie was right opposite, and Diana considered him very much available. If you didn't have a ring, you hadn't closed the deal. And finally, the other side of Claire Downes was Mick Torrance, the arable farmer from Norfolk; an old-fashioned landowner with a wonderful Queen Anne mansion . . .

Any one of them rich enough to keep her in the manner to which she'd become accustomed. Diana squared her shoulders. It was time to start a proper campaign.

Little Claire Downes glowered at her. 'Is that why you never married?' she retorted. 'Didn't want to stay at home and have children?'

Never married? Diana was only thirty-six. But the remark stung.

'I'd be delighted to get married and have children. With the right man,' she said. 'But he'd have to be a perfect fit.'

Claire forked some salad into her rosebud mouth and flung Diana a bitchy little smile.

'I wouldn't wait, if I were you,' she said archly.

'I'm just past thirty, so I have a little time.' Diana smiled, trying to relax. 'And you know, I think men hate it when you're obviously desperate to land them. It looks so cheap and tarty. No man wants a wife who everybody knows is just after a big fish.' She paused. 'Tell me, how long *have* you been dating Ollie?'

Karl spluttered with amusement into his claret. Claire Downes flushed bright red.

'So, Ms Chambers,' Karl said, swallowing his grin. Stepping in before Claire could reply with something even worse. 'What do you do for a living?'

'This and that,' Diana said vaguely. She smiled disarmingly at him. 'I'm lucky enough to have a private income. So it seems a shame to spend my time behind a desk.'

'You might like it if you tried it,' Roden suggested. 'Work is good for the soul.'

'How so?' Diana wondered how quickly she could turn to Mick Torrance, sitting opposite. She wasn't interested in a lecture on the wonders of nine-to-five.

'It's a challenge. Like solving a puzzle. A race. An adrenalin kick.' Roden dipped a piece of focaccia bread in fragrant olive oil and ate it. 'Take the Victrix. I started the hotel in 1990 with every cent I had, and every cent my parents had, and some money from college friends. The first one was in Greenwich Village. A boutique with five rooms, because that was all I could afford.'

'Five rooms?' Diana laughed.

'Five rooms, and two of them were barely singles. But it was the best location, and decorated to the ultimate in luxury. Duck-egg sheets in watered Chinese silk,' he said, eyes glazing over. 'Full room service, twenty-four hours. Real Italian ice cream. Clothes unpacked, folded and ironed. A personal concierge for each guest. And I charged top dollar from the get-go.' His dark eyes sparkled. 'Within a month I had venture capital. Within a year we opened the Victrix on Avenue of the Americas, and it had twenty storeys. Let me tell you, honey. That was the most thrilling year of my whole life.'

Other guests had stopped talking, and were listening to him. Roden was magnetic, Diana could see that. Coarse and New York tough, but definitely magnetic.

'It sounds it,' she said flirtatiously. 'How could any woman ever compete?'

'I'm twice divorced,' Roden replied. 'That answer your question?'

Twice divorced. She did a quick, greedy calculation. That meant he was the type that liked to marry, but also the type that would demand a pre-nup. Loaded, yes, but hardly ideal . . .

'Come over and see the site,' Karl suggested, as she was about to turn to Mick Torrance. 'You know all the hip people in this town. I want it to be the next Met Bar. Or Boujis. As hot as that, but as classic as the Ritz. You can assist me.' He smirked. 'If what I've heard is on point, you'll save me a bunch on consultant fees. I'll gladly pay you.'

'I'd be happy to do it for nothing,' Diana said, trying to get him off the subject. Too late; Mick was engrossed in conversation with a buxom redhead on his left.

'Tonight, then.'

'Maybe tomorrow.' Diana opened her purse and handed him a little business card.

'Girl about town,' Roden read. He grinned. 'You're a kick.'

Diana shrugged, not best pleased. Claire Downes had recovered, and was gazing adoringly up at Ollie Foster, pressing her slim thigh against his trousers. And the other rich men were all being chatted up by the various decorative females Hans Tersch had invited.

Diana had no interest in work. Ugh. Tonight was a bit of a bust.

Across the table, Venus was sitting next to Hans. She appeared lost in him, leaning forward so that her ample cleavage was showing. Diana's annoyance increased. She had moved on to try and grab bigger prey, but she'd have been better sticking with Hans. Now Venus had him all to herself for the entire meal. It wouldn't be worth it to make another play for the film mogul. He was only an indie producer anyway, Diana told herself.

Oh well. Tonight was just one evening. She could pretend she was happy with Karl's interest. And she had learned something tonight. You needed to go to a party like this with a *plan*; a designated man, and a back-up in case he got taken. She took a tiny sip of her Cristal champagne and resolved to shake things up. Starting tomorrow. Diana Chambers was going to do her very own twenty-first-century version of the Season, and just like her ancestresses before her, by the end of it she was bloody well going to be married.

'How's ten o'clock for you?' she asked Karl, with a perfect, bored smile.

'See you then.' He was oblivious.

Chapter Nine

The moon had risen, high and bright over London. The sky was inky black when the revellers departed from Hans's place. Diana was first; angry with Venus, she'd hardly wanted to wait. There was nobody here of any quality. No real *players*, at least ones that were available. She had no desire to watch the teenage chicks in their bad shoes and cheap dresses manage to hog the attention of Hans Tersch's myopic friends. Pretending to be bored, Diana stepped laconically into the road and stole the taxi that was waiting for Claire Downes. Stuff Venus. And stuff her.

Diana watched curiously as the men started to exit, their trophy wives and eager little girlfriends hanging on their arms. How satisfied they all looked, all those couples. The wives especially. They would never have to worry about a lack of embossed invitations on the mantelpiece, never doubt their summers in yachts moored in Capri or St Tropez. The Bulgari handbags, the L. K. Bennett shoes, the precious bracelets by Cartier and the leather Chanel cuffs – all the little things that made life so perfect were theirs for good.

She wanted it. And if Uncle Clem was going to take it away, there was only one way to get it back. Tonight Diana had been sloppy. That could not happen again.

Venus watched Diana leave, without saying goodbye. So, her sister was annoyed. She felt a slight pang of guilt, but she'd just have to make it up to her tomorrow. Venus simply didn't care right now. She was too excited.

As the guests started to drift away, she made herself scarce: frequent trips to the loo, where she splashed on Hans's Molton Brown eau de cologne; plopping herself down on the antique chaise longue and rubbing her ankles; drifting over to the windows to admire his tiny spotlit walled garden, impeccably designed by Rufus Drax with an almost Japanese use of space.

The night outside was crisp and cold. Under her silk gown, Venus's body was warm and tingling. Hans had turned her on at supper. Although she had sat next to him, he had hardly looked at her. He spent the meal concentrating on the other guests, a financier, a Congressman, a little chit of an actress. And he talked about his other projects, his planes, his companies, his estates in Austria. The politician asked his advice on hedge funds. The financier wanted to recruit him for a hostile buy-out he was planning. And he was encouraging to young Melissa, giving her some highly practical advice whilst, Venus was thrilled to see, ignoring the gooey eyes she made at him.

It was conversation that swept across money, stocks, land, and movie star glamour. It reeked of power. Venus knew he was showing off for her a little. It worked.

The dwindling crowd were discussing the Cannes festival and laughing about the impossibility of getting a hotel room.

'So what did you do? Stay in Nice?' the Congressman asked Hans.

'Don't be an idiot.' Hans spread his thick hands. 'I bought a little villa in the hills above the Croisette. Only one point two.'

He didn't need to say 'million'.

Unable to stop herself, Venus heard her breath quicken a little in her throat. She tried to cover it with a sip of champagne, but his eyes flickered towards her, amused, just for a second, letting her know he had heard, he knew. And as the blood flushed to her cheeks, Hans pressed his thigh against hers. He replaced his napkin in his lap, and his fingers trailed, subtly, definitely, across her leg, brushing her just above the knee . . .

It was electrifying. Venus shuddered with pleasure, the squirming feeling in her stomach instantly replaced by a full wash of desire. Everything about him made her feel high, as though she'd just taken a little hit of coke and therefore everything was brighter. She had known richer men, but none who so casually threw their money around. And many of the guys in her circle were actors, who were always that little bit less manly, or moneyed toffs that Juno's parties threw her way. There were few producers like Hans. Self-made and unapologetically ambitious. He was dominant, and his guttural accent made him sound even more masculine. There was something about German. She shifted on her seat, trying to control her breathing, thankful for the strategic tape concealing her modesty, thankful that he didn't have his hand on the flat of her belly to feel the warm blood pooling there.

Hans Tersch had a complete air of entitlement. She knew she should have resented it, resented his easy use of his power and wealth to attract her. But it turned her on. No two ways about it. And the fact that he had power over *her*, particularly, was even hotter . . .

She busied herself with this and that, admiring every antique carved jade statue or sleek modern design piece stacked around his townhouse. Wondering what the bedroom was like. Wondering if he had mirrors.

And she did not, could not, look at Hans. He could damn well broach the subject himself. She was not going to seduce him. Even though her skin, her blood felt as if it was on fire.

Outside the French doors, the designer garden looked marvellously tranquil. The Zen stone water feature on the opposite wall, cast from a single piece of brass and set with crystals and reflecting silver discs, glittered and sparkled as the cool fountain tumbled over it. She tried to focus, but the soothing sounds didn't work for her.

Instead, Venus watched the reflections in the door as they left, one by one; the little actress amongst the last to go. Safely out of sight in the garden, nobody was looking at Venus, nobody noticed she was still there; just as she liked it.

Finally the door opened and closed for the last time, and she was alone in the house with him.

As though carelessly, she sighed aloud and turned from the door.

'Goodness, I think your garden hypnotised me,' she said lightly. 'Lost track of time there. I do apologise, Hans, I should be going. I've trespassed far too long on your good will . . .'

He chuckled. Venus looked up to see him coming towards her, his eyes dark with wanting. And predatory intent.

'Neither of us is stupid,' he said.

She felt like a mouse in front of a snake. Rooted to the spot. With terror, with desire. She simply could not move, could not break his gaze. Hans Tersch came up to her, up close, inserting himself in her body space. Venus's lips parted, almost by themselves. Her heart raced.

He reached out, almost curiously, and rubbed his palm lightly over her ribcage, feeling the bones under the silken gown.

Venus gasped. She couldn't stop herself. Triumphantly Hans's hands slid down her body, his strength, his muscles big and firm against her lightness, and he raised the cream silk up, up over her panties, over her belly . . .

'Upstairs,' Venus croaked, barely able to speak.

He shook his leonine head, smiling triumphantly. 'No time.' And he grabbed her by the shoulders and pushed her to the floor.

When she woke in the bedroom, the clock was blinking three forty a.m. Venus sat up, the cotton sheets pooling around her. His master suite was roomy and opulent, with the walls decorated in brown hessian fabric, a huge en suite bathroom with a free-standing pure copper bath and a vast ornate gold mirror, as well as a wetroom-style shower on limestone. The bed – she couldn't place the designer – had a chocolate leather headboard, and was excessively comfortable. After they had finished having sex, she had fallen asleep, almost instantly, in the crook of his arm.

The crisp white sheets were crumpled and stained. She blushed in the darkness, knowing it was her, it was her sweat. Hans had worked her body expertly, embarrassingly well. Venus leaped and bucked in his arms. Hans seemed insatiable . . . four times he had taken her, pausing briefly, then rolling her back to him to start again. If there were drugs involved, Venus hadn't seen them.

There had been no talk of love. Just urgent wanting on both sides. The fierceness of his desire slightly scared her. But Venus was going to be strong. She didn't want

Hans to wake and find her there, needy, last night's careful make-up job settled into her pores.

Carefully she swung her slim legs out of his bed and padded across the room, retrieving her fallen underwear and scrap of a dress. Out of the door and downstairs, she hastily splashed some water on herself from the kitchen sink, scarfed a comb through her hair, and helped herself to one of Hans's large Burberry macs. No way Venus Chambers could be seen in a used evening gown.

She pulled her glossy phone out of her evening bag and ran her manicured fingers over the screen. Yes, there it was . . . her favourite emergency chauffeur service.

'I need picking up from Alma Terrace,' she whispered.

'We can be there in ten minutes, Miz Chambers.'

'Make it five,' Venus hissed. 'And everybody is asleep, so have the driver dim his lights and turn off the engine.'

It was an anxious few minutes, glancing upstairs, her ears straining for any sounds of disrupted sleep. But Hans Tersch, drained, was dead to the world. Shortly, a black Jag came purring up the narrow road, exquisitely quietly. Venus slipped from the townhouse, closing the door softly behind her. Mystery, she thought with elation. I'll leave him with mystery. Wanting more. Wasn't that the essence of every great actress?

When she got back to Diana's, her sister was already asleep. Venus crept to the bathroom and went through her emergency clean-up routine. She was never too tired for Eve Lom's green facial cleanser, her favourite muslin cloth in warm water, and then lashings of Issima's Midnight Secret. Always go for the classics, that was Venus's motto. She set her alarm for four hours later. It would take a while to make up and get her hair done just so, and present herself to an amazed Hans looking fresher than a bunch of daisies in the dew. Her long blond hair flowing queen-like around her shoulders . . .

She crawled nude into bed. All her tension drained away, and a picture of Hans's chest, ludicrously muscled, covered in wiry dark hair, filled her head as she drifted, sated, into sleep.

Diana staggered downstairs to find Venus already sitting at the breakfast table. Her annoyance of the previous night came flooding back; her sister was sitting there, looking like she was about to pop into a photo shoot. Her hair was blow-dried into Timotei perfection, and she wore a vast, swaddling towelling robe of the fluffiest white; fully made up, she was delicately slicing into what looked like an egg-white omelette with capers. A lemon tisane in a porcelain cup was set to one side.

'What happened to you? I went to bed at midnight,' Diana grouched. Her own eyes were still bleary. She desperately wanted a cigarette.

'I think you mean *who*,' Venus corrected. 'A little tryst with Hans. Nothing important.'

Diana felt a fresh pang of jealousy. Until she'd decided to move on, Hans Tersch had been eating out of her hand. Poor decision. And now Venus had caught him.

'Auditioning?' she asked bitchily.

'I don't need to do that to get the part. Hans recognises talent when he sees it.'

'Evidently,' Diana mumbled under her breath. 'Did you put the coffee on?' she added in a normal voice.

'Coffee? Ugh, no.' Venus shuddered. 'I don't know why you're still drinking that swill. I wouldn't do anything to stain the porcelain veneers.'

'I need something to get going. And anyway, all that false whitening – I think it's a bit Californian. Not my style.'

Venus shrugged. 'What are your plans today?'

'Got to jump in the shower, go and see Karl Roden. New hotel. He wants some advice.' Terminally boring, but still. 'You?'

'Off to sign the deal for *Maud*,' Venus said triumphantly. 'Then I might pop down to my publicists. We'll have to work out how to manage all the press.'

Never mind, Diana thought morosely, as she selected a large mug and filled it with skimmed milk and Nescafé. Karl was a bust, but he might know some people. Definitely *would* know some people. She needed to get on a proper husband-hunting party circuit. The girls at Hans's, even her own sister, were starting to make her shiver. Diana rejected the thought of a delicious bowl of Alpen and instead opted for a slice of low-cal bread with diet spread and Marmite. To keep that figure, there were going to have to be sacrifices . . .

Diana stepped out of the cab two hours later, knowing that she looked good. Damned good. She had her best fake-businesswoman suit on, the gorgeous green Prada jacket, sweetly tailored to show off her waspish waist, matched (brilliantly) with an almost identically coloured Joseph pencil skirt that skimmed her butt and tapered in tightly just below her knees. Then it was Manolo pumps in brown snakeskin, neat Dior tights, a short-sleeved Chanel shirt in cream linen, and a smooth Kate Spade bag in glossy chestnut leather. On her left wrist she'd gone for a crisp gold Cartier watch, and there was a discreet string of Mikomoto pearls around her neck.

Karl Roden was waiting for her. In the daylight, she assessed him critically. Mmm. Certainly *rich*. There was the well-cut suit, the obviously bespoke shoes, a large steel Rolex. More obviously, a racing-green Aston Martin parked on the site was gleaming in the morning sun.

Pity about the ex-wives, Diana thought idly. Great pity.

She moved towards him, smiling briskly. No sense at all in burning bridges . . .

Roden came over and shook her hand. He waved towards the building site behind them.

'So what do you think? There's going to be an underground valet car park. I want to keep the green spaces clear. Lawns in the front with fountains. A landscaped garden in the back. Roof terrace will also be planted, plus there'll be a restaurant up there with wraparound glass walls.'

Diana frowned. She didn't give a monkey's. The point was that he wasn't bloody well looking at *her*. Roden's eyes were fixed on his building, gazing at it distantly. Envisaging the site it was to become.

He was becoming less of a husband prospect by the second. She felt like flouncing off to find a taxi. It was hellishly early for this sort of thing.

'I don't think guests care too much about gardens,' she replied, a little snappishly. 'If you're a rich business-man staying at a hotel, what are you looking for? Central location, luxurious rooms, a hot bar, fantastic cuisine, modern facilities.'

Roden's eyes cleared, and he looked at her. Properly. But he was still only checking out her eyes. His gaze didn't travel to her sexy pencil skirt or her firm calves in their seamed stockings.

'I wanted it to be the best garden in London. A maze, like Hampton Court, and an area of Japanese maples with Zen stones and gravel . . .'

'Tired,' Diana said coldly. 'Done to death. You travel a lot. When was the last time you used a hotel's garden? That's right. Never. And as for Zen, that's so nineties. Any minute now you'll be suggesting growing blades of grass in square white porcelain pots for the front lobby and calling it a design innovation.'

Roden blinked, then snorted with laughter.

'Nobody ever talks to me like that.'

'Well, that's because they all work for you.' She badly wanted a cigarette and it made her even more irritable. 'I don't.'

'So what would you do with the space?'

'Add some value. Give them what other hotels don't. Modern little rooms and flat-screen TVs and broadband all come as standard at the top end. What's going to make you different? We're Londoners,' Diana told him. 'We're demanding.'

'Tell me what would make a girl like you pick my hotel.'

Diana shrugged. 'Health centre. What you want is a state-of-the-art gym. Not one of those tiny ones with three treadmills that most hotels have. Right next to it you want to have the best beauty salon in London. Fantastic make-up artists, masseuses, manicures and pedicures. A top-rated hair salon. And don't skimp on the number of therapists. I can never get appointments when I'm at a hotel because they get booked up days in advance. Your male guests should be able to go and lift weights with a personal trainer without an appointment – almost round the clock. And your female guests should be able to get their eyebrows done on a walk-in basis. Also, offer a diet menu that's healthy and tastes really good. A sort of Champneys you don't need to travel out of town for. That'll be a much bigger draw than some stupid Japanese maples.'

Roden nodded his head slowly.

'Do you know lots of beauty therapists?'

Diana treated this remark with the contempt it deserved. His smile grew even bigger.

'I'd want to keep the wage bills down.'

'That's easy.' She shivered; it was cold out here. 'Most people in fashion work for peanuts. Manicures, pedicures, massages . . . those don't require a huge amount of skill. You want to save the big money for the colorists and hair-cutters. A competent personal trainer will need a little more. There'll be turnover, but your staff will get to work with celebrities. You'll have no problem filling the slots. Maybe you should find one star make-up artist and get them to direct the others. But that's all you'd need.'

'Thanks.' He'd stopped grinning and was looking at the hotel building site again. 'It's a very good idea. Far better use of space. I'm pretty sure my girlfriend would approve.'

Diana's stomach creased in annoyance. 'Your girlfriend.'

For fuck's sake. What a waste of a morning.

'Yes, Suzie Foster, the model. You know her?'

'Not really,' Diana lied bitchily. 'They come and go.'

Suzie Foster was about twenty-four and one of the top

working models on the New York circuit. Just under supermodel status, she was still a name and did all the top shows and major campaigns for Maybelline and H&M. Diana could see her in her mind's eye: blonde, preppy, a sprinkle of cute freckles on her creamy nose, an all-American WASP princess.

And far younger than Diana.

He still hadn't looked once at Diana's outfit. Obviously she'd picked up the wrong signals last night. She wanted to run away, get herself into a spa as soon as possible. Oh God . . . had she waited too long? All the good rich men were dating teenagers. She thought of Uncle Clem with Bai-Ling. Old enough to be his granddaughter.

They had to turn the clock back.

'Anyway, I should be going,' she said. She wanted to get the hell out of here. She needed to see her cousin Juno. They had slacked off on the whole Bai-Ling affair. They couldn't just give up. Juno was very annoying, but she'd know what to do.

'I was hoping for a bit more of your time,' said Karl Roden, regarding her evenly. Slightly surprised.

Diana was angry with him. What the hell would be the point in staying?

'Your girlfriend's a model. Ask her about these things. Sorry, Karl, but it's pretty cold. I have to be going. Busy calendar.'

And she stomped off towards Old Compton Street before he could say another word.

*

Venus floated into her sister's bathroom in an even better mood. Diana had really looked rough. She might be more sophisticated, but Venus was reassured that she was the prettier of the two. And there had been that delicious look of jealousy when Venus told her about sleeping with Tersch. Yes – at one point Diana had looked like she was going off with the prize.

Venus wasn't a mean person, but she did like to think of herself as a winner – the thinnest, blondest, best-dressed girl in any room. And that included her big sister's kitchen.

She was a little hungry, but ignored it. Egg whites and capers didn't go all that far. Still, sacrifice was required for that perfect figure. And the movie cameras, let's face it, were unforgiving.

Oh yes – the movie cameras!

Time to go and secure her future. Venus primped and primed and squirted herself with Clarins' Eau Dynamiste, her lucky fragrance for work-related things. She would pay Diana back; anyway, she thought absently, Diana could run all her parties when she was finally a big Hollywood star. After all, her lead role in *Maud* would just be the first of many . . .

The brass clock on the wall said it was ten to eight. Better motor. Hans wanted them there by half past. Venus knew he'd have to actually hold the auditions, so he could save face; she wasn't about to let him down. Her outfit had been carefully laid out the night before. Time to slip it on and get going. She fished her BlackBerry from her cashmere dressing gown, and called her car service again. An expense, but it was necessary to arrive in style.

The Magnet Productions offices were just fabulous. A nondescript frontage on Wardour Street opened to a TARDIS-like lobby, with sleek, low-slung Eames furniture, white-frosted glass walls, backlit lights that revolved a rainbow of colours soothingly against them, and an achingly hip nineteen-year-old receptionist wearing Jean-Paul Gaultier.

Venus had chosen her LA audition uniform: a sprayed-on pair of low-slung Calvin Klein jeans, and a beautifully cut white silk T-shirt from Katherine Hamnett, teamed with some golden bangles from Morocco and high leather Prada cowboy boots. A white PVC Stella coat was flung over it all against the cold. Effortlessly simple, but leaving zero doubt as to her carefully dieted and surgically augmented curves, her long, glossy buttercup hair, her Beverly Hills porcelain veneer smile, and of course her deep, golden tan. She knew she was a knockout; she liked to think it made her look ten years younger.

'I'm here for the *Maud* audition,' she told the Gaultier-wearing teen.

The girl checked her list. 'Venus Chambers. Sure. If you'll just take a seat.'

'OK,' Venus conceded. 'But let Hans know I'm here.'

'You can go in when they call you,' the receptionist replied flatly.

Venus smiled gently at her, forcing herself to swallow the rage. Insolent little chit; getting her fired would be first on the agenda. She was Venus Chambers, not just another wannabe here for a cattle call.

Not deigning to answer, she picked up her little Gucci bag and went to sit down on one of the Moda Italia leather benches. There were six or seven other girls there, all of them, she was pleased to see, about her age; attractive chicks in their early thirties. Venus did a quick inventory. A few of the faces had had work done, but with somebody far less skilled than her own guy. She could see exactly what was going on: the Botox on the forehead, telltale tightness around the temples, papery skin here and there, colour that was that touch too brassy.

Venus smiled at them all. Most of them nodded and went back to reading their lines.

For want of anything better to do, Venus opened her own copy of the script. Well – at least there was no Lilly Bruin here. She'd obviously come and gone. Venus felt a surge of triumph. She'd done the right thing in seeing that little bitch off.

The words on her script blurred. Venus couldn't concentrate; she stretched luxuriously and drifted away. Thinking about Hans's rough, confident touch on her body. The casual way he'd handled her . . .

He was, she realised, not like any other man she'd ever known. He didn't look up to her. And she liked it. Venus was suddenly shivering with anticipation at the thought of seeing Hans again.

The heavy leather door to the studio opened. Lilly Bruin walked out of it. She was dressed in black leggings and a peasant blouse, and she wore dangling chandelier earrings and a huge smile. Her eyes were alight.

Venus shrugged inwardly. So Lilly got to play some serving wench.

She pasted on a smile and waved at the girl. Lilly bounded over, full of unbridled happiness. Like a bouncy puppy, Venus thought.

'Hi! Hope it went well,' Venus said.

'It did.' Lilly bent closer, lowered her voice. 'Hans told me I got the part!'

'Congratulations!' Venus winced; now she'd have to work with the girl. 'What part were you going for?'

Lilly's eyes widened. 'Why, Maud, of course. I was auditioning for Maud.'

Venus blurted out, 'That's impossible. You must have misunderstood.'

'I didn't,' the young girl said, quite firmly. 'Hans says I'm the one.'

Venus wanted to think she was mad. But Lilly was speaking with such terrible conviction . . .

'But all these other girls are waiting to go in . . . he doesn't even want to see them?'

'Oh no,' Lilly said brightly. 'They're way too *old*. They're here for the part of the dowager queen. Or maybe the old nurse. Like you, right? You wouldn't be here for the lead. Those auditions started at half seven. Hans saw me last.' She reached forward and gave Venus a hug. 'And I'm so happy!'

Venus sat there stiffly. Then she patted Lilly on the back.

Too old. Far too old.

Auditions for Maud started at half seven.

Dowager Queen Matilda . . . a small part, maybe seven or eight scenes.

'I guess I'll see you around. Hey, best of luck,' Lilly whispered brightly. 'And please don't tell a soul till they announce it in the trades?'

'Not a soul,' Venus muttered automatically.

Lilly strutted out through the doors, and Venus lowered her script. Her fingers twisted in her lap. Desperately she tried to remember exactly what Hans said at their lunch.

Had he ever specified what part he wanted her for?

Had she?

No – Venus had just assumed.

The humiliation flooded right through her. All the desire she'd felt for Hans was stone dead in her stomach. She felt her face suffusing with blood, a rich, deep blush. She didn't know if it was anger, or shame . . .

And she'd *slept* with him.

Had he laughed at her? she wondered. Laughed inside while he pounded away at her, while they writhed together on those crisp white sheets?

The receptionist's phone bank buzzed. She pressed a finger to her earpiece, then looked over at Venus.

'Ms Chambers,' she said. 'If you'd go in?'

Venus stood up, holding her script with trembling fingers. She walked across the lobby feeling naked, horribly exposed, and went through the door into Hans's office.

The room was large, with more Italian furniture, and framed posters from his movies hung about it. Hans sat at the head of a polished mahogany table, with a couple of male executives on either side of him. Venus didn't recognise either of them.

'This is Venus Chambers,' he announced. He was looking at her like he barely knew her, with polite detachment. 'She's had some commercial work and small parts in independent films. She understands the script and I think she could make a go of Matilda of Boulogne.'

Venus shook in her shoes. For once in her life she had no idea what to say.

'Do we have your details?' one of the faceless executives asked.

She managed to look Hans directly in the face.

'Hans has all my details,' she said coldly. 'No problems there.'

He lifted his gaze from his notes. No smile, but she

thought she saw his eyes flicker with amusement. Bloody maddening.

'So what scene are you gonna read for us?' the other executive enquired. He pushed his John Lennon specs up the bridge of his nose.

'There's been a misunderstanding.' On the spot, Venus decided not to duck the issue. It was Hans Tersch who was at fault. And her soon-to-be-fired bitch of an agent. 'I came here to audition for the lead.'

The junior prick blinked owlishly. 'For Maud?'

'Yes. For Maud.' She stared furiously at Hans.

'You were being considered for Matilda,' he said patiently. 'Maud is a younger woman's role and we'll be casting Lilly Bruin.'

'I guess you don't know the part,' the first guy said.

'I know it.' Venus tossed her head. 'Matilda has a scene with Maud. I learned that. I'll read it for you.'

Hans's look back at her was impenetrable.

I'll *show* them, those bastards, Venus thought fiercely. I'll show them I can *act*. I'm good at this!

She drew herself up straight, set down her script, looked the spectacled boy in the eye, and started to recite the lines.

'When your father the King . . .'

Venus flung herself into it. She gave the best performance she could. As she acted the scene, playing off the man reading Maud's lines with leaden inflection, she watched Hans from the corner of her eye. He was leaning forward intently, looking at her, a very slight smile playing on his lips. And she could sense the hunger, the appreciation of her body that had been there last night.

'. . . do it,' Venus finished. 'Or you will die.'

The last line. She drew herself up in triumph. Waited for the applause, waited for them to fall over themselves to offer her the part.

The two underlings looked at their boss. Venus did too.

'That was good,' Hans Tersch said evenly. 'Thanks for coming in, Ms Chambers. We'll be in touch.'

Stunned, Venus felt her blood grow ice cold.

What?

Don't call us?

She'd heard that before. In many situations. And she'd never got the part once they talked like that.

Unable to help herself, she flushed again, an unattractive beet red, to the roots.

I hate him, she thought. I just *hate* him.

'Thanks,' she managed, her voice artificially high. She hastily grabbed her script. Her hands were trembling again, and she fumbled with it before she managed to pick it up properly.

Now spectacles boy was wearing a look of pity. Pity! It was too much to bear. Venus turned on her heel and marched stiffly out of the door. In the lobby, the hip little receptionist was asking her something, but Venus didn't want to talk. She strode out, on to the street. Tears of humiliation pricked at her, and she fished in her handbag for her sunglasses. Even on a cold January day, she never left home without them.

London was chilly, but the weak winter sun was streaming down. Soho was bustling. Venus wanted to get out of the area, she knew too many people. She might bump into someone – that would be unbearable. The humiliation of it all, the bitter humiliation! She wasn't lording it over Diana now. How would she explain herself? What could she possibly say? *He fucked me, had me audition for a minor part, then passed me over?*

Shaking with pain, she pulled out her BlackBerry and furiously emailed her agent, manicured thumbs dancing over the tiny keypad.

Hans Tersch is an asshole. You didn't research this. You're fired. Don't call me.

As soon as she pressed send, she regretted it. Damn! What if . . . what if she couldn't *get* another agent? She hadn't exactly had a steady flow of work. She hadn't chosen to . . . wanted to wait for that big break, to be the star she deserved to be . . .

Of course, in the past she'd been able to thumb her nose at gigs.

Because she'd been rich.

Venus thought with loathing of little Lilly Bruin. A freaking teenager. That was who she was losing to. Would Hans ask Lilly out afterwards? Would he take her to bed?

Would they laugh at Venus?

She shivered in the street. A taxi turned towards her from Soho Square, yellow light on like an angel of mercy, and Venus frantically flagged it down.

'Where to, love?'

Venus shut the door and thought for a second.

'Fifty-four Park Street,' she said, in a wobbly voice.

Juno's house.

Chapter Ten

Athena's hands trembled on the steering wheel. It was raining, pouring down in long, harsh strings of droplets falling out of the grey sky; only half three, but as dark as seven. Her headlights were on, and her wipers ineffectually tried to stop the view from the windscreen constantly melting, like she was watching through a thick veil of soup.

Rough conditions. She had to concentrate. The car wanted to slip around under her. Athena made sure to tighten her hands, to control herself.

Control. What she needed. What she didn't have.

Her parents had no money. She'd almost expected that. But to hear they didn't even own Boswell House. Her childhood home – and lifelong dream.

And now developers planned to wreck it.

There was no inheritance. All the money had gone on her and Juno's education. Juno had hung her Masters degree on her kitchen wall; Athena had pursued the life of the leisurely academic. Competing, and being annoyed, but ultimately knowing it didn't matter; that her safety net was woven of the purest silk.

Except it was not. It was illusory. Her whole life was an illusion. Being denied tenure . . . locked out of the old boys' club . . . resented . . . She had nothing.

Athena's mind jumped. One moment she was thinking of her duck-pond at Boswell, concreted over and turned into a car park. The next, all she could dwell on was those men, those smug, self-satisfied academic monkeys, looking down on her, telling her why she'd never make professor.

Money was crucial. Athena realised that now. She wanted her life back. She wanted her home back. And she wanted not to depend on those sexist bastards for her career.

Athena wasn't like the others. A month or so ago in Mahe, Bai-Ling hadn't really registered on her, other than as a mild disappointment.

Now she was a major problem. She was going to wreck all the Chambers cousins' lives.

And as the brains in the group, Athena realised it was up to her to stop them.

Traffic ahead. Her car rolled slowly to a stop. Athena fished out her mobile phone and sent a text to her big sister. *Coming to see you.*

Bai-Ling had to be stopped. Athena needed to get her money back. After that, she could decide what to do.

*

Juno Darling sat in her drawing room, pretending to read a book. Her eyes lingered, unfocused, on her garden. She had not turned a page for fifteen minutes. The maids tiptoed around, desperate to avoid her wrath.

Jack. It was all about Jack. The bastard! He loved to triumph at her expense. Right now, at this moment, she hated him as much as she'd ever loved him.

He'd caught her earlier today; caught her sitting at his stupid computer, trying to work out a budget on his stupid bloody software.

'What's this?'

He peered over her shoulder. Juno tried to close the window, but she wasn't technological, and the mouse dragged.

'Money? Since when do you care about that?' she asked. Tried to keep it light.

Jack frowned. 'What's this?'

'Our mortgage payment,' Juno answered, after a beat. She didn't want to talk about it. Least of all with him.

'You pay that by direct debit. What's the problem?'

She chewed her lip. Wanted to tell him to stay out of it; his asking her seemed presumptuous. Jack never bothered about her money. Why now?

'There isn't a lot more to come,' she replied eventually. What the hell. He would have to know. 'A year's payments.'

'How's that, then?'

'That's why I had to go and see Uncle Clem. He's

getting married,' Juno said stiffly. 'The trust is going to end.'

Jack whistled softly, and stood back from her. Then he grinned broadly. Juno tensed in response.

'I think that's great news,' he said. 'Just us – by ourselves. The way it used to be. No more of these flash parties, Juno, am I right? You wouldn't want to do it halfway.'

'My parties aren't *flash*,' she said, wounded, hating the common way he talked.

'Can we afford the house?' he asked suddenly.

'I – I don't know.' She did know, and they couldn't. Even a fifty per cent mortgage was wildly beyond her personal means. Which, basically, were Jack's means. Juno despised him now, now that he couldn't look after her, that he wasn't rich. Why, why, why the hell had she married him?

'You still have a year.'

'Yes.' She curled her manicured fingers into a fist. 'But there are some other payments that have to be met . . .'

Even at her level of money, Juno had overspent. A house with three full-time staff. His and hers Rolls-Royces. Her gorgeous Tiffany watch. A closet full of jewels from Garrard and House Massot. All bought on credit, all needing payment.

She had been typing out what could be returned. Much of the jewellery. None of the clothes. The Chanel, the Dior, the Robinson Valentine, the Philip Treacy hat . . . that was Juno's, and no way she could give it back.

'Look.' Jack's voice was relaxed, happy even. 'The cash has come between us. Don't worry about it, darlin'. I'll help. We can get top whack for this house. Even fifty per cent of it is a lot of money. You return what you can, we take some of the house money, pay off the debts. With what's left, you can invest in our restaurants. And we can still find a great house.'

'How?' Juno asked. 'How the hell can we find a great house? This one is far too bloody small.'

'We don't have to live in London.' Excited, Jack came around to face her, perching himself on the edge of the desk. 'That amount of money could buy us a gorgeous house in Scotland. With a big garden. For children.'

'You know I'm not ready for children.'

He ignored this.

'And we can take some of the extra and fund a restaurant. All we'd need is to be near a fairly big town. Buckie, maybe. Banffshire's beautiful. It would be perfect for a start-up. Fresh seafood . . .' He fairly crackled with excitement. 'You build a great restaurant, they come to it. Like the Fat Duck.'

'Oh, certainly,' Juno said bitterly. Resentment welled up in her. 'So I get to give up London and my whole life, and fund your little adventures on the stove in the back of beyond. Well here's a clue, sweetie; I'd rather chew off my own arms than live in bloody *Scotland*. Nor do I intend to be chained to the kitchen sink, pregnant by a man who can't put food on the bloody table. Why do we have to sell this house? Because *you* can't help me. Oh no. You quit the City, didn't you? If you'd stayed in stocks . . .'

Jack recoiled, as though she'd slapped him round the face.

'My God,' he said, his Scottish accent thickening. 'Is that what you think? That I'm some sort of failure, because I packed in the trading?'

'No,' she said, and though she could hear the acid, she just couldn't stop herself. 'Not "some sort" of failure, Jack.'

He moved back, startled, furious.

'Life for you is all about money. And position. You don't even see how it's poisoned you, Juno. You're joyless, totally joyless.'

'Spare me the armchair therapy,' she spat. 'I just want to enjoy the finer things, to have fun. While I still can. You have tiny little horizons, Jack Darling. And I bloody don't.'

'Is that why you married me?' he asked, icy cold. 'No – don't answer that. It hardly matters now, does it?'

'What are you talking about?'

'You know perfectly well.' He stood up. 'I'm bringing the car round; I'll be packed in twenty minutes. I'll be in touch to let you know where to send the rest of my stuff.'

'Oh,' she sneered. 'I get it. The money dries up, so you're cutting and running?'

His face darkened with blood. 'No – it's not the money that's dried up, sweetheart.'

'You're moving out?'

'I'm divorcing you.' He hesitated, just fractionally. 'That is what you want, right?'

Juno shrugged.

'Well, fine by me. I won't stand in your way. Perhaps you can do better.'

He was as good as his word. Flung his suits into two cases, left everything else except one thing: their wedding album. It took him ten minutes to pack, and Juno sat stiff and unyielding in front of the computer, wanting to speak, not wanting to speak. Waiting until he had closed the door, and then listening, every atom of her, until she heard his car driving away. His high principles didn't stop him taking the bloody Rolls, she thought bitterly.

Now she was alone.

Juno had fantasised about this moment for months. Even before Uncle Clem's telegram. Her loser of a husband, always demanding sex. Good for nothing else. No social graces. Not *caring* about her life. A constant embarrassment . . .

She wanted a better husband. Somebody rich. Somebody au fait. A good match, dammit. In her fantasies, somebody with a title . . .

But her marry in haste, repent at leisure husband had put paid to that. And now he was gone.

Juno moved away from the computer and picked up her book. The maids knew better than to talk to her. It was fine; she would start firing people tomorrow anyway.

The sun struggled to the peak of the sky, weak behind the clouds. She couldn't think, couldn't concentrate; she felt sick.

The phone, blessedly, rang.

Juno's first thought was: It's him – and her sadness turned back into rage.

But it wasn't him. It was Diana.

'Can I come over?' she said. 'We need to talk. Right now.'

'Sure,' Juno replied. 'Other line. Hold on a second. Hello?'

'It's Venus,' her other cousin said. 'Juno, we need to finish this thing with Bai-Ling. Can I come and talk to you?'

'More the merrier,' Juno said, setting her teeth. 'Di is going to be here.'

Juno cursed herself for her procrastination. Since they got back from the Seychelles, she'd done nothing but worry.

The time for that was finished. No, she told herself. I don't want bloody Jack to come home. I want my life. A new husband can come afterwards. But this time, I won't sell myself so cheaply.

She walked to the cabinet and retrieved her phone. There was a text from Athena. Juno was glad she was coming; they would work through this together.

The phone buzzed. Athena picked up, and there was a telltale silence. She was such a goody-goody, Juno thought. Adjusting her damn hands-free.

'Juno.'

'The others are coming by,' Juno said succinctly. 'To discuss her.' No need to explain who that was.

'I'm driving into London. I should be there in an hour.'

'An hour,' Juno repeated impatiently.

'Just order some lunch, Juno.'

'I want her out, Theney,' said Juno, using her sister's childhood nickname. She was embarrassed to find herself all weepy.

'I know. We all do. She's a gold-digger.' *In our mine*. Athena's voice was strong and confident. 'We'll come up with something. Hold tight, OK? I'll be there in a little while.'

Juno hung up and mopped at the corner of her eyes with a lace handkerchief. She waited till she had composed herself, then called Maria in, her voice steady.

'Maria!'

'Yes, Mrs Darling?'

'Tell Cook I'm expecting three for a light lunch. Ask her to make some soup, a tomato and onion tart, and a chocolate sponge for pudding. And to get me a Sancerre.'

'Very good, ma'am.'

'We'll eat in the dining room,' Juno pronounced grandly. No economies. For today, she wanted to live as normal. Exactly as normal.

The sisters arrived within minutes of each other. Both had miserable expressions on their faces. Juno rang for cocktails; despite the calorie content, she ordered three hot buttered rums. Cook added just the right amount of sugar, and they seemed necessary.

'We're waiting for Athena; she should be here in an hour.'

'That's fine.' Diana nodded, and took her cocktail gratefully. She didn't normally drink mid-morning, but it felt right today. 'Athena's pretty clever. Let her contribute.'

Venus brooded. She accepted her glass mug silently and drank from it.

'Were you going for a part today?' Juno asked vaguely.

Diana looked at her sister, and felt some pity. Honestly, when would people accept their limitations? Venus was pretty, but her belief in herself as Helen Mirren meets Angelina Jolie was completely misplaced.

'I was. I didn't get it.' Venus bit her lip; it was clear she wanted to say more, so the other girls just waited.

'He wasn't even auditioning me for Maud,' she blurted at last. 'He had me in there to read for Queen

Matilda — the aunt. The *lead character's aunt*. This little *teenager* got the lead. And . . .'

Diana minutely shook her head. Venus stopped, mid-sentence. 'Never mind,' she finished lamely. 'The point is I need the money back. I fired my agent. I left my flat. Di is looking after me. The whole thing sucks.'

'Thanks,' Diana said drily.

'You know what I mean.' Venus indulged in a large gulp of smooth, warm rum. 'How about you? How was your morning?'

'Wasted it seeing some bloody hotel with Karl Roden.' Diana scowled. 'Turns out he has a girlfriend. Wanted to hire me as a bloody consultant. As if.' She extended her long legs. 'I have no intention of spending my life at *work*. Please.' She shrugged angrily. 'It's Uncle Clem's fault. He led us to believe that this was going to be here for ever, and then he took it away. People can't live like that. It's not fair.'

'And just to complete the picture,' Juno said reluctantly, 'Jack and I are getting divorced.'

Her cousins rounded their eyes; Juno felt a perverse satisfaction from being in the worst position.

'But why?' Diana asked.

'Money,' said Juno viciously. 'What do you think? I don't have any and he can't make any.' She wound her long string of seed pearls around her finger. 'He wanted me to move to bloody Scotland and fund his new restaurant with the rest of my money.'

'Oh dear no,' Venus said, sounding shocked.

'I can't deal with that. Not now. A woman's got a right to a husband who will look after her.'

'Of course she does,' Diana agreed.

'Jack's been selfish. And stubborn. That's all.' The thought of how he handled her in bed, breaking her resistance, dismantling her control, came back to Juno, but she shoved it aside. 'He also said he felt threatened when I had money. He was *pleased* it was all going down the drain.'

'Ugh,' Venus said. 'And I suppose he's pleased we all have to tighten our belts.'

'I'm going to have to return my jewels,' Juno wailed. 'And lose some of my staff . . .'

They talked, drinking the warm rum slowly, mulling over the ruin of their lives, until a sharp knock on the door, and Athena was announced.

She walked into the drawing room, dripping wet, and peeled off her coat; Juno thought her little sister looked achingly pretty, her cheeks red from the cold, her long hair misted with raindrops; why could she herself never have that spark, that fire? She pulled her ultra-chic little Chanel cardigan around her shoulders to reassure herself. She, Juno Chambers, was a prize . . .

She hoped.

It wasn't good to hear what the girls were saying. All these younger women hanging around. The threats, the endless competition – that was the reason, wasn't it, that she'd married Jack in the first place. To be married, to have that respectability . . .

But respectability vanished if money vanished.

Juno came to with a start. She smiled absently at her sister.

'Hello, darling,' she said.

'Is there lunch?' Athena said, breaking the spell. She stretched and shook herself, like a rangy greyhound, sending drops of water shimmering into the air. 'I'm starving. And cold.'

'It should be ready now.'

'Is that hot rum? I'll take one.'

'If we're eating, hadn't we better move on to the wine?' Juno asked, disapproving.

'Sod that,' Athena said firmly. 'I'm cold, wet and miserable. If you want to move on to wine, give me yours.'

Juno handed her drink across. Athena tossed it back in almost a single gulp. She shuddered, and the others could almost see the warmth of the liquid and the alcohol spreading through her body.

'Let's eat,' Athena said. She looked at the other three. 'We need to fix this. Now.'

Juno made sure the servants left them alone for lunch. They had soup, the delicious-smelling onion tart was cooling gently on the sideboard, and there was a fire crackling in the Victorian cast-iron grate. Juno had three bottles of Sancerre uncorked, and they didn't want to be disturbed.

She updated her sister.

'I'm afraid we've all had some bad news, Athena. Jack has left the house; he and I are getting divorced. There's a mortgage here, so I shall likely have to sell.' Such bald words, and a world of pain underneath them. 'Venus has been turned down for the last acting part she auditioned for, and she's sacked her agent. And Diana tells me her cash reserves are down to almost nothing.'

'Me too. I found out the family doesn't own Boswell House,' Athena replied.

Juno stared. 'What? Oh no, Theney, really?'

Juno knew how much that house meant to her sister. They had grown up there, poor but happy, when every Christmas was spent by the fire with Mummy and Daddy. Juno loved her parents dearly, but she'd always been a bit of a cuckoo in the nest, not quite with the brains of any of the others, and it had left her feeling awkward sometimes, and stiff.

Not so Athena. Bossed around but loved by her big sister, and cherished by her parents, she had been blissfully happy. Before Clem, and before she was sent off to boarding school. And the scene of all that childhood joy was totemic to her.

The loss of that house would devastate her. Juno folded her hand over Athena's, who squeezed back, her eyes moist.

'Mum and Dad sold it years ago. They get a small payment to live in it. They've no money and it's going to be developed. I couldn't stand it if that happened.' Athena reached for the chilled Sancerre. 'And while we're talking reserves, I don't have all that much left myself.'

Juno nodded. Boswell House had always been Athena's obsession. She knew her little sister would not rest until she'd bought the place back.

The four girls looked at each other.

There was a copy of the Chambers edition of *GLITZ* on the sideboard. Venus pointed to it.

'Seems a long time ago.'

Juno shook her head.

'But it wasn't. And it can't be. It's the end of January – we have less than eleven months to stop this thing. And we are all going to have to pull together to do it. Look, are you prepared to give up?'

'No way,' Diana said fiercely. 'Juno, you are one hundred per cent right. We stuck our heads in the sand after we got home. All we did was tighten our belts. That isn't the answer. We have to get together and fight this.' She turned to Athena. 'You're the genius, got any ideas?'

Athena chuckled. 'This is street-smarts, Di. Not my department.'

'But we do need to pull together,' Venus chimed in. 'I've got less left than all of you, and I'm not about to get a job as a temp or something. I know I can pretend to like you three losers.' She grinned. 'I am an actress, after all.'

They smiled at each other. And it was the strangest thing: as desperate as matters seemed, each girl felt her heart lift, just a little.

They needed each other. In a way they'd never done before. And it felt good not to be in this by themselves.

Juno broke the spell.

'So. Bai-Ling. We need to stop her.' She poured out the wine. It was going to be a boozy lunch, but that was OK, she decided; if ever there was a time for loose, lateral thinking, it was now. 'We need to stop the marriage.'

'And stop the sex,' Venus said, daring Juno to tell her off. 'Well, there has to be a reason he'd *want* to marry her. And we can't have her getting pregnant; the kid would get the lot.'

'Uncle Clem mustn't suspect it,' said Diana.

'And then we need to try to restructure the trust,' Athena agreed. 'Get some money in lump sums, up front.'

'One thing at a time,' Diana said. 'There's not much point in tax planning until we've got rid of Bai-Ling.' She leaned forward on the table; when it came to issues of marrying for money, she thought she might have an idea of how Bai-Ling's mind worked.

'Can I sum up how I see it? If we understand the psychology, we may be able to plan how to defeat it.'

'My sister the shrink,' Venus said with a chuckle.

'Go ahead, Di.' Athena nodded. 'I think this is the way to go. Start from first principles.'

'It's not an academic thesis,' said Juno, but she smiled at her sister. There was a camaraderie in the room they had not felt for a long, long time.

'All right. So. Why does Uncle Clem want Bai-Ling?'

'Three guesses,' Venus said coarsely.

'No, try again. Why does he want to *marry* Bai-Ling? She must be more than just a good lover. She must be absolutely sensational. Think about it.' Diana warmed to her theme. 'We all know Clem is a stickler for tradition, he loves the Mad Dogs and Englishmen thing. Why would he marry a foreigner who's half his age?'

'Try a quarter,' Athena said.

'He must be spellbound by her. But he's still Uncle Clem. Which means he will absolutely *hate* to be ridiculed. So how do we put him off her? Want my suggestions?'

'Please,' said Juno, taking a large sip of the wine. It tasted good after the aromatic soup, chicken and vegetable with a little coriander; hell, she would miss her cook.

'First, we need to separate them. Get her here. That takes care of the sex problem, and also of the spellbound problem. Once she's physically not there, her hold will diminish. We need to make the *idea* of Bai-Ling toxic to him.'

'Devious,' Athena admitted, 'but you are making sense, Di.'

'Hold on.' Juno lifted one hand; her engagement ring,

a modest diamond solitaire, glittered in the firelight. She tried not to let it distract her. 'Diana, I'm completely with you that separating them is the first step. But doesn't Bai-Ling know that too? Why on earth would she come to England for any length of time? If you were her, would you leave Clem's side?'

'Oh, she won't want to come,' Diana said. 'She'll fight against it like crazy. We have to *force* her to come by making it Clem's wish.'

'And if she's so hot in bed, why would that be his wish?' Venus asked.

'His image. It all goes back to that. Clem almost never comes to England, but he wants to be well thought of here.' Diana smiled. 'Those bloody lectures every Christmas about representing him? Bai-Ling will be doing that, as soon as word of the engagement gets out. I expect we can make a case that his wife needs to be seen to be a respectable woman, and also that she needs a little polishing to make it in society. After all, she's exotic enough as it is. What do you think, Ju, can you pull that off? You know him best of all of us.'

'Not saying much,' Juno replied. 'Nobody actually *knows* Uncle Clem, do they? But yes, I think we could persuade Clem of that. Pretty easily. He's not the kind to buy a company untested. I think he might want us to put her through her paces. It's just his way. He sets tests. Like going for Christmas.'

'So once she's here,' Diana went on, 'we need to

prove two things to Uncle Clem. First, that she's just not suitable to be his wife – not enough of a lady, a liability socially. Juno, you should take care of that.'

'I can throw a party,' Juno suggested, excited. 'My best ever. An absolutely enormous party with top-drawer guests. Bai-Ling will be out of her depth. And we can make sure she's a social disaster. Then we get it written up. Uncle Clem would be furious with her.'

'Ideal,' Venus said approvingly. She'd known it was a good idea to come to Juno for this.

'Secondly, we should prove she's a gold-digger.' Diana was starting to enjoy herself. Even her clever cousin Athena was hanging on her every word. 'The best way to do this is to get her a young, virile lover.'

'Perfect,' Athena said, impressed.

'Bai-Ling's young enough to be Uncle Clem's granddaughter,' Diana snorted, not caring that she'd happily do the same thing given the chance. 'No way she enjoys sex with him. How could she?'

'How could anyone?' Venus murmured.

Diana warmed to her theme. 'Get her a lover and get it in the papers. If she's too clever for that, there are other ways of doing it. Get her on tape expressing disgust at Uncle Clem, calling him a patsy, and so on.'

'I like both those ideas. But there have to be more.' It was Athena's turn. 'She struck me as not stupid. She's playing for a big prize here, and I think she knows it. So she'll be on her guard. I want to dig around in her past, see if there's something *already* there we can use.'

Venus thought about it. 'Agreed. But she won't buy it, and nor will Uncle Clem, if she thinks we're desperate. It'll scare her away from us. Any overtures of friendship, she'll see through them. And Uncle Clem may resent it. I'm an actress, I know about confidence. If you've got it, people love you; if you're needy . . .' She shrugged. And reached for the wine. She had been needy today.

They toyed with the food a little, eating bites of the delicious tartlet.

'Venus is right,' Athena said. 'Seeing that we're all low on cash, I don't know how we're going to do it. But these plans depend on Uncle Clem trusting us. And for *that* to work, we have got to appear confident. And as if we're still rich.'

'I have an idea,' Juno said. 'Based on Venus's thought. I rather agree – nobody likes desperate women. For any of this to work, Bai-Ling *and* Clem have to think the whole thing hardly matters to us. And yes, for that to work, we have to be the same wealthy, busy women we've always been.'

'Except without the cash?' asked Athena, smiling.

'No. That's the genius of it,' Juno said. '*With* the cash. We don't have a lot left, it's true. But we all have *some*. We all have a little. What we should do is pool it. Rent a fabulous pad in the centre of town. Wear the best clothes. Use what we still own. Keep staff, and live high on the hog. Be visibly, mouth-wateringly *rich*.'

'Now you're talking,' Diana said appreciatively. 'But Uncle Clem knows everything about our lives, Juno. He knows we have no way to support ourselves other than him . . .'

Juno's face fell. She had been so sure rich was the answer. Wasn't it always?

'No, Juno, you're right. We can pretend,' Athena said. 'Pretend to have *careers*. It doesn't matter if they're not real, does it? As long as we look as if we don't need Uncle Clem. We just want some sort of front. Besides, he'll love the idea of us living together. He was always trying to push that.'

'We're ready to kill each other by Boxing Day,' Venus said flatly. 'Every year.'

'I can make the sacrifice in a noble cause,' Juno replied. 'That of getting our lives back.'

'Me too.' Diana nodded. 'I need more space, Venus, more space than the two of us crammed into my flat.'

'It'll be expensive,' Athena warned. 'If this doesn't work, whatever you have right now – you'll have half of it once we're done.'

That halted them. But Juno spoke up first.

'I don't care. I'll do it. Worst-case scenario, we find ourselves in a one-bed in Kensington. I can live with that, if I have to. What I can't put up with is letting my life slip away and doing nothing about it.' She smiled thinly. 'And I have confidence that if we can just fund our *style* for a bit longer, we can make it.'

'I'm up for it.' Venus sounded passionate; she wanted it, desperately, one more year, high on the hog – a year of fun, a year of not looking at her bank account, a year where she could afford not to stress about Lilly Bruin and Hans Tersch – or whoever it might be. For the rest, she would think about it later. Short term-ist, yes, but she just didn't care; anything was better than her current reality: no agent, no part, no boyfriend, and no flat. Her cousin Juno sounded like a prophetess as far as Venus was concerned.

She couldn't *live* crammed into Diana's apartment. She couldn't even think about it.

The juicy alternative danced before her. A year with the girls – and suddenly, after tonight, that seemed quite a fun idea, not the penance it had always been in the Seychelles. And they'd be in a large, elegant townhouse, with servants, and jewels, and her chauffeur service . . .

Hell, yes.

She glanced over at her older sister. Diana would have a plan B, of course: use the window of opportunity to hook up with a nice trophy husband. Somebody with a fat wallet. However snooty Juno was, she hadn't chosen wisely. Diana would, and, Venus decided, she would too. Although her husband would be richer *and* better-looking. And absolutely no pre-nups . . .

But that moment was not on them yet. And something inside her wanted to stop it.

'Let's do it,' Venus said loudly. 'I have a little money left. And a small de Kooning I can sell.'

'I can lose the flat,' Diana agreed.

'The house in Walton Street.' Athena reluctantly spoke up. She enjoyed her Oxford house, loved it, almost. But nothing like as much as she loved Boswell House. 'I get pestered by estate agents almost every day.'

'And I can sell this place. We may as well use my staff. And your butler, Ferris.'

'I already sacked him,' Diana said morosely. 'And I paid him fifty thousand for severance. He was bloody delighted. I wasn't.'

'Well, we can get by using mine. It's still rare enough.' Juno was proud, now, that she'd procrastinated about sacking them; there was a certain cachet to being the one to offer up the domestics. 'And ladies, can I suggest you prepare. Prune your wardrobes relentlessly. There should be nothing second-rate in the house. We want to wear the best of everything, right down to our watches.'

'We can sell the rest,' Athena said. 'I'll do a big auction on eBay.'

'You won't,' her big sister snapped. 'Donate it to charity. What if word gets out? One of the Chambers girls, flogging her stuff on the internet. I hardly think so.'

'Don't get your knickers in a twist,' Athena said, her brow creasing.

'Hey.' Diana put up a hand to stop them. 'We all know how hard it's been in the villa every year. But if this is gonna work, we have to get on. *All* of us. Understand?'

Athena nodded, slightly embarrassed. Why did sisters always rub each other up the wrong way?

'That's it, then.' Juno, bolstered by the rum and the wine, felt a little better; her head was buzzing pleasantly, and Jack didn't seem to matter so much. 'We've got a plan. We know what to do. Houses and flats on the market tomorrow. And I volunteer to find us a house . . .'

'Thanks, but I think I'll do that,' Diana said quickly. 'I know the fashionable neighbourhoods, Juno, you don't. We need to be in a hotspot. And the house needs to say something more than just "expensive".'

Juno opened her mouth to protest, but the other three voted her down.

'Very well,' she said, since there was no alternative. 'Let's move fast, and try to have something settled in a fortnight.'

Chapter Eleven

Amazing how easy it was to dispose of a life, Athena thought to herself. After that drunken, bitchy lunch, their cousins had poured themselves into a taxi back to the West End, and she had asked Juno if she could lie down; she had collapsed on to a daybed, and not woken until six p.m., with her mouth feeling like a dog kennel, thirsty and nauseous at the same time.

Juno had had no sympathy. Get back to Oxford, and get on with it.

Athena had downed two bottles of Perrier, two aspirins and a cup of strong coffee and climbed back into her car, feeling slightly more human. All the way up the motorway she thought about it. And the situation was depressing.

Walton Street. Gone. Which meant that Oxford was gone. She was writing off the last three years. All the study, all the papers, all the libraries. Her friends in the Senior Common Room, her enemies on the tutorial staff. What did she have to show for that academic study? A DPhil. Great. Athena wouldn't say they were ten a penny. But in Oxford they're probably five a penny, she thought.

It was the hypocrisy that pissed her off. All the left-wing bollocks these clubby old men spouted after a fine meal at High Table and two glasses of college port; oh, they were impeccably liberal, devoted to the cause of state school undergraduates, recycling, saving the earth, and local produce. Except when it came right down to it, they only took on a token woman, here or there. Nothing could be allowed to interrupt the boys' club.

She was wasting her time. Banging her head against the glorious old Cotswold stone walls. To them, a pretty girl was just a pretty girl, and the brains in her head didn't matter.

Athena got in late. There were a bunch of fliers dropped on the mat. Students were walking outside her window, rolling drunkenly home to college. She loved it here. She was going to miss it.

She walked up her seagrass-covered stairs to the old, cottage-like bathroom, poured in the Radox, and slipped into her bath. She would set the alarm early. Property in Oxford was on fire, and this place would be sold by the end of the week.

But it broke her heart. Boswell House; now her Oxford home – everything was changing, everything comforting and familiar was crumbling to dust.

She didn't know if she would ever live anywhere so lovely again.

*

Juno waited for Jack to call. She had Knight Frank round first thing in the morning, determined a price, and waited for the offers to roll in; they did, of course: elegant central London townhouses were the hottest commodity in town. Juno smugly raised her price by fifty thousand, and let the agents handle the bidding war.

'Go with whoever will put down the cash,' she said crisply. 'If they want it, let them buy it. As is. I don't have time to waste with surveys. There's nothing wrong with this house.'

They spluttered a little, but she was firm.

Two offers, almost seventy-five thousand above the asking price, rolled in by the end of the week.

Juno was jubilant.

But Jack still did not call. She jumped every time the phone rang, but it was never him. Just a friend, or the estate agents.

Juno wandered around the house, wondering where things had changed. Without Jack there to annoy her, she kept thinking about him.

It had been so different, so new, when they met. She, just turned thirty-seven and still attractive, one of London's premier hostesses, in a private box at Twickenham, last match in the Six Nations, England versus France. Not that Juno gave a damn about rugby. She was in a corporate box with her friend Elise Lowell, wife of a rich American CEO and one of her best contacts; Elise knew everybody on the West Coast, from 'Frisco to Malibu. Elise's husband was offering the coveted tickets to friends and clients, and Juno attended in an informal outfit, an Armani shirtdress with a pretty belted coat.

Jack was there. Wearing slacks bought on the high street and a plain white shirt. He had come back from a holiday in Sardinia, where he was sampling local produce, and he was tanned, with basic sunglasses perched on the top of his head.

'Who's that?' Juno asked Elise in a murmur.

Her friend leaned across disapprovingly. 'Nobody important, darling. Some bloody friend of Michael's. From the local pub. City trader. Cooks on the weekends.'

'Mmm,' said Juno. Elise wouldn't know attractive if it hit her, she thought; Michael was short and goaty, and this man was tall, muscular, deeply handsome.

When he turned round, cursing because England had scored, he stared straight into her eyes.

'Excuse me. I forgot there were ladies here.'

'That's all right,' Juno said lightly. 'It's easy to forgive when your team's winning.'

He grinned at her then, with a smile that knocked her off her feet; Juno was not used to being looked at in this way.

'Jack Darling. Morgan Stanley.'

'I don't believe Jack Darling is your real name,' Juno said, laughing.

He didn't break her gaze. 'You should do that more often. Your whole face lights up when you smile. What's your name, beautiful?'

And with a sudden, heady rush Juno realised that he actually liked her for her, that Jack Darling had no idea who or what she was.

'Juno,' she said, leaving out her surname.

'Forbidding name.' He grinned. 'I like a challenge.'

The first night Jack asked her out, he took her to Gordon Ramsay. He drove them there in his Ferrari.

The second time he took her out, he brought her to his apartment and cooked for her: beeswax candles on the tables, crisp Irish linen, fine wines, and a fragrant truffle oil risotto with porcini mushrooms. They laughed and joked, and Juno felt comfortable with him, completely relaxed, confident in a way she never was. Even her dear parents, as much as they tried to hide it, had been disappointed in her lack of brains. Jack Darling liked Juno just as she was, not for her money, not for who she was. When he reached out to cup her cheek in his rough hand, Juno thrilled to the touch; he made her laugh, he was unique.

And then, when the espresso and liqueurs were cleared away, and Jack moved in, Juno pulled away from him.

'What's wrong?' Jack asked, his breath hot on her skin. 'Don't you like me?'

'Of course I do.'

'Then what?'

'I just met you,' said Juno, sliding out of his grip, a pleasurable sense of power flooding through her. She grabbed her Chanel handbag. 'You'll have to wait a lot longer than that, Jack Darling.'

'You're joking.'

'I don't joke.' And Juno was gone.

The third time, he added flowers to the candlelight, but Juno was still not swayed. Jack managed to kiss her, and the sense of her in his arms, wanting to let go but not daring to, drove him over the edge.

The very next day he came back with a ring.

Three weeks later they were married. Juno didn't want to wait, even to throw a society wedding. She threw money at it instead. She was married in St Etheldreda's, the oldest Catholic church in London, with her sister Athena as the maid of honour and a congregation made up of her parents, his parents, his little brother, and her cousins.

Life was good. Jack Darling gradually realised what he had married into. Sex was frequent, and hot . . .

It was a true marriage, back then. It was vital, and in Jack's arms, when she was laughing, covered in sweat, or arguing passionately, Juno really knew she was alive.

The memories blurred after that. How the hell had it come to this? How had it gone so wrong?

Juno saw it in her mind, as though it had happened to someone else: the hot sex slowing a little, she getting back into her social whirl, Jack hating it; the odd row, at first, when he wouldn't play along with her third dinner that week, or when he wanted to cook for them at home but Juno preferred to go out. She was a snob. He was selfish. He'd even resented her going to Uncle Clem's for Christmas. Perhaps that was it, Juno thought, perhaps that was when we started to crack.

Jack, wandering into their bedroom, finding her trunk open on the bed, the layers of acid-free tissue paper to one side, ready for the maid to pack.

'Suppose I better get some lightweight suits,' he said. 'Your uncle's not a T-shirt and Bermudas type of guy, is he?'

Juno had stared at him blankly. 'What do you mean?'

He gestured at the suitcase. 'We have to pack, for Mahe, right?'

'We – no.' She remembered blushing, realising Jack's assumption. 'Sweetheart, you're not invited.'

He laughed. 'Not invited!'

'I'm serious – I did ask Uncle Clem, but he likes his traditions, he likes having just the girls. I should have told you earlier. Sorry. I'll be back on the twenty-seventh,' Juno said appeasingly. 'We could go off to Paris then, have a late Christmas of our own.'

Jack stared at her. 'You can't mean that, Juno. This is our first Christmas as a married couple. You can't just bugger off to the tropics without me.'

'It's Uncle Clem,' Juno said helplessly. 'He insists. You don't understand. If we didn't do as he asked he'd cut off the fund. I mean, our parents aren't invited either. It's only ever been us four.'

'Then let him cut off the bloody fund.' Jack was easygoing, but he had a powerful temper when angered. 'If I'm not welcome, I'm damned if I'll let him steal my wife. We've got plenty of money, Juno, how much do you need?'

She snapped back at him. 'Don't be selfish, Jack. I *have* to go. You want me to pass up a quarter of his inheritance? Do you have any idea of the kind of sums we're talking about? Two weeks a year seems reasonable enough to me.'

'He wants you to himself – *at Christmas*. That's family time.'

'What, are you religious now?' Juno was cold to him. She hated doing it, hated to quarrel, but Jack was laying a ludicrous guilt trip on her, and she resented it. 'We can take a Christmas break right after I come back.'

'Well, you go ahead,' Jack said, shrugging. 'You're going to anyway, whatever I say.'

And he walked out, not bothering to close the bedroom door.

Two months later, Jack gave up his job. He didn't consult her, didn't ask her. Took it for granted that she would support him.

'It'll be great. I'm going to cook. I was born to do it, Ju.'

'Cook? You make two hundred and eighty thousand a year, Jack.'

'I'll make more once the restaurants are going. Look, we may have to pull in our horns for a while. I need to get some investors. I'm going to start with a sandwich bar, get a feel for running a business day-to-day.'

Juno smiled a furious smile. 'My husband? A sandwich bar? Don't be stupid. You can't resign.'

His enthusiastic face turned leaden. 'I can, and I have.'

'Thanks for consulting me,' she said.

'It's OK. Thanks for supporting me.' He stared at her then, a long look, and she could feel the gap between them crack and stretch, feel the ground moving a little further away from them. 'Maybe we should take a holiday together.'

'I haven't got time,' Juno answered wearily. 'Booked up this month.'

They made love that night, but it seemed perfunctory, and for the first time since they'd met, Juno couldn't wait for him to finish.

The days slipped into weeks, the sex diminished, the quarrels increased. Juno thought Jack was selfish, and a loser; Jack brooded and despised her social climbing. They were falling apart long before the crack ever happened.

So she did not understand why she missed him so much.

On Friday, the doorbell went. Juno knew it was Jack; before her maid could make it, she leaped to her feet and rushed down the steps, pulled the door open with unaccustomed force . . .

There were removals men standing there.

'Mrs Darling? We've come to pack up Mr Darling's stuff. If it's all right with you.'

'Fine.' She wasn't going to let them see her wince. 'Most of it's in the bedroom,' she said carelessly. 'Go ahead.'

Then she retreated to the library for the rest of the morning.

It was nerves, she told herself, just nerves. Jack was not right for her. She'd felt trapped for the whole first year of marriage. Stuck with a real loser. So now he was gone, she had the jitters. But all it meant was that she wished she had done the dumping.

Who might she marry, as the eligible Juno Chambers again? Living in high style with three beautiful relatives? An earl? A baron? A squire from the country with a hundred acres?

Or maybe something different altogether. One of Diana's funkier connections. A major art dealer. An investment banker from Wall Street, looking to wed his money with the epitome of English class.

She would focus on the future, not on some bloody Scottish cook. Yes, go, she thought fiercely, as the men's boots stomped up and down her beautifully carpeted stairs. He doesn't want to call, he doesn't want to talk – let him get his things and get the hell out!

'I'm sorry.' Jacob Sager looked at Venus across his kidney-shaped walnut desk; behind his large windows a restaurant ship processed sedately up the Thames. 'I have taken a good look at your showreel and your credits, Venus, but I don't think you're for us.'

Her impulse was to stand up, shrug, and slap him.

You're too small for me anyway.

That's OK. I don't want to deal with amateurs.

Fine – I need an agency with imagination and flair. Anybody can rep a money-maker. The good places break new talent . . .

Problem was, she'd heard the same at the last six agencies she'd visited. Fletcher Sager wasn't her ideal. They were large, but rather staid, and dealt mostly in serious actors: men and women with nominations for all the major awards, a few winners. They liked up-and-coming talent from the Royal Shakespeare Company. Not hot blonde girls who wanted to star in Hollywood films.

'I understand.' The fight had been beaten out of her; she'd come to these guys last, dead last out of the major players. 'Would you mind telling me why?'

Jacob pushed his chair back and sighed. They were about the same age, Venus guessed, mid-thirties. She hated it that this was obviously an awkward moment for him. That he was embarrassed to hear her almost beg.

'It's nothing against you.' An obvious lie. 'I just don't think you fit with our particular agency. I expect you'll find something good.'

That was it, then, her cue to get up and walk out. Thank him for his time, if she was feeling super-polite.

But Venus didn't want to do that. Not this time. Ever since Hans, her ego had taken a major knock. Since the disastrous *Maud* audition – the friendly rejection letter had arrived in the post three days later – she was a different woman. Her cheerful arrogance was shattered; she was nervous, full of doubt.

Venus had needed that part so desperately. And it hadn't happened, despite everything she threw at it.

Close, but no cigar. It was the story of her acting career. And she couldn't find a replacement agent to take her on.

She was tired, tired of kidding herself that everything was fine, and it was the bonehead agents and casting directors who were the problem. What the hell was the real problem? Venus might not want to know, but she *needed* to know. And she was going to make this squirming little agent tell her.

'I would really appreciate some feedback. You aren't

the first agent to tell me this.' Venus smiled her most confident smile at the guy. 'Believe me, Jacob, I'm tough. I can take whatever you have to tell me. You might save me an awful lot of time.'

His eyes narrowed. 'Are you sure you want the truth?'

'Warts and all,' Venus confirmed, tossing her head a little so that the silky curtain of blond hair cascaded over her shoulders.

'Oh-kay. Prepare yourself,' he said, not unkindly.

This was going to be bad. But Venus kept her smile pasted on.

'Here's the deal: you're never going to make it as an actress. As a mainstream, steadily working actress on TV and film, you stand absolutely no chance. You might – *might* – get a bit of character work here and there, possibly the odd commercial, but I wouldn't bank on it.'

Venus tried to ignore the blood she knew was rushing to the tips of her ears.

'Can you tell me why?'

'An actress needs to be one of two things. Very good. Or very beautiful.'

'Ouch,' Venus said softly. 'No, don't stop. Tell me.'

'You're not a terrible actress. You're a basic journeyman, and it doesn't surprise me you have landed a small part here and there. I think what you have now on your CV will probably be the pinnacle of your career.

You're that bit too obvious; your reel is laboured. On the Streep/Mirren level you simply can't compete. You will never be Patricia Hodge or Brenda Blethyn. Or even Kate Winslet. You just aren't good enough to be a pro in the top flight. What talent you have is limited and parochial.'

That was bitter. But Venus chewed on it and asked for more.

'Go on,' she said quietly.

'Then there's beauty. And you are a very attractive woman. Don't get me wrong. I'm not blind.' He grinned at her, and in that moment she was pathetically grateful for it. 'But the camera needs more. The Californian girls who star in the soaps are attractive on some meta-level that even a girl like you can't compete on. And, not to put too fine a point on it . . .' He hesitated, but Venus waved him to continue. 'You're too old.'

'Too old,' she repeated.

'And if you want the entire picture . . .'

'Why stop now?'

'You probably would have been too old ten years ago. I don't take on a lot of new talent, headed for America, headed for the top, that's as old as twenty-five. The skin is mercilessly revealed under the Klieg lights, you know that, Ms Chambers.'

'Venus,' she said automatically.

'You seem to think you can play the lead. At this age, you can only play her mother. I think Hans did you a big favour in auditioning you for Matilda. Your showreel didn't really warrant it.'

It was so clinical, so brutal that she could hardly focus. But the words were there, drilling into her brain. She hated them, with every fibre of her being. On the other hand, she also knew they made sense.

'You're saying I'm not going to make it,' she whispered.

'No,' he corrected her, and Venus, for a minute, looked up, wanting some hope. 'I'm only saying you're not going to make it *as an actress*.'

'I see.' Venus grabbed her bag and forced herself to her feet. 'I appreciate the honesty, Jacob.'

'Can I say one more thing?'

She smiled ruefully. 'I don't know if I can handle one more thing.'

'You picked good material. The right ads, the right parts, the right directors for your shots, even a good photographer for your headshots. You've got an instinctive understanding of this business. Look, I don't think you have acting talent. But that's not the only kind there is.'

Venus was genuinely surprised. She almost forgot to be offended.

'Thank you,' she said.

But he was already tapping at his computer.

'Have a good day. You can see yourself out, can't you?'

*

Diana sat at home while Venus went out on her agency quest. She was bored, and a little shaken. For a start, things were different: no butler, and a lodger, at least until Juno found them a place. She'd taken an offer on the flat, and half her chic little things sat around, packed into sterile cardboard boxes.

They said moving was almost as stressful as divorce.

Of course, to be divorced you'd have to actually get married . . .

The worst thing was the one she didn't want to face. Her phone. It wasn't ringing. Well, it was ringing – just not so often. And the invitations that were coming in were distinctly second-tier. Nothing for the *Pirates of the Caribbean* premiere, nothing for Guy Ritchie's little bash at Soho House . . . Instead, she was getting asked to club openings and the birthday parties of posh nineties It Girls, Brit Pack rockers and other fading stars.

She had told nobody about the money. Apart from sacking her butler, and she'd given him plenty in severance to buy his good will. But somehow, even if they didn't have all the details, the crowd knew. Collectively. Hot London knew. If it lasted till spring, Diana would be second row at London Fashion Week, and possibly third.

The gold-plated armour of infinite cash had evaporated, and nothing had taken its place.

Desperately, she realised she was actually looking

forward to her annoying sister coming home. And to the move to their big house. Because when the noise and the hectic partying dropped out of her life, Diana Chambers – girl about town, hostess with the mostest, London's answer to Coco Chanel – was just very, very lonely.

Bad thoughts. Diana hated herself for giving in to them. She grabbed her Matthew Williamson coat and headed out of the door, walking to the newsagent. It was an unseasonably sunny day for winter; she might go for a little early-season café culture, wrapped up in her thick faux-fur scarf and cute leather gloves, and sip a cappuccino on the pavement, with her sunglasses and the *Evening Standard*.

Reading material was a great protector. It stopped people from bothering you and gave you a socially acceptable reason to be by yourself. Diana stopped at a stall, picked up her paper; property supplement today. That was something.

She sauntered into her favourite little Costa Coffee rip-off, ordered a giant cappuccino with chocolate sprinkles – what the hell, she was depressed – and found the best table on the pavement outside.

The news was more of the same. Diana sipped her coffee, and flipped through the paper, not really reading it. Drooling over multi-million-pound stucco houses she could never afford seemed much more reasonable.

Then she flipped the page. And her heart slowed.

Karl Roden. Standing outside the building site in Covent Garden. A girl next to him.

Billionaire Karl Roden and his partner, supermodel Suzie Foster . . .

Partner now, was it?

Diana looked at Suzie Foster. She was young. And stunningly beautiful, with even features and a tiny nose. She weighed perhaps two thirds of Diana's bodyweight. She was as delicate as an elf.

Burning with envy and peculiar embarrassment, Diana wrenched her eyes away from Roden's arm candy and forced herself to read the interview.

'It's going to be the most upmarket hotel London has,' Roden told us confidently, 'if you're looking for youth and buzz. No gardens – just the best health spa in London. Free massages, manicures, beauty treatments. Your own make-up artist. A serious gym with personal trainers on hand. I'm bringing New York-style health tourism to the heart of this city. I think we'll be booked up for a year.'

I'm blown away by the spa plan. Roden's ideas are unique. He could be booked up for longer than that. Better get ready for the Roden revolution . . .

Diana's manicured hand curled into a little fist. She was right. And she was angry. He was getting all the credit for *her* ideas. Her casually tossed-out ideas . . . turning into a major business proposition before her eyes. While the young, slinky girlfriend threaded her arm through Karl's . . .

He'd offered her a job. A place as his consultant. And Diana had said no.

She wanted to kick him.

She wanted to kick herself.

The paper hung limply in her hand. Diana's mind raced. She was thinking about her cousins, Athena and Juno. They had purpose, after all. Juno at least was trying to climb the ladder of a stable world; her social stratum was boring but established; an earl would always be an earl, a country estate would always have value. Diana's was exciting, mercurial – transient. Who was hot could vary from one day to the next. And boy, did they cut you loose the second you started to cool down.

Which was why she was here. With a paper.

Even Venus had at least *some* work to her name; when people asked what she did she could say she was an actress. That was something, Diana grudgingly admitted.

She loathed the emotions that were rippling through her. They were unwelcome and unfamiliar. For the first time in her life, Diana Chambers was afraid.

Her glittering life felt tarnished. And she had no way to support herself.

She hoped desperately that Juno would find a place soon.

Right now, their future was bleak.

*

Juno walked up the steps carefully, trying to conceal her excitement. Her plan to derail Bai-Ling required perfect execution. She and Diana had both been looking for a house for six weeks; it was mid-March now, and finally, after countless viewings, the perfect property had shown up.

This was her third viewing. Every time Juno feared it would be wrong, somehow off-centre, not perfect enough. And every time she was mistaken.

The house was slightly oddly shaped, narrow and tall, but that lent it a certain elegance. Gleaming white-washed stucco on a quiet street off Notting Hill Gate, with a generous forecourt for parking and a carefully planted garden, flower-free, in various shades of green and pale wood: birches, bamboo thickets. The garden was simple to care for and effortlessly chic. A gate led around the side into the back garden; it wasn't large, but it was big enough for a generous amount of furniture: a table, chairs and a couch, certainly – a perfect space for entertaining. Spotlights had been planted strategically around the place, which would make for a wonderful atmosphere at dinner; and the garden designer had laid down an actual stream, with an old stone waterwheel, at the other end of the lawn, defining it and giving the place a soothing atmosphere.

And inside – perfect. A flagstone floor in the hallway, accenting the old building; a sweeping staircase that processed grandly up two further floors; five bedrooms, four ensuites; several balconies overlooking the street; a glorious modern kitchen in a smart basement extension, supplied with plenty of daylight from lightwells, and opening on to the green space of the garden.

It married all the Georgian splendour with those modern conveniences that Juno knew were *de rigueur* for Diana's set: underfloor heating; a TV and radio system wired to the whole house; a fabulous modern burglar alarm, *sans* code, where you just wiped your key fob to turn it on and off; and best of all, a darling little home cinema, with ten leather seats, a large screen, and a built-in bar, espresso machine and popcorn-maker. Venus, the actress, would love it. Even Juno was secretly enamoured.

The bathrooms were ultra-modern, with wetroom showers and deep hydrotherapy baths, modern technology set in antique marble or solid, gleaming copper. Juno practically licked her lips as she thought of her dinner guests popping to the loo and being confronted by *that*. Heating under the limestone, strategic windows looking out on to the garden's huge weeping willow – well, it was just perfect. And the bedrooms all had deep closets, or even better, walk-in wardrobes.

The whole house shrieked 'wow' factor.

And it cost. Boy, did it cost. It was eye-wateringly expensive.

But Juno couldn't worry about that. They had a certain amount, from the sale of the properties. Even reserving half their equity, and allowing for hiring her staff and living high on the hog, there was enough. Yes, it was a ludicrous extravagance.

But this year was all about extravagance, she thought ferociously.

She wouldn't tell the girls the price. They were all coming here, in twenty minutes, to view. Juno was relaxed. She knew the Chambers girls. As soon as they saw it, they'd want it, money be damned.

That was the way they used to live, and that was the way they were going to live again.

At six the others arrived. Juno dismissed the letting agent to wait in the car, and regally conducted the other women around. She kept the commentary to a bare minimum; just pointing out a feature here and there, the drop-down TV in the kitchen, the mirror screen in the living room that turned into a television when you pressed a button, the hidden rose gazebo at the back of the stream.

It wasn't necessary. Their expressions, varyingly impatient and disinterested, changed almost right away. By the time she had finished the walk-through, the girls were drooling.

'It is a little expensive,' Juno warned.

'Screw that,' her sister said, and for once Juno didn't wince at Athena's language. 'I want it. Let's take it.'

'Me too,' said Venus, her eyes alight.

'Me three,' said Diana, and comforted herself with the thought that Karl Roden's new hotel would be nothing compared to her bachelorette pad.

Juno nodded. She didn't need telling twice. She dialled the agent, then went and sat in the gazebo while her bank wired the money. No point in hesitating. Their new life started right now.

Chapter Twelve

Bai-Ling moved through the garden with a delicate, studied grace. She was proud of her walk; there was a little swagger in it, but not enough to be unladylike; you could not tell when the old man was watching.

She never let her guard down, not even for a second.

The tropical breeze wafted through the dense vegetation of the mountains and stirred the gardens, lifting the scents of frangipani and roses as they went. But Bai-Ling smelled a trap. Everywhere she looked, life was full of traps. This was just the most serious.

Her enemies. Four pale-skinned, green-eyed, beautiful women. A little older than her. A lot less experienced. But with that animal cunning a woman should rightly have. And worst of all, they understood her fiancé, very well, too well.

The invitation – sent by telegram, of course – burned a hole in her pocket as she walked.

Dear Bai-Ling,
It seems too long since we all met in Mahe. As you

will be preparing to marry Uncle Clem this year, and he no longer travels to England much, we thought you might like to come. Spend the Season with the four of us in London. We'll be very happy to take care of you in his absence, take you along to some parties and concerts, and introduce you to some of the family friends. It may help you prepare for life after the wedding! Of course, we would also relish the chance to get to know you, as ours is a close-knit family.

Do let us know if any of this appeals. The four of us have taken a house together this year — just the girls — so it should be fun!

Yours ever,

Juno Chambers

Of course it had been addressed not just to her, but to Clement. The four English witches had taken good care of that. If she refused to go, Clement would know. And he, sucker that he was, was rhapsodising about it; about Bai-Ling's stupid entry into their moronic society.

Why did the old man care?

But she knew he did care. Very much. And about their warped definition of a family. Bai-Ling knew she was right to suspect them, but she also knew she would have to go.

Never mind. Tonight she would go to him, twice, three times. Yet again try to get his limping old seed to the gold. Just one time would be all it would take. Nobody could ask her to fly halfway around the world whilst pregnant . . .

Bai-Ling knew his warped fantasies. She had the body to make them happen. And she didn't care. Clem was the catch of the century. And she was acting in the tradition, the age-old tradition, of the powerful courtesan. Women like her had risen from the gutter to rule empires and spend the wealth of nations. She was determined her life would be the same way, and four over-the-hill, pasty little white girls were not going to stop her. If they hadn't secured their uncle's cash by now, it was too damn late. Anyway, spoiled brats, they wanted for nothing. Bai-Ling had gotten here doing things, seeing things, those stuck-up bitches couldn't dream of. And nobody and nothing was going to shift her.

She entered the house and looked quizzically at one of the maids.

'He's in the second living room, ma'am,' the girl said, bobbing a curtsey. Just like in the movies. Bai-Ling had taught them to do that, as a sign of respect. If you let these people take one inch they would trample all over you. Bai-Ling had already had four of them fired, including one senior cook who'd been with Clement for twelve years. She picked him deliberately, to flex her muscles; show them all that the only bond with the master that mattered was hers.

Second living room. As she suspected, her fiancé was

fast asleep, dozing in front of a huge open fire in the opulent room, hung with antique yellow Chinese silk, that faced the calm crashing of the ocean on their private beach below the house. The tropical sky was darkening to a gorgeous blue twilight, still streaked with golds and reds. Bai-Ling fanned herself with her hands; even with all the French doors thrown wide open to the patio, it was boiling hot. Clement's skin was papery, and his old blood was cold, she thought, like a lizard.

But she had endured worse.

Gently she stepped over to him; small, mincing, concubine steps, the walk of the Dragon Empress. He was a great one for lady in the kitchen, whore in the bedroom, and Bai-Ling was happy to oblige. During the day, there was no tackiness. She dressed with modest elegance. Aped the old European manners. Studied customs like Ascot, and Wimbledon, and Eton, and Last Night of the stupid Proms. There was nothing about Britain she didn't know. And she felt no need for this field trip . . .

'Darling,' she said, with that low murmur he liked. 'Darling . . .'

Clement's rheumy eyes blinked, and he looked at her, trying to focus.

'You asked me to wake you at six,' she said sweetly. 'Would you like me to draw your bath? We can prepare for supper.'

He smiled, gave a slight cackle of a laugh. 'Maybe later.'

Bai-Ling allowed herself to blush; he liked that. Blushing was his code for sex, for the things he liked her to do, the way he wanted her to act.

'You always make me wait,' she said, pulling a little pout. While she prayed to all the gods in the heavens that he wouldn't be in the mood tonight.

'I'm hungry. What have you ordered?'

'I told Cook to make us some mulligatawny soup. And then a couple of hen lobsters with sorrel butter, and new potatoes.' She smiled. 'A very good Chablis. I hope that's all right, dearest.'

'Sounds delicious.'

'Raspberry fool for pudding,' Bai-Ling added. She had learned fast not to use the telltale words that Clement described as 'common' – 'toilet', 'pardon', 'dessert', 'portion', 'serviette'. These damn English with their stupid rules!

'That's fine,' he said, nodding his approval. Bai-Ling never offered anything other than proper English food; her fiancé wouldn't wear it. 'And the letter, dear. Juno's letter?'

'Oh yes – such a sweet invitation,' Bai-Ling said carefully. As she had feared, she read his wishes in his eyes. 'And I am delighted to accept. So nice to get to know your relations. Family is most important.'

Damn it!

But the deal wasn't closed yet. She had to get that ring on her finger. And if bearding the Four Bitches in their den was the only way to do it, then Bai-Ling was up to the challenge.

If they thought they could derail her now, they were sorely mistaken.

Venus padded downstairs into the kitchen, and was mildly annoyed to find Juno already sitting there. She was used to being the early riser in Diana's flat. This morning had broken clear and gorgeous over her third-floor bedroom, the sun streaming in through the light-well, gently prodding her awake, and she had moved diligently from the bed on to her exercise machines; first half an hour of jogging on the state-of-the-art treadmill she'd splashed out on, and then twenty minutes of Pilates. Half the actresses in Hollywood swore by it. Just pulling on her chic Juicy Couture tracksuit in marsh-mallow pink and white improved Venus's mood a little; she fastened a diamond tennis bracelet around her tanned wrist, to show the world just how glamorous she really was.

Afterwards she escaped to her stylish en suite. There was a low-slung Japanese bath right by the massive window, with direct views on to the garden; the pale green fronds of the grasses and silvery bamboo glades glistened with early morning dew, sparkling in the February sun; she could pick out the soft blues and lilacs of the crocus plants poking up around the trunk of the young oak tree, while the artificial stream glittered in the unseasonably warm light. It was a soft, rich vista, the type she was used to. And was determined to *stay* used to.

Venus's expensive cosmetics also reassured her; the familiar, soothing scents of Clarins and Kanebo and Crème de la Mer, washing and blow-drying her glossy mane, stepping out of the bath on to marble steps and slipping into her fluffy towelling robe. As soon as she was dry, she reached for the La Perla, choosing a tiny brassiere of cappuccino-coloured lace frothed with white seed pearls, a matching thong, and a favourite pair of embroidered Moroccan slippers, the real thing from Marrakech. Then she reached for her cashmere robe, soft as thistledown, creamy magnolia, lightweight, that clung to her hard body and showed off her tan, belted it around her narrow waist, and headed downstairs, glowing virtuously at how early she was up . . .

But Juno was already at the breakfast table. And she was fully dressed, in a chic, severe little outfit, a yellow suit with a white silk shirt, pearls and teetering yellow heels. She reminded Venus of a closed daisy. Juno would be attractive, after a fashion, if she loosened up, she thought idly.

The scent of rich vanilla coffee filled the room. But Venus resisted. No caffeine for her. Juno was toying with half a grapefruit, and had a tiny square of plain wholemeal toast.

'There's more grapefruit if you want it.'

'Thanks, but I need protein.' Venus moved to the cupboards and grabbed some eggs. 'Helps with the weight-lifting.'

'Don't you think that's a little unfeminine?' her cousin asked.

Venus stiffened; Juno was about as feminine as a store mannequin.

'No,' she said shortly, whisking up her eggs. 'What's up?'

'We've had another telegram this morning,' Juno announced.

Venus put the gleaming copper pan on to the Aga, trying to act normally while a shiver of fear raced through her. 'Uncle Clem again?' she asked, tipping her eggs on to the heat and grinding in some pepper.

'No; Bai-Ling.'

'Ah.' Venus sighed with relief. 'And what does she say?'

'She's coming, of course.' Juno was maddeningly confident. 'What else could she do?'

'Morning.' Athena strolled into the kitchen in her grubby tartan dressing gown and pair of men's pyjamas. 'I'm starving. Hope you didn't take all the eggs, Venus.'

'You should be careful what you eat,' Juno said disapprovingly.

'I'm going to be.' Athena grinned. 'Got to get enough food, haven't you? Bacon and eggs, some Marmite toast, Earl Grey, maybe some porridge with golden syrup.'

'Don't be ridiculous.' Juno coloured angrily. 'You're supposed to be raising your standards, Athena.'

'You think I should throw in a smoked kipper?' her sister replied insolently.

Venus tipped her plain omelette on to a plate. 'You two are giving me a headache. Athena, Bai-Ling said yes. She's coming.'

Her cousin nodded as though she didn't care, but Venus knew better. There was something tense about the set of the superbrain's shoulders. She liked to portray herself as above the fray, but Venus knew Athena wanted the money, just like the rest of them.

'Then we have to have a plan.' Athena wandered over to the cupboards. 'Something specific . . .'

Venus sat down, carefully sliced into her omelette, and polished it off in three bites. Damn Athena for talking about food like that. And now she was frying bacon, which when you were dieting was positively sadistic.

To stem her hunger, she took a large gulp of water.

'I'll go and wake Diana,' she said. Anything to flee the delicious scent of Athena's breakfast. 'We should have a council of war.'

Juno started to lecture Athena about her nightwear. Oh God, Venus thought as she escaped upstairs, it's a luscious house, but I don't know if I can take a year of this.

Thank God Bai-Ling was arriving. If they could

dispose of her, they could all get back to normal. Venus could hardly wait.

'We throw a party,' Diana said, simply.

She hated getting up at the best of times, but Venus's news was the ultimate alarm clock. Re-energised, she had thrown off her covers and padded across the thick bedroom carpet to her bathroom, where she washed her hair and dressed within twenty minutes: a simple but sexy Jil Sander shift dress in oyster-grey lambswool, platform clogs from L. K. Bennett, and a cosy pashmina from Liberty in palest silver. Just a touch of neutral Bobbi Brown make-up. Her room at least boasted a fabulous walk-in closet, and she had immediately racked out forty outfits, co-ordinated right on their hangers. All she needed to know was the temperature, and she'd be instantly dressed, fabulously, every day for a month.

For a girl who had grown up for much of her life without parents, without a home, it was good. It was good how in control that made her feel.

The girls had removed to the drawing room, with its huge French doors opening on to the pretty white-washed terrace. Juno had made a pot of mid-morning tea; the antique China Rose porcelain was arranged on a walnut tray, with Juno's exquisite Georgian silver milk jug and sugar pot. She hadn't bothered to lay out biscuits. Nobody but Athena would have touched them, and she hadn't wanted to give her sister that chance.

Everybody was dressed now. Athena had made an effort and put on a Karen Millen dress. It was wrong for her body and colouring, Diana thought, but at least she was trying. Juno in her yellows and whites, prim and proper as ever. Venus in a Matthew Williamson trouser suit in mink cotton; it suited her, better than those ageing micro-skirts she tended to favour, Diana decided, but perhaps still a bit mutton dressed as lamb – was it necessary for the trousers to be quite so sprayed-on?

But her mental inventory was quite satisfied. Four rich women, in a beautiful house. Gold and platinum watches glinted on slim wrists – two Cartiers, a Patek, and a Rolex. Important jewels shone discreetly on lobes and against the hollows of throats. The hair was rich, and glossy. There was the faint tang of expensive scent in the air. For the moment, at least, the spectre of debt and failure had been banished.

'When Bai-Ling arrives, we have to expose her. Make her the talk of London. Somebody Uncle Clem could never marry. He won't want to be seen as her dupe.' Diana went over their goals coolly. 'This is exactly why we rented the house, ladies. Let's throw the ultimate bash.'

'With the best society?' Juno asked dubiously. 'I don't think Uncle Clem will care about your sort of people, Diana.'

She ignored the insult. 'With both, Juno. All the titles

you can get, and I'll bring in the cooler people. We want maximum exposure for her to fall flat on her face.'

'And there will be ancillary benefits,' Venus agreed. 'The snobs will want to meet the rock stars, the hipsters will be fascinated by the countesses. That'll make for a great party. We can show off the house.'

'Launch ourselves while we embarrass Bai-Ling?' Athena asked.

'That is a major part of the plan,' Diana said. 'Successful women, so that Clem doesn't think we are desperate to get rid of his teenage bride.'

'Try to think of something commercial,' Juno pronounced. 'Something Bai-Ling will believe we're good at.'

'Fair enough.' Venus spoke up. She refused to meet anybody's eyes. 'I certainly won't be listing myself as an *actress* any more. It's undignified.' She gave a rather forced laugh. ' "Don't put your daughter on the stage, Mrs Worthington." That's not exactly what Uncle Clem expects of a Chambers, is it?'

Diana smothered a gasp with a cough. What had this imposter done with her little sister? Pride swelled within her.

'But I do still love films. Just not being in them.' Venus shrugged, but she fooled nobody. 'I'm going to start a company that has some kind of involvement in the arts. Maybe something in the film business.' Her face darkened, just a little, and Diana wondered if she were still dwelling on that party at Hans Tersch's house. Her sister had been silent on the subject of Hans ever since the audition.

'*You're* going into commerce?' Athena asked Juno sceptically.

'Of course not.' Juno was cold. 'But we need some sort of cover story, some sort of excuse for why four apparently rich women are sharing this house. That we're all starting businesses works quite well. I think I might pretend to get into property. Diana? Any ideas?'

Diana shrugged. What was she good at, good enough to make money from? It was a depressingly short list.

'Perhaps interior design,' she said. 'Easy to talk about without actually knowing a bloody thing. Lots of my friends do, after all.'

'I like that.' Athena nodded. 'Perfect fake career.'

Juno looked at her little sister, almost fondly. 'Athena, you're fine. For the moment. But you need to think of something.'

Athena glowered. 'OK, OK,' she said.

'Excellent,' Juno said. 'Then we're all set. At the party, we can allow Bai-Ling to embarrass herself, and give the gossip columns something to write about. It's much easier to get coverage when there's something to hang it on.' She smoothed down the glossy fabric of her yellow skirt. 'Just don't get carried away. The whole point of this little exercise is to ensure we never actually *have* to work.'

Diana nodded; the others did the same. There was only one prize here, and they had to keep their eyes firmly focused on it.

Chapter Thirteen

The corporate offices of Roden Realty soared into the sky. Diana stood on the pavement, across the road, looking up at them. Evidently her target didn't believe in half-measures. Even though this wasn't New York, or LA, or Washington, even though Roden had limited interests in Europe, Karl had still purchased a landmark Docklands tower. He'd got in early, and the word RODEN sparkled in the sun above a marble entrance carved in seamless Carrara stone, in brass letters ten feet high. A sheer wall of darkened glass held four invisible doors; they hissed open and shut silently as people entered and left the tower.

Diana had been here before, of course. The ground floor housed a three-star Michelin restaurant and an immaculate luxury car showroom. A grand reception area had Mies van der Rohe furniture, modern classics, looking out over a vast infinity pool, sealed off by more glass for the complex's corporate executives – Roden offered one of his signature health clubs, and it was invariably packed. Visitors could gape at the sleek bodies doing laps in the turquoise water that seemed to flow directly into the Thames. Clever architectural design and a cool palette of greys, olives, and creams soothed the eye, everywhere she looked. Lots of money, and perfect taste.

Diana sighed inwardly, and there was longing in that sigh. Karl Roden was out of her league. Had been, even before the advent of the hideous Bai-Ling. She wondered about money like that. Roden might be the first man she had ever met who was richer than Uncle Clem himself.

And of course, he was dating a twenty-four year old, her inner critic reminded her.

The thought was poison.

Diana glanced at her reflection in one of the mirrored walls. Chic and elegant, certainly. But attractive? Her fingers came up, reflexively, to trace her mouth, looking for minute telltale lines, looking for drooping skin around the eyelids, any trace of age. Her hair – was it still shining?

She had never doubted herself, not like this. But all of a sudden her confidence was knocked. Diana couldn't take her eyes off her reflection. She thought she looked good. But what was missing? What did she need that Roden hadn't seen?

Her emotions churned. Fear, doubt. And then, almost a relief, a pure blast of anger. It was why she'd come. Roden, taking her ideas and announcing them as his own. True, she'd stormed off. But still. Why would such a rich man steal all the credit?

Whatever. Diana shook herself slightly, like a dog after a wet country walk. She was here for a purpose. When she threw that dramatic party, she was going to be more than the hostess with the mostest. She was going to be a businesswoman.

Or at least, look like one.

Karl Roden could help her with that. No more anger. Diana pasted on her sweetest smile, and walked up to the receptionists' desk; there were six of them, all patching through calls on earphone headsets. It looked like the deck of the Starship *Enterprise*.

'Hi.' She gave one of them a confident smile. 'I'm here to see Karl Roden, if he's in.'

The girl arched a brow. She had a sleek dark bob and carefully applied make-up; all of them were wearing slim black jersey T-shirts and knee-length black capris, as if they were assistants in some exclusive Mayfair beauty salon.

'If he's in? Do you have an appointment?'

Diana shook her head, her smile unwavering. 'I'm a friend; he told me to drop by any time.'

'He's in a meeting,' the girl said flatly.

'Great. Buzz his secretary, please, and tell him Diana Chambers is waiting to see him, as arranged.'

The receptionist opened her perfectly made-up mouth, but her eyes met Diana's, and Diana's conquered.

'Just a second.' She punched a few buttons. 'Cynthia, it's Alice. I have somebody here for Mr Roden. She says she's a friend, no appointment. Her name is Dinah Chambers.'

'Diana.'

'OK.' The girl looked at Diana. 'One minute,' she said in a hostile tone.

Diana examined her watch, trying for calm. Damn, it was so much easier when she'd only had to throw lavish parties. If this was how things were in the workplace, they could bloody well keep it. Even setting up a shell company for effect involved tiresome amounts of effort – and now humiliation.

But the girl was nodding into the phone, and a faint blush appeared on her cheeks.

'Ms Chambers, if you'd go right up.' The tone was warmer. 'Mr Roden's office is on the forty-first floor.'

A small burst of triumph hit Diana in the stomach. 'Thank you,' she replied noncommittally. The woman didn't deserve friendliness, but something warned her not to be rude. Besides, the glow of victory settled on her; Roden *would* see her, and now everybody was wondering who she was. She walked over purposefully to the elevator bank. Seamless metal doors hissed open, and she stepped into a well-designed space, with a small bench and black marble cladding backlit with LEDs. Roden's architects had taken care not to overlook the smallest detail, or the most functional area. She made a mental note to go to the loo while she was here. That was always a revealing space for attention to detail.

The forty-first floor was the penthouse. Diana pressed the button, and felt herself whisked smoothly upwards, so high her ears popped slightly after a few seconds.

As the doors opened, a woman was standing there waiting. She was in her early forties and looked very competent; a neat bun, no jewellery, and a good suit, vintage DKNY, with Jimmy Choo pumps. Diana could see the glint of a plain gold watch.

'Ms Chambers, I'm Cynthia Hart, Mr Roden's first assistant.'

Diana smiled. 'First? How many does he have?'

'Six,' she replied, without a trace of humour. 'Would you follow me, please?'

She led Diana through a maze of cream walls and soft dove-grey carpet, past various offices all commanding spectacular views of the London skyline, to a waiting area; there were two large Italianate couches, a small bar with its own waterfall, fruit, mineral waters, and neatly ironed papers from three continents; a sheer wall of glass looked down on the Thames, sparkling in the sunlight, with tiny boats processing slowly up and down it, like toys in a stream.

'Mr Roden apologises; he's finishing up with some Japanese investment bankers. May I fetch you a coffee while you're waiting?'

'Thank you. Just black.' It would give her something to do while she waited. Diana moistened her lips, suddenly nervous. Was the effect of all this wealth to entice, or to intimidate? She liked parties, and hip little clubs, places where she was a player. But Roden's den was out of her comfort zone. Now she had blagged her way in, exactly what was she going to say to him?

A door opened in the wall in front of her. Diana jumped out of her skin. It was so smoothly constructed that she hadn't seen it was there. Roden emerged with three middle-aged Japanese men, who bowed low to him.

He replied, in Japanese, and there was more bowing. Diana sat up a little straighter on her sofa. On his own territory, Roden looked even hotter to her. His salt-and-pepper hair and grey eyes framed with thick black lashes were picked out by a beautifully tailored suit in dark charcoal wool, with a loose palest blue shirt. She could see a chunky platinum Rolex, but no other ornamentation.

The men were deferring to him. Diana read it in their body language; it was more than just the normal Japanese politeness, they were anxious to have his approval. And Cynthia and the other secretaries had sat up straighter; their eyes were on him, their shoulders were drawn back, naturally thrusting out their breasts. A couple of the younger women reflexively smoothed their hair.

It was amusing, she told herself; natural female display behaviours in front of the alpha male. Like they couldn't help themselves.

And she could hardly blame the office girls. He did look devastating. Say what you like, all this wealth, all this power, in his hands . . . it was intoxicating.

Roden turned to her.

'Miss Chambers.' He smiled warmly. 'What a pleasant surprise. Come in.'

She stood, although her legs suddenly felt a little woolly, and followed him through the seamless oak doors into his office.

It was a fantasy: marble walls punctuated with long darkened glass windows, floor-to-ceiling strips. There was a parquet floor that looked as though it belonged in Versailles and a huge, magnificent Persian rug in creams and blues; Roden's desk was large, solid, she pegged it at eighteenth century. Clocks on the wall told the time in New York, Tokyo and Frankfurt. Everything about the place whispered power.

'Will you have a seat?'

Roden indicated a pair of chaise longues in one corner, opposite one of the cathedral windows. There was a dizzying view over London; she could see up the river clear to Parliament.

'Thanks. Good job I'm not afraid of heights.'

'I was.' Roden shrugged. 'Which is why I put my office in the penthouse.'

'To scare yourself?'

'No. To face down my fears. You don't get anywhere in this life by running.' He smiled slightly. 'Heights are second nature to me now. I take the window seat in the plane.'

She nodded, not sure where to start.

Roden's eyebrows lifted. 'You surprise me, Diana. When we met the other day you weren't short of words.'

'It's your office.' She forced herself to look away, to study her fingernails. The last thing she wanted was for Roden to see she was attracted to him.

'You didn't seem so impressed earlier.'

Those words collected Diana. She stiffened. Bad enough that Roden *had* impressed her; a million times worse if she let it show.

'Well, it is a vulgar display of power,' she replied with a brisk smile. 'Which has come to you from the hotel business. And as it seems from the papers that I have made quite a contribution to your new London operations, I thought I should come here and ask for credit.'

He leaned back, and the dark-lashed eyes looked her over speculatively.

'I thought it might be something like that. You want credit.'

'More than that,' Diana said. 'I want to take you up on your offer.'

Roden's smile deepened, and she thought, furiously, that he was toying with her.

'At dinner, and at the site, you gave me the impression that work was beneath you. That you couldn't care less about becoming my employee. Now you've changed your mind, based on five lines of newsprint? Come on, Miss Chambers. I want to know the real reason.'

'This is the real reason.' Diana forced herself to look right into his gaze, not to blink or lower her head. 'I won't be your employee. It's true, I can't see myself punching a clock. The good clubs close too late for the nine-to-five. No, I want to be your consultant instead. I'm starting a firm.' She unclipped her bag, extracted her silver card-case, monogrammed with her initials, and handed across one of her new business cards.

'Chambers Inc.' He read it out. 'That's it?'

'My name and my business. I designed them. Why not?' Diana tossed her dark hair. 'I like it, even if you don't.'

'So what exactly can I do for you?'

'You're going to be my first client, Mr Roden. And you'll announce the commission.'

'And if I say no,' his gaze trickled over her body, her suit, her stomach, causing the butterflies in there to churn, 'you'll do what – sue me?'

Diana shook her head. 'I may not have a degree from Oxford, but I like to think I'm not stupid. You have enough money to hire every lawyer in North America. I'd get crushed.'

'You would,' he agreed coolly.

'It's not what I would do to you if you turn me down. It's what I can do for you if you don't. You know how good my ultimate health club idea is. But that's just one idea. There are more where that came from. Nobody knows London like I do.' Interestingly, Diana heard herself arguing passionately. Now she was here, in front of him, she desperately wanted to win. Wanted his approval. Wanted to close the deal. 'You saw that when you invited me to the site.'

'I thought you might know the names of a few good clubs.' He was toying with her. 'And I was trying to be polite to a guest of Tersch's.'

'Well, now you know better. My ideas are solid for this market. Surely that PR in the *Standard* is enough to convince you to give me a trial.'

'So you want a chance. With no prior business experience other than booking reservations at the Ivy.'

The description stung her.

'Mr Roden,' Diana said fiercely. 'Here's the deal. You hire me. You announce it. I – my firm – will work for you for nothing. I will dedicate myself night and day to your hotel for one month. And at the end of it, you pay me whatever you like.'

His eyes widened, and he chuckled. 'And what if I *like* to pay you one penny? Or nothing at all?'

'I'll take that risk,' Diana said. 'I believe I can please you. And that you'll pay me what I'm worth.'

'Oh,' Roden said, and his eyes danced. 'You can please me. You do please me.'

Diana's stomach flipped over. Was he flirting with her?

'It's a ballsy offer,' Roden said. 'And I like your guts. Very well. You have a deal.'

'You'll announce that you've hired my firm?'

'I will.'

Diana stood up. 'Have your corporate PR people send the release on to me. I'll take it from there.'

Karl Roden followed her in getting to his feet.

'I give the orders around here,' he said. 'Employee or contractor, you work for me. There's social life, and there's business. If you plan on moving into the latter area, you will remember that I'm the boss.'

'Yes, sir,' Diana said.

He smiled. 'I'll have them send it to you.'

She offered him her hand; he shook it, and Diana tried not to shudder at the electrifying excitement of his skin on hers.

'Nice doing business with you. I'll be in touch,' she said, thinking how sensible and Junoesque she sounded.

But Roden had walked back to his desk, and was already tapping at his computer keyboard. He had dismissed Diana, and she hated it.

'By the way.' He raised his head, and she stopped on her way to the door. 'My secretary will call you. Put you in touch with Suzie, my girlfriend. You know her?'

'Not personally,' Diana replied. After all that pleasant sexual tension, it was like being doused in a bucket of icy water. Oh yes, his supermodel girlfriend reared her pretty head.

'She's a model,' he said superfluously. 'Knows a few things. I want you to bring her in on this project. She has some ideas.'

Like hell she does.

'Of course,' Diana said, pasting the smile back on her face. 'It'd be lovely to talk to Suzie . . .'

'See you later,' Karl Roden murmured, and picked up the phone. He was deep in conversation by the time she reached the door.

Juno put it off for as long as she could.

Business. Who wanted to deal with it? Not her. Not ever. Her entire existence had been built around fantasy, the life of the eighteenth-century gentlewoman; she loved Jane Austen books, where a woman could be cold, and respected for it, and look down on those who were 'in trade'. She was an unrepentant snob, and she knew it.

And now that scheming little bitch from Thailand was forcing her down this path . . .

First things first. She procrastinated brilliantly. After all, the party for Bai-Ling had to be a very glittering affair. Juno retreated to the walnut-panelled study to plan her line of attack. She could count on at least one duchess, but for a first-class bash she would aim for three. There were the Arab royals, two countesses, and a Parisian pretender's niece; a few other trust-fund brats of the more colourful sort, an Etonian housemaster, a

Derby-winning jockey, and two Cabinet ministers. Throw in a few of the senior major nation ambassadors and you'd really have the makings of something.

She sketched out a plan: hand-delivered invitations from all four Chambers cousins; the best caterers in London, Dismore & Hawkes; chamber music – her little pun; the garden lighting and design she'd handle herself.

Juno was an expert party-thrower. A few calls, a sketched design for her invitations, and it was all arranged. Diana would add some hip touches: funky types from her showbiz-heavy Rolodex, artists and club owners and cineastes. People Juno didn't even want to know. But people who *would* add spice to her stodgy mix of aristocrats and landowners. She could see that extra ingredient would make this an unmissable party, and then, of course, the next one would be even bigger.

The bigger the party, the bigger the press coverage.

And the more column inches to ridicule Bai-Ling.

But after a morning's work and design, all was in place. Which left Juno with her original problem. She would have to face the world of work.

She sat in the study, sipping a camomile tea in one of the idyllic window seats overlooking the garden. The sunlight dappled the lawn with shadows, and the tall grasses danced in the slight breeze. A perfect London day. In future, might she have to spend it in an office?

She wondered suddenly, fiercely, what Jack was doing. She tried not to think about him, not to miss him.

He was history! But today, with all the other girls out in town, setting up their little fake businesses, she was on her own. What would Jack say if he saw her applying for jobs? Would he laugh? Sneer?

She pictured his handsome, defiant face, that rough jaw that always had an ungentlemanly layer of stubble, the dark Scottish eyes, fierce on her. Unbidden, a secret wave of longing washed through her. It had been weeks now since Jack had left her, longer since he'd touched her. How many months, years maybe, before she found a date, somebody she could marry . . . and then, would they stir her like Jack?

Feckless bastard that he was. Selfish . . . and weak. Juno tossed her head, even though nobody was there to witness it. This line of thought angered her. Was she going to mourn Jack's loss now? She was free, and that was what counted.

She jumped to her feet, reaching across the green baize on her oak desk to her slim Smythson diary, and flicked through its familiar thin blue pages. Forget Jack. She would show him the kind of man a Chambers girl could marry. Peter Lord, she thought fiercely. One of her wittiest dinner-party guests, and London's most eligible bachelors. Arrived a year ago from South Africa, where he owned a huge vineyard and safari park, as well as the premium estate agency that bore his name. Now he had a boutique business relocating some of London's choosiest customers: Russian plutocrats with billions burning up their back pockets, Arab businessmen flush with petrodollars, Chinese entrepreneurs riding the Asian tiger all the way to fabulous high-security mansions in Hyde Park and Mayfair. Peter was a born socialite, and it had been a coup to get him to three or four of her more successful parties. Juno knew he was divorced; a second wife had been left in Cape Town with a consolation villa in Monaco thrown in as part of her divorce settlement. Juno had made it her business to look the woman up. Magazine photographs had shown her dripping in De Beers diamonds. Juno had practically licked her lips.

Of course, Peter was South African himself. So there was no coat of arms. But it was a Dutch family originally. There might be *something* there . . . certainly he had a better quality pedigree than Jack bloody Darling. Juno silently thanked heaven that she'd sat Peter next to Missy Hamilton, the new Lady Cork, at her last dinner in the old house. And he'd been delighted with the placement. New money – it always loved old titles.

Time to call in the favour. Taking a big gulp of camomile tea for courage, Juno rang his office.

'Always a pleasure.' Peter took her hand and kissed it flamboyantly. 'What can I do for you, my darling?'

Lord Estates ran its offices from a smart Mayfair townhouse, gorgeous Victorian red brick at Hyde Park Corner. The ground floor had been remodelled into one large office space, reminiscent of the British Library: Afghan rugs, rows of leather-backed books, mahogany furniture, and girls wearing tweedy skirts and strands of small pearls quietly answering the phone. It was a Disney version of England; very expensive, and what a foreigner might consider classic. Juno could immediately see what a soothing effect it would have on Peter Lord's clients.

'Can we step into your office?' she asked.

'*Mi casa, su casa.*' He giggled and threw open the door to his private space; a soft Wedgwood-blue carpet, an oil painting of a hunting scene, and gold-framed photographs of Peter with various celebrities and politicians. There was a pale desk designed from driftwood, and an uncomfortably solid chesterfield sofa. Juno sat down, and Peter perched on the edge of it, smiling brightly at her, like a crocodile. He had a handsome, clean-shaven face, and his eyebrows were neatly groomed, his fingernails manicured. Beautifully dressed, too, in a Paul Smith suit and John Lobb shoes. The exact opposite of Jack. That thought stiffened her resolve.

'I need a little favour,' she said warmly. 'I need a sort of job.'

'A *sort of* job?' He lifted an eyebrow. 'Rather like being a little bit pregnant, wouldn't you say?'

'Oh, I don't want a career or anything,' Juno reassured him. 'Not exactly me.'

'Didn't think it was, darling.'

'But it's so boring, shopping and throwing parties all day. I love what you do. And you know I'm awfully well connected, and I do have a good eye. I might know of some excellent houses not on the market yet. You would only have to pay me something token.' Juno blushed even raising the subject of money. 'Pocket money for Lord Estates. But I do think it would be fun to learn the letting business, at the top end of the scale, of course. The afternoons can get so terribly dull with nothing to do but potter about.'

'Hmmm.' His smile was just as bright, but he hadn't jumped on the suggestion. Juno creased with embarrassment inside. This was worse than she'd ever imagined. Was she going to have to beg him? 'What kind of properties, sweetie? Can you give me a for instance?'

Luckily, she could.

'Lizzie Lothian wants somebody for her place in St James's. It's got eight bedrooms and two servants' flats, lovely walled garden, permit parking. She hasn't announced it to anybody yet. Dreading having agents walk round her family home. But she wouldn't mind if I took care of it. We've been friends for yonks.'

Peter's eyes sparkled with pleasure. 'So you have.'

Juno recovered. She pursued her advantage. 'Very much up your street, I'd have thought. "On the instructions of the Dowager Marchioness of Lothian . . ." That should get you an investment banker from Wall Street with no trouble at all.'

'Indeed.' He smiled sweetly. 'I can see you'll be a great help. Now I can't offer you any formal pay . . .'

Her heart sank again. There'd have to be *something* in it, or word would leak out. Their jobs could be half-hearted but not completely fake, or Bai-Ling would see through it and tell Uncle Clem they were all desperate for his money.

'. . . but there will be commission,' he added with a jaunty wink. 'And you could earn that on the first deal, if you can deliver Lizzie's place.'

Juno nodded. He was awfully charming. But in her experience, limited though it was, men didn't like a girl to be a total pushover. She wasn't as pretty as her sister or her cousins; she knew that full well. To get a man, Juno Chambers had to rely on the uncertain attractions of her personality. She thought it would be the same to close a business deal.

'If I'm only working on commission, I want ten per cent,' she said coolly. 'And expenses up front.'

'We pay five.'

'Not to me, darling,' Juno answered. 'I'm bringing you a better class of customer. Reflects well on Lord Estates.'

'So it does.' He jumped to his feet lightly. 'Done! I'll have one of the girls add you to the staff list. We'll get you an office of your own, a small one, you understand. And some business cards. Come in tomorrow and you'll be all set up. Hours are nine to four.'

'I'll have to get up early,' Juno drawled, to hide how

much she hated the idea. Punching a clock? Dull! 'I suppose I can manage . . .'

'It will be interesting to see how the fabled Mrs Darling performs,' Peter added.

'Darling? You mean Chambers.'

He tilted his head. 'Didn't you take Jack's name? Handsome devil, your husband. Lucky girl.' Peter nudged her with his elbow, and Juno delighted in the familiarity. He was being very warm now. Well, if he wanted to flirt, she had some good news for him.

'I did, but you must have missed the news. We're getting divorced.'

Peter opened his eyes wide. 'Not really? I assumed that talk was all nonsense. Especially since he's doing so well.'

Juno sniffed. 'You must have a different definition of "well" than I do, Peter.'

'But the new restaurant? Smoked Salmon, he called it, didn't he?'

That was the name Jack had always talked about, for his dream place in Scotland.

'So he finally got it going,' Juno said, dismissing the idea. Really, so what? Jack Darling acting as a maître d' in some godforsaken dump with tartan tablecloths and candles in glass bottles. Big wow.

'Got it going? You could say that.' Peter spoke archly, and his evident delight rattled Juno. Obviously he knew something she didn't. She had to bite down on her own lip to stop herself from asking him the question.

He put her out of her misery. 'They announced last week that the BBC apparently offered him a cookery show. It was in the *Evening Standard* . . . I'm amazed you missed it. He could have been the new Gordon Ramsay. But he chose not to do it. Said he was training sous-chefs instead . . . Wanted this new restaurant of his to win three Michelin stars. They say it easily could, and it's barely up and running.'

'Three Michelin stars?'

Juno was in total shock. She knew what that meant, exactly what it meant. 'But he hasn't even opened it yet.'

Peter smirked. 'The *Sunday Times* property section featured the village last week and said property prices had gone up by ten per cent just from foodie interest.'

'Well, congratulations to Jack.' Juno forced it out. 'I'm afraid I have no interest in cooking. Or cooks,' she added, unable to stop the bitchiness.

'Word on the street is that he'll be a multi-millionaire by Christmas. But he says he doesn't care. He's not doing it for the money.'

Juno gritted her teeth. It was like being doused in a bucket of ice water. Just when she had a plan for dealing with the Bai-Ling disaster, just when she'd found the perfect house, managed to cobble together the appearance of wealth, and felt she was fighting back – this kick in the stomach. It hit her like a horse's hoof to the gut.

She was bitter. Bloody Jack, of course he had to wait till he'd left her to get successful – probably out of spite.

The thought of him owning a chain of restaurants was unbearable; being truly rich, owning a public company, while she was dependent on regaining Uncle Clem's good will. Horrible fantasies danced in her head. Jack buying back their old house. Jack with a much younger, prettier woman on his arm . . .

'I still have his number,' Peter Lord said, evidently amused by the look on her face. 'Shall I call him for you? Try to make amends?'

Juno drew herself up. 'Peter, sweetie. You can't think I miss that Scottish oik. If he's learned how to stop being bone idle, bully for him, but I'm afraid he'll have to waste some other woman's time.'

'Meow,' Peter Lord said infuriatingly.

Juno reminded herself quickly of his net worth.

'I'll be in tomorrow,' she said.

'Here.' Peter reached across the driftwood desk and handed her a contract. 'Get Lizzie Lothian to sign that.'

Juno smiled crisply and handed it back to him. 'As soon as I have my office,' she replied.

Chapter Fourteen

Venus loved swimming at the Victrix Hotel. The eternity pool gave her that fabulous feeling of diving into the sky itself. As she came up from every stroke, London was spread out below her. The exercise kept her trim. It also concentrated her mind.

Jacob Sager's words had cut her to the core. But they were only able to do that because he was right.

Diana and her cousins had been amazed. But Venus was more than bruised. She was at rock bottom. Her rejection for *Maud*, her loss of an agent, her discovery that she wasn't wanted in London. It was the wholesale death of a dream. And even though she hated him, hated him with a brilliant passion, Venus couldn't stop thinking about Hans Tersch. Under the cool, mercifully covering water, she felt herself quiver with pleasure at the memory of his hands on her skin.

And then, as always, her mind stopped drifting, and there was the little shock of embarrassment, rejection, humiliation, as Venus considered how he had turned her down.

Had he laughed? Joked about her, maybe, as he was banging his new Maud, a girl ten years younger than she was?

Her good mood ruined, Venus swam quickly over to the ladder and hauled herself out of the water. Several sets of male eyes followed her, the water pouring down her lean, muscular flesh, as she walked over to her lounger and reached for her fluffy white towelling robe. Her lust had turned into white-hot loathing. Venus wanted to destroy Hans Tersch. But how could she possibly do it? A penniless ex-actress without clout or connections?

She towelled her blond hair dry roughly, causing the watching investment bankers to lick their lips as her Garrard tennis bracelet jangled against her tanned skin. OK, maybe she wasn't *totally* penniless, she conceded. But as good as.

Hans Tersch wasn't dependent on a rich uncle. Or a trust fund. He was a powerful producer . . .

Producer. She remembered what that agent Jacob Sager had told her. The towel halted as she was drying around her ears, sending her solid gold teardrop earrings jangling in the dappled light bouncing from the pool. It struck her with immediate force. Of course, that was what she should do. Forget long, boring courses at film school, trying to become a director late in life. Forget fluttering her eyes at the agency bosses, hoping to get taken on as a trainee working for peanuts, and booking roles for girls much younger than she was. Hell, no. Producing was as easy as owning a great script. And as for overheads, all she'd need was a good telephone connection . . .

She sat in the upstairs study, piles of scripts stacked neatly on the green baize of the mahogany desk. For once, her mobile was switched off. She was trying to concentrate.

Half of the scripts were useless to her, of course. They were studio projects, already bought and paid for. The ones that never got made were languishing in development hell, and Venus no longer had tens of thousands to throw around to buy out the studio's costs – and that was the small Brit film outlets. Hollywood pictures had hundreds of thousands against them by the time they hit the waste-paper basket.

No, she needed to ignore the gold and look through the dross. Stuff she'd been sent hoping to get her attached. Usually with a request to help out with the financing. Some of these had agents, others didn't. Most of them were as unreadable this time as they'd been when they were first sent to her.

Venus sighed. She'd been at this for hours. It wasn't working. She wouldn't find the next *Good Will Hunting* or *Four Weddings* like this. There had to be a better way to get a great script . . .

Idly, she reached over the desk and turned her phone back on. It rang immediately.

'Venus Chambers,' she said.

'Venus, hi,' said a young voice. 'This is Lilly Bruin.'

Venus sat bolt upright, the hairs on her arms prickling.

'Lilly . . . from *Maud*?'

'Yes,' Lilly said, her voice muffled. 'Look, do you have a minute?' She had been crying.

'Of course.'

'It's about Hans Tersch.'

'Has he fired you?' Venus forced herself to sound sympathetic. For a second, a wild hope leaped up in her heart. He'd fired Lilly. He was going to call Venus. The whole thing had been a mistake; she *could* act and the part was hers . . .

'No, nothing like that. I just – I need some advice.' There was a gulping noise. 'You did say you were, like, an old friend of Hans's, didn't you?'

'Yes, we go way back.' Six months at least.

'Do you think we could meet for a coffee? I can get into town in twenty minutes.'

Wild with curiosity, Venus said, 'Absolutely. Meet me at the Groucho.'

Lilly showed up right on time. Venus was pleased to see she looked tarty: a Topshop miniskirt that was far too short, a black boob tube and a smart Armani jacket that couldn't disguise the paucity of the outfit. Her hair had been dyed platinum blond, but not as well as Venus's, and she wore long dangly earrings that Venus thought looked cheap. There was a wild, glittery look in her eyes. Coke, Venus decided, with a rush of satisfaction. Something, anyway. She looked manic.

'Good to see you.' Venus kissed her smoothly on both cheeks, enjoying playing the hostess. 'Can I get you something to drink? Tea, coffee?'

'Gin and tonic,' Lilly said, and laughed at Venus's raised eyebrow. 'Hair of the dog.'

'Why not?' Venus signalled to the barman. 'This is a nice surprise, Lilly. What exactly did you want to talk about?'

'Hans,' Lilly said, and instantly her eyes prickled with tears. 'I need some advice, I just don't know how to handle him.'

'Tell me more.' Venus leaned forward. 'Is he horrible to work with?'

Lilly sobbed, 'Yes.'

Venus put one manicured hand over the younger girl's. 'How? Tell me.'

'He's a slave-driver,' Lilly wept. 'Makes me say the bloody lines over and over again. Total perfectionist. And he doesn't *care* about me. Always getting at me if I'm late on set. Like, I didn't want to be an actress so I could keep office hours.' She dashed her hand across her eyes, and her pretty young face turned from sorrow to petulant anger. 'I'm Maud, you know? I'm a *star*.'

'Absolutely,' Venus said soothingly.

'Venus.' Lilly's red eyes gazed into hers. 'He *slept* with me.'

Venus's stomach turned over. Anger, envy. 'He did?'

'Yes. Twice. So I thought we had a relationship. But he didn't act any differently on set. Just lets the stupid director bark out orders at me.'

'Luke Cantor's directing?'

'Yes, but he's Hans's puppet. He wouldn't bark at me if Hans didn't make him.' Lilly sighed. 'Oh, Venus! Hans is so sexy. He's strong, and he just runs things. You should see him. Snaps his fingers and they all jump. And he's worth, like, *millions* of dollars.' She licked her lips. 'I think I'd be a *great* wife for him, don't you? We just fit.'

'But he's not interested?'

'No.' The tears were back. 'You're his friend, Venus. How can I hook him . . . make him see we're right for each other?' Lilly dabbed at her eyes. 'And that I'm a star.' She pouted. 'He shouldn't bully me. I just want to quit.'

Venus looked at the girl, spoiled, petty, exquisitely attractive. And something clicked in the back of her mind. Revenge on Hans. Revenge on all of them.

'Well,' she said slowly, 'your agent wouldn't like it. But I have to tell you, Hans does sleep around. He probably thinks nothing of it. Discusses you on set, I wouldn't mind betting.'

'That's it.' Lilly sat bolt upright, and her eyes darted to her handbag; she probably had a little vial of cocaine hidden right inside it. 'Screw him.' Her voice was tense with the aggression of the drug, her face tight from her mood swings. 'I'm going to walk out. And if my agent doesn't like it, I'm going to fire him too. Nobody treats Lilly Bruin like that . . .'

'It's a mistake,' Venus said calmly, safe in the knowledge that the girl wouldn't listen. 'You'll get a bad rep.'

'Who cares?' Lilly tossed her head. 'I'm a *star*, Venus. The world will see me that way – even if Hans Tersch won't.' She picked up her glass and drained it in a single go. Then she stood up, shook herself, like a cat stretching, and walked out.

Venus smiled and sipped her mineral water. Suddenly she could see a way forward. There was that script, about the spoiled young model and the blind vicar. A light comedy. Ultra low-budget. And an unproduced writer . . .

She called the number from memory.

Athena pirouetted in front of the mirror.

'It suits you,' the saleswoman approved. 'It's divine.'

'Divine? It bloody should be, at four hundred and thirty quid,' Athena grunted. But she couldn't stop the smile playing on her lips.

The dress, a Versace, suited her perfectly. Chocolate brown and cream, it clung to her curves, ostensibly modest, but actually deeply sexy. It had long sleeves, a scoop neck, and tapered off just above her knees, but it emphasised every lean curve of her breasts, her buttocks, even her calves. The personal shopper had paired it with some Russell & Bromley Mary Janes in chestnut leather with tan detailing, smooth, shiny tights and a chunky gold bangle.

Venus had set this up for her. Athena had resented her cousin treating her like a child, writing down the name and number of her favourite professional shopper, booking her into a hair salon and sending her to a number of serious pampering places: a manicurist, a pedicurist, even a cosmetic dentist. Venus apparently had a separate therapist just for plucking her eyebrows.

But bullied by Juno and her cousins, Athena had had to accept that she must smarten up. It just seemed so superficial. She made the appointments reluctantly. Stupid thing would take a complete day, and she was still working on her second doctoral thesis . . .

The hairdresser was the start. Athena endured the boredom reluctantly. When she went to Supercuts for a trim, it took them fifteen minutes . . . this appointment was for three bloody hours.

But it was a revelation.

The salon itself screamed modern chic. The butterscotch leather chairs, ergonomically designed, sat sleekly on a floor of polished concrete, and the room was dominated by vast steel-framed windows, giving the effect of a very expensive warehouse conversion. The stylists all wore uniform; the girls in pale grey trouser suits and the men in navy shirts and slacks. There was the rich scent of cinnamon coffee throughout the room, and menus were set out, just as if you were in an upmarket café. A huge photograph of Manhattan acted as a mural on an inner wall.

It affected Athena. She couldn't deny the sheer vibrancy of the place. For once she felt the girls were right – just possibly. Her badly cut high-street skirt and comfy jumper with the hole in the elbow, which she had defiantly chosen before leaving the house, now seemed not so much rebellious as ridiculous.

'Oh my goodness.' Clara, the American stylist, was a petite girl. Beautifully put together, Athena had to admit: dramatic white nail polish that looked good against her silver outfit, and a plain face shown to best effect by a clever, lopsided bob of rich honey hair, smoky grey eyeshadow and apricot lip gloss, with nothing but a little shading on her cheeks. But if Athena approved, Clara evidently didn't return the compliment. She took handfuls of Athena's coarse red hair in her hands and scrunched it up in front of the mirror, showing her all the split ends and faded dye and places where she'd missed a spot. 'Suicide redhead?'

'What?' Athena blinked.

'Dyed by your own hand. And not too well, as you can see.'

'Sorry,' Athena muttered. It was like being told off by her mother.

'Your cousin did warn me, but I wasn't expecting this.' The girl scrutinised Athena's face and body, her sharp gaze passing quickly over her outfit. 'You're dressing like a student who buys her stuff at Oxfam. And what are those caterpillars on your face?' She jabbed an unforgiving finger at Athena's eyebrows. 'You bite your nails? What exactly is your beauty routine: wash your face and brush your teeth?'

Athena shrugged. Too embarrassed to admit she didn't usually wash her face as such. The water splashed on it in the shower, that was enough, wasn't it?

'Do all your clothes have holes in them?' Clara stared at her sleeve.

'No,' Athena said defensively. 'I have nice things, actually.'

'Not nice enough.' The stylist moved from brusque to brisk. 'You've been very lazy. If you don't mind my saying.' And I don't care even if you do, the set of her shoulders said. 'You're one of the more attractive girls I've seen this month, and I see a lot of models. But it's like you're on a mission to dress it down as much as possible. I'd kill for your face and hair like that. Really, you have a *duty* to smarten the hell up.'

'OK,' Athena agreed. 'I just want to look professional, though.'

'No.' The clipped New York tones cut her off. 'That's not for a chick with your assets. You want to look drop-dead gorgeous. And believe me, once we've set you straight, you won't want to go back. Here. Put this on. At least it'll cover you up till you can get some decent clothes.'

Clara wrapped a thin gown of dove-grey cotton around Athena's offending garments. She shoved her towards one of the chic little chairs, and Athena found she was looking at her own face in the mirror. Harsh bulbs dotted around the glass showed it for exactly what it was: uncared for, unmade-up, with thick eyebrows and bumpy red blotches on her skin; she didn't get enough sleep and ate too much junk food. Her eyes were a bleary red, and in the merciless glare she could see the bad condition of her hair.

Athena blushed. It *was* rather studenty. She looked like a fresher scurrying through Tom Quad in winter, pretty but totally unkempt, the kind who thought grooming was something you did to a dog.

'How long will this take?' she grumbled, but her tone sounded unconvincing even to her.

Clara was stern. 'Three hours. Now just sit still and read a magazine. What do you want?'

'Have you got the *Economist*?'

'Funny,' Clara said sarcastically. 'Here, have a copy of *InStyle*. Believe me, you need it.'

After the first half-hour, Athena had totally surrendered. Even though she looked worse than she had done before. Clara had painted foul-smelling gloop on her head and was taking for ever to wrap sections of hair in tiny foil strips. But she understood it was necessary. And now she came to look at them, the dresses and bags and heel combinations in the glossy magazines weren't totally stupid. They had a certain élan to them. It almost – almost – made her want to go shopping.

'There,' Clara said, as she lifted Athena's head from the sink. Wet, the hair just looked dark. 'Now Frédérique will do your haircut. Always wet. Then I'll blow-dry.'

There was more snipping and chopping, but thankfully, the next hairdresser had flown in from Paris for just one week and spoke no English. Athena was fluent in French, but it was a relief to shrug when she attempted conversation. The woman was apparently some fashion big-shot, judging by the deference the other beauty therapists gave her, and she worked quickly; little snips and slices around Athena's head, a critical tilt of the neck, her green eyes narrowing, like she was a sculptress working on a bust. When she was done, the hair lay in odd angles against Athena's scalp; it was much shorter, and her head felt lighter; she was nervous, suddenly, having sworn she didn't care, nervous of all that disappearing length, wondering if she would look boyish, or worse, stern and sexless like her big sister Juno.

Maybe it was the loss of her position and her house, maybe it was just a day in a beauty parlour. But Athena desperately wanted to be beautiful. Just like Clara said.

The American girl came padding over to her. 'Let's get you blow-dried.'

'Is it going to look OK?'

Clara shook her head. 'It's going to look fantastic. Should do, honey, the amount you paid for it. Your cousin pulled strings to get you in with Frédérique. Wait till you see this.'

She whipped out a brush like a surgical tool, and deftly started to pull out Athena's wet hair with one hand and blast her with the dryer with the other.

'So what do you do for a living?'

'Not much.'

'You're a lady who lunches?' Clara shook her head. 'Not in those duds, sister. What gives?'

Athena gave her a potted history. Clara listened, while she dried Athena's finely cropped hair. It blew around her skin, but she was starting to see the real colour. And it was glorious: a deep, natural-looking auburn, with glimmering strands of strawberry blond woven subtly through it, waking it up. The cut, too, was starting to surface: an angular bob, long to the chin then slicing up around her cheekbones, throwing them into relief even without make-up. Athena stared at herself in happy fascination while she talked.

'Old boys' club?' Clara summed it up.

'Exactly. They've never quite given up on the ladies retiring as the men smoke cigars,' Athena said, a touch bitterly. 'Despite the politically correct platitudes they like to throw around.'

'And what do the women say?'

'Women? That's the point, there aren't any women.

Not really senior ones. Other than the odd token.' Athena took a sip of the delicious-scented coffee that had been placed in front of her. 'They all network, they all know each other. They're friends, they play golf, they join the same clubs. Clubs women can't be a part of. It's very hard to break in without that social connection.'

'Hmm.' Clara expertly teased her hair some more, then leaned forward and ran her fingers through it. She reached for a can of hairspray and spritzed a burst across Athena's head. 'There now. What do you think? Worth it?'

Athena regarded herself in the mirror and could not suppress a sigh of pure pleasure.

'Oh yes,' she said. 'Thank you.'

The sexy, shimmering bob, its sharp grade cut with microscopic precision, defined her face and made her green eyes even larger. The colour was bold and seductive, the tones like nature only better – a lot better. It was a traffic-stopping cut. And Athena decided she loved it.

Loved it. She wanted more, right now.

She jumped up, tugged off her gown, and gave the surprised Clara a hug.

'You're a genius. The colour's perfect. Now I actually want to do the rest of it.'

'Even the manicure?' The stylist grinned.

'Especially that.' Athena grabbed her battered old handbag from the coat-rack, thrust her bitten nails inside it and fished out three twenty-pound notes. 'These are for you.'

Clara blinked. 'That's much too big a tip, Miss Chambers.'

'It's Athena. And no, it's not. You see, you've given me more than a fabulous hairdo. You've given me an idea.'

As good as her word, Athena had submitted meekly, even enthusiastically, to the rest of the appointments Venus had set up for her: the fake nails, brilliantly deceptive, that were fixed on to her hands; the five minutes it took to turn her unibrow into two clear, aristocratic arches; strangers dabbing at her toes, buffing the rough skin off her heels, and wrapping her feet in gloopy moisturiser; and last, but not least, this marathon session at Liberty. The personal shopper brought out row after row of clothes, and Athena was starting to be impressed. Clothes that looked like absolutely nothing on the rack, or the hanger, things she rejected as drab or dull, when tried on transformed her body. The woman's name was Esther. She was middle-aged, a short woman from Finchley, and she had, Athena was discovering, a perfect eye.

'Fantastic.' Esther nodded, pursing her lips as she appraised Athena's body, in a new dress. 'Modest . . . but every man will stare as you enter the room.'

'How much is it?' Athena murmured.

'If you need to ask . . .'

She remembered she was meant to be keeping up appearances. 'Of course not. I was just curious.'

'That one's cheap,' Esther shrugged. 'Seven hundred . . .'

Athena lifted her head. She was learning not to be shocked. The pampering that had changed her completely, and in one single day, was expensive. She had already worked out that with the new wardrobe, the Manolo Blahniks, the Christian Louboutins, the Chanel bags and Kanebo make-up, she was into her grooming for about fifteen grand.

'Let's keep going,' she said.

Esther patted the pile of dresses, jackets, the odd trouser suit beside her. Athena Chambers was a dream client; she hoped she came back. Stunning haircut, beautiful face, slender, athletic body, attractive nails and soft skin . . . and she didn't argue or bitch or complain about the prices.

She also didn't second-guess. Esther was used to dealing with divas. Athena Chambers treated her like a professional; she tried on what Esther asked her to, and didn't insist on dresses that were too small or too young. And as a result Esther was trying her very hardest. Miss Chambers would be dressed in a drop-dead gorgeous wardrobe. Esther was determined she should not own a single outfit that wasn't breathtaking.

'How long have you been working here?' Athena was asking her. The younger woman peeled off the tight dress and accepted the fresh sage-green silk skirt that Esther handed her; it would match gorgeously with the cream cotton leotard with the pearl button detailing, and a young-looking pair of glossy chestnut leather stacked wooden heels.

'Eight years, ma'am.'

'Please call me Athena.' She tugged on the skirt and twirled in front of the mirror, the motion lifting the scalloped edges of the fabric; the garment danced, it looked sensational on her. 'Would you consider another offer? I think I'd like to hire you.'

Hire her? Esther had dressed some of the richest women in the world, billionaires' wives and sheikhs. Been offered jobs as valet, personal dresser, many times. But Athena Chambers didn't have enough vanity for that. Esther could tell that immediately.

Esther blinked. 'To be your personal assistant?'

'No.' Athena shook her head. 'I want you to run a programme at my club.'

'Your club?'

'Oh, I haven't bought it yet.' Her customer shook her beautiful head. 'But I'm just about to. Do you think you might be interested?'

Esther had a small mortgage, but her husband's company pension was looking a bit shaky. She wanted to be able to go on cruises when they retired. And she was sick of waiting on spoiled young women with no sense of style.

'Certainly, if you double my salary.' She shrugged.

Athena Chambers smiled. 'How about if I *halve* your salary, but offer you half a per cent of the company?'

Esther felt an unfamiliar emotion prickling at the bottom of her stomach. This young woman was fascinating. There was just something about her, something deeply impressive, something that made Esther want to break the habit of a lifetime and gamble. Gamble on Athena Chambers.

'I'm listening,' she said. 'Tell me about your club.'

Chapter Fifteen

Bai-Ling put out one manicured hand and steadied herself against the wall of the lavatory. It was about as spacious as they got in a commercial aeroplane, but she still felt hideously cramped. Despite the soothing first-class accoutrements, the expensive toiletries and warm towel railings, she was tense.

An impatient passenger was talking outside the door, wondering how much longer she would be. Screw the old bitch, Bai-Ling thought. She could wait.

One minute and three-quarters. The second hand on her platinum Tag Heuer ticked round infinitely slowly . . . two minutes . . .

She turned her head and studied the little plastic stick laid out on the bowl in front of her.

One line.

One goddamned line . . .

This time she had thought it might be different – she had believed there was a faint tinge of pink, a crease, below the main indicator.

But no.

Bai-Ling shuddered with fury as she thought of what she'd had to do, how revolting and humiliating sex with Clement had been, just to be able to look at this stupid stick . . . same as she'd looked at the others for the last four days.

No line. No baby.

The woman outside banged on the door.

'Just coming,' Bai-Ling cooed sweetly, swallowing her rage. It would not do to lose control. She was Clem's woman now, ambassadress for that old, wizened, perverted, *impotent* bastard. 'One second . . .'

She felt wet . . . had she lost control? Splashed some water on her hugely expensive trouser suit? Bai-Ling tugged at the zipper on her white Chloe trousers and pulled down the clean ivory cotton panties that Clem liked so much.

There it was, staring her in the face, a badge of defeat . . . that ugly little spot of blood.

Gasping in disappointment, she yanked open her bag and reached for a tampon. Damn it, damn it to hell. Now she really had to take on those Chambers bitches. If they thought they could scare her off, they were about to get a lesson.

They were fucking with the wrong girl. Bai-Ling was not in the mood.

'Champagne, madam?' The stewardess was leaning towards her with a bottle. Bai-Ling checked – it was vintage Veuve. It was unfortunate – not to say annoying – that Clement would not let her use the private jet until they were actually married. But first class was getting a lot better these days.

'Thank you.' She held out her glass. No point in staying away from it now.

The cashmere blanket was draped comfortably over her knee, and she took out her in-seat phone. Eight dollars a minute, and worth every cent. From memory, she dialled Clement's own chauffeur service, arranged for them to pick her up at Heathrow. Bai-Ling never took the generic airline car. Next, a reservation at the Lanesborough Hotel; Clem's name instantly freed up a suite. Again, she would have liked to have stayed at his house in Eaton Square. But Clement had said no. Until she was legally lady of that house, he thought it improper . . . And this way she was still, for a time, her own mistress. She would sleep for five hours exactly, then have a beauty therapist attend her.

Juno Chambers wanted a private dinner at their new house in Notting Hill. That was fine with Bai-Ling. She intended to look perfect. Her first phone call would be to Clement, to tell him she'd landed. Her second, later, to inform him she was running straight over to the girls. Just a hint, the barest hint, of exhaustion . . . make him feel they should not be imposing on her . . .

War between women was a subtle game, and one Bai-Ling had played many times before. You needed to take the long view. She would undermine these girls in their uncle's eyes. And he wouldn't even know she was doing it.

'Miss Bai-Ling . . . Woohooputu,' stammered the butler.

Bai-Ling flashed him an icy stare. 'Wuhuputri,' she corrected him. Her name had several syllables, so what? It wasn't that difficult to pronounce. She was sure they'd put their servant up to it.

The house was illuminated by a series of pretty wrought-iron garden lamps; it was an elegant building. She wondered how they could afford it. Bai-Ling's eagle eye had noted the sumptuous decor, the French antiques, the glorious washed-silk chaise longues. Somebody with real talent had gone over the place.

Her blood quickened a little. As an opening salvo, it was effective. So the Chambers women had money. Money they'd sucked from their uncle. She was more determined than ever that the life-giving spigot should be cut off from them.

'Bai-Ling.' Juno Chambers took the lead and came forward, giving her a very faint hug indeed; more a sort of gentle touch to the shoulders. 'How nice to see you.'

'Likewise,' Bai-Ling purred.

She quickly took them in. Juno had retreated to the safety of Dior, and looked polished and elegant in an A-line jersey dress with a cut-off bouclé jacket. Impressive sapphires, a rich cornflower blue, glinted at her ears.

Venus was wearing a skin-tight Azzedine Alaia vintage skirt, deepest black, and a black-and-white Versace blouse. It looked good on her, as did the chunky men's Patek she had dangling from her left wrist. Diana had chosen a beautifully cut Joseph trouser suit in a dusty pink, with nude leather strappy sandals and a white cotton vest. She had no jewellery on at all, and Bai-Ling reluctantly conceded she didn't need it. The greatest shock was Athena. The younger woman had to look twice to be sure it really was her. Her wild hair was now cut in a razor-sharp elongated bob, her brows were arched, she had a modest French manicure and she was wearing a va-va-voom Matthew Williamson strapless dress in bright red that showed off her large bust and narrow waist. Bai-Ling instantly coveted the dress, the hair, and her make-up artist. Her stomach tightened with a burst of adrenalin. What the hell? Why was Athena Chambers all dressed up like this? Her sloppy manners and couldn't-be-bothered appearance bugged Clement no end. She was glad he couldn't see the way Athena had changed.

Clearly they meant business.

Fine. So did she.

'You remember my sister Athena, and our cousins Diana and Venus.'

The other three girls murmured a welcome.

'Please don't mind Jameson.' Juno nodded at the butler.

Bai-Ling smiled bitchily. 'That's fine. Soon it'll be Chambers, which is a lot easier, isn't it?'

Diana laughed merrily. 'It certainly is. And will you change Bai-Ling as well?'

Bai-Ling flushed. 'Clement likes it. It really depends on your uncle. I do everything to please him.'

'I'm sure you do,' said Athena. Venus covered a snort.

'Shall we go in to dinner?' Juno rose and ushered them into the dining room. 'Bai-Ling must be exhausted – we don't want to keep her out too late.'

'A delicious meal, thank you.' Bai-Ling wasn't quite sure how to react. They had offered her a good, light supper, not too much wine, and the maid had served her promptly and respectfully. Plus, none of the girls had doled out the insults. There was too much of that dull British chit-chat about nothing, but that was the way these people were. Cold fishes. She was almost lulled by all the attention. 'So tell me more about this little dinner?'

'It's a major party, actually,' Juno said. 'Welcoming you to London. Uncle Clem's been so good to us all these years and we want to repay him.'

'By throwing a party?' Bai-Ling asked.

'It's just a start.' Diana took over. 'You are going to be Mrs Clement Chambers, Bai-Ling, so that means you have a certain position in London. Even if Uncle Clem rarely shows up here, he likes to keep up his reputation in Britain.'

'You could say it's why he keeps tabs on our activities,' Venus agreed.

Bai-Ling nodded. 'This is traditional, the party?'

'Think of it as your coming out,' Athena said. 'There will be many very important people attending. Juno seems to have listed half the aristocracy. And Diana is bringing some movie stars and musicians. And financiers . . . it should be a good mix.'

Movie stars. Financiers. Aristocrats. Bai-Ling's eyes glittered with greed. The one thing that was wrong, so wrong, about being Clement's fiancée was that she couldn't *enjoy* it properly. Dancing attendance on that old goat meant putting up with his reclusive ways. There were no nights at the Cannes film festival, no masked balls in Venice, no thousand-dollar-a-plate charity dinners in New York . . . she couldn't spend his cash properly. It was one thing to live in luxury, but you had to be *seen* to live in luxury. She envisaged herself in a drop-dead-gorgeous ball gown, something bespoke from Atelier Versace, dripping with Clement's diamonds, queening it at this bash . . . Certainly, pretty as they were, the Chambers girls couldn't compete with her. Bai-Ling was younger. Hotter. And infinitely richer . . .

She took another sip of her Chateau Lafite. Mmm. Doubtless they had designs in throwing this party. But she could use it to dazzle London and make them all see how futile it was to fight her.

'It sounds a bit of a chore, actually,' she drawled. 'Are you really doing it all for me?'

'Mostly for you,' Athena said. 'Of course, we are celebrating our various projects. The Chambers girls are career women, you know.'

Bai-Ling blinked. Instantly, the pleasant fog of alcohol lifted. She was alert, her skin prickling. Career women? How? Weren't these the ultimate trust-fund brats?

'You have careers?' she blurted out, unable to stop the overt rudeness.

'I know.' Juno shrugged. 'It's rather enjoyable. I work in property management. I find darling little places around town for some of the world's richest people to rent. Tremendous fun sticking one's nose into other people's houses.' She smiled. 'And quite lucrative.'

Juno Chambers, a working woman? Bai-Ling tensed; that went against everything Clem had ever told her about his eldest niece.

'Well, I suppose you are nearly divorced now,' she said sharply. The idea of these girls having jobs – especially well-paying ones – grated. She'd been looking forward to watching them grovel and twist as she took the money away. Never thought they might make their own. That wasn't the Chambers way.

'It's fun,' Juno said, her dark eyes ignoring the insult. 'And I am meeting absolutely tons of eligible young men – if I ever want to tie myself down again.'

There was a subtle emphasis on the word 'young'.

Bai-Ling tensed. She hated to think of Clement's old, saggy body heaving on top of her. And she liked others referring to it even less.

'I've started a design consultancy.' Diana leaned forward intently. 'I do interior design for major hotels, and serious private projects. My first client is the Victrix Group. I'm overseeing their hotel in London. Karl Roden will be coming to the party.'

'Will he?' Bai-Ling murmured. She was starting to feel her competitive hackles rise. The Victrix hotels were her favourites across the globe. Nothing said luxury like the Victrix. And Karl Roden . . . one of the richest unmarried men still on the market. He would certainly spice up her party.

How on earth did a wastrel like Diana Chambers get a gig like that? she wondered. Was she banging Mr Roden? Hell, Bai-Ling hoped not; that would be dreadful.

'Well, I expect I can make it,' she announced. 'And Venus . . . Athena? You are still doing whatever it is you were doing?'

Venus's blond head tilted with anger, Bai-Ling was pleased to see, but Athena remained quite calm.

'I have a project,' she said. 'I want to raise some finance to see it through. And the party will be an excellent networking opportunity.'

'And I've moved on,' Venus snapped. 'I'm not acting any more.'

'Perhaps you've decided to make pop records,' Bai-Ling

teased. 'Like Kylie Minogue. Just older.' The wine made this sound highly amusing, and she laughed.

'I'm going to be a producer. Films. And I already have my first deal lined up.' Venus bared her white teeth in an approximation of a grin. 'You could have a cameo, Bai-Ling, if you liked.'

A cameo! She wondered if Venus meant that. Her . . . a star.

At any rate, it was quite clear Bai-Ling *had* to come to the party. All those duchesses and rich men. All the networking . . . and she wanted to see if the girls meant what they said. Were they all self-sufficient now? Telling her they didn't need her lousy money?

She was wary, sure. But definitely intrigued.

'You've talked me into it,' she agreed. 'I'll come and let you ladies introduce me.'

'Marvellous news,' Juno said. 'And now, Bai-Ling, let me call your chauffeur. I'm sure you'll be wanting to get that beauty sleep.'

Bai-Ling eyed the eldest cousin suspiciously. But Juno's expression betrayed nothing. Perhaps she was now engaged full-time on a husband hunt of her own. Whatever, Bai-Ling thought, suddenly exhausted. She would find out soon enough.

Chapter Sixteen

It was the first day of February, and unseasonably warm. Venus woke to the weak winter sun streaming through her skylight; in a few seconds she remembered what she had to do today. Her bare feet swung instantly out of bed, on to the carpet. She was full of energy, raring to go, her whole body crackling with adrenalin. It took discipline to force her on to the treadmill. Half an hour, no longer; she didn't have the time. Venus cranked up the speed, sweating the intensity to make up for it. Yes, today was a big day for her. But she still wanted to look *good*. There was the party for Bai-Ling coming up, of course. And even more importantly, she had a feeling she'd be seeing somebody else today.

If she encountered Hans, Venus wanted to look good.

Achingly good.

As the last track on her MP3 player faded away, she dialled down the speed, spending a few minutes on cool-down. No point ripping her muscles, and anyway, the workout had helped her to think. The bloody writer had an agent, so that meant she was paying Guild minimum;

daylight robbery for a stupid script that had languished in a drawer for eighteen months. Nevertheless. Writing the cheque had felt good, in a perverse way. She had scorned to attach herself when it was a no-hope project, but it was a good comedy. Now it was hers; her first act as a producer.

Step two was a director. And Venus already knew who she wanted. Keisha Roland, a young black woman fresh from film school, also with an agent, but on the very bottom rung of the ladder. Venus had worked with her on the Oxo commercial. She hated that bloody spot, but it had worked as an advert – cleverly shot and lit, well edited. And Hans Tersch had rated it. So the director was cheap as chips, but very very talented. As she was a woman, nobody had promoted her yet. Women found it harder to break in. Venus had sent over the script, knowing that Keisha would be excited if offered the chance to direct the traffic. Last night's desperate, grateful call had confirmed her judgement.

I'm not stupid, Venus congratulated herself, as the water from her shower sluiced over her relaxing muscles. Hans is a genius. I'm just going to borrow his ability to spot talent. And it won't cost me a thing.

She jumped out of the shower, towelled off, and reached for her cashmere gown. She opened the wardrobe and picked carefully: an elegant buttercup-yellow dress with a knee-skimming saffron coat and butter-coloured heels, a light spring outfit that she teamed with an outrageous strand of golden South Sea pearls, real in-your-face jewellery. She carefully curled her long hair with a round brush to make it bounce. Excitement knotted in the pit of her stomach. This morning's meeting was absolutely crucial.

Sir Leo Fabricant was a legend, and like most legends, he lived deep in the past. Once upon a time – in the sixties – he'd been an important British director. But times had moved on, and by the time Burt Reynolds was box-office gold, Leo was history. His social climbing instincts had not abandoned him, though. Well-connected government chums got him a sinecure passing out government grants to British film-makers. Leo enjoyed being sucked up to. For decades he'd clung like a limpet to his post at the Film Council.

But the last year had seen him ousted in a coup. The British Film Commission, Channel Four and the rest of the Young Turks were players in the domestic market. Leo's own credit had all but disappeared. He could hardly green-light a thing. Producers were giving him a wide berth now, men and women who'd fallen over themselves to flatter and cajole him, to buy him lunch at the most expensive restaurants and supply limos to the best premieres.

Venus knew all this. She had chosen her target carefully. Was Sir Leo available for lunch? Nothing special, just the Ivy. She'd be *so* grateful. And apparently, he was.

Venus checked her reflection again. This was calculated to push all the buttons. The randy old goat would leer at her beauty, and his ever-present inner snob would approve of her elegance; sexy and demure, not her normal MO. But Venus was shifting her image – actress to businesswoman. The clothes must shift with it.

She slipped her phone into her Versace handbag. Maybe even before lunch, she was expecting a call. Perhaps two . . .

'I can't believe it.' Janet Syms, blithely ignoring the law, clicked hard at her platinum lighter and fired up another of her trademark cigarillos. 'Fucking girl. Fucking stupid little girl.' She sucked viciously and blew a stream of fragrant smoke out towards the window. 'Why would she *quit*?'

Venus nodded in sympathy. They were sitting together in the ultra-modern offices of ICP, one of the largest acting agencies in London. Janet was an experienced, hardbitten agent; she favoured mannish jackets and had a face that was leathery from drinking, smoking, and utterly ruthless deal-making. She handled big stars and a handful of actors on their way up. Until this morning, Lilly Bruin had fallen into the latter camp. As soon as she got the lead for *Maud*, Janet pounced, poaching Lilly from the two-bit little agent who'd repped her since she got out of theatre school.

Then she had been a valuable asset. Today, she was nothing.

'She's a junkie. Loves the coke.'

Venus shrugged. 'Hardly unique amongst actresses, Janet.'

'She didn't know when to stop. Then she was mooning after Hans. Coming to the set late. I told her, I warned her. Don't blow your big shot. But one lead and the fucking idiot thinks she's Lindsay Lohan.'

'She really quit?' Venus asked innocently.

'Gave Hans an ultimatum. He told her to get lost and get her ass on the set or she'd be fired. She threw a tantrum, he sacked her.'

'But the production must be hugely over budget . . . can they replace her?'

'He's shutting it down. The whole project's a write-off.' Janet, tough old bird that she was, shivered in fright. 'If you could have heard him . . .'

'So what next for Lilly?'

'Who gives a fuck? She's toast. History. Nobody will touch the brat who blew up a Hans Tersch movie. He's already put out word that she's coked up to the eyeballs. I'm dropping her as a client.'

Venus smoothed her dress down across her knees, suppressing a sly smile.

'How did she take it?'

Janet's face did not soften. 'Badly – kid was bawling in my office, did everything short of drop to her knees, it was fucking embarrassing. She's tried to call up Hans and beg him to take her back, but he's having none of it. Swore she'd lay off the drugs, but I told her it was far too late. Her career's finished.'

'That bad, huh?'

Janet shrugged. 'Look, I tried to place a couple of calls for her elsewhere. Nobody wanted to take her on. I couldn't get her cast in a commercial.'

Venus nodded seriously. It was time to strike. Her prey was at rock bottom.

'I have something that might interest you, in that case. A rom-com, excellent script. The British Film Association is financing it,' she lied. 'Very small project, and I want new talent. I'd pay her only scale and minimal residuals, but I do think Lilly has something.'

Janet was incredulous. 'You want to cast her?'

Venus nodded. 'The director is Keisha Roland. I worked with her on the Oxo commercial.'

Janet's eyes narrowed; Venus could almost see the wheels turning in her head.

'I know her work. That's a smart play, Venus, a very smart play. You got her cheap?'

'First gig.' Venus shrugged.

'I think you might be good at this,' Janet decided. 'You know you've got me over a barrel.'

'It's a second chance for Lilly. If you're the one who saves her career . . .' Venus stood up. 'Basic money, no perks, and she submits to having a urine test on set daily.

Tell her that if she's so much as one point over the limit for booze, I'll broadcast it to every producer in town.' She gave Janet a brilliant smile. 'But on the plus side, good script, hot director, and we're working on indie money so the shooting schedule is only eight weeks. Which is why I have to be ultra-tough on her. We can't burn days on an actress. It's serious shoestring time. From your point of view, she makes it through an eight-week boot camp with me, she's rehabilitated as a working actress.'

'You got it.' Janet shook her head. 'You know you're taking a risk, though.'

Venus stood up, delighted. 'That's what life's all about. Bye, sweetie.'

Janet air-kissed her cheeks, and Venus swept from the room feeling a lot more like a real producer than when she walked in.

'Sir Leo.' Venus pitched her voice low and deferential. 'Wonderful to see you. So good of you to make the time.'

His rheumy eyes roved over her trim body and swelling breasts. He obviously approved; Venus winced a little, being nakedly appraised by this randy old goat. Was this what Bai-Ling felt like, in bed with Uncle Clem? She certainly earned every penny she got.

Venus forced a smile and pressed her elbows together to give him a good look at her cleavage.

'Anything for you, my dear,' Sir Leo rasped. He hadn't seen her in over a year, but he acted like they were the best of pals. 'To what do I owe the pleasure? I've ordered some champers, a magnum of vintage Krug.'

Because *she* was paying. Venus loathed people who said 'champers'. It was low class and snobby at the same time.

'Fabulous,' she trilled. 'What's good here? Tell you what, Sir Leo, would you order for me?'

He smirked; Venus was an expert at flattering men.

'Delighted.' He chose a small Dover sole, no butter, and a leafy salad for her, whilst indulging himself with the beef Wellington.

'I have a project for you,' Venus said. 'It's unique. It's a first-look deal. This film is going to be huge. It needs minimal financing, and I promise you, Sir Leo, everybody involved will make their reputations.'

She laced her words with heavy significance.

He snorted, white whiskery face scrunching itself up.

'I made my reputation many years before you were born.'

'Ah yes,' Venus said soothingly. 'But this film will, shall we say, *cement* it. Sir Leo,' she announced dramatically. 'This is your way back in.'

'Back in.' He stared at her, but at least he was listening. Venus seized the moment.

'Yes – you provide the money, we deliver a knockout movie. It goes big, we sell the distribution. You'll be seen to be on the ball.'

He blinked. 'Perhaps you haven't heard . . . the Film Council . . .'

'Sacked you, yes, I know,' said Venus brutally. 'But you still have your position with the BFA.'

It was a tiny quango, with a minute budget – hardly worth bothering with.

'I only need a million. We can get it done on the cheap. Keisha has access to discounted film stock. Everybody's on minimum. Skeleton crew. Limited locations. Eight-week shoot.' Venus leaned in to him. 'You still have one million in the kitty. Spend it on us.'

'And why should I do that?' Sir Leo laboriously sliced himself off a piece of meltingly soft beef Wellington, and chased it down with a swig of Krug. 'When you've been in this business as long as I have, dearie, you'll know that every producer swears their project is the next *Star Wars*. Or *Four Weddings*.' He sighed. 'Do you know how many times I've heard "This is the new *Four Weddings*"?'

Venus reached into her bag and passed over the script. 'Judge for yourself. And bear something in mind. I've got the hot new director Keisha Roland, smart kid, does commercials. *And* I poached Hans Tersch's star, Lilly Bruin, from *Maud*. They had to shut down production.'

'Bruin?' Sir Leo considered the name. 'The junkie girl?'

'She's no junkie. That's Hans bitching. Anyway, she'll be taking dope tests. Janet Syms is thrilled. Just think about that, Hans Tersch's hand-picked star for peanuts.'

Sir Leo nodded, slowly, and turned the script over in his hands.

'I'll read it,' he agreed. 'First thing this afternoon.'

Of course you will, Venus thought. It's not like you have anything else to do.

She lifted her champagne flute, clinked it with his. 'Cheers.'

Venus floated back to the house. She had her first deal as a producer. Lilly was signed up, and Janet reported her breathless, slavish gratitude; Keisha was thrilled to have a shot; even old man Leo had read the script in one hour and messengered over his contract.

It was a go project. Now she had to concentrate on casting the smaller parts. She couldn't afford a casting director, but after years on the scene there wasn't an up-and-coming, hungry, underpaid actor that Venus didn't know about. She already had ideas.

The thought occurred to her that maybe, just maybe, the movie might actually live up to her billing. Not that it mattered, of course; the point was that she should have some sort of vaguely believable role as a career woman, that Bai-Ling should assume she was independently wealthy.

In that regard, today had been an unqualified success. She would go to the little welcome party, dazzle, shine, and act up the lady producer. Bai-Ling would never guess that Venus Chambers was hurting for money.

She walked into the kitchen with a swagger. Juno was already there, looking tired; she offered her cousin a martini, and Venus nodded, ready to celebrate.

'Hard day at the office?' she asked.

Juno shrugged. She was wearing a coffee-coloured suit with a marron glacé silk shirt and a necklace of brown quartz and seed pearls. It was subtle power dressing, Venus realised, and it looked good on her; easy wealth, it said.

But despite the elegance, there was something drained about Juno. Venus recognised the concealer under the eyes, blocking off the shadows; Juno's skin was dull, and she seemed subdued, resigned; like nothing had zest for her any more.

'I closed a few deals. You?'

'Not so bad.' Venus exulted privately. 'How's the Bai-Ling party coming?'

'Sewn up; almost all the invitations are out there, and we're starting to get acceptances. Polly Sheffield, for one.'

Venus tried to look casual. 'Will you have room for one more on the guest list?'

Her cousin eyed her speculatively. 'Who now, a boyfriend?'

Venus blushed bright red. 'Oh, definitely not. Actually, a rival. I just want to rub it in.'

'Well, why didn't you say so?' Juno was all smiles. 'This is our little bash for Bai-Ling, sweetie – rubbing it in is the *raison d'être*. Anyway, if he's connected to you he's bound to be a player, and we want Bai-Ling to see us in all our glory.'

'I'll just go and call him.'

'When you get back, stick around. We're all in tonight. We need to plan Bai-Ling's evening.' Juno smiled wickedly. 'I have some *sensational* outfits for her.'

Venus nodded, almost absently. Her mind was already on Hans. She escaped to the privacy of her bedroom, flopped down on the oyster silk coverlet, feeling like a naughty schoolgirl in the sixth form. Of course, this was just playing, just a cover story, a bit of fun. But she could still tease Hans over it. And getting rid of the humiliation she'd felt after the *Maud* audition was a massive extra bonus.

Her stomach pressed to the bed, manicured nails tapping out the number on her phone, the gesture of making the call suddenly seemed very intimate.

'Tersch Productions.'

'Hi. Is Hans about, please?'

'I'll check.' Venus could see the cool young receptionist in her mind's eye.

'It's Venus Chambers.'

'Oh. Venus.' There was an audible note of pity, mixed with just a little contempt. Venus flushed with anger. 'I'm afraid Hans is a very busy man,' the girl said. 'I don't know if I can reach him for you.'

'Try,' Venus said sweetly. 'Tell him I'm calling as Lilly Bruin's new employer.'

There was a long pause. 'One moment, please.'

Yeah, that's what I thought, Venus told herself.

A click on the line. Then his voice.

'Hans here.'

The impact he still had on her surprised her. The memory of his hands on her, confident, powerful, came back as though nothing else had passed between them.

'I want to invite you to a little party I'm having on Friday,' Venus said. 'For my uncle's fiancée. I hope you can come; you can give me some tips on handling Lilly.'

'Handling her? I don't understand.' His voice was clipped. 'I sacked her.'

'Yes, and I hired her again.'

'To do what?'

Venus stretched out her legs, starting to enjoy herself.

'To act, of course. And you know, Hans, Lilly's a very talented girl. I'm going to have to thank you for making her available.'

'You've hired her to act?'

'I'm a producer now, didn't you know? I have a rom-com set up. Lilly's the star. Very hot script. Good director, small budget.' Venus sighed with pleasure. 'It's a career-making film.'

He chuckled softly. 'Everybody with a phone's a producer these days. It doesn't mean anything without cash.'

'Oh, I forgot to mention that. I have the cash.' Venus

saw herself, mentally, smashing an ace into the far corner of his tennis court. 'It was Lilly's involvement that clinched the financing.'

Tersch chuckled. 'You're joking, of course. What is this, some vanity project? Looking for ways to get back in front of a camera?'

That stung. Venus composed herself, hating him and wanting him desperately all at the same time.

'No. Another favour you did me, Hans. Making me see how untalented I am.'

'You have talent.' A beat, then he said softly, 'In more ways than one.'

Venus struggled against the pulse that throbbed in her belly. He fucked Lilly, she reminded herself. Young, stupid Lilly. He'll sleep with anyone. That worked, and she recovered her poise.

'Like Lilly?' she asked tartly. 'Anyway, you should drop in. I hear your film's shut down now, so perhaps you'll be at a loose end. You can tell me how to handle this great young actress, and I can give you some tips on making a small-budget film work.'

Tersch growled. 'Don't challenge me, Venus. I'm not interested in petty games from a trust-fund brat.'

'Don't challenge you? I think I just did.' The blood was singing in her veins now, the adrenalin of battle pumping through her. Courage; it was an unfamiliar sensation, and she liked it. 'Come along, Hans, if you dare. Otherwise, see you at the BAFTAs.'

Her heart thumping, Venus hung up. Then she rolled on to her back.

So this was dealmaking. The strangest thing. She *loved* it.

Athena put her red spotted handkerchief to her mouth and coughed.

The hall had fifty years' worth of dust in it. She peered into the gloom. Marble floors and brass rails were barely visible under a thick coat of white; the occasional weak beam of sunlight that streamed in through the boarded-up windows illuminated more fluff as particles danced in the still air. She longed for an industrial-size hoover. Or failing that, to open a window and let in a blast of traffic-choked air; it would still be fresher than what was inside.

'We've had offers,' the estate agent said, with a marked lack of enthusiasm. Athena could tell the man thought she was just another time-waster. 'But nobody wants to conform to the council plans. They all want to turn the place into flats, or develop it into a large private house. The council thinks it's a landmark, but the big cinema chains are only interested in multiplexes these days. And the small independents are offering peanuts . . .'

Athena nodded. The boarded-up cinema fell between two stools. The left-wing council refused to sell it for development, and the heritage people didn't want it touched; to locals, it was just an eyesore.

'I'm going to put in an offer,' she said.

He sighed. 'I told you, they won't permit residential development.'

'I don't want to do that with it.' Athena glanced around, her eyes getting accustomed to the dark. 'It still has that car park underneath?'

He nodded. 'They won't let you make it a multistorey either, so don't think you're the first person to come up with that idea.'

'Who's the person on the council to speak to about it?'

'Her name's Maxime Chilcott.' The young man cast an admiring eye over Athena's sprayed-on hot pants and tight tartan sweater, teamed with Jimmy Choo boots and a glossy French plait. 'She won't like you.'

'And why's that?'

'Go and meet her.' He sniggered annoyingly. 'You'll see.'

The planning department of Toxheath Council was exactly as Athena imagined it: cramped, soulless and industrial. The secretaries all wore cheap clothes and an air of hating their jobs. Maxime Chilcott's office was littered with Styrofoam cups. There was a poster of Che Guevara tacked on to a pinboard.

Maxime herself sat resplendent in an old swivel chair with holes picked in its fabric back. She wore what looked like a hand-knitted sweater in grey and sludge green, and a voluminous pair of jeans to swathe her massive legs, while her unkempt hair was drawn back in a ponytail. Athena tried not to stare at the luxuriant moustache that grew on her upper lip.

For Maxime, the revolution was just around the corner. She glared accusingly at Athena's sexy clothes, shiny lipgloss and perfectly plucked eyebrows. The younger woman could not mistake the waves of disapproval that emanated from her.

'Miss Chilcott . . .'

Mistake. 'Ms,' the woman said fiercely. 'You know, *Ms* Chambers, this is a serious office. We're on local government business. What's your idea?'

'I want to restore the Regal Palace.'

'Another developer wanting to profit from local heritage. That makes a change,' Maxime added sarcastically.

It was a ratty old cinema that had been past its glory days in the sixties, and was now an eyesore. Athena smiled ingratiatingly.

'Not planning on developing it. Just restoring it. It'll be a private club. The interior feel will be kept just as it is; all I'll need to do is rip out the seats. We can even keep the velvet curtains.'

'A private club.' Maxime looked like Athena had just sworn in church. 'Fancy millionaires ripping off the workers; no thanks, not the council's sort of thing.'

Athena refused to be cowed. She squared her shoulders in their trim little sweater.

'Ms Chilcott,' she said sternly. 'This is going to be different. It's going to be a feminist club. Women only.' She only just stopped herself saying 'girls'.

'A feminist club?' Maxime raised a bushy eyebrow. 'Explain.'

'Well, I'm an academic.' Athena gave her a brief sketch, going hard on her qualifications and the old boys' network that was keeping her out. 'So you see, it can be impossible for women to get these opportunities. We need a way to network. And it needs to be made attractive, to tempt the female high-flyers in.'

'Full of beauty parlours,' Maxime snorted. 'Manicurists . . .'

'There may be some of that.' Athena inclined her head. 'But there'll also be a state-of-the-art internet and communications centre, a private jobs board – not just any old job, opportunities for major players – a property network, and opportunities to lobby, whether it be female MPs, diplomats, or chief executives.' Athena took a breath. 'An Athenaeum – for women. And who better to start it than someone called Athena?'

Maxime chewed on her lips, which were the only thin part of her body.

'There are the obvious benefits for your town centre. The club would be an equal-opportunity employer. We would pay council tax and bring a cachet to the area. And,' said Athena, leaning in to close the deal, 'I would want to include prominent local politicians and top civil servants. Your superiors in Parliament would be members. Of course, as the visionary planner who gave us the go-ahead, we'd want you as a member for life – fully complimentary, you understand.'

She had her. The antagonistic light in Maxime's eyes quivered and blinked out, to be replaced by something else . . . a wary look of greed and hope.

'A life member,' the planner mused.

'Think of the networking opportunities. You'd be smashing the old-boy network. Think of the money we'd bring to the council.' Athena had never seduced a woman before, but she knew she was winning here. 'Say yes, Ms Chilcott. The acceptable face of capitalism is wearing lipstick.'

Chapter Seventeen

'So I've been thinking,' Suzie Foster said.

Hard to believe, Diana thought cynically. But she swallowed the response.

Suzie Foster, supermodel. Anorexic waif with big plastic tits, eyebrows dyed to match her platinum-blond hair, and tiny, expensive clothes to fit her size two frame. She chain-smoked frantically, but her procelain veneered teeth stayed Barbie-doll white. Diana had been afraid to shake hands, in case she fractured Suzie's bones. Roden's girlfriend had big doe eyes of perfect blue, thick lashes, collagen-enhanced stripper's lips, and maybe one and a half brain cells, Diana thought bitchily.

All the men they'd passed on the way to the Covent Garden site had leered and drooled – and not at Diana.

As a pretty girl herself, she wasn't used to being outdazzled. But the combo of flawless skin, flaxen hair and surgical curves was making her almost invisible. Diana could just imagine being Karl Roden with this beauty on his arm. It was a statement of domination, she perceived at once; that he was the richest, most powerful man in any room, and bedding the hottest woman too.

Diana knew she couldn't possibly compete. She hated it.

She looked at Suzie with loathing.

'Yes? What have you come up with?'

They were standing in the hotel ballroom, which was going to be converted into the health centre. Diana could already see it all in her mind's eye. The spinning bikes at one end, the Pilates studio at the other. A rock-climbing wall. Gleaming, top-of-the-range treadmills. A sumptuous shower suite right next door; individual power showers with massage jets. After that she wanted the guests to be channelled out via the spa; massages, beauty treatments all available . . .

This would be a destination hotel for chic health freaks. Just as punters stayed at the Mondrian in LA so they could use the Sky Bar, Londoners would book into the Victrix Covent Garden just to use the spa. She could see it now, Gwyneth and Madonna, Tom and Katie, William and Kate . . . it would be wall-to-wall celebrities and moguls.

'Well, you know.' Suzie blinked her baby blues. 'I just can't go for a gym.'

Diana blinked. 'I beg your pardon?'

Suzie patted her arm. 'I know you mean well, sweetie, but folk don't want to sweat when they're staying someplace nice. What we need is a really good restaurant! Excellent food. It'd be like totally original.'

'Original.' Diana couldn't keep the sarcasm out of her voice. 'Like, say, Gordon Ramsay at Claridge's?'

'Yes!' Suzie beamed at her, irony free. 'Just like that! Except it'll be all protein Like an Atkins restaurant! Scrambled eggs and steaks! And meringue made with Splenda for dessert.'

Diana choked back a snort of laughter. 'Suzie, I really don't think that's the best idea. The hotel is going to be themed on the ultimate health club experience. It's cool, it's unique in London and it's—'

'Not going to happen.' The big blue eyes narrowed, and Diana took a step back. All of a sudden the blonde was looking at her with naked dislike and suspicion. 'Karl is *my* boyfriend, he put *me* on the project and *I'm* going to design the hotel, so if you want to get on board I suggest you start looking for protein-based chefs.'

Diana lifted her chin. Nobody spoke to a Chambers like that.

'I'll continue to design the hotel I promised Karl,' she replied.

Suzie gave a mean little shrug.

'I *said*, get looking for protein chefs.' She reached up and rudely snapped her fingers in Diana's face. 'What are you waiting for?'

Diana laughed aloud. 'I don't take orders from you.'

'*Excuse* me?' Suzie demanded, her thin face going puce.

'No,' Diana said. 'I don't think I will.'

Suzie snarled, 'So you quit, do you? Limey tramp! I'll tell my boyfriend.'

Diana's pulse was racing, but she forced herself to stay calm.

'I most certainly do not quit. I don't work for you, Miss Foster, I work for Mr Roden. He owns this hotel – you don't. If he wants to fire me, he can.'

'Damn straight he can.' Suzie was almost spitting. '*Bet* on it.'

'If you'll excuse me,' Diana shut her folder with a snap, 'and even if you won't, I've got work to do. There are gym suppliers to get quotes from, and at lunch I'm interviewing six Hollywood personal trainers.'

'If you don't leave this hotel,' Suzie hissed, 'I'll get my personal security – *our* personal security – to throw you out.'

Diana felt a wash of despair rock through her. She was going to lose her commission, lose her gig. And suddenly, even though it was just a cover story for Bai-Ling, she truly wanted it. She had a talent for this, she just *knew* it, and a life of parties hadn't exactly prepared her for anything else.

But faced with this triumphant bimbo looking down her pert little nose, Diana Chambers was just not prepared to buckle, cry or beg. If Karl Roden sacked her – too bad. She realised she'd rather starve in the streets than crawl to this blonde bitch.

'Have a nice day,' she replied coldly, and walked

straight out of the hotel. There was a taxi in the street, and Diana jumped in; she gave their address in Notting Hill. Best to wait there for the inevitable call. At least she would be on friendly territory.

As the taxi ploughed through the streets, Diana half-heartedly made some calls. She did have connections at the hottest workout spots, not just in London but in Paris too, and there was this amazing new place in Berlin run by a former welterweight champion, where movie stars liked to work out, very cool and underground. It was just an exercise, but she went through the motions all the same. Call it stubborn pride.

By the time they reached Kensington, Diana was done with her calls. She wondered, depressed, how the other girls had been getting on. Venus seemed to be more excited these days, Athena was full of mysterious plans, and Juno was as pompous as ever. Diana had the ugly feeling that by the day of Bai-Ling's party, she'd be the only one whose career had died at birth. And she had absolutely no idea what else she could do.

Her phone buzzed; she looked down and saw she had voicemail. Her heart in her mouth, she lifted the phone to her ear. It was Karl. Her stomach did a sick, slow flip.

'Diana.' His voice was flat. 'Come over to the office when you get this, would you?'

Sighing, she gave the order to the cabbie to turn the car around. Oh well. Better face the music . . .

*

The secretaries, eyes averted, ushered her up to the top floor. Defiantly, Diana lifted her head. She was determined not to cry. Besides, Suzie had probably got there before her, and there was no way Diana was going to give that cow the satisfaction. She called on her public-school training. If there was blubbing, Diana thought, she'd damn well do it at home. It amazed her how much she cared.

Karl Roden was sitting behind his desk. Suzie, she realised with relief, was not with him. He gestured for her to sit.

'You know why I called you in?'

Diana nodded. 'Of course.'

His gaze flickered across her assessingly. 'You had a blazing row with my girlfriend.'

'I did,' Diana replied coolly.

Roden's eyebrow lifted. 'And that's all you've got to say?'

She shrugged. 'Karl, if you want to fire me, do it now. I don't mind incorporating your girlfriend's whims, as far as is practical, but she wanted to blow the entire point of this hotel. She came up with an idiotic alternative, and then she snapped her fingers at me as though I were a waiter. I told her where to get off. If that's unacceptable to you, so be it. I can't work with her.'

Roden's face was impassive.

'Is that all?'

'No.' The imminence of her departure made Diana

suddenly brave. 'She's a conceited gold-digger without a brain in her head and I can't believe you're going out with her.'

She saw him fail to conceal a slight grin.

'Suzie's very beautiful.'

'So was Samantha Fox,' Diana snapped. 'Don't you think a man like you should be dating a woman who can pass the time of day with him once he's finished in bed?'

Roden's dark eyes bored into hers.

'Diana, my private life is really none of your business. You wanted to be a design consultant to Victrix Hotels.'

'But it *is* my business. You made it my business when you asked me to work with that bimbo. She'll ruin this project if you let her. Free advice, even though you're firing me.' Diana jumped to her feet. 'I wish I could say it's been fun.'

'Where are you going?'

'Home,' she said. Wanting to get out of there before her fragile composure cracked.

'But we're in a meeting,' Karl Roden responded. 'And I haven't fired you.'

Diana sat down heavily. Blinked.

'I have, however, fired Suzie,' he said. 'She barged in here earlier, demanding your head. She cursed and screamed at me when I refused. In fact, I told her she'd have to apologise to you.'

Diana blinked. 'Really?'

'Yes.' His gaze was starting to unsettle her. Diana was

266

regretting her loose tongue. How could Karl work with her when she was giving him relationship advice?

'How did she take that?'

Karl smiled openly. 'She said it was you or her.'

'And you chose me?'

'I don't take ultimatums. From anyone.'

Diana blushed. 'I see.'

Roden stood up. 'And I don't like being made to look stupid. Suzie had been whining about getting involved in the business. I thought it might freshen up the relationship – things were somewhat stale. Besides, if there's one thing Suzie knows about, it's working out. She's the ultimate body fascist. So I sent her off to work with you. I guess I forgot her terminal case of jealousy.'

'I'm sorry for mouthing off about your relationship.'

'It was refreshing.' He looked at her, and Diana shifted uncomfortably in her seat. 'Tell me what you've been working on.'

Safe ground. She started to recite the offers she'd had from suppliers, her design vision for the hotel, and told him about the hip European trainers. Amazingly, as she heard herself talk, Diana realised she was making sense. And Roden noticed, too; he was nodding and making notes.

'How quickly do you think you can pull this together?'

'Judging from what they were telling me, three months.'

'Make it two. I want to be opened faster than that.'

'I'll try.'

'Don't try, baby. Get it done.' Karl Roden snapped the file shut. 'And stop by accounts on the way out. Fourth floor. They'll cut you a cheque. I'm starting small until I see the final result, and I'm warning you, don't try to bargain.'

'I won't.' Relief washed over her. 'Whatever you decide is fine with me.' She paused. 'We're having a little party at my house next week, for my uncle's fiancée. Would you like to come?'

He shook his head. 'I rarely do parties.'

Diana nodded, trying not to feel too gutted.

'Maybe lunch,' she said casually.

He smiled at her, looking right into her eyes with that laser-beam stare.

'I don't think so. I just got out of one relationship. You're too beautiful; I'd try to take you to bed, and that would ruin everything.'

Diana flushed scarlet.

'Don't worry,' Roden added. 'I leave for New York tonight. You'll have full budget approval on this hotel. Get me the best, and get it as cheaply as possible.'

'I will.'

'We'll see if you have a talent for this or not.' He tapped the desk. 'Hotels are big business, Diana. There are consultants out there who would kill for a break like this.'

'Thank you, Karl.' Diana jumped to her feet. 'I won't let you down.'

He swivelled the chair away from her. 'See you in a couple of months.'

Diana fled.

The accountancy department on the fourth floor was very different from the corporate fantasy of Roden's suite. Brisk young men in grey suits and efficient-looking women busied themselves in glass-walled offices. Diana presented herself to the receptionist.

'Diana Chambers. Karl Roden sent me down here for a cheque.'

The woman tapped at her computer. 'Oh yes. Chambers Inc?'

Diana nodded.

'Take a seat. Somebody will be right out.'

Diana perched on an industrial dove-grey sofa and wondered what was coming. Of course, it was all about prestige. She wouldn't dream of arguing with Karl; he was the boss, and she'd taken the job to attract other clients. But still. These days, everything was about money. Fighting Bai-Ling would require lots of it, and even though Diana had taken the gamble, she still hated seeing her savings trickling down the Juno-sized hole: lavish parties, excessive rent, the best clothes . . .

She hoped Karl would give her at least five thousand.

'Good afternoon, Ms Chambers.' A young man with a

white envelope. 'Your fee. Mr Roden reminds you it's non-negotiable.'

'Yes, I got that,' Diana said crisply. She took the envelope. She wouldn't allow him to see her face if she opened it and found a cheque for a few hundred pounds. 'Good afternoon.'

Diana waited until she was safely ensconced in another taxi, and on the way back to the house, before she ripped the envelope open.

She stared at it disbelievingly. Karl Roden had written her a cheque for twenty-five thousand pounds.

Twenty-five grand! Her share of the rent for an entire year.

Emotions ripped through her. Sheer relief. Then gratitude. Then pride. And finally excitement.

'I've changed my mind,' she told the cabbie. 'Take me to Covent Garden.'

It was a good thing Roden was headed off to the States. He could pick up another piece of arm-candy there, and Diana could do her job without worrying she was about to fall for the boss. Besides, Roden said himself he didn't want a relationship. She needed to find a billionaire who was actually ready to marry.

And one who didn't mind his wife having a career, she added silently. Because the strange thing was, this was rather fun.

*

'Juno,' Fatima al-Abdul purred, moving forward to kiss her on both cheeks. 'You look marvellous.'

'So do you, darling,' Juno said lightly. 'How do you like the flat?'

She was sitting in her office in the Lord Estates building, with the door open and the computer on. The telephone lights kept flashing; Juno pressed a couple of buttons to divert them to voicemail. She was delighted Fatima had come here. A recent acquaintance, her husband worked for the Qatar embassy, and Fatima had that glorious air of serious money all around her: the elegant Lacroix suit, the large diamond studs in her ears, the handmade shoes and Fendi bag; her hair shone, and her skin was luminous. Oh, and her car, with the diplomatic plates, was parked right outside the front door, immune to the double yellow lines.

'Hello, hello,' Peter Lord said heartily, coming into her office without knocking.

'Come in,' Juno said, a little coldly.

He ignored that. 'Who's this, Juno? Introduce me.'

'My friend Sheikha Fatima of Qatar. Fatima and her husband have taken that penthouse I found in Chelsea Harbour. Fatima, this is Peter Lord.'

'It's amazing. Juno was so clever to find it.' Fatima beamed. 'World-class security, wonderful views. You're lucky to have her, Mr Lord.'

'Peter – please. And she's lucky to work here too,' Peter said with a taut little smile.

Juno stiffened. This was starting to be a pattern. Peter shoving himself into her space, ingratiating himself with the contacts she brought to the job, both landlords and tenants. And she resented it. The career might all be an act, but she was finding that her skill in putting parties together – which was all about people, after all; introducing people who would find each other fascinating – worked with houses too. Just as she had a sharp mind for her guests, their interests and obsessions, Juno quickly found out what her social circle wanted in a pied-à-terre, a long-term rental, or a love nest for the girlfriend.

She worked the phones for this just as she had done on the social circuit, and with a good deal of success. And Lord was trying to jump on it.

It was quickly clear to Juno that flirting would do her no good. Peter Lord was not that way inclined. Within a day she understood why his marriage had broken up – that he was gay.

And indeed, his first love object was himself. Peter was greedy – greedy for credit, greedy for clients. Torn between celebrating all Juno's new business and wanting every scrap of it for himself.

'Peter, Fatima and I are going to lunch.'

'Shall I pop along with you?'

'Oh no,' Fatima said. 'In my culture ladies do not eat with single men. Nice to meet you, though.'

'Are you coming along to Juno's little party for her uncle's fiancée?' Peter asked, immune to the snub.

'Of course. It's the event of the spring,' Fatima laughed.

'Then I will see you there. Lovely to meet you, Fatima. *Ciao!*' Peter said, and turned on his heel.

Juno gritted her teeth. That was ten minutes of her life she'd never get back. And for the first time ever, ten minutes mattered to her. She had a window for a short lunch with Fatima, and then it was back to organising this bloody party as well as closing three other leasing deals. The red lights flickered on her phone again.

Bringing down Bai-Ling was proving to be a *lot* of work.

Chapter Eighteen

The afternoon of the great event was a glorious March day.

The sun was shining, the flowers were starting to bloom, it was warm with a light breeze; if Juno could have chosen her weather, this would be it. Ideal for maximum attendance.

She stood on the terrace and overlooked the scene with a critical organiser's eye.

The caterers were in place. Juno had hired not the most expensive but certainly the most chic firm in London; they were run by an ex-Grenadier guardsman, and did eye-wateringly delicious dinners, perfectly traditionally. Brilliant flames from crystal torchères lit up the garden, and there was a large, open-sided silk tent set up in the centre of the lawn. Tables were laid with white linen, antique silver candlesticks and sorbet roses; the champagne was Laurent Perrier, and the sound of a harp duet serenaded the still empty marquee. Everything was just so. Juno had personally conducted the diarists for the *Evening Standard* and *Vogue* around the garden. The guest list, well; she did think she had outdone herself. Two Arabian princesses, three ambassadors, a duchess and sundry other titles; two movie stars, and more billionaires than you could shake a stick at. Nothing so infra dig as models, but Juno had ensured some of the prettier young wives on the society circuit were there to add flavour. Attractive girls kept a party buzzing. And, of course, journalists; plenty of journalists.

There was even a young London freelancer who worked for the *Seychelles Nation*, the islands' local newspaper. Juno had also invited some of the capital's nastiest, hungriest paparazzi. She shuddered to think what the party had cost, but doubtless it was all going to be worth it.

'What do you think?'

She turned to her younger sister. Athena nodded.

'It's perfect. You'll have all of London here.'

'The Foreign Secretary and his wife are coming.'

'Never mind, it'll still be a great party,' Athena deadpanned.

Juno could not get annoyed. 'You look exquisite,' she said, and was taken aback to discover a surge of sisterly pride. Her sibling was always the scruffiest, rattiest of the cousins. Today she looked steely; the goddess not of wisdom, but of war, resplendent in a gun-metal silk sheath dress, with thick armlets of silver, and dangling platinum earrings set with icy diamonds. Pewter satin heels from Chanel propped up her long legs; her hair flowed, shining, in a straight curtain, held in place with a mother-of-pearl headband that gleamed like a diadem for some ancient queen. With a make-up palette of dusty pink and charcoal eyes, Athena was quite breathtakingly beautiful.

After the pride, there was a slow pang of jealousy. In other company, Juno would have glittered tonight; but she knew she was comprehensively outdazzled. She had picked an Alexander McQueen coat dress in a daring combination of tangerine, cream and palest green; she had burnt-orange Dior pumps on her feet and wore an emerald and zircon pendant with a matching tennis bracelet. Despite her stern features, she was sure she'd have turned heads, if only for sheer elegance.

It was exactly the kind of outfit Jack had loved to rip off her; feminine, forbidding. The more ladylike she looked, the more he'd love to warm her up.

Juno surveyed the richness of the scene before her, trying to wrest her thoughts from her ex. There was no use at all in pining for him. He was gone. He had money, now, and growing fame; she'd read about him in the most annoying places, the *Sunday Times* supplement, the *Evening Standard*, even her Waitrose food magazine. His restaurants were popping up all over Scotland; there were two in Glasgow, a huge one in Edinburgh, another in Fife – writers were complaining Jack wouldn't come to England.

Well. Juno hoped he never did. She hardened herself and stared out at the garden.

'Looking good.' Her cousin Diana interrupted her

reverie. 'Lovely dress, Ju. What do you think?'

Juno nodded, very pleased. Diana wore an ankle-length skirt and matching boned bustier in dusty pink chiffon, embroidered with tiny pink roses; a silk shawl was draped beautifully across her neckline, and she had long coral earrings dangling from her lobes; her handbag was a tiny, sparkling Judith Lieber piece, and she had on flat mink leather Moroccan slippers. The whole effect was very Pre-Raphaelite.

'Tremendous. Bai-Ling will look utterly out of place.'

'What did you send her?'

'A few outfits,' Juno said slyly, lifting her head. 'Let me see: there was the avant-garde translucent cheese-cloth gown from Chloe . . .'

'You mean it's see-through?'

Juno smirked. 'And the halter-neck by Versace; let's just say she'll need bloody strong nipple tape for that one . . .'

'Daring outfits.'

'Daring. Yes. That's the word.'

'And I've asked heaps of titled people, diplomats and so on. She'll be getting all that quite wrong. The social diarists will be there to hear her do it.' Juno gave a fierce nod of her head. 'By this time next week she'll be on her way back to the island and Uncle Clem will have dumped her as an embarrassment.'

'Let's hope so,' Diana mused. 'We wouldn't want to rely on our bloody jobs, would we?'

'How is that going?' Juno sniffed. 'I do hope you've got something to tell the guests.'

'Yes – the cover story is quite plausible, actually.' Her socialite cousin smiled, and Juno thought she detected a hint of pride. 'I'm in the middle of designing a health spa for the Victrix in London and I've made rather a large fee. You?'

Juno thought back on her past week. 'Yes, one or two commissions.' She shrugged. 'I don't enjoy work, you understand.'

'Of course not.'

'Look, here's your sister.'

Venus sauntered up to them, and Juno noted with disapproval that she hadn't quite managed a perfect relaunch; there was no new, demure Venus on display. Yes, the dress was modest, but only just; it perched precariously right on the dividing line. Venus had chosen a light gold silk as an alternative to her favoured palette of creams and whites, the colour still pale enough to offset her tan; the dress was knee-length and off the shoulder, but the fabric clung to her as though it were making love to her curves; nothing about her taut, silicone-enhanced figure was left to the imagination. She had a sinfully rich fox fur stole draped around her shoulders, a choker of diamonds, and teetering Jimmy Choo stilettos; all in all, she looked like a goddess of old Hollywood, Lana Turner for the new century, her platinum hair waved forties-style to match.

But still, Uncle Clem was used to Venus.

'You look hot,' Athena said approvingly.

'Hot isn't the point.' Juno was quite cross.

Venus shrugged. 'I'm doing more at this party than sticking it to Bai-Ling, ladies. I'm promoting a movie. So I want to stir up some interest.'

'You do recall these things are just cover stories.' Juno was firm. 'Don't believe your own publicity, Venus, don't get sucked into the hype. You know the likelihood the movie will actually get made is not that great, and distributed probably even less.'

Athena laid a restraining hand on her sister's arm, seeing Venus's face cloud over.

'She has Hans Tersch attending,' Athena said, with heavy meaning.

Juno ran the name through her mental Rolodex. Tersch . . . producer, big one. Reputation as a wolf. Perhaps Venus was trying to land him. Well, certainly that would be a notch for the Chambers sisters. Since they were all single . . .

Again she felt a tug of envy; when she had been with Jack, there was nothing but a benign interest in the other girls' love affairs. Now, she wondered why she had nobody at this party. Since Jack left, she'd thought only of him. And the move, and getting Bai-Ling . . .

'Well, that's different, I suppose.' She tried to smile. 'Happy hunting.'

'It's going to be a terrific party.' Athena thought of

Boswell House, and her heart steeled against the interloper. 'Best behaviour, girls. We belong, remember. Bai-Ling doesn't.'

Bitches, Bai-Ling thought. Bitches, bitches, bitches.

They were defeated, but they couldn't accept it. They wanted to get her money, her man. It wasn't going to happen.

But, she thought, as she stroked a hairbrush reflexively through her long hair, they certainly weren't going down without a fight.

Juno had lulled her into submission after dinner at their house. And it was a blow to see that all four girls apparently had money, their own damned money. No denying, their place was spectacular.

But clearly they wanted more. Clem's money. *Her* money. The old pervert wasn't long for this world, and his legal, rightful wife was going to give a new definition to the term 'merry widow'.

Juno was the ringleader. She'd been relentless. Inviting Bai-Ling to little suppers and tea parties. At the Savoy and the Ritz. Testing her on everything. Did she crook her little finger when she drank her tea, how did she handle a cucumber sandwich, did she know how to eat quails' eggs with celery salt? But Bai-Ling was way ahead of her. She'd studied, mugged up on the form book. Clem was going to get just what he wanted, the perfect little English wife, in every way other than the bedroom, where she could delight him exactly as he wished.

Whatever it cost her. But he was just the ultimate john. Bai-Ling told herself she'd suffered far worse. She would not let anything split her from her prey.

She looked at the dresses the maid had laid out on her hotel bed, and laughed. It was almost insulting; they really thought she was that stupid? Cheap little hooker clothes, plunging, sexy Hollywood dresses, a couple of ethnic outfits chucked in for good measure. And Juno had tried to camouflage them with a good selection of jewels! As if! Why not offer her a fan, and be done with it?

So the girls wanted to embarrass her. That was the strategy: show the exotic trophy girlfriend up. Well, they had telegraphed that now. And two could play at that game.

Satisfied, Bai-Ling regarded the outfit she'd bought in New Bond Street today. A perfect, classic little Chanel suit in pink tweed, with a matching tan leather quilted bag. The longer skirt length, of course, and low, dull court heels. She'd been professionally made up in muted colours, was wearing Clem's favourite, personally blended perfume, and stuck to her colossal red diamond engagement ring for jewellery – other than the string of whopping South Sea pearls, each individually fished and as large as a marble, that peeked out from her classic cream silk shirt. Her raven-black hair was neatly coiled into a bun, without other ornamentation; Bai-Ling knew she looked like the first lady of some Far Eastern country, her wickedly sexy curves tucked right away, and nothing flashier than her general youth and beauty.

The Chambers girls thought they could embarrass *her*? They were about to find out what war meant.

'My goodness,' Peter Lord said. He looked past Juno, eyes bugging out of his head. 'Isn't that the princess . . . Dubai, right? And Hans Tersch? You've pulled so many names here.'

'We like to have a good mix of people,' Juno agreed. She despised him; he was such a grubby little man. 'Do have some champagne.'

'Is it vintage? I don't like drinking a blend.'

'Of course,' Juno said serenely.

Peter's greedy hand grabbed a crystal flute from a passing waiter.

'He's a bit dishy,' he remarked, eyes on the younger man as he walked across the room.

Juno looked around hastily for a reporter – none near, thank goodness.

'Please behave yourself,' she hissed, 'and don't hit on the staff.'

Peter scowled and drained his glass in one go.

'Well, we are uppity, aren't we? Look, darling, you've had a couple of good weeks at work. A bit early to be talking back to your *boss*, don't you think?'

Juno turned to face him. Her pulse quickened, but she could not risk a scene. What this party had cost . . .

'Just relax, Peter, this is a social occasion.'

'And you should be accommodating.' His handsome features drew together cruelly. 'Get me his phone number, there's a dear.'

'Don't be pathetic,' Juno said, her voice ice cold.

'I *am* your boss.'

'No you're not.' Juno smiled. 'I quit. As of tomorrow, I'll be founding my own firm.' As she turned to face him, the words seem to come from someone else altogether – someone who wasn't tired, scared, anxious about money. Her sister was doing it, her cousins were doing it. Why not her, why not Juno? 'And you have two choices: behave, or be thrown out. There's quite a lot of press attending. Peter Lord getting drunk and embarrassing his hostess wouldn't be good for business, now would it?'

'You know, you can be quite a cow,' Peter slurred. But his gaze quailed. 'I'll be good. *Pax.*' He held up his crossed fingers.

Victory. Juno dismissed him with a wave of her hand. Just in time, too; Penny Matlock, the *Evening Standard*'s diarist, sidled up, overseeing the gathering.

'Darling. Fabulous party.'

'Thank you,' Juno said modestly. 'I try.'

'Wasted no time getting over Jack, have you?' the reporter asked. Juno struggled; she bit back a sharp retort. She could almost see Penny writing her copy.

'Divorce happens,' she said lightly. 'I'm sure Jack wishes me well.'

'Do you talk often?'

Hell! Get her off the subject.

'Not really.'

'Frosty relations, then.'

Juno forced a laugh. 'I believe Jack's a little tied up with the restaurant business, and I'm founding a property company myself, so there isn't much time. Plus, my cousins and sister and I are having so much fun sharing a house. We're just happy and busy.' She made herself add, 'If you see Jack, do pass on my regards.'

'Not love?' Penny said cattily. 'And so where's the guest of honour? Your aunt-to-be, is it?'

Juno sighed theatrically and consulted her gold dress watch. 'Oh dear; rather a little past fashionably late, I suppose. Oh, but you must make allowances,' she added quickly. 'Bai-Ling is trying to get the hang of English parties.'

'Mmm,' said Penny, picking up on Juno's tone. 'Slightly rude, though.'

'I wouldn't say that,' Juno demurred unconvincingly.

'Who's that in the silver gown?' Penny was distracted. 'The one with a bevy of men gathered around her? I don't think I've seen her before.'

'Of course you have, millions of times. That's my sister Athena.'

The journalist's eyes widened. 'No! It can't be . . .'

*

Athena was enjoying herself. This was quite a new situation. Of course, she kept a weather eye on the door; when Bai-Ling appeared in whatever outlandish dress she had chosen, Athena wanted to be able to draw attention to it, eyes widened, a sharp look of horror, perhaps a shocked hand over her mouth. Why should Venus be the only actress in the family?

But until then, she was very pleasantly distracted.

Men were competing for her attention. And not in the way the dons did it: a drunken fumble on a college stairway, a hand 'accidentally' placed on her knee; these were sophisticated entrepreneurs, gentlemen, oil barons, movie moguls. They laughed at her jokes, made small talk, enquired after her business ideas, offered to fetch her drinks. It was a heady mix.

'A club for women? That's a frightfully good idea,' said Lord Freddie Wentworth earnestly. 'Will you have a cigar room?'

'Athena, your champagne is getting a bit low.' Pieter der Saar, the South African wine magnate, reached out for her glass. 'Let me get you another.'

'You know, that's an incredible dress.' Rick Stellis, the Texan oil baron, was more direct. 'Brings out your eyes. Where'd you get it? I might have to pick up shares in the designer.'

Athena laughed and joked with them, but deep inside herself she was resentful. Sure, she enjoyed the flattery, who wouldn't?

But where had these guys been when she was struggling, and lonely? Why hadn't they ever been interested before? Was that all it took to transform her romantic fortunes, nothing more than a makeover? She'd been the same person when she was a gangly academic. But when she was scruffy, when her beauty was not that apparent, nobody asked her out except losers, and even then it was half-hearted.

She loved the attention. She despised their weakness.

Athena accepted a chilled flute of champagne from the wine magnate. Well, she couldn't stand here all day allowing the drooling, could she? Juno's coterie of society hacks were out in force, and any fast behaviour would defeat the object of all this. The Chambers girls must behave impeccably, bordering on the prudish. Uncle Clem's world hadn't moved on much from Jane Austen. He would not approve of reports of Athena encouraging a gaggle of beaux.

Slightly light-headed from the booze, Athena put on her academic's hat. She would conduct a little social experiment, she thought cruelly. A touch of revenge for all those sexist bastards in Oxford had put her through. Not having any desire to settle down yet, she could still use a man; another cover story for Bai-Ling. Why would Athena want to detach her from Clem if she had a rich fiancé of her own?

These boys wanted to use her; well, she'd use them. She'd allow one of them to fall madly in love with her and then dump him the second Uncle Clem dropped his gold-digger.

What was worse? Athena thought furiously. A woman who was only after a man for his money, or a man who only cared about a woman for her looks?

The answer was they were both appalling. And Athena Chambers determined to ruin one of each species.

She sipped her champagne delicately, her eyes roving over the menu of egotistical lechers on offer tonight: the vintner . . . no, she couldn't take that accent, not long term; the oil magnate had a paunch; the film star's teeth were disturbingly bleached. Which of these would be the least unpleasant to put up with for a few months?

Her sharp brain weighed the men up in a few seconds, and she was done. Athena turned to Freddie, giving him the full benefit of her dazzling looks.

'Freddie,' she said, with a smile that sucked the breath right out of him. 'Your people come from Northampton-shire, is that right? I hear it's a beautiful part of the world.' She focused on him, blocking out the others. 'But I've never been there,' she said with a pout.

The other boys got the message; she heard the sighs as they melted away into the crowd, murmuring their fare-wells. Wow, Athena thought, that's the male equivalent of a beauty contest and I've just picked the lucky winner. She leaned forward, to encourage him. His eyebrows had lifted into his thatch of russet hair, and a broad grin wreathed across his pale face, as though he'd just won the lottery.

Lord Frederick Wentworth. Younger son of the Marquis of Gretton; Eton and Durham, a degree in agricultural studies and estate management. His father's seat was Farnsworth House, a hundred acres of rolling English countryside and an Elizabethan manor house; his sister, Lady Felicity, was a notorious wild child with a very public cocaine problem, and his older brother Christopher was cut from the same cloth.

Athena had been updated on all this by Juno. She'd announced the party guest list to the girls, and Freddie was one of her better aristo catches.

Athena cast an eye over him. He was short, for a man, perhaps five nine. Dark red hair, pale skin, freckles. He was also barrel-chested, and clearly worked out with weights, or something. To her gaze, he looked like a warrior from another age, a Viking or a Norman perhaps; he'd fit right in a medieval house with low ceilings, she thought meanly. And his manner was just too deferential and moony, like a puppy. She hated that in men.

Yes, Lord Freddie would do just fine.

'Oh. Well.' He leaned forward, knocking over a wine glass in his eagerness. 'Bother. Clumsy of me . . . Anyway,' he added, mopping up the spillage with his handkerchief, 'we can fix that. You must come. Come for the weekend.'

Athena batted her long lashes.

'But we haven't even been out yet.'

Freddie blinked, as though dazzled by his good fortune.

'*Would* you?' he asked. 'How about Maxim's, tomorrow night? Eight suit you?'

'Just fine. You can pick me up.'

'Course, course,' he said. A flush of happiness spread right across his bulldog face. 'Terrific.'

Athena nodded and took another sip of her wine. Oh, thank goodness; Juno was trying to catch her eye from across the room.

'Excuse me,' she said, heading for the marquee. The crowd melted as she passed; there was a real buzz about this party. And it looked as if the guest of honour was about to make a monumental social error. Bai-Ling wasn't even going to show up. Athena exulted, fiercely. The girl had just snubbed the cream of London society.

Knowing Clem, she was as good as gone.

Venus didn't share her cousin's resentment. She and Diana had been tiny little things when they lost their parents, when her father had drunkenly killed himself and their mother. Now, she was like a sunflower, basking in the warmth of male attention, turning inexorably towards it. Even when she was a toddler, flaxen-haired Venus had been a terrible flirt; while Diana obsessed about keeping in with the biggest gang of girls in school, Venus had wanted to go co-ed. Unlike her sister, she cared hugely what men thought. And she was never afraid to admit it.

The other girls disapproved, but Venus did not care. She dressed sexy, as sexy as she could get away with without being cheap – and even that was a matter of debate, she thought, knocking back a gulp of chilled white wine.

'I want to read the script,' an admirer was saying.

'Not before we get into production.' Venus was firm. 'It's high-concept. Got to protect my intellectual property.'

'Fair enough.' The speaker was a thin, ferret-faced man with eager eyes. His name was Eric Draper, and he ran a small distribution network, the kind of set-up that would be ideal for micro-budget projects like hers. 'You know, Venus,' he said, his eyes running lovingly over the gold silk sheath, 'I'm sure we can come to some sort of deal.'

'Like what?'

'I buy the rights to your picture, and you have a working breakfast with me.'

After we spend the night, said his eyes.

She loved the admiration, but loathed the presumption.

'Eric,' she cooed, 'I don't think so. I'm afraid that what *you*'ve got to offer is far too small.' She looked right at his groin, then back in his face. Some bystanders sniggered. 'I'm looking for major distribution for this one,' she concluded, moving the conversation back to business. 'A studio.'

Eric opened his mouth to reply, but he was cut off. A large shadow fell across them both. Venus looked up, and her heart skipped a beat. It was Hans.

She hadn't seen him come in, hadn't seen him walk over to them. The shock of his nearness, his physical size towering over her, was enough.

He was wearing an American-style dark suit, which picked out his eyes, with their dark lashes. His skin was tanned, and there was a glint of thick gold on his wrist, an Oyster, she thought. A white shirt was open at the top, revealing wiry black hair; how erotic it had been when her fingers trailed across it . . .

Venus felt a warm surge of lust. She struggled for composure, and took refuge in her drink.

'And what on earth makes you think,' Hans asked softly, his eyes on her, trickling over her, letting her know he saw her reaction, 'you would manage to achieve that?'

She sucked the air in. His voice, full of amusement, told her he realised exactly what she was feeling. It was a dominance he didn't deserve. The question angered her. So, she wanted him. Venus had never deceived herself on that score. She had a powerful sexual pull towards Hans Tersch. But so what? She had made a fool of herself once. No more. He'd jumped right into bed with Lilly, and how many others after her?

I'm Venus Chambers, dammit, Venus told herself. I don't stand in line with a number.

'We'll shoot the film and offer them the print.' Venus smiled coldly. 'It's going to be sensational, Hans. A Venus Chambers Production. And the most bankable element is that *you* spotted the talent.'

'Yes.' His eyes narrowed, switching from desire to anger. 'I've had a couple of conversations. Apparently you had something to do with Lilly's behaviour.'

Venus shrugged. 'If you can't handle one young actress, Hans, perhaps you're losing your touch.'

Immediately ignoring Venus and her insults, Eric Draper flung himself at the big name in the crowd.

'Eric Draper.' He thrust his arm across Venus's body, grazing her breasts. 'Good to meet you at last, Mr Tersch, heard a lot about you. Maybe we could do some business together . . .'

Hans glanced at Eric, shoving himself in front of Venus.

'You appear to be blocking our hostess,' he said flatly.

'Oh, excuse me.' Undefeated, Eric tried again. 'You're so right, though: every tiny indie producer thinks they'll hit it off with the studios. We players know otherwise.' He turned to Venus. 'You'll learn, honey.'

'It's Venus,' she said.

'Whatever,' Eric replied. 'So, where are you sitting, Hans? I'll drop by to say hello.'

Tersch looked at his hostess. 'I'm sitting with Venus,' he said.

'You're not.' She was burning with rage at these two men. Use it, she told herself. Let it help you to succeed even more. Let it get you up in the morning. 'You're sitting at Eric's table, actually.'

Eric beamed with delight, but Hans looked at Venus searchingly.

'I put a lot of the film people together,' she continued carelessly. 'And I sat you with Sadie – an established star, but you have to pay to get quality. Perhaps you can recast her for Maud, now that I have Lilly.'

Hans shook his head.

'I'm sitting with you,' he said. 'I switched the place cards. Your guest of honour's bodyguard is now sitting with this schmuck.' A strong hand indicated Eric, who flushed beetroot.

'Excuse me?' he spluttered.

'Certainly,' Hans said. His tone did not change. 'Now fuck off, if you know what's good for you.'

Eric's mouth opened, but he thought better of it. He hunched his shoulders up against his ears and scuttled away from them, spider-like, into the crowd, heading for the exit.

'You don't mind making enemies?' Venus asked, trying to conceal her pleasure. Whatever his personal beef, Tersch had not permitted that little jerk Draper to mess with her at her own party.

'You didn't.' His dark eyes were on her. 'I caught the end of your conversation.'

Venus tensed. What could she say? That she wasn't the sort of girl for a one-night stand? She had been with Hans. And never forgotten it, either.

'I hate it when men toy with me,' she snapped.

'And I hate it when women make assumptions,' he replied. Very cool. 'You were more than fairly treated at the audition, Venus.'

'I don't want to talk about it.'

'No; just act on a false scent. You think you're entitled to be cast as the lead in a film by me? A major movie. And you, an untested actress. I saw something in you for a character part. In fact, you never lived up to that potential.'

Her fist curled. 'Oh yes, your movie,' she replied with acid sweetness. 'Not so major any more, is it?'

She was rewarded by seeing his poker face flash with sudden answering anger.

'You will pay for that,' he said shortly. 'I have a reputation to keep up. Nobody sabotages one of my films and gets away with it. No matter how beautiful she is.'

'Are you sure you want to sit with me at dinner?' Venus asked, her chin tilting up defiantly.

She was certain she registered lust in his eyes, but really, who cared?

'Of course,' Tersch said, and his tone was menacing. 'Keep your friends close. And your enemies closer.'

*

Diana made her way across to Juno. She worked the crowd, ever the consummate hostess, accepting compliments and passing better ones on.

But her heart wasn't in it. For once, socialising seemed empty, a waste of time. Diana's mind kept wandering to her new obsession: work.

She had already lined up five interviews on the state-of-the-art Victrix facilities. The workmen were coming on at lightning speed – Diana had made the decision to hire five crews simultaneously, promising further contracts to the best, and the competition was doing fantastic things for the build schedule. Next week she'd be able to start the photo shoots. The hotel would feature in *InStyle*, *Heat*, *Glamour* and the *Evening Standard*, and that was just for starters. She didn't like Karl's publicity people. Let Roden do its own in-house thing, Diana decided; she was determined to get the lion's share of the PR herself.

She wanted to impress Karl. The Covent Garden hotel was going to be stunning, but it was a boutique. He was renovating his European flagship, the Victrix Roma. Diana had ideas. This project was almost wrapped; she wanted another.

'Darling.' She kissed her cousin, who was surveying the party like a conductor looking over an orchestra. 'Job done, I think. Who would have imagined it'd be this easy? Silly cow doesn't show.'

'Almost too easy,' Juno replied anxiously.

'Let's get them seated.' Diana signalled to the maître d', and the waiters began ushering the guests to their tables. As the linen-covered chairs were pulled out and the crowd sat down with a rustle of silk and lace, Juno noted the eyes turning to the top table: the Chambers girls, the producer Hans Tersch, Penny, the diarist from the *Standard*, and one very obvious empty chair.

Juno glided over to her place and sat down, Diana right behind her. Penny was deep in conversation with Athena; Venus and the Austrian were looking daggers at each other, but they seemed perfectly civil. Juno signalled sharply to the waiters to start the service, disapproval etched bright on her face. Anybody could have seen it, and she was determined that Bai-Ling's faux pas would be rubbed in for the writers.

'We can't wait any longer, I'm afraid,' she said with a sigh.

Penny gave her her full attention. 'Yes – isn't it terrible?'

The waiting staff moved in, laying bowls of mock turtle soup at every plate, pouring wine, offering warm herby breads.

Suddenly Penny dug Juno in the ribs. 'Who's that?' she asked.

Juno turned her head, and a little chill ran through her blood.

It was Bai-Ling. Beautifully, in fact impeccably, dressed

in a perfect little Chanel suit, with every classic accessory, her hair in a sober bun, her make-up subtle. There was a murmur in the crowd as people turned their heads to look at her. In a fraction of a second Juno decided that she'd picked close to the perfect outfit. She tugged her own tangerine and cream combo a little closer; Bai-Ling's haute couture made it look rather flashy.

Unable to stop themselves, the Chambers girls swapped looks of dismay. Juno watched as Penny pursed her lips. She had picked up on their unease.

'Is that the guest of honour?' she asked sweetly.

Juno nodded. 'Yes,' she said, pushing back her chair. 'I'll go and get her.'

But Bai-Ling was already on her way over to the table. She stood for a moment behind her chair, next to Juno, so the journalists could get a really good look. A few of the snappers clustered round; Bai-Ling smiled serenely and inclined her head.

'Juno – Athena – Diana – Venus!' She turned to each one individually. 'So sorry I'm late, but I was delayed.'

Bai-Ling waited; Juno realised her lack of courtesy and hastily ordered a waiter to pull out her chair.

'I'm Penny.' The society hack was drinking her in. 'I write for the *Evening Standard*. So good to meet you.'

'Delighted,' Bai-Ling said graciously. 'And you're sitting with my in-laws-to-be. You know, Penny, it's dreadful to be late. But I think there was some sort of mix-up.'

'Oh?' Penny asked archly.

Juno had a bad feeling about this. She shook her head at the other girls, an infinitesimally small gesture. Diana picked up on it and started to eat her soup; the other two drank some water.

'Yes. Juno and the girls sent over a few dresses to wear, but they were completely unsuitable. One was see-through.' Bai-Ling's tone was light, but her eyes were like flint. The *Standard* diarist was hanging on Bai-Ling's every word. 'I'm afraid their uncle wouldn't have liked that at all.' Then she gave a little shrug, and added sweetly, 'Perhaps it was a little joke?'

'A see-through dress!' Penny exclaimed theatrically. She looked at Juno. 'You didn't!'

Juno felt horribly exposed. She flailed about for something to say.

'No, of course she didn't,' Venus said, and gave an easy laugh. Juno turned to stare at her cousin, but Venus didn't catch her eye; she was focusing wholly on Penny. 'Bai-Ling, I'm terribly sorry,' she said. 'I'm so embarrassed. If there was a see-through dress in that delivery it was intended for me. I was meant to send over the outfits to your hotel and instead I must have given you the costume package for my auditions. We're making a movie. I truly am sorry, to think I delayed you like that.' She shook her head, as though disgusted at herself.

Wow, Juno thought, the girl can act after all.

Diana took up the baton. 'But what about the cocktail dress from Givenchy? You didn't send it?'

'I meant to,' said Venus defensively, with a perfect little touch of ire. 'Anybody can make a mistake.'

'I spent half a day picking that dress,' Diana snapped. 'And the Marc Jacobs suit.'

The sisters glared at each other.

'Oh well.' Penny was visibly disappointed. 'You certainly look beautiful in that.'

'Doesn't she?' asked Athena, casually sipping her wine.

Bai-Ling's eyes flashed with rage, but she carefully swallowed it, and sat down. Juno effected the remaining introductions; but as Bai-Ling nodded, and smiled, and launched into her anodyne small talk, she radiated loathing at each of the Chambers girls.

Well, there it is then, thought Juno. She'd had the narrowest of escapes, and her prey was alerted. But so what? Uncle Clem wanted Bai-Ling to mix with his family, meaning the girls. Without proof, she was absolutely trapped.

She met Bai-Ling's look with a carefully blank stare. All of them would be actresses tonight.

The rest of the night passed without incident; Juno was supremely careful not to let rumours get started. She posed with Bai-Ling for all the society pages, she proposed a toast to her, with a heartwarming speech about the woman who had brought their uncle such happiness. She had the staff all serve her first, and after the Jamaican Blue Mountain coffee had been finished, she made up for lost time by introducing Bai-Ling to all her more glittering friends; the other Chambers girls hung behind her like the Three Graces, and the journalists couldn't get enough of it.

'And this is my friend Poppy Sheffield,' Juno said.

Bai-Ling smiled. 'How do you do, your grace.'

Damn. 'And Prince and Princess Pieter of Lichtenstein . . .'

Bai-Ling gave a perfect bob curtsey, just enough for respect, not so deep it looked stupid. 'Delighted, your serene highnesses . . .'

Juno's stomach creased in annoyance; the woman was a bloody machine, and she, Juno, was guilty of underestimating her. Not only had Bai-Ling turned up to the party beautifully dressed, she knew the correct form of address for every ambassador, duchess and minor European princeling Juno could throw at her. In fact, to add to Juno's misery, she saw the freelancer for the *Seychelles Nation* open-mouthed with admiration at her poise.

'It's such a pity your fiancé couldn't make it,' Melissa Cork said to her.

'Well, Lady Cork—'

'Melissa, please.'

'Clement is a very private man; he just wanted me to

get to know his family a little better. And it's such fun to be here.'

Yes, Juno mused, this would be written up as a triumph. But she wasn't finished, not by a long way.

Bai-Ling left early, the height of good manners, so others could go. Juno said goodbye to the guests, with Diana assisting her; the two socialites each handling their own stream of friends. Athena had Freddie's card in her pocket, and a date to look forward to. At least she'd managed to flirt lightly with him in front of Bai-Ling; there had been at least one success for the Chambers girls, because Freddie had a title, and it was instantly clear to all of them that Bai-Ling wished she had one too, the one thing Clem couldn't buy for her.

She'd actually made some suggestion about a large donation to the Prime Minister's favourite charity; Juno laughed it off as a joke. Any further attack on Bai-Ling would set Penny racing on quite the wrong scent. She was forced to defend her for real.

But she was even more determined to get rid of her. Now Juno had broken with Peter Lord, the trust fund was even more essential.

Venus stood at the back, waiting for Hans Tersch to leave. Damn, he infuriated her. He had watched the little tableau with Bai-Ling with endless amusement and, she feared, total understanding. During the meal, he'd driven her mad by refusing to say one thing about her movie, his movie, Lilly, even the business in general; he'd stuck to polite conversation, and forced her to do the same. And pretend she didn't care about it.

They were next to each other, and his hard, muscular thigh was close by hers; his thick fingers brushing against her arm; his eyes on her, on her body. Even when he handed her the bread basket, she felt the endless pull, the tug of wanting him.

Well, she thought, determined not to give him the pleasure of seeing her break, it's good training. He thinks I'm just like that sex-crazed little Lilly. Forget it. I will not be added to his harem.

But it stung that he wouldn't fight on her turf. She wanted to talk to him as a producer. A tiny one. But a woman on his level.

When Hans spoke across the table to Bai-Ling, Venus found she was burning with jealousy. Clem's fiancée could beguile a man with the best of them. She basked in Hans's attention, the trollop, and laughed a tinkling little laugh, and batted her dark lashes, and tried to be vivacious. Ugh, Venus thought with dislike. Bai-Ling was acting like a dumb brunette, an old-fashioned coquette. And the way Hans smiled back at her, she thought he might even be stupid enough to fall for it.

Thank God, she thought, that Uncle Clem has so much money even Hans cannot compete. She would have hated to see Hans Tersch with Bai-Ling.

Frustrated and ignored, Venus was forced to make

conversation with a diarist on her right, and she resented every second of it. She knew she ought to be paying more attention, looking for fresh ways to trip Bai-Ling up. But she couldn't be bothered. Not today. Not even for the sake of Clem's millions.

She just wanted to get the hell out of here, and prove Hans wrong.

Bai-Ling peeled off her clothes and dumped them on the floor, leaving a trail of couture behind her as she stamped off into the bathroom. Bloody witches. Costumes! And what was worse was that that idiot tabloid writer had actually *bought* the line.

Frustrated, she turned on the taps and ran her bath, tipping half a bottle of Floris bluebell essence into it and allowing the fresh spring scent to fill the entire room. So, they had planned to humiliate her, to make her wade in social ostracism. Stammering in front of the Eurotrash royalty, being photographed in some hideous dress. She, the exotic foreigner, too low-class for an old pervert like their goat of an uncle. Such an obvious strategy . . .

As the water swirled around her, Bai-Ling considered exactly how she could have her revenge. There were several delicious possibilities. She must make sure Clem was happy; open warfare wouldn't do. But a battle of attrition, with the four women humiliated and defeated . . . Clem wouldn't just disinherit them, he'd cut them off as embarrassments. The ties of blood he liked to talk about were all, really, a reflection on him. If the fabulous Chambers girls became the notorious Chambers girls, he'd drop them like a hot potato.

And she could start, Bai-Ling decided, with exposing these little 'careers' of theirs. Could the girls really be doing so well? Of course not. It was an act, all an act. They were trying to play a player. She herself had had to scrape every penny she had stashed away to create an impression for Clem of prosperity . . . If he knew her background he would never have touched her.

Well, then. Her long, tanned limbs shifted in the soapy water as she luxuriated in the heat. Clem liked her ultra-skinny, with no womanly curves at all, and Bai-Ling lived a life of constant hunger; heat was one pleasure she could truly indulge in, which was another reason to resent the English witches who had dragged her to this freezing dump of an island. She had her plan, anyway. She would expose the Chambers girls to the whole of society. And once they were seen as money-grabbing frauds, just for good measure Bai-Ling's cash would put a stop to their nascent careers. Just in case they *were* genuine. She intended that the four of them would damn well wind up ruined.

Better women than they had crossed Bai-Ling. She was determined to make them regret it.

Chapter Nineteen

The morning sun streamed through the windows of Juno's bedroom. She woke slightly disorientated, thinking she was late for work; but as she struggled to consciousness, she realised she'd actually resigned from her job at the party.

The party. Ouch. All that money spent to show up Bai-Ling as an unsuitable wife, all of it down the drain. The younger woman had triumphed, in a quiet, under-stated, fundamentally English way. The journalists would be working on their laudatory copy now.

Juno was back to square one. Minus about forty thousand pounds. And one job.

Depressed, she lay on her back for a few moments, allowing herself to wake slowly. The room was exquisite; a country-house fantasy of heavy chintz curtains tied with a green velvet sash, a Persian rug laid over the softest cream carpeting, a pale yellow sofa with Wedgwood-blue cushions, and a kidney-shaped dress-ing table in walnut. She had an antique escritoire in the corner, one of her favourite pieces of furniture from the old house. Jack had picked it for her.

Of course, the trouble was that however beautiful, the house wasn't hers. It was rented. And only for one year. They were already in March . . .

Distressing thoughts raced through her mind. What if she could not prise Bai-Ling away?

Juno shook herself slightly, ashamed at her weakness. Of all the cousins, she was the stiff-upper-lipped one; she was the eldest, the leader. She never lost control. She wasn't allowed to have doubts. She reached for her kimono-style dressing gown in watered silk, put her feet into her calfskin slippers, and headed downstairs to the kitchen.

Athena was there, finishing a cup of espresso; she tossed it down in one gulp, Italian-style. She was wearing a sharply cut trouser suit in sage green with a pale pink silk shirt, and Stephane Kelian heels; it looked fantastic on her. Juno instantly resolved that she'd have tea for breakfast and half a grapefruit with Splenda; not a calorie more.

'Bit of a disaster,' her younger sister remarked.

No need to ask what was. Juno's stomach creased in annoyance.

'Thanks for pointing out the obvious,' she snapped. 'The woman is cunning. We'll get her.' She looked around the tidy kitchen. 'Diana and Venus are still in bed?'

Athena shook her head. 'They left hours ago. Venus first, if you can believe that.'

'Why?'

'Work,' Athena said simply.

Juno chuckled. 'They're taking it very seriously. It's only a front for the real job.'

'Of course,' Athena agreed vaguely. 'I've got to go,' she added. 'Got a meeting. See you for dinner?'

'Absolutely,' Juno said, to her sister's disappearing back. The Stephane Kelian heels clicked purposefully out of the door.

Why is everybody taking this so damned seriously? Juno thought petulantly. But she knew the answer: because they could.

Her brave words to Peter Lord came back to her. It had seemed like the right thing to do at the time. But now she was stuck. No job; no man; Bai-Ling still in the picture; and savings that were rapidly dropping.

What if . . . Juno couldn't help the thoughts. What if Clem didn't come to his senses? What if Bai-Ling pulled it off? What if she got pregnant? What if Jack remarried, and nobody else wanted Juno?

What if *nobody* was around to look after her?

The idea she'd been trying to suppress could be stifled no longer. It swam up to the front of her mind, vicious as a shark. The girls were serious about these jobs because they had to be. It wasn't a cover story, not any more. It was their backup.

She was going to have to face it. Juno Chambers needed to join the twenty-first century. Getting a job –

that was not for her. Her golden twenties had been spent in a wash of money and prestige. Juno knew instinctively that she couldn't work for a boss; Peter Lord had been a disaster.

She was going to have to set up for herself. An entrepreneur. The thought provoked a bitter smile. Exactly what she'd despised Jack for doing. And despite what she had told her drunken ex-boss, she didn't want to get into the rich rentals business; far too much danger of turning into an oily little suck-up like Peter. Rich people wanted too much; she knew, none better, what demanding primadonnas they could be. Juno shuddered. She couldn't face a life that involved toadying to others. It went against her whole character. Good heavens, what if some of them were her friends? Inconceivable.

No. There had to be a better way to make money. Juno stood up. She would go and dress, and decide what to do. It was frightening, but she was not about to give in. Frankly, she thought, I can't afford to.

She chose her navy Dior suit. It was vintage, from the forties, with a crispness to the colours and a precision to the cut that Juno thought couture today lacked. Her reflection in the mirror had a sharp waist and definite elegance. She fastened a string of freshwater pearls around her neck; they were cheaper than her normal jewels, but exceptionally luminous, and flattered her skin with a soft glow.

All the while she was thinking. Finding those properties for rentals had been hard, but rewarding, for the short time she had done it. But the trouble with rental was tenants. Top end, low end, they were all demanding.

Better to satisfy the demands of buyers. The house talked for you. Get the house perfect, and you were done . . .

The trouble was, London was full of upmarket estate agents. And home-search firms. What Juno needed was something completely different. Something that filled a gap in the market, something that nobody else would touch.

She remembered Claudette de Vere from that film company, her little snub nose in the air, complaining that her corporation paid way over the odds, but that was the price of housing film stars.

And Emily Wayberry, moaning about her pied-à-terre. Her court case had crashed. She'd been suing her ex-husband for a year now, but it had been thrown out of court. Large legal bills were due, and Emily complained she couldn't sell her flat – because the lease was just too short. Juno chewed the conversation over in her head. There was something there, something . . .

And suddenly it burst on her, like a firework exploding over Hyde Park. The possibility. Something that would require creative thinking, creative banking, and a lot of hard-nosed negotiating.

Excited, she walked to the drawing room and curled herself on the couch, picking up the phone. There was a lined pad next to it, and Juno grabbed a Mont Blanc pen, starry-eyed with the possibilities. Complex, yes, risky, of course, but if it worked, so very profitable.

She punched out Emily's number. Two rings, and there was her old acquaintance on the phone.

'Hello?'

'Emily, darling. It's Juno.'

'Juno! Nice to hear from you. How are you?'

She sounded strained, Juno thought. She got right down to business.

'I'm very well. Look, it's about your flat.'

'My flat?' Emily gave a bitter laugh. 'You don't know somebody with more money than sense, do you?'

'Does it have restrictions on subletting?'

Emily sighed. 'No, but that's no use to me, I need to sell. And no tenant's going to pay enough anyway.'

'Well, darling, as you say, it is unmortgageable,' Juno agreed. 'But I need a pied-à-terre of my own. Somewhere to think quietly. I might like to buy it, if we can come to some sort of deal.'

She could hear Emily's eagerness right away.

'Really? Don't joke, sweetie. You'd like to buy my flat?'

'Not for half a mill, though. Without a mortgage I couldn't go any further than three hundred.'

Emily pouted down the phone.

'But it's a two-bed in Mayfair . . .'

'On a fifteen-year lease.' Juno felt herself breaking out

in a light mist of perspiration. 'Darling, you want to dump it, I just thought I could do you a favour. If it's not for you, just tell me. I saw another in Foxton's—'

'No, no. Three hundred's fair,' Emily said hastily. 'And you *are* doing me a favour. How quickly can we close?'

'Well, I have to get the surveyor booked, but I expect quite fast. I'll just pop round now, shall I? Discuss things.'

'Now? I have to go to my yoga class.' Emily was a fitness fanatic. 'But the doorman will let you in.'

Even better. Juno desperately wanted to see the place for herself.

'That's fine,' she said. 'We'll chat this afternoon.'

Juno hung up and raced into Athena's room. She kept her digital camera hung on a loop at the end of the bed; yes, it was still there. Well. Ten o'clock in the morning. New York would be open for business at two. She could have most of this deal done by then.

Park Street was exquisite. Tucked away behind Marble Arch, steps from Hyde Park, it was quiet, residential, and full of Victorian houses and old money. Emily lived in an upper-floor maisonette in a building towards the end; it was narrow, with a heavy, black-gloss-painted front door and a bronze knocker in the shape of a laurel wreath. Juno felt a little foolish taking a snapshot of the outside, but she got over it. She pressed the buzzer and explained herself.

'Juno Chambers to visit Mrs Wayberry's apartment.'

'Certainly, madam,' came the mechanical voice, and she was buzzed in.

The doorman turned to fetch the lift – she was pleased to see it was modern – and Juno quickly took shots of the lobby: old English, with marble flooring, statues, and crisp white walls. She followed in behind him. The elevator was upholstered in plush red velvet. No expense spared. They emerged into a narrow, plastered corridor, and the doorman opened number 6 with a skeleton key.

'Mrs Wayberry asks that you lock the door behind you, madam,' said the doorman, tipping his hat politely.

'Of course,' Juno murmured. He disappeared, and she stepped through, into the flat, on her own.

Juno looked around. Her practised eye made the judgement in nanoseconds. Yes. It was perfect.

The walls were white plaster, hung with old prints. Emily's taste ran rather modern, a look that showed the smallish space to best advantage: Eames couches in leather on stilted metal legs, lots of reflective paint. Large sash windows, but a modern real-flame-effect gas fire; the remote control was on her oak coffee table. A galley kitchen, with top-of-the-range appliances built in; perfect for a rental. The kitchen didn't swallow up the space, and as a result there was a large living area.

Juno took up Athena's camera. She snapped, again and again. Making sure to get the light-filled living space, the granite countertops in the kitchen. Bathroom – down the corridor – nice and modern again, a basalt basin hanging in space, the loo concealed in the wall, a deep, square, almost Roman bath, with recesses in the walls to hold shampoo or candles; a separate power shower, lined with grey stone tiles and embossed with a motif of moons picked out in mother-of-pearl.

Increasingly excited, Juno went into the second bedroom. It was a good size, with built-in closets and a row of bookshelves, and high over the street. The master was one and a half times as large, with a small walk-in wardrobe and an en suite shower room; everything in pink Carrara marble.

She moved around, taking photographs. Everything had to be clear. But she didn't waste time. The flat was perfect, just perfect.

In less than five minutes, she was on the phone to her solicitor.

'But I don't understand.' Emily blinked her heavily mascaraed eyes, and Juno suddenly found it very annoying. When had Emily Wayberry become this stupid? 'This isn't buying the house?'

'No, it's called an option to purchase. You give me the right to purchase the house exclusively, just for a month; it stops me being out of pocket on surveys if you sell to someone else.'

'But there is no one else.'

'Just to be sure,' repeated Juno firmly.

Emily's eyes narrowed; Juno could almost see the

hamster wheels turning. She quickly moved to press the deal home. 'And of course, there's a consideration for you. I give you five thousand pounds for the option, refundable against the three hundred thousand when I buy.'

'I don't understand,' Emily repeated.

Juno sighed. 'If I pull out, you keep the five thousand. Just so we're both committed for the next month.'

'I keep the five thou?'

'Absolutely,' Juno encouraged.

Emily smiled then, like a little girl who'd just been given an ice cream. 'Well, darling, you should have said so!' she said, and reached across her desk for a gold Parker pen.

Juno went home in a taxi, the precious document clutched to her chest, looking at her watch. It was one thirty – she had half an hour to go. Another expensive morning – her solicitors didn't come cheap – but Juno had her option agreement and a company registered with Companies House: Goddess Lettings.

Now she had to put flesh on the bones of the deal. If it went wrong, she was out five thousand, plus fees.

And if it didn't?

Already there was a small stormcloud gathering in the back of her mind, but Juno refused to look at that, not right now. She fixed herself some coffee downstairs, delicious American cinnamon coffee, aromatic and calorie-free. The house felt very quiet without the other girls.

She couldn't believe how slowly the clock moved. Juno imagined Claudette, in her cramped modern apartment on West 16th Street, pulling on her slacks, choosing a pair of Manolos, checking her Patek Philippe, eating half a bagel, perhaps, or a large pot of yogurt. Already busy, already frazzled. What demanding star would be forcing her to jump through hoops this morning?

Ten to. Juno couldn't take it any more. She imagined Claudette, flicking hastily through the *New York Times*, grabbing her keys, on the way out the door. She dialled. It rang, that single tone that the Americans used. Juno's mouth was dry with nerves. Thank God, she thought, that it was the phone. Claudette couldn't see her.

'Hi.'

'Claudette, it's Juno Chambers.'

Her own voice sounded calm and cool to her. Amazing what a little social training could do.

Claudette sounded just as rushed as Juno had imagined.

'I'm on my way out. Call you in the office?'

'Actually, I'm working on my own now,' Juno said, and moved on so Claudette didn't have time to process it. 'Don't you have Kevin Blaney shooting in London next month?'

'Yes. And he's a terrible snob. Said no to everything Peter's got.'

'I have the perfect place.' Juno described it briskly. 'Mayfair, doorman, two-bed, en suite, power shower, all new everything. Gigantic hidden cinema screen.' There wasn't, but she'd install one. 'It would do you fine for him. And afterwards for any of your clients. I thought you might want to take the headache away, rent it from me for a year, full service of course. That way you always have an emergency apartment for executives, stars, whoever.'

'Gotta be chic,' Claudette said, but at least she didn't hang up.

'It is. I sent you the pictures,' Juno said. 'They're sitting in your inbox. This is very private, very old-money stuff. But I do have interest from Warner's if you don't want it.'

'How much?'

'Discount. Four and a half a month, including fixtures, maid service and a full concierge.'

Juno's heart was in her mouth.

'Let me see. Hold on.' There was a pause, and she could hear Claudette walking across to her computer, tapping at the keyboard. 'Oooh.' There was an intake of breath. 'Now that is very nice. But Juno, we'd want some security. Two years' firm.'

'Two years at the same rate?' Juno sounded reluctant. 'Claudette, that's unheard of.'

'That's my deal.'

'Well, I'd want a year in advance.'

'No problem there.' Claudette heaved a deep sigh. 'Kevin will love it; so will our CEO . . . Great job, Juno. Can you fax over the paperwork to Business Affairs?'

'Of course.' Juno pressed her elegant fingertips to her forehead. This was all going a little fast now. She had her credibility on the line. But it was good, it was what she wanted.

Provided she could come up with the cash.

'Do you do other cities?' Claudette was asking.

'I beg your pardon?' Juno tore her mind away from mental sums and the contemplation of her dwindling bank accounts.

'Other cities. I need somewhere in Edinburgh. And Paris, and somewhere in Rome.'

'Soon,' Juno heard herself saying. 'Very soon.'

She hung up. Her emotions were swirling. So far, so good, but that was the easy part. The sums added up; it was a winner, an absolute winner.

Three hundred thousand, divided by fifteen years, divided by twelve months. She'd done a deal to buy a lease worth sixteen hundred quid a month and sold it on for four and a half thousand – give or take. Quickly she pulled up the little calculator on her computer. The difference in profit over fifteen years would be half a million pounds.

Half a million. And that on a flat that nobody would touch.

Just one problem. Juno Chambers didn't have three hundred thousand in cash. She had less than half that remaining, and she had to live on it.

Filling with anxiety, she considered her options. Ask the other girls? No good; they were all as broke as she was, equally unlikely to surrender their cushions. Go to her bank manager? After Juno's profligacy, he wasn't going to agree. No, there was only one thing for it: to borrow against the profits from her London house, held in a trust.

Her lawyers had insisted she do that. Jack was to be her ex-spouse, and despite the fact that he hadn't asked for a penny, he could. Until the limitation period ran out on their divorce, she'd been told to leave half the money alone.

But now she needed it.

Juno shrugged. There had to be a way out of this, there just had to. She rang her solicitor, Richard Freeman, again.

'Juno.' He was there at once. 'What can I do for you now?'

'I like to keep you busy, Richard,' she said lightly. 'I need to get at the money in the trust.'

'But you can't. You know that.'

'It's my money – from my house.'

'We've been over this, Juno. Your former spouse has a claim.'

'I don't need to spend it, just borrow it.' Juno's toes

curled in frustration. 'It'll be paid back with interest. Why can't the trust loan it to me?'

'Unfortunately, that would be illegal.'

'To invest the money?'

'In one of your personal business ventures, yes, I fear so.'

She exhaled, disappointed beyond belief. She needed that money. It was the only way.

'I can't accept that,' she said crossly. 'There has to be a way to get at the money from my own bloody house. There just has to.'

'Well, there is,' Richard agreed. 'Quite a simple one.'

'Go on, then.'

Juno knew what he was going to say before he said it.

'You need to talk to Jack.'

Juno breathed in sharply. Jack. Talk to Jack. Ask Jack for her own money. Of course, it really was that simple. And she knew that he'd give it to her, there would be no problem at all there; Jack was far too proud to accept it in the first place.

She just wasn't sure she could cope with seeing him again, cope with seeing Jack rich, successful, everything she had always nagged at him to be.

Hell, it was worse than that. Juno wasn't sure if she could cope with seeing him at all. The rough, rugged man she had given her tight little heart to, only to close it off again. Even the thought of shaking hands with him made her heartbeat race in her chest. She was afraid for her composure, afraid she would blush, or get light-headed.

Or, God forbid, cry.

She missed him so dreadfully. When he wasn't in front of her, if she kept busy, she could cope. And now she would be confronting that awful loss.

'If you feel you can't do that,' her solicitor said, into the silence, 'then I'm afraid you'll have to give up the idea of the money.'

'No. Fax across an agreement, could you? Something watertight. And your contact details for my ex-husband.' Juno could hardly bear to say his name.

'I have a meeting. There's no hurry, is there?'

'Of course there's a bloody hurry,' Juno snapped. 'Get it done now, Richard. I have to be on a plane.'

The Royal David Hotel was luxurious, at least. Juno had booked it at the airport, in a little kiosk, wondering what the hell she was doing. But paying top dollar would guarantee her a fax machine and an internet connection. Plus, this place was close to Jack's flagship restaurant, in the heart of the Royal Mile. Juno's suite overlooked a cobbled street; unlike the bitterly cold spring day outside, Edinburgh in the grip of an unseasonable fog, her room was warm, and the staff had laid a blazing fire, which crackled merrily in the grate; she might have enjoyed herself, she thought, under other circumstances.

But there were no other circumstances. She'd driven

herself out to Heathrow, and a few hours later she was here, in Edinburgh. Sharing a city with Jack. About to see him again. About to ask him for a favour.

She was ridiculously, childishly nervous, she decided, angry at herself. Jack Darling was part of her past. What was the problem?

The fax from Richard was in her purse. Juno took it out and dialled the number before her nerves got any worse.

'The Smoked Salmon. Good afternoon.'

'I'd like to speak to Jack Darling, please.'

'Are you with the press?'

'No.' Juno forced herself to sound calm. 'This is his wife, Juno Chambers.'

There was a pause. 'I'll see if he's available. Hold please.'

She found herself listening to chamber music. Within a few seconds, the girl was back on the phone.

'He's in a meeting. May I take a number? He said he will call you back.'

Bastard! In a meeting, yeah, right. Juno wondered bitterly if it involved some young Scottish beauty.

'That's fine,' she managed. 'I'm staying at the Royal David.'

'Thank you. He'll call you back.'

Juno hung up and stared into space. The feeling of anticlimax was palpable. She didn't know what she'd expected. A torrent of rage? Pity, or scorn? Something, though; some violent confrontation. Now she had no idea what to do. There was no way she could call back, begging Jack to see her. Turn up at the restaurant? That would be even worse. Juno imagined her humiliation, being thrown out by security . . .

Well. Another expensive dead end. Disappointment leaden in her stomach, she wondered if her deal was over, or if there was any other way . . .

The phone rang. Juno jumped out of her skin. She stared at it, almost afraid to pick it up.

It kept ringing. She reached for the receiver, her hands slippery with sweat.

'Juno Chambers,' she said.

'It's Jack.' His voice was cold, but just the sound of it made her light-headed, almost dizzy; she was glad she was perching on the end of the bed. 'What do you want?'

'I need you to sign some papers.'

'It'll have to wait. I have a civic banquet tonight. I'm cooking personally. The Crown Princess of Sweden.'

'I need it today. It's very important to me, Jack.' She loathed having to do this, but there was no help for it. 'Please do me this favour. I flew up to Scotland to get your signature, and I'll come to wherever you are.'

There was a pause, and she waited, heart in her mouth.

'You won't,' he said eventually. 'I'm at Holyrood, and security won't let you in to the palace. I'll come to your hotel.'

'When can you come?'

'Still nagging,' he said, angrily. 'I'll come as soon as I can.'

Juno forced herself to accept that.

'I'm sorry. It's very good of you. Thank you, Jack.'

There was a click; he'd hung up. She numbly replaced the receiver. Juno had an overwhelming urge to run to the mirror and check her make-up, but she resisted it, miserably. She still had her pride; Jack Darling would take her as he found her.

When he rang from the lobby, she decided to go down to meet him. Seeing him in her bedroom would be far too intimate. She took the paper with her, and told herself to be scrupulously polite. Jack was doing her a favour; she had to remember that.

He was standing by the front desk, tapping his fingers in that impatient manner she knew so well. Juno drank him in, just for a second; he was wearing a very expensive, well-cut suit, his dark hair had become threaded with grey, and it looked good on him. She checked for an expensive watch; no. But then Jack had always avoided ornamentation.

She walked over, not wanting him to catch her staring.

'Thank you for coming,' she said, with a nervous smile.

His light eyes held hers, expressionless, and something folded up inside her heart.

'I'm very busy, Juno. What do you want?'

She gestured to the tea room. 'Can we sit down privately?'

He nodded. She picked a table not far from the open log fire, and ordered a pot of Earl Grey to keep the waiters happy.

'So what's up?' Jack asked, not meeting her eyes.

'I need you to sign this paper. It will allow me to borrow against half the value of the house. It's been kept in a trust.' Juno blushed, richly. 'In case you sued.'

That got his attention. Jack blinked. 'What?'

'In case you sued for maintenance.'

His face darkened. 'My God, woman. Your arrogance has no end, does it? You thought I would sue *you* for one damned penny? My, my, I'd almost forgotten how high and mighty the Chambers girls are.'

Juno thought he looked sensationally attractive; yearning for him boiled up, and she could hardly look him in the face.

'No,' she managed. 'I never thought that. I knew you were too stubborn. You'd rather die in a ditch.'

'Damn right.' He was still furious. 'So why the trust?'

'My lawyer insisted.'

'Give me the bloody papers.' Jack practically snatched them from her, scribbling his name with a platinum pen he kept in a jacket pocket. 'There you are. Tell your lawyer mine will be sending something to him, absolving you of any future claims whatsoever from me. As it happens, I'm somehow managing to feed and clothe myself.'

'You've been very successful.' She felt small. 'Congratulations.'

'Yes, I have.' Jack looked at her, and his face was flint. 'The restaurant in Banff was booked solid from the first week it opened. I got finance for another, too. I train all the chefs personally. Underpaid kids from the better hotels. They all get stock in the company. I'm already worth more than a million, and I've only just started.'

'Where are you living?' she asked, folding up the paper and slipping it into her handbag.

'I have a country house in Banffshire, not far from the first restaurant, and a flat in town.' He smiled thinly. 'What's it to you?'

'I suppose I'm just curious.'

'Small talk was never your strong suit, Juno. Not with me, at least.' His eyes swept over her forbidding, elegant dress. 'Are you engaged yet?'

She pulled back, shocked. 'Of course not, we just got separated. I'm staying in a house with the other girls.'

'How fabulous,' he mocked. 'I thought you'd have bagged a billionaire by now, at least.'

'I'm working,' Juno snapped back, provoked to anger. 'That's why I'm here. For my company.'

'Well, best of luck with it.' Jack didn't even ask her what it was. 'I have to get back to the palace. Got a dish of sugar mice for the pudding, hollow sugar mice with redcurrants. Delicate stuff. I don't trust the sous-chefs.'

He stood up. Juno wanted to stop herself, but she couldn't. The curiosity was too great. She blurted out, 'And you, Jack? Are you seeing anybody?'

He turned, almost in slow motion, and looked back at her, an unreadable expression on his face.

'Oh yes,' he said. 'There have been a couple of girls. But I'm with somebody now, and it's a bit more serious. Her name's Mona McAllen. I think you'd approve of her, Juno, I'll introduce you some day.'

'Oh.' She couldn't think of a comeback; her throat was dry again. 'That's nice,' she managed lamely. She patted her bag, the signed papers peeping out from it. 'Thanks for this,' she said. 'I should get going too, before the banks close.'

'See ya,' Jack responded, and with a harassed glance at the grandfather clock in the lobby, he was gone, walking out of the revolving door without looking back.

Juno wanted to wait, to stare after him, but she managed not to. His words had sliced surgically into her heart. The pain was overwhelming, but, and she thanked God for it, she had only a few hours left. She needed to get back to her room, fax this to Richard, then call her bank manager. Emily's solicitors were waiting by the phone. And so was Claudette, in her office in New York.

By the time she got home it was almost eleven, and she was exhausted. Athena was in the kitchen, in her dressing gown, stirring a mug of cocoa and chatting to Diana.

'Where's Venus?' Juno asked, peeling off her coat.

'Still out. I think she has a night shoot.'

Juno blinked. 'She's actually shooting the movie?'

'They started today,' Diana said. 'Where have you been?'

She opened her handbag and pulled out a set of keys. 'I bought a flat. On a fifteen-year lease.'

'You're mad,' Athena said anxiously. 'What did you do that for?'

'To rent it out.' She was too tired to explain. 'It's already rented, actually. I need to find some more.' A yawn stole up on her, and she swallowed it. 'I'm going to be away for a few days, in Rome.'

Diana flashed her cousin a small smile. 'I'll take you to the airport. I have to go to Paris.'

'Well, well,' Athena remarked. 'Look at us all. Working women.'

'The embarrassment,' Juno agreed, but she didn't feel it. In fact, she had a small glow of satisfaction. Something to hold on to, when she thought of Jack, and realised her heart was broken.

Chapter Twenty

Clement Chambers paced in front of the vast windows in his enormous private office. His staff scurried outside the room, afraid to attract his attention when he was in this mood. There was something going on here, and he did not like it. Not in the least.

A seagull banked and soared in the air in front of the house, just over the cliffs. Usually he enjoyed watching their flight; they were such canny predators. Clement identified with animals, pitiless survivors, like himself. Not with people, unless they were useful. Or amusing.

The scene in London was not to his taste, because it was not following the script.

Of course, there were some predictable aspects. The girls were trying to detach him from Bai-Ling. Her complaints about the party, the unsuitable dress, had provided him with great enjoyment. Clever little Juno, striking back in her own, infinitely pathetic way – through a party. And clever little Bai-Ling, dodging the trap as deftly as a monkey swinging past a crocodile. The girl was agile. He liked that. He liked the catfight. This was planned, and it was fun to watch. His brother would hate it. That meant a good deal. Let them all torture themselves. All those pieties about family he'd had to swallow, all just so much froth when money was involved.

But there were things he did *not* enjoy. The fact that his lawyers and contacts informed him that apparently all the girls were working. Working seriously. Small projects, but ones that were advancing. They had sold their properties, they lived together in one house. This, he detested. It did not fit with what he knew about his nieces: that they were selfish, spoiled, annoyed each other – every girl for herself.

He could look on it as desperation. That by suffering each other's company, they were showing how badly they needed his money.

But he received no reports of fights. And now the working. The girls had not been in touch with him, not to beg and not to plead.

He hated that. He needed to control all four of them. They were very important to his psyche; the girls were his heirs.

They were his triumph over his brothers. He would have to think this all through again.

'I think you're better off with the beige,' Athena said, flicking through the samples.

'Nothing flashy, then?' Serena Mack asked.

'No.' Athena gestured towards the colour wheel, showing the other girl what she meant. 'I want it tone on tone, no flowers, no pink. Lots of chocolate and mahogany near the floors, then hessian, toffee, all the way up to pale beige; sophisticated browns, even some greys possibly for contrast, little strips of white and cream.'

'I understand.' Serena nodded. 'Sounds cool. You'll like my painters, though they're not all women.' She grinned.

Athena shrugged. 'Nobody's perfect. As long as they work fast.'

'Hey,' Serena told her, 'when you handle as many Hollywood prima donnas as I do, you learn to work fast. And cheap.'

Athena smiled. Even though she was breathing through a mask and shouting to make herself heard, this was quite thrilling. The old cinema was mired in chaos. There was grime and dust everywhere, the hammer of drills, the shouts of workmen. But she could see through the filth, she had to; she could imagine what this place was going to be.

They'd been here almost a month and already the seats had been ripped away, the peeling wallpaper stripped, the projection rooms removed. Now wireless cables were being laid, council inspectors were everywhere, and Athena was project-managing. Her friend, Serena, was a contact; not your typical interior decorator, with overpriced style and a cut of the costs. Serena had worked on a BBC series with Athena once. Athena was a historical consultant, and Serena the set designer. She had a great feel for colour and mood, and with her job serving demanding directors, she knew how to get things done in record time.

'When are you going to start recruiting members?' Serena asked.

'Soon,' Athena replied. 'It's something I have to tackle. We'll be ready in a month but I don't have that kind of time. We need cash.'

Furiously, her mind leaped on to Bai-Ling. That damned woman! If she would just bugger off, Athena could have had anything she wanted from the banks. But instead, last night, when Venus had arrived home, there had been a little letter waiting in the hallway; hand-delivered and written on scented paper.

'There's a letter.' Venus had walked into the drawing room, where Athena was sitting slumped on the couch, drinking decaf espresso. She held it up. 'A pretty little letter, pink embossed monogram. BL.'

Athena started. 'I didn't hear the bell.'

'She had somebody post it,' Venus said.

Athena sat bolt upright, tiredness forgotten; and Venus felt the same adrenalin race through her own blood.

'Well, read it, Venus,' Athena said. 'You're the actress. Let's hear what she has to say.'

Venus sliced the envelope open with one manicured fingernail and drew out the crisply folded paper. Athena was the ideal audience; Venus had her total attention.

Dear Juno, Diana, Venus and Athena,

Thank you so much for welcoming me to the family. Dinner the other night was wonderful, and your little party was delightful. Such a muddle with the costumes for Venus's movie, but all quite understandable. I explained the mistake to your uncle, and also told him about your marvellous careers. He's delighted that we all continue to be such friends. I suggested to Clem, and he agreed, that as you are doing so well at work, there wasn't a lot of point in continuing the payments to the trust until the end of the year. However, your dear uncle feels that there ought to be a small transition period, so we compromised; this note is just to inform you that until Christmas, when the money stops, your payments will be halved.

I hope we will all meet again soon!

Best wishes,

Bai-Ling

There was no point in calling Juno or Diana. They were in Europe, chasing deals; Athena was vague on the whole thing. No, for once she did not want to delegate to her big sister. Juno's plan had been far too subtle. Bai-Ling needed something a little more obvious. And after this insult, Athena was ready to play dirty.

*

Clement was watching the figures on his screen. The latest fire sale had gone particularly well; two hundred seventy mil for the opal mine in New South Wales. That must have been forty mil or so more than it was worth. He could visualise the seams in his mind's eye, dark, almost tapped out, with a paucity of rough that had real fire to it. The money had gone directly into his New York account, and from there, with the punch of a button, his senior accountants had sent it spinning across the world, squirrelled away into companies, foundations, secret and unnumbered accounts, government-backed securities, and other instruments. His wealth was as widespread as it was huge. If one account were closed down, there were hundreds of others, in eighty-four countries.

Clement Chambers had learned to trust nobody.

The staff walked around his house quietly, in the little slippers he made them wear. There were enough of them for him to feel secure; a fair army of bodyguards outside, various firms employed at the same time, to prevent corruption, and the domestics were there for company. Not companionship; Clement almost never required that. Rather, he wanted people in his house. To jump to his whims, prepare his food, bring him things. To be there should he hurt himself. Or fall ill, or have a heart attack.

He had read, whilst younger, about rich people whose domestics abused them when they got old. Clement structured his house in such a way as to prevent that.

There were too many people around, coming from too many companies, all of whom had a vested interest in keeping Clement Chambers well, and happy.

Time to study the situation in London in more depth.

He snapped his fingers; an impossibly quiet gesture, yet somebody heard it, of course: the young maid who hovered outside the door, checking every thirty seconds if the master wanted anything.

'Bring me today's paper.'

'Yes, sir,' she said, with that heavy Seychellois accent, running off to the front of the house. She returned, a little out of breath, within twenty seconds. He enjoyed having his staff jump to serve him.

The girl laid the paper out smoothly in front of him, then retired. Yes, there was the picture of Bai-Ling. Clement studied it carefully. It was blown up on the front page. She was wearing a pretty little suit, obviously Chanel, and the jewels he had given her. What an interesting diversion she was.

Society report, page 12. He flicked to it. A breathless account of the party. A picture of his nieces, all well dressed, except perhaps Venus; there was a slice of the vulgarian in her, bad blood somewhere. Clement read closely. The careers Bai-Ling had bored on about were being described. Hotel designer, movie producer, estate agent, club owner. Really, his fiancée was not as clever as she supposed. As if those lazy, selfish women had learned a damn thing about business. No, like her, they relied on him . . .

His heart quickened, and he lifted his leonine white head, careful not to upset himself. How ironic if his little project should upset him enough to cause a heart attack. He had to be careful. He looked again at the black-and-white shot of Juno. Her smile certainly looked a little frozen. Bai-Ling had clearly won the first round.

He chuckled, a nervous, whistling sound, high-pitched and womanish. The girls fighting, all of them fighting. Exactly as he had predicted. Exactly as he had intended. Every one of them thought they were playing him, but in the end, he, Clement Chambers, was going to be the only victor.

The girls would lose.

Bai-Ling would lose.

And he would win.

He smiled as he thought of Bai-Ling's latest shot in this very feminine little war. The girls' allowance, halved. That would put paid to their pretensions; what would happen when they couldn't pay the bills? The very idea of their independence from him angered him. Clement wanted, needed to be in control. He had planned that they should hate Bai-Ling; jockey, and jostle, and offer him the spectre of a well-mannered catfight. Which he knew would end in the manner he had defined. But that they should take jobs, well. Ludicrous. It was an insult. They were, as the world knew very well, his dependants. After all, Venus and Diana had had no one but him for most of their lives! Their parents, gone . . . So tragic, how that had happened . . . He chewed his thin lips thoughtfully.

The girls thrilled and repelled him equally at present. He was enjoying the little puppet play he'd set in motion, but of course it depended upon a terrible insult; the idea that he, Clement Chambers, would unite himself in marriage with a girl like Bai-Ling, a foreign chit of no family . . . why had they all believed it? Clement scratched the delicate fabric of his tropical-weight suit; his old skin crawled and itched when he thought himself laughed at. The girls imagined he was losing his marbles. They thought he was a foolish old man, like that dribbling fool who had married Anna Nicole Smith. Ingratitude, he decided, hateful ingratitude, and now they were all circling like pretty little vultures . . .

Clement was determined he would teach them all a lesson. These idiotic stumblings around the world of business must be the first thing to go. When they were properly humbled, properly scared, the girls would be back on a plane here. And they would then discover what it meant to do things his way.

Bai-Ling looked around her hotel room, bored out of her mind. A porn movie was playing on the TV, but it had failed to arouse her. Idly, she switched it off. How much longer did she have to be here? She'd been to every musical worth seeing, trawled around a million dull galleries. Talking to Clement's accountants about shutting off the girls' money had been the only fun she'd had all week.

She slid off the bed and went and looked out of her window. The hotel looked on to Hyde Park; it was an overcast spring day. Gloomy and cloudy, that was Britain for you. She wanted to be back at Clement's compound, where at least she could walk in the sun, and she had all her things just the way she wanted them.

That cow Juno hadn't even called. Bloody women, doing the stiff-upper-lip thing. She wanted to see them, wanted to know just how much it was hurting.

Bai-Ling thought about the porn movie. Was she shutting down? she wondered. She hadn't felt anything, no lust, no shivers of desire. The only good thing about England was that she was away from Clement. Unable to get herself pregnant, but at least she didn't have to suffer the man's perversions. She briefly imagined the tanned, muscled bodies on the screen and compared them to Clement, the randy old bastard, his chest hollowed with age, his papery skin loose on his bones, soft and wrinkled; everything sagged . . . He needed to use drugs just so he could get it up . . . and yet he was still goatish, still wanting her to act out his fantasy . . .

Ugh. Bai-Ling shivered. She lived in a perpetual state of nerves. First, that she should inch towards the altar, towards that blessed piece of paper that would bestow rights, money, a name on her. And even more importantly, that she become pregnant, with Clement's heir. When she had that DNA evidence, then she was golden. Clement seemed frail to her – no, he was frail. His wizened old body was clawing on to life. She had to pray for his good health. Every moment mattered – every moment until she got pregnant, that was.

After that, he couldn't die fast enough. She felt no remorse in thinking such thoughts. He was a bitter, cruel old man whose brilliance in making money had turned him in on himself; his snobbishness and greed made him petty, and that made him hate. The world would be far better off without him.

And as for the billions? Well, she thought with her stomach churning at the revolting memories, last time she'd gone to bed with him she'd earned every cent . . .

She was going to have to wear him out. That shouldn't be difficult. The ageing husband and the horny, grateful young wife . . . Just get his child, so she could not be written out of the will, and then exhaust him!

Sometimes, in her blacker moments, Bai-Ling considered adding a little coke to the Viagra . . . just enough to push him over the edge. It was so tempting. She had never killed anyone, but Clement was practically dead now.

In the end, she always decided against it. What might an autopsy show? No, Clement was old enough. Time was always fatal, in the end. Bai-Ling was going to have to wait it out. With her body, with her sensual self, totally shutting down . . .

The phone rang, startling her.

'Hello.'

'Bai-Ling, it's Athena. Chambers,' the girl added, unnecessarily.

'Oh, hello, Athena.' Delighted to be pulled from her gloomy thoughts, Bai-Ling curled her tiny frame into a ball on the blue velvet chair. 'I take it you got my note?'

'Yes thanks,' Athena said lightly. Bai-Ling suppressed a snort; the bitch didn't fool her.

'I'm sorry if it causes you any financial difficulty,' she purred. 'I'm sure your little party for me was quite expensive.'

'Not in the slightest. Uncle Clem has left us all very well off,' Athena told her. 'And you know, it does remind us all that there's a wedding coming up. Two of the girls are in Europe this week. I wondered if you'd let Venus and me help you with your planning? There are some tremendous places to get gowns.'

'Not see-through ones, I hope.' Bai-Ling gave a little giggle of her own, and was rewarded by hearing Athena suck her breath in.

'Not at all. No.' Her future niece could certainly stonewall. 'All very modest and traditional. Exactly what Uncle Clem will love. My club's being renovated at the moment; can I pop round to your hotel? Or send a car to pick you up? Venus will take time off for this too.'

'Very good of her, to interrupt her little movie,' Bai-Ling purred.

'She feels terrible about what happened at our party.'

I bet she does. Bai-Ling stretched her limbs. She was starting to perceive desperation in Athena Chambers's voice. Obviously the girls had realised that their stunts were worthless; she *was* going to be Mrs Clement Chambers. And she was going to cut off their access to their uncle's limitless cash. Their best hope would be to crawl to Bai-Ling, to suck up to her, to curry favour. She would soon be in a position where she could cut them out – or toss them a couple of million.

Bai-Ling smiled. She would enjoy this surrender immensely. Almost as much as the day she would become the world's happiest widow.

'Well, I expect I can see you both,' she agreed. 'What time would you like to come by?'

'How about in an hour? I have an appointment booked for you at a couple of places.'

'That's absolutely fine.' Bai-Ling hung up, and smiled to herself.

'Not another wedding salon,' Bai-Ling said, affecting a sigh.

Venus smiled warmly at her. 'Last one, I promise. I need to get back to the set.'

'And I have meetings too.' Athena glanced at her Patek Philippe. 'But you *have* to see this one.'

Bai-Ling arched her neck a little, like a supple cat presented with a raw steak.

'I suppose I could manage one more,' she conceded.

The Chambers cousins had certainly managed to please her. They had sucked up divinely, and she got the sense they were beaten; a certain weary resignation when they talked about the wedding. Today, there had been no attempts to trip her up, no journalists employed to watch her fall flat on her face. Instead, Athena and Venus had taken her to Harrods, to Basia Zarzyka, to Vera Wang, to Jane Packer . . . all the top bridal outfits, the best florists, the ultimate shops for tiny bejewelled slippers.

And Bai-Ling had enjoyed it; slipping into minute dress after minute dress, playing with tiaras, sniffing expensive bouquets of waxy blossoms full of twigs and glossy foliage. After all, she was actually going to need a wedding dress. And Clement had to be happy. If these wretched girls co-ordinated a proper English wedding in the tropics, no expense spared, then he'd be happy. They had crowded around her, demanding fabric swatches, cake samples, photographs of exotic boutonnières, upbraiding the serving girls if they were slow.

Mmm; it was fun to have the company. Bai-Ling adored it when she could hold court. And it was especially nice to lord it over these two proper English ladies, although they were perhaps a touch aggressive, not like Juno.

'You'll *love* this place,' Athena promised. 'It's the ultimate wedding prep salon.'

Bai-Ling tossed her head. 'It doesn't look like much.'

'That's because it's discreet,' Venus emphasised. 'And you want to be discreet. It's just the English way.'

They were standing outside a white stucco building in Belgravia; it looked just like a normal house, except for the small brass plaque that gleamed in the warm sunlight. The clouds had cleared up now, and Bai-Ling was enjoying the rare sight of some English sunshine.

'The Maxim Studio,' she read aloud. 'Never heard of it.'

'You wouldn't have.' Athena gave her a wink. 'That's the point.'

They rang the bell, and a woman admitted them, dressed in a surgical receptionist's gown. Bai-Ling was ushered into a corridor lined with eighteenth-century oils and fitted with soft carpet; there was the instant, reassuring smell of money about the place. The reception room to the left was lavish, twin receptionists at walnut desks, with chintz sofas and a glossy array of magazines laid out on glass tables.

'Yes, madam.'

'Athena Chambers.' The younger cousin took charge. 'We have an appointment for Miss Bai-Ling Wuhuputri.'

Bai-Ling noted that Athena pronounced it perfectly. Good. Another sign of surrender.

'Of course. Somebody will be right out.'

'What is this place?' Bai-Ling demanded.

'It's a beauty salon. But so much more.' Venus

beamed enthusiastically. '*Very* private; Hollywood stars use it when they're filming in England, royalty, everything. I've had stuff done here myself. They simply have the best of everything. Make-up artists, manicurists, waxing . . . and a little plastic surgery office for Botox or an eyebrow lift.'

'Plastic surgery?' Bai-Ling wrinkled her nose. 'I'm twenty-five,' she lied. 'I don't think Clement would like that one bit.' She looked patronisingly at Venus. 'Now for *you*, dear, well – I can see how an older girl would find it useful.'

Athena glanced at her cousin, but Venus was inscrutable; nothing more than a slight hardening of the eyes.

'Oh, goodness, no,' Venus said sweetly. 'You're perfect, Bai-Ling, and obviously Uncle Clem thinks so. You don't need work. What I'm talking about is maintenance. They have this marvellous trainer here who can keep your figure perfect while you're in London. *Everybody* uses him. Kate, Sadie, Keira.' Venus tossed her blond head. 'He doesn't get many spots, but I'm determined to book him.'

'I want him.' Bai-Ling's eyes lit up. One thing that was tough was keeping her weight at that perfect minimum. Without Clement there all the time, she could forget exactly how . . . *gamine* he wanted her to be. Bored in the hotel, she'd started to eat – yesterday she'd actually had a bread roll with dinner. Yes, if she was stuck here for the summer she would need help. A sadistic personal trainer used to keeping supermodels trim – that was perfect.

'Oh, don't be silly, Venus,' Athena said acidly. 'Bai-Ling couldn't take that sort of regime. And Bob is *so* expensive. She'd better have Emily or Tina. Besides which, Uncle Clem might not approve of her seeing a man.'

Bai-Ling tensed; the younger girl was in danger of forgetting her place. Athena did not rule in this family. She would help her to remember that.

'I think I know exactly what *my fiancé* would approve of. My darling Clem wants me to keep healthy. And I can certainly take any amount of discipline.' She looked disparagingly at the rounded curves of Athena's bottom. 'You might want to consider this Bob yourself.'

She enjoyed watching Athena scowl.

'I can't afford him.' The English girl tossed her head.

'Ah, well.' Bai-Ling smiled sweetly. 'I would offer to pay, but Clem does want you to stand on your own two feet . . .'

An immaculately dressed girl in a Juicy Couture tracksuit walked up to them. Bai-Ling noted she was lean, with glossy hair in a sleek ponytail, ultra-flat abs, and Hollywood-white teeth; an impressive transformation of rather ordinary raw material into something a millionaire might marry.

'Good morning, madam. I'm Cece. I believe you might want to see one of our trainers?'

Bai-Ling nodded. 'I want Bob.'

The girl was apologetic. 'I'm afraid his schedule's full.'

Athena dared to smile, which incensed Bai-Ling.

'Then clear it,' she said. 'If you get me an appointment this morning, I'll give you a thousand pounds in cash.'

Venus gasped, and Bai-Ling smiled triumphantly. 'I'm a very rich woman,' she added to the blinking girl. 'So I advise you to give me what I want.'

'Of course, ma'am,' she said. 'Just one second . . .'

She stepped away into the shadows, pulling a mobile phone from her top pocket. For a minute she talked animatedly into it, then she came hurrying back to them.

'Bob would be thrilled to have you on his client list, Miss Wuhuputri. He's finishing up with a client and he'll be right with you.'

Athena sounded cowed. 'I can't believe you did that. It's impossible.'

Bai-Ling looked her dead in the eyes. 'Impossible's a big word. I always get what I want.'

She gestured for them to sit down. The Chambers cousins looked crestfallen – but let them watch her in action. By the end of the day she would have them properly house-trained.

As she expected, within five minutes there was the sound of heavy feet arriving, thumping down the corridor. Whoever it was was in a hurry.

The heavy mahogany door swung open, and Bai-Ling looked up. There he was, standing in front of her like a tanned, bronzed god. She opened her mouth, then hastily closed it again. Bob was six foot two, strong but not muscle-bound. He had shining platinum-blond hair, white teeth, gleaming eyes that were bright and wide-awake, and soft, even features like a Renaissance prince. He looked like something out of a boy band, but with added strength. Young, fit, taut and healthy.

She immediately wanted to see him with his clothes off.

'So, Ms Wuhuputri.' He was American; she loved the confident, sexy burr to his voice. He was ageless and polished, a million miles from Clem's sagging body and crooked British teeth. 'I guess we're going to be working together?'

'Yes,' she said crisply. The two Chambers bitches were watching her. 'I'm told you're the best.'

'That's right. I am,' he said easily. 'And will I be training these two young ladies as well?'

Athena clicked her tongue with annoyance, and Bai-Ling enjoyed pretending not to hear it. 'Do you have workout gear for sale on the premises?'

'Absolutely. We can get started right away.' His eyes assessed her, and she liked it. 'You're very slim, but I can harden you up a little, maintain a good tone, good elasticity.'

'Perfect. I need to look just right on my wedding day,' she said primly. The two English girls were stuck on the couch like lemons; Bai-Ling had had enough, she wanted to be shot of them. She turned round, and addressed them as if they were her personal shoppers.

'Athena, Venus, dears, I think that's enough for today,' she pronounced. 'Your uncle wouldn't want me to be tired out. And you have your jobs to get back to. I think Bob and I can take it from here.' She nodded to the girl, Cece. 'The concierge from my hotel will send your tip over.'

'Thank you, ma'am, thank you very much,' the girl said deferentially.

Bai-Ling smiled; at last she was getting to enjoy her position.

'OK.' Venus sounded dejected. 'Have fun, Bai-Ling.'

'I will.' She tossed them a bone. 'You girls can call me tomorrow morning. I'm going to have you all as matrons of honour.'

'Bridesmaids,' Athena said automatically.

'Well, I think you're a little old to be bridesmaids, Athena.' Bai-Ling gave her a sharp smile. 'But whatever; you will be attendants at the wedding, and that's what counts.'

Victory was hers. Athena and Venus stood up, blushing, not able to look at her.

'See you tomorrow then,' Athena mumbled, and the two girls left.

Bai-Ling waited until the door was closed, then turned back to Bob. He hadn't given his last name, and she wasn't interested. She just wanted him to take that

T-shirt off, so she could watch him sweat. The thought of his young, firm body, glistening in the studio lights, sent a tingling feeling through her she almost thought had gone for ever. Lust. Desire.

She lifted her young face to his, drinking him in. He smiled back, and Bai-Ling thought she saw a gleam in his hazel eyes: appreciation of her beauty.

'Are you ready, Ms Wuhuputri? You could pick an outfit, and then we can get started. I'd like to begin with weighing you, measuring your body fat.'

The way he talked about those clinical details, Bai-Ling had the definite impression he was flirting.

And she liked it.

Chapter Twenty-One

Diana hesitated, then put the phone back down.

She was nervous. Was this a mistake?

Last night, in the house, she'd sat up talking with Venus, late. Just chatting – about Hans and Karl, about the film and her business. What a shock it was to have to work. And more of a shock to enjoy it.

Mostly, she'd just loved the change in them. The friendship between all the girls was solid now, better perhaps than it had ever been. There were no recriminations over the bad scene at the party; Juno had done her best. They weren't catty with each other any more. There was a bond, that sense that the Chambers girls were more than a marketing concept, more than a glossy magazine cover.

And even more than the fun of enjoying her cousins, Diana cherished the relationship she was having with her sister. She'd stopped seeing Venus as slutty, and started thinking of her as stylish and fearless. And Venus openly admired Diana's skill in design, the way she pulled her company together, ran the accounts, worked the suppliers. They'd had only each other before Clem came; and it was starting to feel like that again.

'For myself,' Diana geared up to make the confession, 'I almost – I almost don't care any more.'

There. She had said it.

'Really?' Venus's eyes widened.

'Maybe we could make it. On our own.'

'It's possible.' Her little sister sipped her champagne. 'But Di, it's a hell of a gamble.'

'It would be good to have the money back . . .' She thought longingly of Karl. 'Then I could meet Karl as an equal. I hate seeing myself the way I saw those girls at Hans's party.'

'Maybe you should forget him.'

'Easier said than done,' Diana replied. She sighed. 'Venus, we should do our bit to stop Bai-Ling; we can't leave it all to those two.'

'Family honour?' Venus grinned.

'Too bloody right.' But Diana was only half joking. 'Juno needs that cash, Athena too. So we have to be helpful. You know what I think, I think we're doing it all wrong. We're amateurs, and something tells me Bai-Ling is not. She must have planned it very carefully to get to where she is with Clem.'

'What's your idea?'

'You've heard of Klaxon?'

Venus's eyes widened. 'You wouldn't, Di.'

Klaxon were an extremely high-priced, extremely

ruthless firm of private investigators. They worked out of New York, and dealt mostly with corporate espionage. Companies could afford their fees. But there were some high-profile divorces, some corrupt politicians. Their reputation for black ops and total client secrecy kept them in demand.

'I'm not ordering a hit on the bloody girl. Just a report. If she has secrets, they will find them.' Diana shrugged. 'Look, Venus, we're wasting time. Running a small business is teaching me things. I suppose the most important one is that you delegate. I don't hang wall-paper myself; I'm not an expert plasterer or electrician. So why not hand Bai-Ling to the professionals?'

Venus thought it over. 'You have a point. I'm not sure Clem would like it . . .'

'So we don't tell him. The fee is expensive, though. I'd need you to go halves with me.'

'Delighted.' Her baby sister yawned. 'Then I've done my duty in this and I can get on with the bloody film. The shooting schedule doesn't leave time for mucking about.'

Now, though, in the cold light of day, Diana was dithering. Klaxon. They were so powerful. She and the rest of the girls took turns to have lunches and dinners with Bai-Ling, to take her to galleries, to show her round London. They had to keep up the front of introducing her to London society. But underneath the hard shell, Diana thought she saw frailty.

What the hell? If Bai-Ling was innocent, somehow in love with Clem, they would find out. She picked up the phone again and dialled the number.

'There.' Athena closed the door of the taxi behind them triumphantly. 'I told you it would be worth it.'

'You're lucky you were right.' Venus extended her tanned arms, and yawned. 'Four *hours* with that silly little tramp. I'll be lucky if the set hasn't burned down. And one more crack about my age and I was going to scratch her eyes out. Let's see Uncle Clem marry her then.'

'Bob will put a stop to that.' Athena was firm. 'I know his reputation. She doesn't. And you saw her reaction.'

'When the cat's away, the bitch will play?'

'Something like that.' Athena thought aloud. 'Now we let her get settled. Let her get comfortable. When he makes his move, I need pictures.'

Venus shrugged. 'It's a tiny bit sleazy, don't you think?'

'Maybe.' Venus was surprised to see her cousin's face was hard. 'It has to be done. I *need* my trust fund, I have to buy back Boswell House. And I hate her attitude. Uncle Clem won't want her, once we're through. If I have to bribe Bob to use his cell-phone camera, I bloody well will.'

Venus glanced over uncertainly; this was a whole new Athena.

'Blimey, I'm glad you're on our side,' she said. 'I take it marrying Freddie Wentworth is a non-starter?'

'Absolutely.' Athena laughed. 'No lifeboat there. We had our first date the night after the party.'

'How did it go?'

'Boring.' Athena made a face. 'He took me to Maxim's, and he didn't have much to say. Nice kid, but he seemed nervous to me. Nope – I still need to get rid of Bai-Ling. Juno took her shot, but it's going to need more than bad etiquette at a party. We don't want her with us for the whole summer. Worse, through the winter. This romance has to die.' Athena glanced at her watch. 'Now I need to go over to the House of Commons.'

'The where?' Venus blinked. 'What on earth for?'

'I'm meeting some women I want to join the club. We launch in six weeks, and I need it to be perfect.' Athena sighed with sheer exhaustion. 'Groundwork, a lot of groundwork.'

'I understand.' Venus nodded. 'And the filming's going pretty well. It's a tight script. We're aiming to get it all finished very soon, and then another five weeks for the edit.'

'That fast?'

Her cousin stretched. 'I don't have enough money to be slower.'

'And then what?' Athena was interested; Venus, selfish, vain, sexy Venus, was starting to sound quite professional. Of course, Athena didn't really believe she could pull it off, but it did appear Venus was at least going to try. 'Once you have the film done, then what? Do you enter it for Cannes or something?'

Venus shook her head. 'I sell it. Get distribution. We will keep a percentage of the profits, but it's all about getting something on wide release. The movie's a romantic comedy, very low budget. It doesn't have to do that well to make money.'

'Thinking big,' Athena joked.

Venus shrugged. 'Everybody's got to start somewhere. Next time I'll have the money to buy an even better script.' She extended her nails, painted scarlet. 'Do you think Bob will be able to get Bai-Ling?'

'I do.' Athena was cold. 'Either that or we imply he did.'

'You don't think we're being a little . . .'

'No. I do not.' Athena looked Venus straight in the eye. 'Tell me, you think that girl feels anything for Clem, or vice versa? It's disgusting, an old man like him and a woman younger than us. She wants the money. It's family money, it's *our* money. She's completely cynical about getting him, and I'm completely cynical about stopping her. That's why we sold our houses, that's why we're wasting all this cash in Notting Hill. Don't take your eye off the ball, Venus.'

'Well no, ma'am,' Venus said smartly, annoying her. 'And after your meeting, you're seeing Freddie again?'

Athena sighed. 'You really know how to pour cold bloody water on a productive day.'

'I can't help it. He's perfect.' Venus grinned. 'Poor, dumb Freddie Wentworth trying to date you. It's like Rain Man going out with Carol Vorderman.'

'He isn't *that* thick,' Athena said, surprised to find herself defensive. 'He's not a bad man, overall.'

'Just your type?'

'Of course not.' She was sharp. 'I could ask the same about you and Hans Tersch.'

'He's never been my boyfriend.' Venus bit her lip. 'Just a rival.'

'Uh-huh.'

'He's hot,' Venus admitted, 'but so are lots of guys. I just think of him as somebody I need to teach a lesson to.' She fidgeted with her shirt cuffs, uneasily, and changed the subject. 'You know, you're right about Bai-Ling. You've come up with Bob. I've done something too.'

'You?'

It came out a little disbelieving, and Athena regretted her cattiness.

'I'm not Freddie Wentworth, you know,' Venus said acidly. 'I don't see why it should be down to just you and Juno. Diana and I have a stake in this. We've hired a private investigator. Diana was discussing it with me, and I agreed to split the cost with her.'

'I don't know.' Athena was anxious. 'Some bumbling guy rooting around the Seychelles – you think that's a good idea, really?'

'Diana knows some people. A firm called Klaxon. They split off from Kroll, in New York. Very serious, very heavyweight stuff. They'll be discreet, and they won't go anywhere near Uncle Clem.'

'Expensive?'

'Yes, but Diana and I are funding it jointly.' Venus frowned. 'That's the drawback; they are very expensive, but you get what you pay for.'

'A solid morning, then.' Athena leaned back against the worn leather seat of the taxi and exhaled. 'Our little gold-digger's on her way out.'

Athena paused on the pavement and looked up.

Wow, she thought. Just – wow.

The Houses of Parliament. She'd driven past them a million times, never really stopped to look. Now she was here, at the St Stephen's entrance, and the Palace of Westminster was towering over her. And she was suddenly in awe.

There were tourists streaming past, and protesters on the other side of the street; uniformed police officers, and crowd barricades. Amongst the chaos, the grey stone walls of the palace thrust upwards into the cloudy spring sky; glorious gothic turrets, surrounded by small scraps of manicured lawn.

Athena stepped into a little Portakabin while her briefcase went through security. She told an armed policeman whom she was visiting, was searched, and then walked through an open door into Parliament itself. Her mouth opened; the building was breathtaking, long grey stone steps rising through a medieval hall towards the lobby. It was a large octagonal space with a soaring, ornate ceiling and stained-glass windows; journalists, schoolchildren and lobbyists milled around, being greeted by MPs. A harassed-looking man in a dark suit tried to muscle his way through the crowd. Athena recognised him; he was a minor government minister. Immediately a security guard was there.

'Make way, make way for the noble lord,' he shouted.

The crowd melted, and the peer stomped off down the red-carpeted corridor that led to the House of Lords. Athena was charmed; it was all so old-fashioned, yet the place bore the unmistakable smell of power.

Yes, she thought. Like Oxford. Clubby, exclusive and masculine.

'I'm here to see Sue Pritchard. It's Athena Chambers.'

'Name of your organisation?'

Hmmm. She hadn't come up with anything yet.

'Miss?'

And there it was, in a flash of inspiration.

'The Bluestocking Club,' she said.

Athena had chosen her target well. Sue Pritchard, the Liberal Democrat MP for Bootle, was one of the most glamorous women in the House. Thirty-seven, she had sleek auburn hair, piercing blue eyes, and a penchant for sharply designed trouser suits, which she famously paired with teetering Jimmy Choos. The second she'd arrived in Parliament, she'd been subjected to wolf-whistles and muttered comments. These were par for the course for any woman MP under fifty, her whips' office told her. Newspaper gossip columns reported that the Honourable Lady had replied, 'Fuck that, I'll sue.'

She was no longer harassed. But she was also not liked. There was a subtle punishment meted out for kicking up a fuss. Sue had languished in a minor front-bench role in Transport, and apart from fawning pieces in the tabloids about her beauty and style, her career was going nowhere fast.

'Tell me why I should join.'

'Because women need this club. And it needs you.' Athena realised she was getting passionate about this, leaning forward, her eyes flashing fire. 'I was passed over for tenure because I wasn't one of the boys. The press is interested in you because of your shoes. It's the same all over. Women need to network. We need something for high-flyers, some place we can beat the men at their own game.'

'I don't know.' Sue stirred her black tea. The tearoom in the Commons was packed; familiar faces were slouching in every chair. Athena noticed how they leered across at her and Sue, when the MP had her back to them. 'I'm pretty busy here. Not much time for socialising.'

'Socialising is work, if it's done right. You could come into Bluestocking to get a document faxed out, or to have lunch. While you're there, you might talk to the CEO of Amazon or Hewlett Packard. You could meet with Indira Knight, the film director, or Emily Larson, the Nobel-winning physicist. *And* the two of you could get your nails done at the same time.' Athena's passion blazed out of her. 'This is going to be a revolutionary concept – it'll keep you looking fabulous, and it will supply the networks women need. Bluestocking will help you stay in the game and refresh you so you look and feel the part.' Athena laughed. 'I'm installing massage chairs in the front room, so members can get a ten-minute neck rub at any time.'

Sue stretched her neck. 'OK. Sold. How much is membership?'

'For you, a thousand a year.'

The MP blinked. 'Ouch. Expensive.'

'Oh, that's just the introductory rate. After we open it for general applications, the price for the first hundred members is a thousand a month. The next nine hundred will pay double that. This club is for high-achievers only.' Athena took a sip of her tea. 'I guarantee you, we'll be full.'

'With footballers' wives and trust-fund Sloanes?' Sue asked dismissively. 'I wouldn't want to network with some billionaire's wife.'

'No.' Athena blushed; she was a trust-fund baby, she

had been vigorously fighting for her fund to go on. 'Money won't be enough. Applicants will be judged on their career, a bit like the Groucho Club for media types. We'll take women from business, politics, academia, even sport, but only women who achieve.'

'No WAGs?'

Athena shook her head. 'None. And I want you to be one of the founder members. If you like, you can sit on the membership committee. Ms Pritchard . . .'

'Sue.'

'Women are going to push themselves harder in their careers just so they can meet the threshold to get into the Bluestocking.'

Sue was smiling softly now, as though she couldn't help herself.

'I do like the idea,' she admitted.

'We open in a month. Full wireless internet, a financial ticker, a media room, beauty salon, gym.'

'And massages.'

Athena grinned. 'Yes, ma'am. Will you be there?'

Sue pulled her Fendi bag on to her lap.

'I sure will,' she said, taking out her chequebook.

Athena floated home. She was so distracted with pleasure, she nearly walked into the Tube. Juno would have had a fit. Cabs swarmed around Westminster, and she grabbed one, leaning her head against the window. Sue's cheque for a grand was folded neatly in her purse, and there were six others next to it. Her personal appeals to these women were paying off. She had enough in her corporate account now to start hiring staff. In a month, she might be running a viable business. Losses would be limited, with the prospect of a profit in a few months . . .

This is crazy, Athena thought. I can't believe I'm getting so excited about making a loss!

Tomorrow she would go to the bank, put the cheques in. She idly wondered what Bai-Ling was doing now. Had Bob got her into bed yet? How much would his bribe cost? She should be desperate for news, but just now, with her high from the club, Athena didn't care.

Her phone buzzed in her coat pocket, vibrating against her. She fished it out and felt her good mood evaporate.

Hi Theney. Can't wait to see you tonight. Love Freddie.

Oh bloody hell. She'd almost forgotten. Her date with the Wentworth boy.

'Actually, forget Notting Hill. I need to go to Sheep Street. Mr Wong's.'

'No problem, love. Romantic dinner, eh?' the cabby asked. 'Lucky for some. 'E must be rolling in it.'

Athena smiled weakly at this casual impertinence. 'Suppose so.'

Sue Pritchard's words stung her. *Footballers' wives and trust-fund Sloanes.* Whatever she pulled together with the club, getting Bai-Ling dumped was supposed to be her main focus. It was a nasty thought that the politician didn't want to mix with the girl she was hoping to be.

But what the hell. She *needed* that money. To buy back Boswell House. To get back her place in Oxford. To fund her independence . . .

Still – was it really necessary to actually date some loser, just for cover?

The first date she'd had with Freddie had been awkward. He'd booked a table at Maxim's, coughed nervously through the evening, and asked her a few lame questions about her studies. After he paid the bill, he hovered uselessly around while Athena got a cab, then just ummed and aahed when she said good night; not exactly a date to set the world on fire. But he'd still asked her for another one.

This time Athena insisted on picking the restaurant. If she was going to be bored out of her skull, she at least wanted to be well fed at the same time. Mr Wong's did the best dim sum in the city, and a fantastic sake. But it wasn't enough to make her want to keep seeing Freddie.

Athena decided. She would end it with him tonight. Dating a man to make Bai-Ling feel comfortable was a step too far. If they'd played it right, Bob would be making the girl very comfortable indeed.

'Wow.' Freddie breathed in. 'You look wonderful.'

The comment annoyed her. She hadn't taken any trouble to look special. She was wearing the same clothes she'd picked for work, a sleek Donna Karan suit with a pleated skirt, and a tight black silk vest underneath it. Her sole concession to this second and final date had been a spritz of Molton Brown perfume on her wrists.

'Thank you.' She deliberately decided not to return the compliment. Freddie was wearing a nondescript dark suit, and it didn't fit him terribly well. The shirt cuffs gaped, and the material was too tight around his muscular chest.

He was relaxing against the red leather banquette at one of the restaurant's best tables. In fact, with a quick glance round the room, Athena noted they were better placed than a record label president and two movie stars. She was late; he'd been here for ten minutes.

'Did you decide what you're having?'

'Oh, no. I don't normally eat Chinese. I was hoping you could help me, maybe order something good,' Freddie said. He was completely unembarrassed. 'Something with meat in it; I'm bloody starving.'

'Really? Long day?'

He nodded. 'Problems with the house. One of the outer walls in the East Wing apparently has dry rot.'

'Ouch.' She had the good grace to wince. 'That is nasty, I'm sorry.'

'The architects want us to knock it down and restore it. I'll be damned if I do.' His jaw tensed. 'That house has been in my family for three hundred years.'

'Isn't it going to your brother, though? You're the second son.'

Freddie nodded. 'But it's my childhood home; I still care.'

'You're an estate manager?' Athena asked. 'What does that involve?'

Yawn. Now she had to hear some little rich boy blather on about his pheasant shoots and his walled herb garden. She loved Boswell, but houses were like children, Athena thought; you could be obsessed with your own, but you'd have to fake interest in everyone else's. The waiter came, and Athena fired off two generic orders. The quicker she could eat, the quicker she could leave.

'A lot of money. A lot of conservation. The estate employs over two hundred people, we've got a small-holding producing organic food, the house is open to the public in the summer . . . Essentially I run a medium-sized business.' Freddie spoke confidently. 'People depend on me for a living. We want to keep Farnsworth as a true English country house, not some toytown mansion run by the National Trust.' He poured out some sake for them into two eggcups, and tossed his back. 'People think that estate management is about organising your next croquet party, because they can't imagine that the rich work. I do eighteen-hour days sometimes.'

Athena felt slightly embarrassed. 'I see.'

'I'm not brilliant like you, of course.' Freddie shrugged. 'But we all do the best with what we have.'

'Doesn't your older brother want to run the estate?'

His face clouded. 'Chris is a bit of a waster, to be honest. Dad's very worried about him. We all are. I wish I had been the oldest, sometimes – not for the title and the house so much, but just so the burden didn't fall on Chris. Dad forced him to go into the army; he was badly bullied in the Guards, and then when he came out, it was all nightclubs and coke. My sister dabbled in that as well, but at least she's clean now.'

'Sorry.' Athena found she'd actually stopped thinking about when would be a good moment to dump Freddie; she was listening to everything he said. He wasn't bright, true, but he was honest and at ease with himself. And pretty good-looking, in an earthy way.

'Not all men can take being in the forces. I did it myself for a few years, served in the first Gulf War.'

'Did you kill anyone?' Athena joked.

'I'm afraid I did,' he said, deadly serious, and she blushed, silenced. 'It was the hardest thing I've ever done, and easily the best. I wish I was out there serving now.'

'Then why aren't you?'

'Because of Farnsworth. If I left it all to Chris, the house would be in ruins, and Chris would be dead. At least daily contact with me keeps him from the worst sort of dissipation.'

'Can't your parents cut off his money?'

Freddie shook his head. 'Some of it only comes when he inherits, but there was a nice chunk the second he turned eighteen. My brother's laden down with the weight of ermine and money. I wish to God he didn't have a trust fund. It can suck the creativity out of a man.' He looked at her admiringly. 'Not you, though, Athena. You're a businesswoman, and a professor. You could have sat there and spent your money in nightclubs, like my brother. But you haven't let it suck the soul out of you.'

He was making her uncomfortable.

'And you – don't you have a trust fund?'

'Nothing special. These things are archaic, it all goes to the heir. Younger brothers were expected to make a fist of it in the army, or maybe the Church.' He looked at her, his eyes glinting. 'Although I don't think I'd have been well suited to the Church.'

Athena was twisting in her chair. She wondered if Venus would make fun of her. What, the superbrain was finding the farm boy attractive?

But she was seeing him differently; a man with his own ideas. And one who was comfortable in his own skin.

She found it was rather difficult to hold his eyes. The waiter came by with the food, and Athena took refuge in that, thanking him and pointing out the dishes to Freddie.

'That's crispy hoi sin duck. It's good. And that's the coriander and coconut parcel with spiced beef. Squid in satay sauce . . .'

Freddie put his hand on hers. 'Relax, I can eat any-thing. And I have, on manoeuvres.' He grinned. 'I don't know what was worse, roasting a mouse on an open fire or school lunches at Harrow.' He grabbed two or three little dishes and wolfed them down.

'You're meant to savour them,' Athena said, smiling. He did make her laugh.

He looked her right in the face. 'I'd rather savour you.'

She blushed.

'Of course, I mean your company. Honestly, I can't imagine why a girl like you would go out with me.' He flushed a little himself.

'You seem completely different to when we met at the party,' she said. 'And even last time.'

'Well, I was nervous then.'

'I don't bite.' Athena smiled.

But his eyes slid off hers, embarrassed.

'When you're me, you'd be surprised how girls will date you just to make a point. You know, going out with a lord. The title is a real draw to a certain kind of girl. And you're so brilliant – I was never good at school, the forces saved me from college. I almost thought you were doing it for a bet. But since you said yes a second time, I suppose I've concluded that perhaps you're not *that* brilliant – you're dumb enough to want to date me.' He spread his hands. 'Full disclosure, now – Chris gets the fortune, the house and the title. I can only offer you a rented cottage and seventy grand a year. A rich girl like you would be dating beneath herself.'

The words were humorous, but, Athena thought, there was precious little warmth behind the smile. He was testing her. And she thought there had been a decent amount of pain before that. Girls who had dumped him on learning he wasn't rolling in it like his father and brothers.

'I'll be the judge of that,' she replied coolly. 'You know, you were the one that asked *me* out, Freddie. What made you ask?'

He inclined his head. 'Touché. Yes, you're obviously very pretty. I suppose if there are girls chasing money, then men are superficial too.'

Athena lifted her sake and waited.

'But you see, I *asked* you out because you're stunning. I wouldn't have continued with it if you weren't more than that. Cool. Interesting. You're your own girl, and I like that. The serial shoppers get very boring very quickly. And I can't afford them anyway.'

'But why pick a girl for her looks? Isn't that exactly the same as a woman hitting on you for your title?'

'Well,' he said, slowly, 'consider: women want their men to be faithful. That's a lot easier if the girl's attractive. Maybe it's sexist to say that, but at least it's the truth. If I ask a girl out and she's ugly, I'm not going to stick with her. There needs to be some passion.' He lifted his sake cup to her. 'So please don't be offended if I find you beautiful. Too beautiful and too clever for me, perhaps, but maybe you got tired of boffins.' Freddie shrugged. 'Women are a bloody closed book anyway. If you get to date a nice one, you don't question it too closely. At least, I don't.'

Athena smiled. He was completely disarming. She wasn't used to this sort of honesty. And there *was* a difference between Freddie and those leering, condescending dons and mature students up at Oxford; he was attracted to her, but he didn't treat her like some trophy.

'So what do you say? Do I get to take you to Farnsworth for that weekend?' Freddie asked hopefully.

'Easy, tiger,' she replied. 'It's still just the second date.'

'If we go up to Northamptonshire it'll be the third.'

Athena bit back a smile. 'Maybe.'

'I'll pick you up on Friday,' he said triumphantly. 'Five o'clock?'

'Five o'clock it is,' she agreed.

And for the first time in weeks, she found she didn't give a damn about Bai-Ling, or her uncle.

Chapter Twenty-Two

Venus leaned against the wall of the prefab and regarded the sobbing Lilly. This was the last thing she needed. She'd taken Bai-Ling out to four society bakers this morning to sample bloody cakes. There were just a few weeks to go before the end of the shoot, and now this?

'You have to help me.' Keisha, the director, had stormed into Venus's hut, where she was haggling on the phone with the Mayor's office over a shooting permit for the City of London. Fucking bureaucrats, didn't they have even a tiny bit of imagination? 'I can't take this bitch for one more second.'

'I'll get back to you,' Venus said hurriedly into the phone, hanging up.

This was bad. Keisha was the best decision she'd made since starting this project. Used to the micro-second discipline of commercials, she was an astonishing talent. She framed and shot perfectly, she made the rag-tag of minor-part actors look good, and she knew how to get things done in the fewest takes. Keisha liked to have the writer on set, and the two of them had formed a real bond. She was prepared to work all hours for Guild minimum. When Venus thanked her, Keisha pushed that aside.

'Fuck that, honey, this flick's gonna make my name too. The business don't like women in the chair. But they *do* like money. So – I make you rich, I make me rich.' She examined her long, fake, blood-red nails; Keisha Roland didn't do subtle. 'This is all about me, baby.'

And Keisha made the most of the rare bit of talent Venus *had* been able to provide, for the micro-budgeted movie. Which was Lilly. Temperamental, vain, spoiled, but in the end a very scared young girl; she had pissed off Hans Tersch, and this movie was her very last chance. Lilly worked for Keisha, although the older woman often told Venus she pitied her next director.

'When she's a star, that little cow's going to be impossible.'

Venus was thrilled. '*Is* she going to be a star?'

'Of course, honey. This movie's a hit.'

But Lilly had been off, lately; flaking out of her schedule, needing four takes instead of two; even her skin was dull in her close-ups. And now Keisha was standing in front of Venus, so mad you could see the veins throbbing in her smooth black neck.

'What's up?' Venus asked, her heart sinking.

'What's up? Little Miss Hollywood out there.' Keisha scowled. 'Where the hell *were* you today? I needed you this morning.'

Venus thought of Bob, and devoutly hoped he was giving Bai-Ling the workout of her life. This job was meant to be a distraction, but right now she felt guilty for diverting her energy towards dealing with that poisonous little dwarf. The trust fund gave her more money, but, she suddenly realised, sitting here, in a cold little prefab hut, nursing a mug of Nescafé in a chipped mug and watching her first-time director rant about her ex-junkie star, for the first time in years she felt totally fulfilled.

She fucking *loved* producing. Venus had no idea why so many actors and writers wanted to direct. Producing was where it was at. The director was hired by her and reported to her. She had to put out every little fire, negotiate with everyone from the caterers to the government, tease, cajole, bully and sweat. The phone was glued to her ear, she was utterly exhausted, and she loved it.

'Sorry. I'm here now.' Venus leaned forward, giving Keisha her undivided attention. 'Tell me exactly what the trouble is. She's not back on coke, is she?'

Keisha shook her head. 'Nope. Not on booze either, far as I can see. You scared her straight on that. Plus we make her do the dope tests daily. Blood samples, not urine, so she can't cheat.'

'All right.' Venus relaxed fractionally. If Lilly wasn't hooked again, maybe they could fix it. Scrap that – they *would* fix it. They had to. The movie was all about the star, essentially a vehicle. 'Then what?'

'She's depressed.'

Venus blinked. 'Huh?'

Spoiled, bitter, fame-hungry Lilly Bruin, depressed? Why? The film was hard work, with long days and a slave-driving director, but it was pulling together nicely. The dailies looked terrific, as though far more cash had been spent on the production. The jokes made people laugh, and when Venus showed the shots to the crew she'd caught a burly grip snuffling at one of the sad scenes. The actors were jazzed; everybody understood in their DNA that this flick was pulling together.

'De-pressed,' Keisha said slowly, as though Venus was being stupid. 'She wants to hang around between takes, she's moping, the light's gone out of her eyes, she's fluffing her fucking lines, and she's got the presence of a block of wood. It's like somebody gave me a different chick. I can't do this and keep this movie on schedule. I already shifted the scenes around so I can do a few of the buddy shots with Oliver and give her time to recover. But she's always sniffing and crying.'

'Does she say why?'

'Man trouble.' Keisha rolled her eyes. 'She's no fan of *you*, either.'

'I haven't taken her man. I haven't got a man.' Venus suddenly understood. 'You mean she's still on about Hans Tersch?'

'Never fucking stops, babe. I can't get her to give me an opinion on what she wants in her sandwiches, but she'll drag Hans into every conversation. And she thinks he's in love with you.' Keisha shook her head. 'You ask me, she's deliberately trying to ruin this film because she's obsessed. She thinks if it's a hit, you'll become a player, and you'll see Hans all the time. She's not mature enough to cope with it, you know.'

Venus sighed deeply. Hans would have enjoyed that tremendously. Two women fighting over him. He might yet have his revenge through Lilly.

'Send her in here.'

'What if she won't come?'

'Make her come.'

'Yes, boss,' Keisha said sarcastically, but she disappeared, and within half a minute there was a knock on the door.

'Come in.'

Lilly slouched into the office, glaring at her.

'Shut the door.'

Venus was shocked. Her slim, gorgeous star was now gaunt and pallid. Lilly's eyes were red, and she had dark circles under them. Her hair, which had been glossy, always blow-dried, was greasy, unwashed; Venus could see a rats' nest by her left ear, where Lilly hadn't been brushing.

'Take a seat.' She was playing for time.

'Don't want to,' Lilly muttered.

'Sit,' Venus barked. Lilly stumbled forward, into the plastic chair set in front of Venus's cheap Ikea desk, and looked daggers at Venus under her half-hooded lids.

'Keisha tells me you won't work.'

'I'm here. I show up every day. I say my lines.' Lilly shrugged aggressively. 'I'm fulfilling my contract and if you fire me I'll sue.' She scowled. 'You've got plenty of money, you can afford a big payout.'

'Lilly. I expect Keisha has been giving you pep talks?'

Lilly tossed her head, sullen. 'A lot of bullshit about how I'm only letting myself down. . .'

'You're right. It is bullshit.' Venus's eyes narrowed. 'And don't expect it from me. You're letting everybody down – the other actors, the crew, Keisha, me. But in the end, this movie is what stands between you, serious depression and a drugs overdose in some skanky rented flat in the East End.'

Lilly gaped at her.

'Yeah, that's right, I said it. So Hans Tersch fucked you and dumped you. Welcome to the club.'

Lilly gasped. 'What?'

'Something wrong with your hearing?' Venus knew she was laying herself open, wide open, to articles in the press, snide comments in the gossip columns. A Chambers girl admitting a one-night stand? And what if that got back to Uncle Clem? Would he wait to take the poker out of his arse before cancelling what remained of her trust fund?

But Venus couldn't think with her heiress hat on. Right now she was a producer, just a producer. And she had to shock Lilly out of this. If it took a little humiliation, then fine.

'It's what Hans does. Bangs girls, then dumps them. You know why we're sitting here? I slept with him, that night at the party.'

'When we met?'

Venus nodded. 'And I assumed he was going to cast me for Maud. When I get there, the audition's for an older woman's part. And he cast you anyway. So you think you got problems with the guy, take a number.'

'But . . .' Lily twisted in the chair, clearly unready to give up her prejudice quite that quickly. 'He went to your garden party. The one with all the royalty and millionaires. I *know*. I've got *friends*. I know he sat right next to you all through the meal.'

'He invited himself. And he didn't ask me out. He wanted to know how I'd landed you.'

Lilly almost jumped up from her seat. She sat straight, and the light flickered back to her eyes.

'He was talking about me? He was interested in me?' she asked eagerly. 'Do you think he might want to get back together?'

For a second, Venus debated yes-ing her to death. After all, she only needed the girl to keep it together for a few more weeks. It was a short shoot – after that, if Lilly went to pot, who the hell cared?

But her conscience stirred. Just a little. Enough not to lie. Lilly Bruin was talented. She was also very fragile. Venus couldn't take risks with her psyche. Hollywood littered the funeral parlours with its suicides and overdoses; she didn't want to get rich that way.

'You're not stupid, so don't act that way. Hans has zero interest in getting back with you. You were just a lay to him. He fucks starlets like you as often as he can. He's a goat, Lilly, and he's powerful and handsome and good in bed, and he thinks as long as the girl enjoyed herself, no harm done. But we know better,' she added with fellow feeling, and saw the tears brim in the younger girl's eyes.

'I liked him too. He's a very cool guy. Very masculine. It's just that he needs to be taught a lesson. You moping around and wrecking the one project that could revive your career, that's not going to help.'

'Do you think if I . . . got pretty again, and I was a big star, and rich, that he'd—'

'Absolutely not. He doesn't love you, Lilly. He might fuck you again, but he'll never love you.'

'But why not?' she wailed.

'Look. You're gorgeous. *Usually*. Have you had boys fall for you but you weren't interested in going any further? Maybe even ones you'd slept with?'

Lilly dashed away some tears, and stuck out her lower lip mutinously.

'Who the hell knows why we do anything? The heart wants what it wants.' She thought of Bai-Ling, Bob and Uncle Clem. 'Right now, Hans Tersch is just enjoying his virility. He doesn't want to commit. He especially doesn't want to lose – to you, or to me. The best thing you can do for yourself is smarten up and act your arse off. Then you'll be beautiful and famous, and before you know it you'll be Brad Pitt's next Hollywood consort.'

Lilly managed a tiny smile.

'Hans is too old for you. Believe me, you get yourself known and you can have your pick.'

'And you?' Lilly asked, still suspicious.

Venus was hoping she wouldn't ask. The answer would not please her. And furthermore, the question was going to force Venus to be honest with herself.

'I have a crush on Hans,' she answered simply. 'If he wanted to go out, I'd date him. But only if he was serious, Lilly, and I can assure you he's not. He'd like to bed me again, as well. But I wouldn't be his girl if he was unfaithful, even if he had a roving eye. One thing this whole episode has taught me is that I can only really rely on myself. So I have to respect myself, just a little bit. You do too.'

'What whole episode?'

Venus passed her a packet of Kleenex, realising she'd voiced her thoughts out loud.

'Never mind. Nothing that concerns you, I'm sorry.'

Lilly blew her nose and dabbed away more tears. She was a red-nosed, bleary-eyed mess.

'I'm sending you over to the new Victrix Hotel in Covent Garden.'

Lilly stared. 'It hasn't opened yet.'

'That's right. But my sister's designing it, and they're testing the spa. Very exclusive. You can take a shower, then they'll massage you, do your hair, nails, feet and make-up. Keisha will shoot around you. When you get back here, get ready to work. You're Lilly Bruin, not some rich old producer's plaything. You're a star, Lilly. *Be* one.'

'Wow.' Lilly nodded slowly, and Venus saw that the loathing in her eyes had been replaced by a kind of dim respect. 'You're right.'

'Of course I am. I quit acting because I didn't have what you do.' Venus waved her hand. 'Now get the hell out of here. Get over to Covent Garden.'

'OK,' Lilly said, and then, more definitely, 'OK! Thank you, Venus. I'll be fine now.'

'Better be,' Venus replied sternly to Lilly's departing back.

But she leaned back in her chair, and a deep contentment spread through her. That was my first big test as a producer, she thought, and I bloody well passed.

She was going to have to deal with Hans Tersch at some point. She realised that now. But she mentally shoved it on to the back burner. She needed to get the film done, get it into the edit suite, and then get it sold.

There was a knock on the trailer door.

'Come in,' Venus said.

It was Rio Jackson, their enthusiastic young runner; first-year film student, just thrilled to be on a set.

'Ms Chambers . . .'

'I told you, it's Venus.'

'There's a call on hold for you. Name of Paul Westfield. Said he was calling from New York.'

Westfield. The name took her right out of her reverie. He was her point man from Klaxon, the firm she'd hired to investigate Bai-Ling. Hell, Venus thought resentfully. She really didn't want to speak to him. She'd wasted too much time on Bai-Ling already. But he only rang when it was really important.

'Give me the phone.'

Venus took the mobile from him. 'Venus Chambers.'

'I have interim results.' The voice on the phone was clear and direct. Obviously these people did not waste a lot of time on small talk. 'We would like to present them to you in person.'

'Can you give me a summary?'

'I'm afraid not.'

Venus started to get angry. 'I'm the damned client, Mr Westfield.'

'You and your sister, Ms Chambers.' He was calm, obviously with no intention of backing down. 'The matter is highly confidential, and this is an open line. My judgement is that it needs a personal presentation.'

'I can get Diana conferenced in to the call.'

'That would not work either. We feel there is an issue of client safety.'

That took Venus aback.

'Safety?'

'As I said, this is a public line. Miss Chambers, you agreed to our policies when you signed the contract. We never do anything to imperil either our clients or the case they hired us for.'

Venus wanted to ask if he was joking, but his tone assured her he was not.

'Very well. Personal presentation.' She thought of her schedule. 'I'm a little busy right now. And I'd like my cousins and sister to be there too. Diana's in Rome.'

'How about next week? Monday?'

'Monday's fine. Can you come to our house, say eight p.m.?'

'Perfect. You have our number.'

Venus hung up. Monday. Well, at least she could get the other girls in, and Diana would be thrilled they'd made a contribution. She wondered anxiously what he'd have to say.

Venus grabbed the receiver on her phone and buzzed Carlton Bart, her editor; a precocious kid from film school who'd already impressed Keisha on an Apple commercial shoot.

'Carlton. Get in here,' she said.

Chapter Twenty-Three

The sun was setting over Rome. Diana stood against a railing at the top of the Campidoglio, looking out over the Roman Forum. It was a warm spring evening, and the stones beneath her feet seemed to radiate the heat that had soaked in during the day. She was high up here, and the view was spectacular. The Arch of Domitian reared in front of her; she could see past the Senate House, past the ruins of Caesar's temple, all the way to the walls of the Palatine Hill. It was spectacularly beautiful, and a wash of pleasure settled over her, sinking into her bones like the heat that permeated the ground.

She'd worked her arse off. There was no lounging about in restaurants, enjoying *spaghetti al'erbe* or *fragile di bosco*. Diana had taken over the building site that was the hotel, opposite St John Lateran, and over the last few days had designed in a frenzy. There would be no gyms this time, no spas. Diana thought about it deeply. Karl had told her this was big business, and not to fuck it up. The Victrix brand would be different from the others, the Hiltons and Savoys and all the upmarket chain brands. It had to encapsulate two things: first, ultimate luxury, and second, a sense of place. In Covent Garden, guests would be sunk into hip, modern, healthy London, the hub of consumer society. In New York, the hotels were already geared to the businessman. In Rome – well, in Rome she wanted the ultimate gastronomic experience, and the sense of the Eternal City.

Diana had brainstormed it out. Then she had jumped into action. Italy's traditionally sluggish workers stood no chance. Karl Roden's money would buy fast service. She insisted on that. The centrepiece of the Victrix Roma would be a fabulous restaurant, the best in a city that specialised in glorious food. She drew up contracts with the best *gelato* parlour in Rome, outside the Fontana di Trevi; she poached the most famous chefs, not just from the other great hotels, but also from the tucked-away little *trattorie* where the menus were in Italian and tourists didn't come. There was a Michelin-starred chef lined up, but she preferred the spectacular food from the sixty-year-old *nonna* who ran a little café in Trastevere.

The restaurant she placed on the top two floors, with windows floor to ceiling; guests would be able to drink in the beauty as they drank in their wine. And then there was the decor. How could she distinguish the Victrix? Every hotel in Rome used prints of the city, old framed drawings and paintings. Diana determined she would do better.

The Victrix Roma would *be* history. She hired two

curators and embarked on a major purchase of antiques. They would be displayed in the public spaces, in the restaurant, in the lobby, even in the most expensive suites. Walking into this hotel, guests would breathe in three thousand years of beauty. Diana bought statues, weapons, coins, jewels; from the Empire to the Renaissance, prehistoric to the war years. It would be a hotel, and it would be a museum. And on top of that, Diana thought, grinning, it would serve the most glorious Bellinis, made from fresh ripe peaches and vintage Krug.

Her excitement infected the site. The cooks, the curators, the interior designers, everybody got into the spirit. This would not be just another hotel.

'People will come to visit it even if they aren't staying here,' Diana vowed. 'We're outside the centre; this has to be a destination hotel.'

Giovanna Berlucci, the artistic director of the Museo della Repubblica, was standing beside her; she admired the bust of Brutus Diana had acquired at inordinate cost.

'*Sì. E magnifico,*' she purred.

'*Grazie.*' Diana inclined her head – and she did feel satisfied. The hotel would take months to decorate, staff and equip, but the vision was there – the theme, the all-important plan.

'You will be pleased,' Giovanna attempted some halting English, 'that Signor Roden will be able to see this himself *questa ventura.*'

'What? No.' Diana smiled ruefully. 'He'll see it when it's done. He's in New York, at head office.'

'No, no.' Giovanna smiled, her teeth crooked. 'He call me at the Museo. Want to know about your purchase of the *Roma Victrix* statue.'

Of course. The key piece for the central lobby. She had to buy it. How could the Victrix Roma not have *Roma Victrix*, divine *Rome Victorious*? But it had cost a major chunk of the budget; nine hundred thousand euros. Her confident mood evaporated. If Karl Roden thought she was being rash, a stupid spendthrift; worse, a dilettante . . .

'What did you tell him about it?' Diana asked, trying to sound casual.

'I tell him is major piece and you get for bargain.'

She relaxed, just a little. '*Grazie*, Giovanna.'

'*Ma è vero.*'

'*Io lo so . . .*' Diana agreed. 'So he was pleased?'

'Yes. And he come to see statue. Also, hotel.'

'He's coming here?' A flood of adrenalin hit her in the pit of the stomach, and she was instantly glad of the workmen and cleaners gathering around her in the chaos, which meant nobody could see her blush. 'Well, the project managers will show him around. I leave for England tomorrow, got to finish up the Covent Garden job. I'll be back when the hotel is ready to dress.'

'What time you leave tomorrow?'

'I have a flight at seven p.m.'

Giovanna smiled again, disturbingly; she was a hunched old Roman woman, toothy as a witch, but brilliant. 'That OK, you see him. He's coming here *a l'undici*.' At eleven. Diana opened her mouth. Giovanna was watching her carefully; she closed it hastily, trying to look composed.

'Then I suppose I'll just catch him,' she said.

'Uh-huh,' the curator replied, and the amusement in her tone needed no translation.

Diana had knocked off at five p.m. and walked back into the city. There was no point getting a taxi in Rome; everywhere you walked it was gorgeous, and she could keep the *gelato* off that way. She had invested in the latest limited-edition Marc Jacobs flats, and combined with a light silk trouser suit by Armani, she was cool and collected even under the Italian sun. Her own hotel was a tiny *albergo* next to the Theatre of Marcellus, and so she made the Forum her destination. Five minutes on the ledge, gazing out at the faded beauty here, restored her calm. Rome had once been the centre of the world. Now New York was. Her hotel for Karl Roden would marry both these together.

She chewed her lower lip. Would he see it that way? Covent Garden was an easier sell; the hotel had been almost fitted when she got hold of it. The Victrix Roma was still in construction chaos. Diana wanted Karl to see her vision finished, triumphant.

Instead, she was going to stick him in a hard hat and take him round a building site.

She wondered if she'd look good in a hard hat . . .

Come on. Don't be childish, she lectured herself, turning away from the iron railing. The Michelangelo-designed square of the Campidoglio was thinning out now, the tourists on their way back to their hotels to catch a bite to eat. She had not truly had a chance to enjoy Rome. But now she just wanted to get out, as quickly as possible.

Karl Roden. She had been icy cold about him the night they met. Not a suitable candidate for marriage. Not fit to replace Uncle Clem's trust fund . . .

And now?

Now she was feeling ashamed. She'd misjudged Roden, the guy who'd given her a chance – a chance to put aside the pampered, spoiled little party animal and actually *do* something with her life. She was working, and she relished it. Diana blushed for herself of a few short weeks ago. Marrying for money sounded like a great idea; all the girls on the circuit wanted to bag a billionaire. But now she didn't want to be Karl Roden's wife. She wanted to actually *be* Karl Roden.

Come on, she lectured herself, and started to walk briskly down the long stone staircase that descended from Santa Maria in Ara Coeli, the glorious church that had once stood as the temple of Juno Moneta. What would her own Juno, her cousin, say about this attitude?

Diana actually not wanting a rich husband . . . and hardly caring about the trust fund either. Away from England, Bai-Ling and the house in Notting Hill, all their little games appeared just that, games.

The sun started to sink, sending long shadows down from the neo-facist mausoleum of Victor Emmanuel II. Next to her hotel was a restaurant she loved, dark and a little claustrophobic, but it served the most fantastic food. She was going to enjoy a bottle of Brunello, a little bit of luxury, and a jugged hare, with a pasta starter of truffles and mushrooms, just a tiny helping, the way the Italians ate.

Diana tried to concentrate on that. She was getting carried away. This was only her second commission. She couldn't run her life on fifty thousand, even if Karl Roden did like the results. And she only had the one client. Whom she was starting to fantasise about . . .

Karl told me, Diana thought. He's not interested.

Besides, she'd seen the living-Barbie girlfriend. And even if this model had been dumped, an identical one would have taken her place; a girl with a skinny, lanky frame, not the wasp-waisted curves Diana was so proud of, her 1940s look. If Karl Roden preferred that model type, she could not compete.

And he'd already said he couldn't bed her and work with her. She had no other clients. The Covent Garden hotel wouldn't open for a month, the Victrix Roma another six. If you like your job, Diana lectured herself, don't even think about messing this up.

Fine. She strode along, acknowledging it. She was trying to reinvent her life. There was no place for useless crushes. She would go to the meeting tomorrow in her plainest suit and with no make-up. Meet Karl, describe what she was doing, excuse herself and leave.

Diana decided to skip the jugged hare and go for room service. She would get an early night. Maybe even try to call the house, talk to the other girls about Bai-Ling.

Anything to distract herself.

Nervous, Diana woke early. She pulled on a shirt dress, brushed her hair, applied a touch of tinted moisturiser and left for the Victrix. Roden would not arrive for several hours; she had a chance to set out the hotel. He had to see what she planned in the dust and rubble, while tiles were being laid and plumbing being piped. Diana had ordered plinths yesterday – she wanted to lay them in their places, hoped he had an active imagination. The windows, brand-new expanses of glass fitted into the building's Victorian frames, were in place in the upper floors; Diana would clear out the workmen, she thought, and at least show Karl the glories of the space, the view of St John Lateran, the great basilica, right in front of them, and the ancient walls of the city to the east.

After that was done, she would run back to her hotel, shower again, scrub her face and wear her ugliest outfit. There were some brogues packed, walking shoes, and a long skirt suit by Jean Muir that was, at least, a little shapeless. She didn't own anything truly ugly, and there was no time for shopping. But Diana was going to look as dowdy as she could. She walked fast; Rome was chilly in the early morning, but speed brought colour to her cheeks. She hadn't bothered with tights; her long legs were smooth and tanned, and her hair was shining, its chestnut base tone gleaming with natural coppery highlights, streaks of auburn and caramel from the sun.

But Diana couldn't pay attention to her appearance. She had grabbed her Gucci bag and a large pair of sunglasses, and she was half running out of the city. When she arrived at the hotel, she was a little out of breath. Flustered, she spied the tiny café opposite, with its breakfast bar where the Italians came to take their morning refreshment: a sweet pastry, possibly, but certainly a gorgeous little cup of espresso, thick and strong, served in a glass no bigger than an eggcup. It delivered that necessary jolt of caffeine in ten seconds flat. She made a mental note to stick such a bar in the lobby of the Victrix; the Americans and English would want full breakfasts in their room, but the locals, the Romans, whose seal of approval she desperately desired, would want their coffee.

Right now, she agreed. She ran across the road, interrupting the desperate flow of traffic, drivers suicidally careering through the main route into town, and ducked into the bar.

'*Buongiorno . . . un caffè, per favore*,' she gasped.

'*Ecco.*' The waiter slid a porcelain cup across to her, and Diana opened her handbag to pay.

'You're starting early.'

She jumped out of her skin. Karl Roden was standing right behind her. He was tanned, and wearing a sharply cut light wool suit, with black shoes and a thick platinum Rolex at his wrist. His dark eyes narrowed with amusement as she blushed.

'Karl! What are you doing here?'

'I believe I'm allowed to attend my own hotel,' he said mildly.

'I – yes, of course.' Diana fumbled in her purse for a couple of euros to cover her embarrassment. '*Grazie.*'

'*Prego.*'

'But I didn't expect you until eleven.' Diana knew she was flustered. Her cheeks were glowing from the dash across the road, her hair was tousled, she was wearing make-up, just a little, but enough. And she desperately wanted to do up the top button on her shirt dress.

'I prefer to come early. That way I can see the site before anybody gets a chance to pretty it up.' Roden looked at her, his eyes flickering across her. 'Is that why you got here so soon? Going to dress the site for me?'

Defeated, she admitted it. 'Of course.'

He nodded towards her espresso. 'Drink it. It's good.'

Obediently, Diana tossed it down. The liquid was hot and fragrant, although she didn't feel like she needed any more energy right now. Oh God! He was so attractive, standing there with his salt-and-pepper hair and that sensual, cruel mouth. A rush of excited nerves was making her jittery; she avoided his gaze.

'We'll go over now.' Roden moved past her, put his own tiny cup back on the counter; Diana had to force herself not to start when his sleeve brushed against her dress. 'You can talk me through what you've done. Let's see if you've earned your commission.'

'But it's not ready,' Diana protested. 'It's a building site.'

He shrugged. 'Do you think I'd wait till you had finished a costly refit to approve or disapprove? I do this for a living, Diana. As much as it may surprise you, I do have *some* experience.'

She gulped. 'Yes – of course.' Got to stop saying 'of course'. 'I'll show you then.'

Karl opened the door and walked out. Diana followed him, glad of a moment's respite to collect herself and stop acting like a giggly schoolgirl. She knew she was sweating and warm from her brisk walk; not perfect, not groomed. So much the better. Look on the bright side, she thought. At least you can go to the airport a few hours earlier.

The hotel site was almost deserted. Nobody was there but two security guards, who yawned as they waved Diana through.

'Where are the workmen?' Karl asked, as they entered the cool marble shade of the lobby.

'You have to be kidding.' She was glad of the chance to talk business. 'It's not even eight a.m. You're in Italy, Karl. Price of doing business.'

'Then they're slow?'

'My crew works longer hours than any in the city, but it's still slower than New York or London.' Diana shrugged. 'Look, they also take more care with the craft and conservation of the building . . . they truly love this place. It used to be a *palazzo*. I don't think you'll be disappointed.'

He didn't reply. 'Tell me about the Victrix Roma. This will be one of the main flagships on the Continent, after Paris and Berlin.'

Diana found she was terribly nervous. Karl was not flirtatious in the least. He was looking down an empty corridor, where nothing was beautiful other than the dusty marble walls and the elegant proportions. Would she be able to make him see it, thronging with well-heeled tourists, filmmakers, and captains of industry?

'I see the hotel as expressing Rome. We're not in the centre of town, so it has to be a destination hotel. My themes are history and luxury.'

'Go on.' But his expression was impassive.

'The hotel will have the standard five-star fittings. But you need something else, something no other place in Rome has. On one level we're going to compete on competence; I'm fitting out and staffing the best restaurant in the city.'

He looked sceptical, and Diana felt her heart sink just a little. 'A bold claim,' he said.

'I've poached all the most famous chefs, and then the Italian ones only the cognoscenti know. I've even invested in *gelato* makers and cocktail mixers. The Victrix has offered them a platinum compensation package.'

'At my expense?'

Diana didn't flinch; he would eat her alive if she did.

'Yes, boss. At your expense.'

For a second, she thought she saw a flicker of pleasure in the chestnut irises when she called him that. Her heart thrilled, and she lowered her gaze in case he saw it.

'The walls on the upper floors are being replaced with glass, so diners can look out over the city while the sun sets. American luxury, Italian cuisine.'

'We'll have a look at that later. But you said "on one level".'

She nodded. 'Knockout food depends on the chefs. The other aspect of this hotel is going to be history. That's expensive, a lot more so than the restaurant. In fact,' she blanched slightly, 'I've allocated every penny of the budget to it and I want to spend more.'

'Describe history.'

'The Victrix as museum. All the best rooms will have real antiques from the various periods in the city, but the public spaces will have truly spectacular pieces. From *Roma Victrix* in the lobby to our bust of Brutus in the main corridor on the ground floor; sightseers will come just to view the pieces, and take tea in the orangery – at great expense. Staying here will be the ultimate class act.'

'Yes.' He nodded. 'Walk me around the placing of your major artefacts.'

Diana led him around the site. 'There's a third-century Apollo here, and there's a sketch after Michelangelo over on the far wall . . . I'm bidding on a helmet and sword from Caesar's Gallic legions for the entrance to the dining hall. This niche will hold a fine statue of the empress Julia Domna, nothing missing but the tip of the nose . . .'

They finished in the back garden. Diana showed him her design: rich box hedges, lavender, orange and lemon, and papery white olive trees.

'Giovanna told me about your plan for this spot.' Roden sat down on the antique iron bench, imported from Spain, that Diana had installed next to the fountain; great arches of water sparkled in the sun. 'You were going to put in statues of goddesses, based on you and your cousins: Diana, Juno, Athena and Venus.' She blushed, caught out in her moment of vanity. It was true. But she had intended it to be a private joke. They were fine specimens, the statues, and she had billed his company for tens of thousands. Karl's gaze was impenetrable. She wondered with horror if she was going to lose her commission over this.

'You look shocked. Those are the names, right? The famous Chambers girls?'

Diana nodded, dry-mouthed.

'What, you thought I wouldn't check up on you? Your little refit job has already maxed out our budget for this site.'

'I'm sorry. I just thought it might be amusing . . . They really are very fine statues, Karl, and they'll look beautiful in this garden . . .' Diana's voice trailed off. 'Look, it was a joke, but not at the expense of the hotel. I take this very, very seriously.'

'Hey.' For the first time he smiled, and she suddenly heard the dry, mocking tone that had crept into his voice. 'I'm not mad. I'm . . . intrigued.'

A wave of relief washed over her, and Diana found her legs were dissolving into jelly. She reached out discreetly and steadied herself on a stone wall. Hoping he wouldn't notice.

'So.' She forced herself to sound brisk and business-like. 'What do you think? Early stages, but the Victrix Roma should be distinctive.'

He smiled openly then, like the sun bursting out from behind a tall building.

'Yeah, very good. The museum concept is perfect. People need to get perfection at all my joints, but not in a cookie-cutter way. I'll up your budget, another million euros. Get some quirky artefacts, as well as the high-class pieces. Talking points. Water-cooler art.'

Diana got it at once. 'A child's toy, an ad for a brothel . . .'

'Bring Ancient Rome to life.'

She glowed. 'Thanks, boss. I will.'

'And don't call me boss,' he said.

'Why not?' she laughed, delighted to have pleased him.

'Because it turns me on when you say it.'

Diana froze, hardly daring to breathe or meet his eyes. Slowly she dragged her gaze up to face him. Roden was looking at her, assessingly, deliberately. She tried and failed to stop the rich, deep blush that spread up her neck to her cheeks. And as for her dress, Diana thought, it might as well have been made of lace; her body tensed and responded to his stare as though she were wearing nothing more than a bikini.

'Oh dear,' Roden said unrepentantly. 'Come back with me to the Hassler. We have to talk about this.'

They sat together in the lobby of the hotel, the finest in Rome; Diana could not match its location at the top of the Spanish Steps, but she was sure she would destroy it as a destination hotel. But she could not think about the job here. Karl had checked his messages and joined her, sitting opposite, close enough for their knees to touch. And Diana had no idea how to think; her heart was thumping, her breathing was shallow. She could lose her job, or lose her heart. And she wanted neither.

'Karl . . .'

He lifted one hand. 'Age before beauty. I'll go first, then you can say whatever you like.'

'OK.' She shrugged, surrendering. He would have his way.

'You've had an inspired idea for two of my hotels now. I've just discussed your meals-and-monuments thing with a couple of people. They all loved it. You got paid twenty-five last time because you came in late and improved my hotel. This time you designed it. You get a proper commission. Here.'

He reached into his jacket pocket and pulled out a brown envelope. 'In Italy they call this a *bolla*.'

Her hands trembling, Diana opened it, and gasped. There was a check for a hundred thousand pounds, made out to her little company.

'You can't be serious. This is too much money.'

Karl shook his head. 'You have to do some research, Diana. You've got a talent for this field, but you'll need to study up if you want to make some money. Actually, that's a pretty small commission for the size of the job. Most interior designers might make that on an upmarket Fifth Avenue condo. They'd take a percentage of the overall budget.'

'So it's too little money?'

'It's a respectable fee because you've got no track record, and because I always buy at a discount. I'm in it for profit, too.' His voice roughened a little. 'In fact, I'm being tougher on you to prove that I never let other considerations get in the way of business.'

'Then thank you for the fee,' Diana said softly. She

slipped the envelope into her Gucci bag. In under a month she'd made one hundred and twenty-five thousand pounds. It still didn't compare to Uncle Clem's trust fund, but this money was infinitely more precious.

'Let me give you a little advice: use the cash to hire a great PR. Get the word out. Your toughest time will be now, finding another commission.'

'But you have more hotels to renovate.'

'Yeah; and I don't know where I'm going to find anybody with your touch. That's my big problem.'

'I can suggest somebody sitting right opposite you,' Diana teased. But she knew where he was going with this, and her body tensed with anticipation, waiting for him to say it.

'I can't work with you. I'm extremely attracted to you.'

'But you went to New York.'

'It didn't work,' Roden said, with a shrug. 'Thought about you all the time. I guessed it was rebound stuff from Suzie. So I came over here. Partly to see the hotel. A lot more to see you. Remind myself you weren't all that hot, get you out of my system.' He grinned. 'Only you are all that hot.'

Diana touched her hand to her throat, feeling herself break out into a light mist of a sweat. 'Don't be dumb.'

'Interesting way to talk to your boss.'

She drew back her shoulders, sitting upright. 'You're not my boss any more. You're an ex-client. And I know the kind of chick you date. I met Suzie, remember? She's straight out of the Barbie factory. Look at me. I'm not super-skinny, I have dark hair and curves, I'm not even made up.'

'Fishing for compliments doesn't suit you,' Karl replied. 'You must know how beautiful you are.'

Diana paused. She wanted him, desperately. But she was starting to see herself differently, and she liked it. She didn't want to stop now. Bravely, she lifted her chin.

'I know I'm a pretty girl, Karl. But there are degrees of these things. The day I was with Suzie, I was invisible, pretty much. She stops traffic. A man like you typically dates a woman like that. I don't want to be anybody's one-night stand, and I don't want to be dumped when somebody introduces you to a twenty-two year old on her first major modelling deal. So while yes, I admit I find you . . . somewhat attractive,' she could not stop the blush, but kept her voice steady, 'and yes, I would like to go out with you, I'm not going to.'

He sat back in his chair and stared at her. Then he laughed.

'You're a very strange woman, Miss Chambers.'

'Thank you.'

'What would your parents say?'

Diana's pretty face clouded. 'My parents are dead, Karl. My father was a drunk driver. He killed himself and my mother.'

'I'm very sorry,' he said sincerely.

'I looked after my sister Venus. We're the only family we have. Until my uncle . . .' She stopped herself. 'Growing up without parents changes you, it shapes your whole life. I want to stand on my own two feet. You see, I'm not ready to be somebody's diversion, even yours. I want marriage, a family, the whole bit. What my parents refused to give to me.'

Roden smiled. 'You blame your father; I understand that. But it sounds like you're refusing me before I've done anything wrong.'

'Sorry,' Diana said, and this time she managed to hold his gaze. 'But it's for the best.'

Roden chuckled. 'That's sweet. You're under the impression that this is over. You don't know me too well, Diana. I don't tend to give up easily.'

'Maybe not, but you don't know me either. I mean what I say.'

'You're not exactly giving me a chance to get to know you. Look. How about this? You let me take you to dinner. You owe me that much, at least.'

'I don't know.'

'Your reputation won't suffer. Client and designer having a meal together. If you don't want to see me again, I promise not to bug you about it . . . for at least two weeks.'

'Two weeks!'

'Like I said, I'm not giving up. You're giving me a reputation I don't deserve. Yes, I've dated women based solely on looks, but as you rightly point out, Suzie was exceptionally gorgeous. I'm not with her now.'

Diana hadn't thought of it that way before.

'And this is Rome. I could make a call, go to a nightclub and be surrounded by fifty aspiring starlets, assorted models and Eurotrash socialites with platinum-blond hair down to their asses. Men like me always have that option. A beautiful girl isn't a rare thing in the world I move in. But you're different; you have fire.' He leaned forward, and looked directly into her eyes; his assured, confident manner was turning Diana on, and she reflexively pressed her knees together. 'When I first met you, I thought you were good-looking. At that dinner party. If you thought I was flirting with you, I was. I might have wanted to take you to bed. But I had no real respect for you. You reminded me of my first wife, elegant, polished, turned out to be a gold-digger.'

'Don't sit on the fence. Tell me what you really think.'

He grinned again. 'You can take it, baby. You dish it out easy enough.'

'Why did you marry her, then?'

'I was young, and she was sexy. But when my business started to go wrong in its third year, when we had a credit crunch and overextended, and I lost a hotel in Boston and had to raise cash against my own houses . . . she went very cold, and she cheated on me. Hence my divorce. Now when I met you, I was attracted, not a lot more. It was when you came to see me in my office that that started to change. I'd thought you were just another pretty husband-hunter; evidently not. You surprised me, Diana, and not too many women do that.'

She didn't know what to say. She could hardly protest; it had been true, hadn't it? And now she was glowing from his compliments. She had slaved to win his respect, and in doing so found a little of her own.

'You'll come to dinner,' he added, and it was a statement, not a question.

'Yes.' She surrendered. 'I'll come to dinner. But not tonight. I've got to get back to London; my flight is booked.'

'I'll take you back. My private jet flies to Heathrow tonight.' Roden smiled. 'You can multitask: fly back and have dinner on the plane. There are plenty of staff to chaperone you, don't worry. And if you're ashamed to have a date with a playboy, there's the added advantage that only the stewardesses will see you.'

'OK.' Diana relaxed slightly, allowed herself to smile back. She wasn't going to let herself fall for Karl Roden. She liked him too much. She had anxiety deep in her belly as to what would happen when he found somebody else; if she allowed herself to get in too deep, she would drown, her heart would break.

But it pleased her very much that he liked her. It wasn't one way; he was attracted, he was actually chasing her. She was proud of herself for not jumping when he offered. One dinner wouldn't hurt. Diana would enjoy being wooed by a man like Karl, even if it was for a single night. She thought she deserved it.

Diana picked up her Louis Vuitton case and carried it downstairs. It was light enough; she had packed intelligently, and all her clothes were neatly folded away between sheets of acid-free tissue paper. The drying-up of Uncle Clem's money could not be allowed to affect her sense of luxury. Diana knew she had to be immersed in that because of her job, to give herself the finest things and expect them from others. A great hotel was only as good as its fussiest customer. She would stay in the best places, drink the best wine, wear the best shoes, and pack the ideal summer wardrobe elegantly, with tissue paper, the way her butler had once done on her behalf.

She felt a little excitement. A taxi to the airport, and then seeing Karl again. Everything she'd done that afternoon had failed to distract her. A walk around the Forum; yes, very lovely, but her eyes had hardly focused. A trip to the Vatican, ditto; a waste of time to queue in St Peter's Square for an hour when she'd got inside the epic glory of the basilica and was still counting the minutes till she could check out. In fact Rome could offer nothing. At four o'clock Diana had cracked, and hurried back to her hotel to blow-dry her hair and triple-check her make-up.

'I hope everything was to your satisfaction?'

Diana blinked; the desk clerk was asking her a question.

'Oh yes. Very much so. If I could just have the bill . . .'

The receptionist stared blankly.

'*Il conto, per favore.*' Perhaps his English was limited. The Victrix Roma's reception staff were to be recruited from the language departments of Roman universities and trained up.

'No, the bill, I understand, madam. It has already been paid. Mr Roden has taken care of it.'

She blushed. 'I would rather pay myself.'

He spread his hands, a particularly Latin gesture. '*Non posso.* Signor Roden is very powerful, I don't make him mad – *per piacere?*'

Diana nodded. 'No problem.'

'*Grazie,*' he said gratefully.

'Could you just call me a taxi?'

A little nervously, the young man shook his head.

'No taxi either?'

'He sends a car for you, madam, very nice car, limousine.' He looked at her pleadingly. 'He give me big tip if you take his car. Very romantic, madam, *il signor Roden è molto simpatico . . .*'

Yes, well, she was sure he was very *simpatico* indeed if you were getting a massive tip for strong-arming your customers into his cars. But Diana couldn't get angry. The boy was poor; she had no right. And anyway, he was smiling at her with real warmth, appreciating Roden's romantic streak. This in a country where they adored every toddler and applauded every bride.

'*Non c'è problema*,' she shrugged.

The door to the hotel swung open magically, and a uniformed chauffeur appeared, touched his cap, and picked up her case.

'Good evening, Ms Chambers.' His accent was perfect New York, and Diana thrilled with excitement to hear it. 'Mr Roden sends his compliments, ma'am, and asks if I can take you to the plane. He asked me to tell you he's seen how the Italians drive and he'd prefer it if you got there alive.'

'Fine.' Diana nodded, let herself be led out to the car; a luxuriously equipped Lexus. He opened the door, and she slid into the cavernous back seat. There was a silver bucket full of ice and chilled vintage Pol Roger champagne, and, her heart beat faster to see, an elegant bouquet of long-stemmed roses in sorbet colours, tied simply with a green grosgrain ribbon. She tried to tell herself that it was corny, only it didn't feel corny. And as she settled back against the buttery leather seats, the interior of the car filled with the scent of the blooms, Diana struggled mightily against a rising sense of joy.

'This way, madam. Thank you.'

A courteous steward was ushering her across the tarmac. Diana had been whisked, incredibly fast and discreetly, through the airport. The stars were out now, and it was a cold evening. Her Burberry mac wasn't up to the strange chill of a brisk Italian night; but an air hostess, dressed in the Victrix insignia, had rushed up to her with a huge, thick brushed cashmere cape, the softest grey, that draped around her like a blanket.

'I know,' Diana said, 'with Mr Roden's compliments.'

'*Sì, signora.*'

Now she was walking slowly over the floodlit ground, the stars receding against the artificial light, swathed in pure cashmere. The corporate jet was enormous; it looked practically like a passenger plane. And there was the familiar Victrix logo emblazoned right across it. It was incredibly impressive.

Diana tugged the soft cloak tight around her. A whirl of emotions chased themselves across her heart like autumn leaves blown up in a storm. Excitement. The stirrings of arousal. This display of wealth was like a peacock fanning his feathers, she knew that, but it still worked. How could a woman not be attracted to such a visceral display of dominance? Karl Roden wanted to show her he had taken on the world and conquered. And then there was fear, and nerves. She had to keep her cool, keep her resolve. He might conquer Wall Street, but not her. Nothing's changed, she told herself firmly, as she stared up at the jet. Nothing at all . . .

Roden was still a lone wolf. Jetting all round the world, buying hotels, attending the biggest parties. And she wasn't interested in being any man's arm-candy. She wanted a career at home, and eventually more. Like marriage. Diana carefully voiced the thought in her head. Karl had called her a 'husband-hunter', dismissively. Maybe she wasn't the same billionaire-seeking missile she'd been at Hans Tersch's dinner, but she was still husband-hunting. For very different reasons. And Karl Roden was not the type to be tied down to wedding cake and nappies.

It's a fantasy, she thought, and there was a stab of sadness in the midst of all her jittery nerves.

Because the more she saw of this guy, the more she liked him.

The metal steps up to the front cabin door were lined with soft blue carpet in the Victrix colours. No expense spared even there, Diana thought. She walked up them with trepidation, wondering if her hair was all right, if her make-up was perfect. Roden was standing in the open doorway, waiting for her. He caught sight of her, and desire leaped into his eyes, naked and intense.

Under her cloak, Diana's skin flushed hot. Forget rationalisation; she was unbearably thrilled to see his reaction to her.

Three hours to Heathrow. She hoped her self-control could last that far.

Chapter Twenty-Four

'I'm sorry.' The voice on the end of the phone was soft, modulated, English and absolutely firm. 'I cannot put you through. Ms Wuhuputri is asleep.'

'I told you, I'm her fiancé,' Clement rasped, his papery voice lifted with rage. He controlled his world, every element of it. Now some wretched functionary was refusing him. 'I'm Clement Chambers. Of the Chambers Corporation.'

'Yes, sir.'

'Do you know who I am?'

'Yes, sir, I do, but our guest has placed an absolute privacy block on her room, sir.'

Clement patted his wrist, stroking the blue vein to check his pulse. He did not want to set his heart racing. He must monitor his blood pressure. This bitch could kill him.

'It's not her room, it's my room. I've paid for it. My credit card. So put me through to my room, damn you!'

'The room is booked in Ms Wuhuputri's name, sir.

That is the policy of the hotel. We don't interrupt our guests.'

'Put me through to the manager, goddamn you!' Clement snarled.

'I'm afraid he's in a meeting, sir, but I can take a number and have him call you back.'

Clement slammed down the receiver, seething. He would find out who that woman was, and have her fired. Trembling with rage, he started to gnaw at his finger-nails. What the hell. Was his little joke going desperately, embarrassingly wrong? He imagined his fiancée cavorting with her stud at this very minute, in one of London's most prestigious hotels. A woman everybody knew was his fiancée. Fucking some moron from the health club. The staff would be chuckling, society would be sniggering. He, Clem Chambers, would be a cuckolded old fool.

Stupid, stupid Bai-Ling. She thought she was being discreet, of course. But Clement's tails were good, very good. Ex-CIA, recruited in the Lebanon and used widely all over the world. It had given him the ultimate advantage in business many times. And now he'd decided to play around, in his old age, three of the best were set to watching Bai-Ling.

They were there to ensure that she did not embarrass him. To check whether she was hellishly out of her depth in London society. She was useful, useful in his relationship with the girls, but obviously that depended on Clem reading her right. And he'd been certain he'd got the measure of her. She passed the first test beautifully, knocking back Juno's obstacle course in etiquette. Since then, his spies had filed reports that pleased him: Bai-Ling half starving herself, trying to diet her razor-thin body into nothing, eliminate her small curves, so she could be the way he liked her. But then . . .

The gym. She was working her body, but with a man. A straight man. A man with a reputation, as Clem quickly found out. Sessions at first once daily, soon three times. And then one of his operatives photographed the man's hand travelling towards Bai-Ling's buttocks and caressing them as she worked a weight machine.

Oh, she was careful. Which made him angrier. The way the trainer left separately, then met her in cafés and hotels far from the original workout spot; how they never ate in public, merely disappeared into various places, where Bai-Ling inevitably paid in cash.

His fiancée was screwing some young stud. Once the business press got hold of that . . .

Today he was going to call her, summon her home, and deal with her. Bai-Ling knew enough about Clement Chambers not to mess with him. The end would have to be managed, so that no scandal, no taint of mockery, attached to it . . . The old fool and the young girl. But she was the fool. Risking everything, he thought with utter contempt, for the sake of a little friction.

And now it had escalated. His most trusted man had

called with the bad news. The woman had taken her trainer, Bob Russell, to her *own* hotel. At night. Filled with horror at her inanity, Clement had called her direct.

To find the block put on her room.

Was she in her room, paid for by him, screwing this man? Was the little tart that infatuated? Conspiracy theories, the sound of mocking laughter, filled his head.

And the girls. Why hadn't they cracked, why hadn't they called him? By now, with their allowances halved, they were supposed to be on the phone, or better still, on a plane. Wheedling and begging. He was looking forward to that, had been for a few years. Watching to see if they proved themselves worthy heirs to his fortune. Wanting them to pay him the proper respect. Juno to get pregnant; Athena to groom herself like a lady, and stop hanging around dusty classrooms; Venus to give up acting and behave like a girl of breeding; Diana to find a decent husband before she got too old and drop the trashy parties with the trashy people.

If only there had been a boy. But there was no boy. Clement was a dynast, and the Chambers girls must learn that they took their name, their fortune, their very *raison d'être* from him. Before he died, he would mould them in his image.

And, of course, the ultimate choice. Clem had no intention of dividing the estate. His brothers had never actually asked him, of course, but he knew they had resented it. Resented his great rise to wealth and power, resented his life of complete luxury; even resented his bankrolling their disappointing sets of daughters. But true dynastic power didn't allow great fortunes to be split up. One of his yearly pleasures had been watching the four cousins attempt their best behaviour in his presence whilst indulging in little catfights all around his estate. They could hardly spend a couple of weeks together without scratching each other's eyes out.

Wait until they understood his purpose.

That just one would inherit the lot.

The other three would receive sufficient money to live well: a couple of mil apiece. But one consequence of wealth was that you always, always wanted more.

The fight would be bitter. It would be epic. It would be highly amusing. He would relish it.

But what was going on? The girls were not writing. They were not calling. They were seeing Bai-Ling, taking her to wedding parlours. One of his men had remote mikes; Clem had listened to a couple of the conversations. It was obvious to him they hated Bai-Ling; he could tell from the inflexions of their voices. Yet the battle to remove her had slowed.

It was almost as if they didn't care.

They had to care. They simply had to. Clement breathed in, aware he was getting agitated. It was defiance, that was what it was. Bai-Ling reducing him to ridicule, his chosen heiresses indifferent. What means did they have? What were they prioritising over him?

He pushed the chair back on its well-oiled wheels and lumbered slowly to his feet. Clement loathed taking his plane anywhere. The divisions of his empire, jewels, gold mines, shipping, all of them were run now by excessively well-compensated corporate titans. He was retired, and reclusive. The Palms was his retreat, and it was his tropical world, ordered precisely as he wished it.

When you stepped outside, you faced dissent. Rebellion. *Disrespect*. The way he had just done from some two-bit little receptionist. That was why Clement loathed the idea of leaving his safe haven.

But . . .

The thought came, unbidden, of the trainer fucking Bai-Ling, in the room that he'd paid for, the staff knowing about it.

Of Diana in Rome, and Juno in Scotland, not pursuing her, not bloody *caring*.

Venus on set with some junkie tart, Athena running around the House of Commons . . . both of them taking Bai-Ling along to get her trousseau, as though the loss of Clem's cash really didn't bother them.

He hated it. The women were slipping from his control. However distasteful, there was only one thing to do. He had set the hare running, and he was going to have to finish it.

He cleared his throat. 'Mendelsohn!'

His private secretary, a distinguished American lawyer, raced into the room.

'Yes, sir?'

'Order my jet to be ready. I may go to England.'

'Excuse me?'

'Are you deaf?' barked Clement.

'No, sir. Your jet. Right away.'

'Advise the people in Eaton Square that I may be coming. Get my measurements across to them and make sure there is a first-class valet in place for when I arrive.'

'Absolutely. How long might you be away, sir?'

Clement thought about it. How long would this take? The quicker, the better. He wanted the girls in hand and Bai-Ling disappeared.

'Two weeks,' he said, shrugging.

That would be long enough. It had to be.

The house was well lit, even though the nights were already getting longer. Juno liked to keep the lights blazing. If there was the slightest chill in the air, she had the maid lay fires in all the downstairs room; when it was bright, and warm, the place kept her depression at bay slightly.

It had been a hard couple of days. Long and busy. She had taken a full afternoon with the bank manager, showed him the completed contract for her first apartment, then used it as security to borrow against the place in Paris. It was a brilliant idea, and Juno was now shopping to order. She had the client lined up before she signed an option to purchase. In four days, she had bought three apartments on ultra-short leases. And she now had money in the bank; not much, a total of forty-two thousand, but it was money of her own.

She had even leased a room in a house in Richmond that rented office space and a desk. And she had already hired a temp from an agency. It was a start in business, just that, a start. But it made Juno feel good.

Face it. She needed all the work she could get. The confrontation with Jack was necessary, but it had been terrible. Juno tried, but she could not forget him. The man was locked in her brain.

Worse than that. Locked in her heart.

And of course, he was gone for ever. He was dating a younger woman. He had plenty of money of his own. If Juno even tried to get him back, it would look like gold-digging. Her pride absolutely forbade it.

And it still hurt to think of him, around, in the country, succeeding, happy. Without her. The invitation to meet Mona had burned her heart like a red-hot brand searing the side of a cow.

Venus had called Juno with the news. Her private investigator had a case to present. Had Juno known about it before Diana and Venus clubbed together, she would have stopped them. A sleazy detective digging around the family's affairs? But it was too late now, and Juno's heart was aching. She was busy. In fact, she hardly cared. If Uncle Clem was stupid enough to get engaged to a gold-digger young enough to be his granddaughter, then maybe he deserved it.

The hideous thing was that even if her uncle dumped Bai-Ling tomorrow, all the money in his bank account wouldn't fix Juno's problems now.

She had finally fallen in love with her husband. Just as he was gone.

But the other girls were coming home anyway. Numbly, on autopilot, Juno laid out a tray of drinks, some olives and cheese biscuits, and a silver coffee service. She was still the natural family hostess. They would hold this meeting, listen to their guest. They might as well.

Athena parked her Aston Martin in the drive and rested in the seat for just a second. She was wiped out with exhaustion; they had been decorating all day long. She hadn't told Juno, but just about all her remaining nest-egg was now sunk in the place. It was crazy, maybe, but Athena loved the concept and she was desperate to get going. She'd torn up the rule book. There was no reason building had to take months. That depended on how many guys you had on site. In a burst of inspiration, she had hired four separate crews, and within days the club's wiring and plastering had all been finished; they painted, hammered, sawed, moved like an army of constructive termites across the old cinema. And she paid well and treated them better, ordering pizza, Cokes, water, beer at the end of the day. A team of decorators were in there now, carefully placing her interior-designed furniture. Every piece in the club, every sofa, every painting, every rug, had been designed or made by a woman. It was her theme, and it was almost ready to go.

Tomorrow the place would open. Not a grand opening. Quite the reverse: discreet, no journalists allowed, unless they were members, in which case they had to sign a confidentiality agreement. No, the press would come through rumours, word of mouth. If she'd done her job right.

It was all Athena could think about right now. Not this, not Bai-Ling. She'd done her part, setting Bob on the girl. Soon it would be time to see what money could buy. But there was an unspoken partnership amongst the Chambers girls; they were living in the house together, for a reason. And Diana and Venus, her cousins, wanted to contribute. The investigator was their shot. She had to be here, had to waste time on this. It was family business.

Athena sighed and got out of the car. Juno would have everything ready. It was only April, and already Athena was sick of this life. She had the disloyal thought that perhaps it'd be wonderful if Bai-Ling and Uncle Clem just got married anyway. And the Chambers girls forgot all the games . . .

But no: Boswell House was in danger. The Bluestocking Club wouldn't make a dime this year. And Freddie . . . well, they had only just started properly dating, and he had no money anyway.

She shrugged. Guess she had to go through with it. Athena tossed her cashmere shawl over her shoulder and strolled in through the front door.

Diana tried to concentrate. This was her meeting, hers and her sister's. It mattered, of course it did. Karl Roden wasn't the only man in the world with a private jet. And what could she do with the business with her half-mil a year restored to her?

But her heart wasn't in it. There was the matter of the advert to think about. She'd spent a thrilling day in the boutique Soho agency of Carter, Burghley & Corton, the hottest little shop in London, and given them what she could afford. They had come up with a smart photograph of the Victrix London gym and the restaurant in the Roma hotel; the spaces looked effortlessly chic. Underneath, cursive script declared *Chambers Design. Public and Private Commissions*. Then there was a phone number and the fax for her tiny office in Islington.

It looked very cool, very professional. Where to place it? Diana had decided on her market: upscale and niche. She was spending half her commission to date advertising in *Wallpaper*, the funky design mag, in the *Standard*, and in *House Beautiful*. A risk, sure, but you had to spend it to make it . . .

Karl had offered to introduce her to more clients. It took all she had, but Diana turned him down. If she got her commissions through him, she would be even deeper in his pocket. And Diana didn't trust herself to think straight.

She walked in through the front door; Athena was hanging up her coat.

'Coming in?'

'I'll be right there,' Diana promised, running up the stairs to her room.

She wanted to get changed. Something light for the evening, for their warm drawing room. New clothes might take her mind off the design business, help her to concentrate. Get her mind off Karl.

She pulled off her trouser suit and selected a shirt dress in watered yellow silk, with a matching cardigan by Karen Millen. Perfect; add some Jimmy Choo platforms, and she was dressed. Carefully, Diana laid her BlackBerry on her bed. The text messages from Karl Roden had kept coming. She couldn't focus while they were in her handbag, and she couldn't quite bring herself to delete them.

Hell, Diana thought regretfully. I have *got* to stay away from that man. He was too sexy, just too powerful, too everything. She silently thanked God for the little summit downstairs. Anything to get her mind off him.

Venus arrived in Notting Hill late. Shit. There were the girls' cars, and a black limo with foreign plates. Must be the spook. She imagined Juno's thunderous disapproval. They'd all be in the drawing room, making strained small talk over a glass of Chablis and waiting for her. But she had an excellent excuse: the movie had wrapped, and she'd spent her very first day in the edit suite. It was looking good, even at this raw stage, looking *really* good. Lilly was luminous, a bona fide star. Much more than a looker; the girl could absolutely act. And her very desperation leaped off the screen, made the performance more than comic. It was a funny film with a dark heart. And it was going to rock.

She shrugged. Well, the other girls could be as mad as they wanted. She, Venus Chambers, was going to earn her reputation as the bad seed, she thought defiantly. Because right now she couldn't care less about Bai-Ling, the money, the wedding, or anything other than getting this done so she could get right back to the edit suite.

She needed that print. Once she had it, she thought fiercely, it would be time to teach Herr Tersch something of a lesson. For Lilly's sake. And her own.

Venus slipped off her coat as she walked into the drawing room. Yes, the other three girls were there: her sister, Diana, looking like a particularly gorgeous buttercup, and Athena and Juno sitting together on the chesterfield sipping long gin and tonics. Juno frowned, on cue, but Venus didn't get the death stare that she had expected.

Paul Westfield was standing in front of the fireplace. He was short, and wore a beautifully cut relaxed suit – Armani, she thought.

'Sorry. Edit problems,' Venus said.

She waited for somebody to challenge her, but nobody did. That came from her lack of parents. She was always waiting to be challenged, scolded, given boundaries. But her father had crashed the car, and Venus had taken a lifetime, up until now, to learn – very slowly – that she had to discipline herself.

Diana looked around and cleared her throat.

'We apologise for keeping you waiting, Mr Westfield. Please go ahead.'

'Thank you,' he said. Venus noted he was giving no sign of impatience. Maybe you had to deal with things like this in his job.

Besides, she thought tersely, Diana and she were paying enough. A hundred thousand between them for three weeks' work.

'This assignment was far more difficult than usual,' Westfield said as Venus slid on to the sofa, and Juno handed her a glass of champagne, her favourite in the early evenings.

'Really? You must be used to travelling long distances, surely?' Diana asked.

'Oh, that wasn't the problem. Rather, it was avoiding detection ourselves. Your Uncle Clement has hired operatives to follow his fiancée around.'

Venus gasped; there was a murmur of shock from the other girls.

'He's having her tailed?' Athena asked.

'He is.'

The girls looked at each other. What did that mean?

'He also has men watching you when you meet her.'

'Spying on us!' Juno exclaimed.

'We believe he has a tremendous interest in your affairs. His operatives have been seen by our men taking photographs at your various places of work, as well as of Ms Wuhuputri. We think he receives reports on the whole family.'

'Bai-Ling's not family,' Athena said automatically.

Juno laid a hand on her knee. 'Let's hear the man out, Athena. Tell us everything you know.'

'Bai-Ling Wuhuputri is her real name. We haven't been able to construct much about her childhood or family, not in so short a time. We could, eventually. She was born in Thailand, we know that. She has lived in Jakarta for the last five years, in a comfortable house; she dated at least two local politicians. For an amateur, the woman is pretty discreet. It's unusual that she wasn't married, and we suspect she was some sort of high-priced escort. She met Clement Chambers in the Hilton Jakarta after a major gem industry fair at which he was being honoured with a lifetime achievement award. After that, she came and went regularly at her house and didn't see either politician again; she lived a very pure life. Clement flew her to the Seychelles and installed her in November of last year. She lives in one of the smaller guest cottages on the grounds. They dine together and sleep together occasionally. We have an operative in the house, as a gardener. Staff wouldn't talk much; they all fear your uncle, but our man does report a general climate of surprise.'

'Why?' Juno asked, leaning forward in her seat.

Venus was fascinated too. Suddenly even her movie seemed less important.

'Firstly because your uncle has never had a woman in the house. Secondly . . .' He hesitated. 'I should stress I only relay what we are told.'

'Go ahead,' Diana said firmly.

'Secondly because the staff believed your uncle was homosexual. He has not, however, been openly seen with a partner of any kind for at least ten years. Or if he has, the staff are not talking about it. We would need longer, and a much higher budget, to establish that.'

Juno shook her head. 'We are not investigating my uncle,' she said, blushing slightly. 'His private life is his business. We just suspect Bai-Ling.'

'She keeps to her cottage quietly unless summoned by your uncle. The impression is of a woman desperately wanting to marry. In England, there is no doubt she perceives your hostility. Hotel staff report she was contemptuous when you tried to dress her in embarrassing clothes. She bought Chanel with Clement's card. She has also called him frequently and a maid overheard her complaining about your attitude. She persuaded him to end your allowance.'

The Chambers women all nodded. Yes, Bai-Ling was a gold-digger, but not a total bimbo.

'You introduced her to a personal trainer?' Westfield glanced at Venus and Athena. 'After taking her around wedding boutiques?'

The girls nodded.

'And then stayed out of her way. If that was a deliberate ploy, it worked.'

Venus shrugged. 'Not really. I've just been busy.'

'Me too,' Athena said. 'In honesty, I kind of forgot.'

'Well, Bai-Ling apparently took it as surrender. Her calls to the house to complain about you dwindled away to once a day. She began by entering an intense training regime. There seemed to be a genuine wish to lose weight; she half-starves herself, and exercises obsessively. But there was a clear sexual attraction, and although she was *very* careful,' Venus thought she detected a note of admiration in the tone, 'we do have clear evidence of a sexual relationship between her and Bob Russell.'

He reached behind him and picked up a slim folder from the table. There were glossy pictures inside it, blown up large: Bob at the gym with Bai-Ling, her on an exercise machine, his hand between her legs, a caress at a running track, against a wall in a dark London street, unmistakably kissing.

'Well.' Juno exhaled. 'That's it. We did it. We got her. When Uncle Clem sees these . . .'

'My opinion, if you want it . . .'

'We do.' Diana grinned. 'We paid enough for it.'

'You ought to do very little. Your uncle will already have these pictures, or ones very like them. His main tail is on her twenty-four hours a day. We recognised one of the men, because he worked for us after he left Mossad. Glad I fired him,' Westfield added, a touch smugly. 'He concentrated on his target and never saw my men. But he is more than capable of pinning her down, as we have. No. In my opinion, your uncle is interested in her behaviour, but also yours. The more you push to remove Bai-Ling, the more you defy him. Remember, ladies. He isn't just watching her. He's watching you.' He handed Diana the rest of the folder. 'Our notes are in there. To take the job any further, I'd need a lot more money. Our man in the Seychellois compound may be endangering himself.'

Juno opened her mouth in amazement. 'Endangering himself? You think Uncle Clem might hurt him?'

'I don't know,' Westfield said, impassive. 'But it's my job not to take risks.'

'Thank you.' Diana got to her feet. 'No – we won't need any more from your firm. This is enough, more than enough. Are there any outstanding expenses?'

Westfield shook his head. 'The initial fee covers everything.'

'Then please destroy all the records you have, and anything listing this commission.'

A thin smile. 'We always do, Miss Chambers. Good evening, ladies. I'll let myself out.'

He walked from the room, and Juno rose and went to the heavy curtains, drawing them against the darkness. She held up one hand, preventing the others from speaking.

A moment later there was the shuddering sound of the car roaring to life and crunching away out of the drive. Without a word, Juno disappeared to the kitchen. The other girls sat on the couch, waiting. They heard the sound of the cook and the maid getting their coats, closing the door. Now they were all alone in the house.

Juno reappeared.

'Well,' she said, and a look of deep weariness spread over her face. 'Now we have a problem.'

They discussed it for hours. Bai-Ling. Her history. Clem spying on her. Clem spying on them. The money, and what would happen to it if they did not chase it.

'Thing is,' Venus said eventually. She was on her third flute of champagne, not drunk, but feeling very relaxed, almost detached. 'I feel sorry for Bai-Ling. So she's been a hooker, so what?'

'So what?' Juno spluttered.

'Yeah. So what?' Venus looked at her cousin. 'It's easy for you to say, Ju, you don't live in grinding poverty. We're rich girls; even now we're rich. This woman comes from an undeveloped country, she has no family alive now to speak of or the detectives would have found them. She dates men with money, she gets her own house. She meets Clem, tries it on; he moves her in and proposes. What would you do?'

Juno shook her head. 'Not every poor girl sells her body.'

'We haven't been poor,' Venus repeated.

'But she's using Uncle Clem.'

'And are you sure he's not using her, Ju?' Athena asked. 'I mean, he's following her. I know we did, but we didn't propose to her. How can he love her if he treats her that way?'

'He's following *us*,' Juno pointed out. 'Does the same apply? Does that mean Uncle Clem doesn't love us?'

There was a heavy silence. The fire had burned low in the grate, and they were no further forward. But unspoken, they all agreed to go on; Juno's question hung in the air.

'Love.' Diana spoke slowly. 'It's hard to tell. Has he shown much love? I've had love from Venus since Mum and Dad died. Sure, we drive each other mad, but we do love each other. From you two as well, to a lesser extent. After that, we see Clem each year, but all I can remember is being on my best behaviour.'

'He's been generous. The money's been there,' Athena agreed. 'But every year, weren't we really thinking about the cash? What did Uncle Clem do when we got there? It was awkward little parties, dressing for dinner, talking about nothing, all social graces and trying to keep on his good side.' She made a face. 'I don't know, when you look at it I'm almost embarrassed.'

Juno bit her lip. She heard what the others were saying, and it was true, she knew it. But she was also tribally loyal. And Clement had treated them well, more than well.

'You say he's been generous. That's not up for debate.'

'No.' Athena nodded. 'Fair enough.'

'Then why would we allow Bai-Ling to get away with it? Doesn't Uncle Clem deserve something from us? Loyalty, at least? We can't let him marry her. We've happily accepted his millions. Do we really want to let him sleepwalk into this marriage?'

Venus sighed. 'Juno has a point.'

Her cousin looked relieved. 'Then we will tell him.'

Venus nodded. 'But give Bai-Ling the chance to come clean first. Confront her.' She squared her shoulders. 'And look. Maybe this is crazy, maybe I'm the mad rebel. But I feel sorry for Bai-Ling even if she *is* fucking around . . . OK, OK, no if,' she added, at Juno's look. 'And I don't appreciate the fact that Uncle Clem's sending his goons to my film set. Look, nobody's perfect here. Bai-Ling isn't, but nor is Clem. And nor are we. Let's not rewrite history. We suspected Bai-Ling, but wouldn't we have tried to break up the marriage if his choice had been some sedate upper-class English widow? We'd have found a reason because we wanted the money. And I used not to care. But maybe Clem did me a favour. I was forced to take up a job, and I find I love it. And I'm going to be good at it,' she said bravely. 'I'm willing to bet on myself. So here's where I am. You can tell Uncle Clem, by all means, but I'm not going to take his money any more. I don't like being spied on.'

Juno stared. 'Not take his money? It's half a million a year.'

Venus nodded. 'I know. But Juno, I'd rather make it on my own. Call me arrogant, but I think I can.' She smiled wryly. 'Although we could do with half a mil. And I don't propose to give any of it back, either, so I'm not running for sainthood or anything.' She exhaled loudly. 'Imagine that, no more having to shop for dowdy clothes at Christmas!'

Diana stood up from the couch, excited, and moved to pat her sister on the shoulder. 'Venus is right, Ju. I don't want the money if being spied on is the price. I did before, can't deny that. But today things have changed. I wouldn't marry for money and I don't see why I should live my life to get it. Uncle Clem shouldn't have to marry Bai-Ling. Fair enough. We'll make sure he knows. But I'm not going to be his performing seal one minute longer. Juno, don't get angry; it's all the more for you and Athena.'

Juno sighed deeply.

'I was worried you were going to say that.' She looked over at Athena. 'If Diana and Venus take that line, I think we must.'

Athena set her mouth mulishly. 'Ju, I want Boswell House. And the garden. I need to buy it back from the developers and I don't have that kind of money.'

'How much money do you need?' Juno blushed slightly. 'My new company . . . I mean, it's early days. But I have made a bit of money. There's a niche out there, and nobody's thought of it.'

'Tell me,' Venus said, genuinely interested. Of all of them, she thought, Juno was the least likely to make it on her own, the most wedded to the trust fund. And now she was offering to bail out her sister. 'What exactly are you doing?'

'I'm essentially trading in leases for a profit. I buy flats that nobody else wants and rent them out to upper-end agencies. They aren't properties, because the leases are so short.' Juno smiled. 'It's honestly quite easy money. And I think I actually prefer it to holding dinner parties. I've made almost seventy thousand on just three deals. When I've got some money, I might actually expand into longer-term rentals, buying and holding. I do know exactly what a certain class of client wants.'

'Honey, that's very sweet,' Athena said, unfreezing with a smile. 'But Boswell's going to need a lot more money than that. And the Bluestocking's going very well too, but it will lose money the first year and I'll only start to make it in the second. The bankers are happy, but I know it'll be a slog. I can't live like this . . .' she gestured with one manicured hand at their gloriously chic surroundings, 'without the trust money. The bank loan gives me nothing but a grand or so to live on. I'd be stuck sharing a bedsit in Hammersmith with a student – if I was lucky.'

'Well, you have to think about it.' Her sister shook her head. 'I can't live tied to Uncle Clem. I think these last few months have made me look at life quite differently. Daddy always used to tell me that the money was no good for me.'

'He said that to me too,' Athena admitted.

'I know you loved Boswell more than I did. And I know it'll kill you to see it turned into flats. But in the end, Theney, it's only a house. For me, even a nice house in London isn't worth being tied to someone else.'

'So you're going to give up society?'

Juno shrugged. 'I'll see who invites me. But yes, I suppose I will give up chasing the approval of people who don't actually care about me. It just no longer seems important.'

Athena gave a deep sigh.

'I hate it when you're right. Maybe you and I can share a flat. A two-bedroom in Fulham, perhaps,' she said gloomily.

Diana smiled at her cousins. 'Hey. We're not taking a vow of poverty. I *love* being rich. As far as I'm concerned, we're just tweaking the method.'

Athena got up. 'Anybody want coffee? Jamaican Blue Mountain. Get it while you can; it's Nescafé next week.'

'Me,' Venus said, grinning. 'Hey, how d'you think Uncle Clem will take it?'

Juno thought about it, and then gave a little shiver.

'Not well,' she replied.

Chapter Twenty-Five

Bai-Ling stretched out in her bed and looked down at Bob. He had fallen asleep sprawled across the mattress. He had a habit of dropping off in the most awkward positions, and now, to compound things, he was snoring slightly.

With effortless silence, she slipped her tiny body out of bed and headed for the shower. She was getting very hungry; soon it would be time for just a little protein, maybe a couple of eggs, and a vitamin pill with some vegetable juice. She had designed the perfect programme for Clement; little enough to keep her body curve-free and boyish, but not so bad as to starve her menstrual cycle out of existence. It was no good heading for anorexia; she could never get pregnant that way.

Carefully she stepped into her power shower, the black marble reflecting her slim body back at her. The luxurious jets of warm water blasted away her tension, and more importantly, the lingering scent of sex. Bob would have to go. It was four a.m.; he could slip out quietly and avoid being seen; she had prudently bought him a greatcoat and scarf to muffle his face. This really must be the last time, Bai-Ling thought. Yes, she'd said that before; tonight she meant it.

There was a maid in one of the hallways watering a pot plant, and she had seen them coming in together. Of course Bai-Ling was in her workout gear, but still . . .

And besides, after a sexless year, she was sated now. Bob had no brain. A superb body and a talented lover, but he bored her. It simply wasn't worth the risk. Her craving for a man's touch had evaporated, and now she was feeling stupid. Of course they had been exception-ally careful, but Clement . . . She knew him, he wasn't a soft touch. If he became angry with her; if he suspected, of course not sex, but even impropriety . . .

She could be replaced. Bai-Ling knew he didn't love her. That was clear. But he wanted a woman to control, a woman he could actually get an erection with. She had decided that Clement wanted an heir. There were no male Chambers left, only the girls. Not good enough for a man like him.

And she could see clearly through all the money, the Christmas ceremonies and the formal letters and telegrams. Clement Chambers didn't *like* his nieces. He would take a sharp, bitter pleasure in the sudden conception of a boy who could disinherit the lot of them. Why else had he agreed to cut off the trust fund? All that guff about his wife needing the money. That trust fund

435

was peanuts. He never revealed quite how much he had, but it was billions, she was sure of that.

Despite the hot water sluicing down her back, Bai-Ling shivered a little. Clement didn't like the girls. Actually, she was pretty sure he didn't like women at all. That was all right with her. She wanted the money, and if he wanted a child she would damn well find a way to give him one. Nobody and nothing could get in the way of her inheriting that money; not the Chambers bitches, not stupid, sexy Bob, and not Clement himself.

The old man was the trick of a lifetime, and he was the last one she would ever have to turn.

She switched off the powerful jets, towelled herself down, and slipped back into the bedroom, getting changed into the soft cotton waffle karate suit she'd had made specially. Then she walked over to the bed.

'Bob.' She shook him by the shoulder. 'Bob, wake up.'

'Uhh,' he grunted, shaking his head.

She dug her sharp nails into his shoulder. He yelped in surprise, and his eyes opened wide.

'What the fuck did you do that for?'

'Time to go. Get dressed, go before somebody sees you.'

'It's early.' His groggy eyes focused, and travelled over her trim body. 'Come here, baby. Wanna work out? I'll work you out good.'

A spasm of distaste seized her. For this fool she had jeopardised all that wealth?

'Get up,' she hissed. 'Get dressed. You have to leave, right now.'

He sat up in bed, the sheets slithering around his impressively worked-out chest.

'You can't order me around. I'm not some whore.'

Of course you are, she thought, but bit it back.

'Please, Bob. You have to go.' Saying please came hard to Bai-Ling these days, but she forced herself. Honey was better than vinegar in a situation like this. 'I'll give you a call in the morning.'

Sullenly he jumped off the bed and started to dress. Bai-Ling tapped her fingers impatiently.

'When am I gonna see you again?'

She hated his voice when it was whiny. Pleading, submissive men did nothing for her.

'You're not.' Better to get this over with. 'We're done, Bob. I want to go back to the Seychelles as quickly as possible.'

He squared his shoulders, and his dark eyes narrowed. She could see the greed written right across his face, the horror that his super-rich meal ticket might be going to walk out on him.

'Baby, I don't want you to leave your fiancé.' Of course not. Bob knew where the cash came from. 'Just let me hang around,' he wheedled. 'I'll be there when you need a friend. Need a little *relief*.'

'Grow up,' Bai-Ling hissed. 'We're through.'

'You'd better be careful how you speak to me.' Bob

pulled on his trousers, grabbed his white T-shirt. 'In case you forgot, lady, I could blow your marriage to Mr Moneybags right out the window.'

Bai-Ling allowed the fear to course through her. Of course she'd expected blackmail, but it made it no better when it actually arrived.

'Let's get this settled.' She drew herself up to her full height. 'You're a good fuck, but that's all. I knew you wanted my money. Very well, here's the deal. You go away and say nothing and I will send you one hundred thousand pounds.'

Bob's eyes flashed fire.

'That's a one-time payment. And I never hear from you again.'

'You hope,' he said slyly.

Bai-Ling's dark eyes turned ice cold. 'Understand this, Bob. I am a very determined woman. I already have a sizeable amount of money of my own. And if you *ever* come between me and Clement, or try to shake me down for a penny more, I will have you killed.'

He sucked in his breath. 'You're joking.'

Bai-Ling turned away, already bored with him.

'Try it and see.'

There was silence while he grabbed his shirt and slid on his shoes.

'Use the coat and scarf,' she ordered. 'Nobody is to see your face. That includes the CCTV cameras in the corridors. And on the street. Don't unwrap until you're in a taxi.'

Bob nodded. 'When do I get the money?'

'Soon,' Bai-Ling said. 'And use some of it to go on holiday. Disappear for a while. A month should be good.'

She went into the bathroom, turned on the gold-plated taps over the sink and ostentatiously started to brush her teeth. A few seconds later, she heard the door slam.

He hadn't bothered to say goodbye. Fuck him, like she cared. That little diversion was done with. Bai-Ling would train herself, the simple way; just keep running, keep up with the constant weigh-ins. And she would go to the travel agent first thing in the morning and book an open first-class flight back to the Seychelles. With the Chambers girls giving up, she just had to persuade Clem that she should come home.

This visit to England was one giant distraction. She didn't need it. Bai-Ling rinsed, then crawled back into bed and switched out the light. The bride-to-be had to get her beauty sleep.

Juno took charge in the house. The first thing was to separate out their stuff. The girls would all find places. Athena offered to share, but Juno didn't want to; being with her sister would expose her pain. She wanted time and space to get over everything. Get over Jack.

'Everybody call me when they have something. I'll get the movers booked, and once we're out I'll hand it back to the letting agent.'

'And you're sure they'll give us the money back?' Diana asked doubtfully.

'Pretty sure. This is easily rentable. If they refuse, I'll simply sublet it, and I'm sure they don't want that.'

'OK.' Venus grabbed the tiny China Rose porcelain coffee cup and tossed down the fragrant vanilla-scented brew Athena had made. 'Gotta go, got to get to the edit suite. I already know the place I want. It's small, but it's gorgeous.'

Juno nodded. 'Fine. But please all go as quickly as you can.'

'When do we talk to Bai-Ling?' Athena asked. 'Before we move out?'

The girls looked at each other.

'Tonight.' Venus spoke decisively, and the other three agreed. 'It can't wait. Uncle Clem deserves to know and we should see her first.'

'Who's going to do the honours?' Diana asked. 'You, Juno? That seems right to me. You were always Uncle Clem's favourite.'

'We should all go,' Juno said. 'The whole family. It's a family matter. Go to the hotel, give her the pictures. I don't mind doing the talking, but you should all come.'

'Fair enough.' Athena nodded.

'Seven p.m., and Venus, don't be late. You can go back to work afterwards, but this is serious.'

'I know,' Venus said, faintly offended. 'I'm not completely flaky any more. I'll be there.'

'I'm not looking forward to it,' Athena said. 'But it has to be done.'

She grabbed her coat and headed out the door. Juno watched her sister go. Did Theney still want the money? Probably. But she was wrong. It was tainted, it was poison. She thought of Jack, and how her own unearned riches had made her despise him, just because he wouldn't play a certain part. Ironic that he could now buy and sell her ten times over.

And much worse that he didn't want to.

She stood up, to break the train of her thoughts. There was no point brooding. She had to find a house. And then do a couple more deals. After all, nobody was looking after her now.

In the non-rarefied world of ordinary flat-hunting, Juno discovered, the whole thing was quite painful. Two high-street agents turned her down, because she was self-employed; the third agreed to take her without references, if she paid six months in cash up front. Juno stiffened her spine, and settled on three. She took a one-bedroom cottage in Richmond, with a parking space, sight unseen. It was close to her new office, had decent shops, and was gratifyingly far from the centre of town and embarrassing meetings with her erstwhile friends.

Juno transferred the money. She couldn't wait for a cheque to clear. As soon as she was moved in, she decided, she would start looking for a house. Her budget was decent; the remaining savings would enable her to spend about eight hundred thousand. It had to be a house, and not a flat. She still had some friends in the upper echelons of London's property search companies.

'Don't worry, Juno.' The Honourable Thomas Kircaide was an erstwhile dinner-party companion, and she was ridiculously touched to hear an air of concern in his voice. 'I can find you something really good, if you can close quickly and waive the survey. There's a little unmodernised one-bedroom mews in a quiet close off the King's Road . . .'

'Perfect. Start the ball rolling, would you?'

'It has to be a house?'

'Yes. A freehold house. No flats, no leases.' She pressed one manicured hand to her eyes, thankful that she was on the phone and that he couldn't see the tears welling. 'I want something I can own outright. For the security of it. And I simply can't share.'

'If you go further out, I can get you something charming, even with a garden. Eight hundred goes a long way in Fulham, or West Ken. Three or four bedrooms, possibly.'

'No.' Juno was firm. 'I don't care how tiny it is, but I want a house somewhere really smart. Chelsea, Kensington, Mayfair, the Pimlico Grid. I'm starting out again, and I want to start with the best. Small, but perfect.'

'Leave it with me,' he said, and then paused. 'And

Juno. My wife asked me to tell you . . . you have guts.'

'Thank you,' she said, and managed to put the phone down before dissolving into tears.

Juno reached for a tissue and forced herself to calm down. At least there would be plenty to do. Move into the cottage, and then buy whatever Tom found for her. She would feel a little better once she owned her own place again. Let it be a shoebox; it would be a bloody smart shoebox. She felt a sudden rush of gratitude towards her Uncle Clem. Yes, he might be a bit of a controlling old sod, but she still owed him – this house would be bought with the remnants of his money, a lot of money that had been flowing freely for many years and which she'd blithely wasted.

At least she would be able to afford a house in town, free and clear. And that was thanks to him.

She was glad they were going to see Bai-Ling tonight. The whole business would be finished. Diana was more compassionate than she was, possibly. They wouldn't shame the girl – just demand she call off the engagement. Protecting Uncle Clem from this unsuitable marriage would at least be a start in repaying their debt. He'd be a laughing stock – and Juno knew the old man would hate that above everything. None of this was pleasant, but better to face it now than later.

Juno looked out of the window of her tiny Richmond office. It faced on to a green; sometimes you could forget you were in London. Her computer was springing into life. Time to find another couple of blockbuster flats on tiny leases. The good ones weren't advertised, of course, but she was building up her contacts. Maybe she'd call Tom back, see if she could take a difficult property off his books, return the favour . . .

Her phone rang, startling her. Juno jumped out of her skin. Who could be calling her? It was quarter to nine and Tom was an exception; most estate agents didn't answer their phones until half past. And New York was fast asleep. One of the girls, maybe. She hoped it wasn't Venus cancelling for tonight. Better not be, she thought darkly.

'Hello. Chambers Lettings,' she said.

'It's Jack.'

Juno collected herself. 'Hello. What can I do for you?'

Her knuckles whitened on the phone, but she kept her voice steady.

'Do you think I could make an appointment to see you? Mona is pressing me to speed up the divorce.'

Mona. The divorce. Of course. For a wild second, as tears welled up in her eyes, Juno thought about begging him to come back to her. Or even threatening to delay. But her head, painfully reasonable, told her heart it was no use, no good. She had pushed him out, and the only control she had now was to spare herself humiliation.

'That's fine. I'll come to you.' Juno dashed the tears from her eyes as briskly as she could. 'There's a flat on the Royal Mile I want to take a look at anyway.'

'Can you come today?'

He sounded eager. Boy, was he in a rush to get rid of her.

'Not today.' She had Bai-Ling tonight. All my birthdays are coming at once, she thought. 'But tomorrow is fine. I'll grab a plane. How about two o'clock?'

Better get it over with. You had to have the death before you could mourn.

'That's great. Thanks, Juno. I'll email you my solicitor's address.'

'Tomorrow, then. Goodbye, Jack.'

'Wait.' He paused, and sounded awkward. 'I hope – hope you're keeping well?'

The concern in his voice was too much. To her horror, Juno felt a sob well uncontrollably in her chest.

'What is it?' Jack asked, almost like he was anxious.

She gave a violent cough. 'Nothing. Touch of flu. I'm too busy to chat, Jack, goodbye.'

She put down the receiver firmly, not slamming it, and rested her head in her hands for a moment. The desire to cry had gone when his voice did, but Juno felt her heart gripped in a deep, calm despair, smooth and cold like ice over a pond. She composed herself, then reached for the phone again. Time to call Bai-Ling. Because life went on, even when you didn't want it to.

'I don't believe it,' Freddie said again.

Athena shrugged. 'Believe it. It's true.'

'But all that *money*. And your beautiful house.' He

fell silent, and Athena could see he was searching for something encouraging to say. 'Well – you've got money left over, haven't you? Enough to buy somewhere of your own.'

'I do. But I'm going to rent instead. I found a nice modern one-bedroom apartment, close to Hyde Park Corner. The building's got a gym.' Athena forced a smile. 'At least I'll get fit.'

'But renting . . .'

'It's cheaper. I'll need money to live on while I get the club off the ground. It's going to run at a loss, so I can't take on more debt.'

Freddie nodded slowly. 'No point asking you to move in with me, is there?'

She smiled at him. 'Not yet.'

'But you're still coming to meet my parents?'

'Yes. Looking forward to it,' Athena lied. His parents . . . that wasn't going to be much fun, was it? First their son was dating a major heiress; next minute she was a pauper with penniless academics for parents and no steady job . . .

'Let's have dinner tonight.' Freddie moved in, put his hands on her waist; his strong fingers splayed lightly over her ribcage. 'Take your mind off it.'

Athena thought of Bai-Ling. 'Can't tonight. I have an appointment.'

He was disappointed. 'Can't you cancel? How urgent is it?'

'Unfortunately not. It's very urgent.' And to her surprise, Athena found she was actually looking forward to getting it over with.

'What do you think?'

Carlton, her editor, was looking at Venus nervously. He'd just finished showing her the final print of the movie.

'You have to say *something*,' he prompted her. 'We're renting this suite by the hour, remember?'

'I remember,' Venus said. 'Pack it up, Carlton, we're done. It's fantastic. You're a bloody magician.'

Joy suffused her. The film was better than she'd dared to hope. It was a strong story, well acted, and cleverly shot. It looked like a major budget movie. Venus believed, in her heart, that they'd hit paydirt. At this moment, she had absolutely no doubt the thing would sell. And she felt prouder of this movie than anything she'd ever done in her life. No party, no magazine feature, not even an acting job could compare with it.

The movie was hers. Her first. Conjured from nothing. And it was excellent.

Bai-Ling – Venus would see the girl tonight, and send her packing with the others. But she felt a weird moment of gratitude. Without Bai-Ling, she'd have been just another trust-fund brat, in a golden cage for the rest of her life. Instead, she was an indie producer. No money to speak of, no sale, and no connections.

And she absolutely *loved* it.

*

Diana couldn't concentrate. The fabric swatches swam in front of her eyes. Zoffany or vintage Laura Ashley? What would go best with the authentic Georgian paint colours she was using in the study?

'I favour this,' her client said with a heavy Texan accent, pushing forward a piece of candy-stripe cotton. 'Mixed with plaids.'

The fat housewife, Betty-Lou Freedman, smiled smugly. She had a million dollars to spend on this renovation of her holiday home. The dot com boys liked to swagger, but oil still made good money. And hiring a fancy aristocratic English broad to put the apartment together was the height of good taste. All her friends would be desperate to copy her.

'That's horrible,' Diana said absently. 'Totally clichéd.'

'Excuse me?' Betty-Lou demanded, outraged. Her fat cheeks went purple. 'I'll have you know I took a course in interior design in Austin last summer. Graduated top of the class.'

'Yes. I know. I'm sorry.' Diana bit on her cheek, hard, to stop herself from laughing. 'It *would* be lovely in Texas – it's just that Europe has a different vernacular. And you're paying for the edge over ordinary good taste, Mrs Freedman.'

'Yes. I suppose I am.' Betty-Lou sniffed, as if to tell Diana to watch her back. Diana forced herself to concentrate.

'I think the Zoffany would be better.'

'Do they use that in the Victrix hotel in Rome?' Betty-Lou enquired.

'No . . . but that demanded a different style again.'

'I want what that Karl Roden had.' Betty-Lou sighed, and her blue eyes lit up with a disturbing lust. 'You know, he is one smart-lookin' man.'

Diana was instantly focused. Her heart gave a little lurch. Pathetic, she knew. She tried for casual. 'You know him?'

'Well, not personally. My husband met him at some business thing a few times.' Betty-Lou patted her hair proudly, remembering it. 'He came over and talked to us. Very nice man.'

'Yes, he's not bad.' Diana put her fabric book away. 'Have you decided on your budget for the bathroom? I think we should do something quite striking, with hessian-covered walls and stone flooring, underfloor heated, of course . . .'

'He makes you feel like a woman,' Betty-Lou gushed. 'Holds your eyes, and *so* polite. I saw him just last week, in fact, just after he came back from doin' your little project in Rome. That's why we hired you, you know. When we saw the ad and realised you did a Karl Roden hotel. That's what I call class.'

Diana tried to resist, but failed. The lure of discussing him openly was just too great.

'How interesting. And what did you talk about?'

'I asked him where his girlfriend was. The model. He said they broke up, so I offered to introduce him around. I know some very pretty young ladies. One of them's even a Cowboys cheerleader.'

Diana turned away so that Betty-Lou wouldn't see the curiosity written bright across her face. 'And what did he say?'

'Well now. He told me that he wasn't interested because he found somebody already. But he didn't bring her along to the party,' Betty-Lou announced, 'so she can't be that important.'

'No.' Diana didn't even try to stop the surge of happiness breaking over her like a wave. 'I expect she's not. Anyway, we've made a lot of progress here today, Mrs Freedman, and I'll be on site next week to start the fitting. I always hire multiple work crews, so given the delivery of the antiques from Paris, we should be good to go before the end of the month.'

'I'll have the keys?'

'You will.'

'And it'll look great?'

'No.' Diana favoured her client with a warm smile. 'It'll look spectacular. My first private commission. You'll be the talk of Fifth Avenue.'

After Betty-Lou had waddled out of the door of her new office, a bijou studio flat in Notting Hill, Diana called a few suppliers, then made a large pot of coffee. Anything to distract herself, really. Karl just wouldn't give up; he kept calling. And although Diana was worried about letting herself go, letting herself believe, she couldn't help it.

She was falling for him. A bit more every day.

What would Juno say, what would the girl think, if Diana moved straight from Uncle Clem to Karl Roden? She was doing well, but her business was still a start-up. She poured the cinnamon coffee into a large mug and sipped, thinking it over. She loved her independence. She'd only just begun to stand on her own two Manolos. It was a problem, and she didn't know what to do.

For the first time, she began to look forward to tonight. Bai-Ling was what she had aimed to be, and what she now despised. Diana would go there and use it to put a little steel into her spine. She had to find herself, before she could settle with Karl. If it came to that.

Although there were big differences between Karl and Uncle Clem. Karl was gorgeous, for a start . . .

Stop that, Diana lectured herself. She grabbed the phone and called Juno in the office.

'When are we meeting her again? I have to get this done.'

'Seven,' her cousin replied. 'I just called.'

Bai-Ling hung up the phone and sat on the end of her bed, staring into space.

There was a sharp knock on the door. 'Housekeeping.'

'Fuck off!' Bai-Ling screamed. Then she grabbed hold of herself. At least she hadn't spoken in English. 'That's fine, I don't need service, thank you,' she said, in her politest clipped aristo tones.

They wanted to see her. Juno Chambers. The rest of the bitches. All together. Despite Bai-Ling's delicate hints, Juno had refused to say what it was about. But Bai-Ling had a sixth sense for danger, after years on the street. And she already knew.

A solitary tear rolled down her cheek. Well, they had won. They had trapped her. The handsome piece of meat had been her undoing. She racked her memory, trying to think where she had slipped up, where she could have been spotted. She had tried to be *so* careful. But it hadn't been enough. Nothing like.

She had only herself to blame. Years, decades of patient scheming, waiting for a moment like this, and she'd blown it over something as stupid as a smooth body and a good technique. Bai-Ling did not kid herself. Clement would not stand for it, not for a millisecond. The Chambers girls were coming here at seven, coming for a 'family conference', coming to gloat over her ruin, no doubt. They would giggle and laugh. They'd be happy to see her like she was at sixteen, Bai-Ling thought, in a wave of hatred, stuck in a brothel in Kuala Lumpur, terrified and in pain . . .

No. She would not give in. Maybe Clem was over, that revolting pervert, but her life was not.

The moment of self-pity passed, and fear replaced it. Her life wasn't over – yet. Bai-Ling did not trust the tender mercies of Clement Chambers. He would not just drop her. He would, she knew at once, attempt to punish her. Ruination, possibly worse . . .

Possibly a *lot* worse.

An old, deep survival instinct sprang into action. She pulled out her BlackBerry from its bespoke Versace case and tapped out a few numbers from memory.

'Christian? Hi, it's Bai-Ling. How are things at the *Post*? Fabulous . . . Look, I'm in a bit of trouble and I need a favour. Yes, there could be a story in it. Perhaps front-page stuff . . .'

Six forty-five p.m., and the last streaks of sunlight were still in the sky. Venus, Juno and Diana were standing around on the pavement outside the Lanesborough; a limousine pulled up, and as the doormen sprang forward, Athena got out. She was wearing a fantastically high pair of leather boots under a long pale grey jumper dress by Jil Sander that clung to her body in all the right places. In her classic Dior suit, Juno sighed inwardly; hell, her baby sister just looked so *beautiful* since she'd smartened up: the wild auburn hair was now sleek and chic, the just-right Armani mac gave definition to the informal dress, she was made up, her lips were a glossy peach . . . Athena just glowed. And she, Juno, was merely prim and proper.

Oh well. At least she was presentable. At least, Juno thought with a faint trace of self-mockery, the Chambers cousins could say that. Their world might be falling apart, but not their style.

'I'm early,' Athena said defensively, rushing up to them. 'Still got ten minutes.'

'You are.' Venus grinned. 'I'm just glad I'm not the last, for once.'

She was wearing a coat dress by Armani and tailored Christian Louboutin Mary Janes; the tulip style emphasised the va-va-voom of her body, but, Juno realised, there was no overenthusiastic cleavage, no sky-high skirt slit to the thigh. Not even some fishnet stockings. No, Venus was apparently growing up. And she looked all the sexier for it. Diana, perhaps, had changed the least of them; she wore a simple shift dress by Ghost, dark tights, towering Jimmy Choo heels, and a chunky mother-of-pearl cuff; modern elegance, with her dark hair worn loose across the shoulders, just pinned back from her face by a fabric rose in mink silk. But Diana was calm, and there was a deep joy about her at the moment; Juno saw in her cousin the reverse image of herself. You only looked that way if you were in love, just as she was grey and tired because she was heartbroken. No cream or blusher could put that back into your skin.

Good for Diana, Juno thought, and wondered at herself. Four months ago, in December, she'd been dreading another Christmas with her wayward relatives.

And now everything had changed. When she looked at these three, she understood: she loved them all – actually loved them. And perhaps more, she was proud of them.

It was something to cling on to. And she'd take what she could get.

Uncle Clem had had strong ideas about family. But that was all etiquette. This was the real thing.

'Come on,' she said to the others. 'Let's get this done.'

And the four of them strode through the doors of the hotel, past the admiring doormen, who were bowing and grinning.

'Juno Chambers, Diana Chambers, Venus Chambers and Athena Chambers. To see Ms Wuhuputri.'

'Yes, madam.' The receptionist was marvellously impassive. 'She left instructions to ask that you go up to her suite when you arrived.'

'To her suite.' Juno glanced at the others; they gave little shrugs. 'Very well.'

They walked together to the elevator, without speaking. But Juno could tell from the way they held themselves, the set of the shoulders, the slight shortening of breath, that they were all as tense as she was. She had a set of the photographs in her large Prada satchel. With any luck they would not get that far.

They stepped out on the eleventh floor. Bai-Ling's suite, one of the best in the hotel, was at the end of the corridor. Juno led the way, and the others fell in behind her.

Before she could knock on the door, it opened. Bai-Ling stood there, beautifully dressed in a sari. Her hair was loose, she had almost no make-up on, and she looked achingly young.

'You had better come in,' she said. 'And sit down.'

Chapter Twenty-Six

The suite was immaculately made up. The Chambers women settled themselves; Diana and Juno on a chaise longue, Venus and Athena in armchairs. Bai-Ling remained standing, propping herself against an antique walnut table.

'I know why you've come,' she said.

Juno sensed a flood of adrenalin course through her. She welcomed it; battle was better than misery.

'Tell us.'

'You want to prevent my marrying your uncle.' Bai-Ling glared at them with true loathing; Juno felt Diana shrink back a little beside her. 'You are selfish, greedy bitches who are determined to have every last cent of his millions for yourselves. And you will do anything to stop him marrying or fathering an heir.'

Juno rested one hand, very lightly, on her cousin's arm.

'You are quite correct, of course. And I speak for us all when I say I'm glad you're dropping the pretence.'

'Like you were so very sincere. That little dinner. The

letters. The luncheon party. The trips to the bridal salons.'

'Fair enough.' Venus spoke up, unembarrassed. 'We thought you were a gold-digging little tramp, and you were trying to get us disinherited. Of *course* we did whatever we had to. We lied, same as you did. But you lied first.'

'Pretending to love our uncle,' Athena agreed. 'He's old enough to be your grandfather.'

Bai-Ling lifted her dark head, and her eyes flashed fire.

'If I pretended to love him for a year or so, what of you four? You've been pretending to love him for years. Ever since the money started flowing.' Juno winced, and saw triumph spring into the younger woman's eyes. 'Sure, you come for Christmas,' Bai-Ling sneered. 'You dress up for dinner and pretend you're all living under King George, but afterwards, do you give a fuck about him? Hell, no. You don't call, you don't write. You don't *care*. You just turn up when he asks you to so you can keep hold of the money.'

The attack found its target; Juno blushed, and watched Athena drop her eyes.

'Maybe.' Venus jumped up. 'But that's between him and us. We are his nieces, his brothers' daughters. We're family. You're nothing but a predator.'

'So sharing some genes makes it all right? Think again,' Bai-Ling said, and a terrible hardness came over her face. 'Your family can betray you. Mine did. And you're predators too. You don't give a damn about Clement.'

'Enough.' Juno shook her head. 'We're not here to bargain with you. We have photographs of you with your trainer. Kissing.' She didn't mention the worse ones. 'We didn't come here to humiliate you, Bai-Ling. You just break it off with our uncle and we'll call it quits.'

'Just break it off. Like it's that easy.'

'What do you mean?'

Bai-Ling stared. 'Oh yeah, his nieces, his brothers' daughters, the happy family. You don't know him at all, do you? You little fools! You imagine he'll take that lying down? All the man cares about is himself. His reputation, his legend. In his mind the world keeps spinning just because he wants it to. Why do you think he gave you the money? Why did he keep having you there for Christmas? It's a game to him, stupid bitches, all just a game.'

'Explain yourself,' Athena said sharply.

Bai-Ling gave a wild laugh. 'Why the hell should I? You'll find out.'

Juno was disturbed. Not by the insults and threats, but by the manic, driven look that had suddenly appeared on Bai-Ling's face. She was amazed to find her emotions had changed. When it came right down to it, she didn't hate this woman. She pitied her. She remembered what Paul Westfield had said. It had been just a set of facts, drily recited in their drawing room. But now those facts had a human face. She wondered what life had been like for

Bai-Ling, to turn her into this ruthless, calculating, diamond-hard machine of a woman, armed with nothing more than her beauty and her cunning.

'Bai-Ling. Did our uncle harm you in some way?' Juno asked.

The softness of the question hit. Bai-Ling reacted as though struck. Anger, hate she was used to; pity hurt.

'Harm me?' She dropped her eyes, hissing. 'Your precious uncle loves to degrade. He made me stop eating, starve out my breasts. Then bind them close to the body. He makes me tell him about . . . bad things that happened to me when I was a girl.' Her eyes half closed. 'It's the only way he can get aroused with me.'

Venus opened her mouth, then closed it again. 'But you're beautiful.'

'Yes. And he's bisexual. Prefers boys.' Bai-Ling tossed her head. 'You didn't know? He chose a woman just to get an heir. And he can only get aroused if I look close to a boy, and tell him . . .' She shuddered.

'Why should we believe you?' Diana said. 'Uncle Clem wouldn't . . .'

But her voice trailed off.

'You believe me,' Bai-Ling said fiercely. 'You all believe me. He wants you around because you make him look respectable. He's not respectable. He's a bully. He loves nobody but himself. OK, I went for the money, but I *earned* it. It was a transaction. I gave him what he wanted. I deserve to get paid.'

Juno stood. 'We can't be sure of anything, except this: our uncle gave us lots of money over many years, and we owe him for that. We will not expose him to ridicule by allowing him to contract a loveless marriage with a woman who hates him. You must withdraw from the relationship or force us to expose you.' She paused. 'I am sorry, Bai-Ling. For all the wrong that people have done to you. But you must see that marriage to Clement would destroy your soul.'

'So it's for my own good now, is it?' Bai-Ling snarled. 'Very nice, Miss Juno, very noble, with your designer housewife suit and your thousand-dollar bag. I'm sure you can all rejoice over the state of my soul as you suck Clement dry of every last pound.'

'You're wrong,' Venus said hotly. 'We're going to tell Clement we can't take his money any more. We don't want to be controlled. It's not worth it, not for us.'

'Sure.' Bai-Ling's voice was high with contempt. 'Oh, absolutely, Venus Chambers with the plastic tits and laser smile, she's going to tell her darling uncle where he can stick his half-million a year. And what sugar daddy's gonna look after you now?'

Venus flushed with rage. 'I'm no whore.'

'Whoring's an honest living,' Bai-Ling said. 'And you girls have been doing it for years.'

'We're here to come to a settlement,' Juno interrupted. 'One that preserves his dignity; yours too.'

'I can look after myself.'

Venus said, 'I'm a producer. I've made a film, and I'm going to sell it.'

'Right,' Bai-Ling said sarcastically. 'Without Uncle Clem, you maybe star in porn.' Her eyes narrowed, and she smiled bitterly. 'I can set you up.'

'I have an interior design business,' Diana chipped in. 'Athena's started a club. Juno is working in property. None of us is going to touch Uncle Clem's money any more. And if we go to see him, it'll be as his nieces, nothing else. You're an intelligent woman, Bai-Ling. You should turn your mind to that. Start a business.'

Juno said, 'You can come and work for me.'

The other three girls turned towards her, staring. 'What?' Athena said.

'I believe her,' Juno said simply. 'I hate to say it, but I do. Even if she can't marry Uncle Clem, I see no reason why she should suffer. Bai-Ling, I can pay you something – not much, but something. Until you get another job, or decide what you want to—'

Bai-Ling laughed. 'Oh, that's rich. You force me out, then try to tell me you give up all the money.' Her accent increased with her stress. 'Now, instead of a billion dollars and control of his diamond mines, you offer a consolation prize. I can be your secretary, get to make your coffee. Well guess what, Miss Juno, you can keep the fucking dignity in that.' She stood up. 'I speak to your uncle right now. You can listen, stupid bitches. Then you leave me alone.'

'We don't need to be here,' Juno said. 'Bai-Ling . . .'

'You *stay*,' she hissed. 'You *listen*.'

Bai-Ling picked up the phone receiver from the table behind her and pressed a speed-dial button.

'Maria, it's Bai-Ling. Put Clement on.' She paused. 'I don't care if he's not there. Patch me through to the limo.'

There was a delay. Bai-Ling's fiery gaze swept each of them, and Juno saw that none of the girls wanted to move. They were transfixed by her rage, by the drama. No way they could walk out now.

'Clement, this is Bai-Ling. I'm not marrying you any more.'

As Juno watched, Bai-Ling pressed the speaker button. And their uncle's reedy, watery voice, which they were used to hearing as petulant, or chiding, came through the speakers; old, yes, but crackling with loathing, clear and strong.

'You never were.' The disdain made Juno flinch. 'Did you really think I'd marry some foreign whore? Did you believe I didn't know what you were?'

The Chambers girls gasped in horror.

'Uncle Clem!' Diana said.

'What the fuck? Who is that?' Clement spat.

Bai-Ling smiled a terrible smile. 'Your nieces, you bastard, your precious heiresses. They are all here with me. And I have told them everything about you. All your secrets.'

He gave an inarticulate cry of hatred, so dark the Chambers girls shrank away from the sound.

'They came to blackmail me,' Bai-Ling said. 'So I give you up and all the money.'

'I have pictures of you,' Clement barked. 'Fucking some monkey. My female, my fiancée. Or you thought you were. As though I would ever tie my name to that of some slit-eyed bitch . . .'

Juno groaned. She raised her voice. 'Uncle Clement. That's quite enough. This is Juno. You are acting shamefully, just shamefully.'

'You had better keep a quiet tongue in your head, you wretched little embarrassment,' Clement bellowed. 'It's my bloody money, and you'll remember that.'

'No. We don't want your money. None of us.' Juno said it now, clearly and without a trace of regret. 'Nothing could persuade me to take one more penny from you.'

'Ungrateful *slut*!' he screamed. 'I've given you millions . . .'

'And we've saved you from a fake marriage. Saved your precious reputation. I'd say we're even,' Juno responded.

'Your sister and your cousins won't be so proud.'

'Yes we will,' Venus shouted. 'We're all here. And you're a blot on this family . . . *Clement*.'

'I'm a blot? *I'm* a blot?' Clement's voice rose in near-hysterical fury. 'Coming from the tramp, the slutty little orphan who's penniless without me? You think you're going to get away with this, any of you? Do you think you can pit yourselves against Clement Chambers?' He suddenly cackled, gulping weakly with laughter. 'Try it,' he said, enjoying himself. 'Try it. Ask Bai-Ling what will happen to you.'

'I thought you would say that.' Bai-Ling stuck herself back into the conversation. 'You will leave me alone. I have contacted two journalists with a file on you. If anything happens to me, they publish. And don't try to find them, because I will do it with twenty more if I hear of it.'

'You publish anything, and you're dead,' Clement said flatly.

'And if I'm dead, they publish. So it works two ways.' Bai-Ling smirked. 'I start again, Clement. With some of your money. I better not hear anything bad about myself. I *like* your society. I will put out a statement saying we drifted apart. You gave me money for the trip; it is now in my account. I'm going to find somebody, not a sick fuck like you. And if I hear one bad thing about me, I will make you the contempt of everybody that ever read the *Wall Street Journal*. You'll be a punch line on a chat-show monologue.' She tilted her head, listening with pleasure as he drew in his breath. 'You leave me alone, I leave you alone. Deal?'

Clement coughed; it sounded as though he were almost choking with his anger. But in the end he spat out, 'Deal. Now leave the room. Before I change my mind.'

Bai-Ling smirked. 'I leave you in the arms of your loving family, asshole. At least you didn't leave me needing an abortion.'

She bent over and reached out for her Marc Jacobs coat, slipped it on, and picked up the incredibly expensive Henk suitcase standing by the door. She looked at the Chambers girls, her face hard with defiance. 'Tell that walking corpse he's paying the bill,' she said, and stormed out, slamming the door behind her.

'Is she gone? Juno, are you there?' Clement barked.

'I am. We all are.' Juno moved next to the phone. 'How could you do that to her? She's a human being. Is what she told us true?'

'I don't give a damn what she told you,' Clement said. 'You girls will get in line and you will smooth this over for me with the press back home.'

'Maybe you didn't hear us, Uncle Clem.' It was Athena. 'We don't want your money. We won't accept it. And frankly, you have a lot of explaining to do. What do you think Daddy would say to you?'

'Marcus? Marcus would say *nothing* because he *is* nothing. Like you. Like all of you.' Clement's voice was lower now, calmer, but more threatening. 'I will not be defied. We're going to ignore that slut and go on exactly as before.'

'We're not.' Athena was cold. 'We have our own careers. And don't speak about my father like that. You aren't worthy to pronounce his name. I can't believe you're brothers.'

'This is Diana.' Her cousin came and stood next to her. 'I am embarrassed we ever did take your money.'

'You took it, you spent it, you asked how high when I said jump,' Clement roared at her. 'And you will continue to do so.'

'We're going to stand on our own two feet. All of us,' Venus said. 'And as for you, we'll have to think about whether we want to see you again. And how. Because you're still our uncle.'

The unspoken 'unfortunately' hung in the air.

'Don't lecture me about family,' Clement spat. 'Don't think you can run things your way. I'm on my way to the airport. Now.'

The girls glanced at each other, stunned. Clement was a recluse. He never left the Palms – at least, they didn't think so. But then again, he was not the man they knew.

'What are you going to do at the airport?'

'I'm coming to England. To see you. To deal with Bai-Ling. And to return things to normal.' His tone was heavy with menace. 'And you had better not anger me any further, girls.'

There was a click, then a buzz. Uncle Clem had hung up.

*

467

They left as one, not speaking by mutual consent, and walked around the corner to a restaurant. Juno, in a daze, got them a table and ordered a bottle of wine and four glasses. She waited for the waitress to leave before nodding at Venus, who was obviously bursting out of her skin.

'Told you. I told you,' Venus said. 'Tainted money.'

'You were right.' Athena shrugged. 'I was wrong. I'd rather sweep the streets than get anything from him.'

'Do you think Bai-Ling was telling the truth? That he might . . . might try to hurt us?' Diana asked.

'He can try,' Venus said. 'He won't succeed. This is England. And we're well known.'

Juno thought of her tiny fledgling company. It was pretty much all she had left to be proud of.

'And what if he tries another way? Hurts our businesses? He sounds like a man who just needs to control everything. I'm only starting out,' she said fiercely, 'but I love it, I love what I'm doing. And I'm bloody good at it. I don't know if I can afford a billionaire competitor.'

'We'll deal with him,' Venus promised. 'Not sure how, but we will. He's a cockroach, and cockroaches hate daylight.'

'My advice is that we get on with our lives.' Athena sipped her Pinot Grigio. 'We're moving house. Juno's winding up the lease. Let's just ignore him altogether. And as for Bai-Ling, she's going to do her own thing. If anybody asks, our understanding is that they grew apart and decided to call it off. Leave it at that.'

'But he is still our uncle,' Diana said. 'And he's a very old man.'

'No excuses,' Venus replied. 'I agree with Athena, Di. Bai-Ling was a nasty piece of work, but she was still a person. He has a hell of a lot of explaining to do if he wants to regain any affection from me.'

'But did he ever have our affection?' Juno asked slowly. 'She had a point there, didn't she? We turned up, we hated it, we didn't even like each other much.'

'That's one way to put it,' Venus agreed drily.

'We didn't offer much in the way of love to Uncle Clem, either.'

'You can't be blaming us for what he did, Juno?' Athena asked incredulously. 'We're not racists, we're not perverts. We haven't used some ex-hooker just so we could laugh at her.'

'I understand there's no equivalent,' Juno admitted. 'Thank God. But I am blaming us for what *we* did. We let the money blind us. We're as guilty of that as anyone. Nobody's perfect here.'

The four girls sat in silence for a moment; they all knew it was true. Athena spoke first.

'Fuck it,' she said, ignoring her big sister's raised eyebrows. 'So we acted stupid before. But I can't change that. I can only change where I go from here. And I want to get my own place and launch the Bluestocking. We may have messed up the past. But the future is wide open.'

The other three smiled.

'You're a hundred per cent right.' Diana grinned at her cousin. 'No more regrets. I'm not going to let him control me for one more second.' She thought about Karl. He wasn't Clem, he was a good guy, and Diana wasn't going to live her life based on what other people thought. As soon as she got home, she was going to call him. A surge of excitement rushed through her, and she lifted her glass. 'Our money. Our family. Our future.'

Juno announced, 'A toast. To the Chambers girls.'

'The Chambers girls,' they said, and drank.

Clement slammed down the phone.

'Maria! Get my car and my goddamn jet! Consuela! Pack my London wardrobe!'

'Yes, sir.'

'Yes, sir!'

His maids ran off to do his bidding. They worked fast; he knew he would be in the air within the hour. How he hated the necessity of this. But Clement was in crisis mode. They were running away from him, things were running away from him. It was time to end this joke.

The girls thought they could make it. As though, even if their various little businesses survived, he could not strangle them.

The joke of Bai-Ling barely entered his mind. She

would be rubbed out. No, the important thing was the girls. And what they meant to him.

His brothers' daughters.

His aged mind drifted back, back, back. To his childhood, where he had always been emotionally detached. To growing up with two brothers, who laughed, and smiled, and were close. Marcus and Rupert looked up to him; he rebuffed them. When they played with each other, hugged his parents, Clement had always understood, on a basic, biological level, that they were normal and he was not.

His focus was intense. And he was withdrawn. The overt love of his parents and brothers he did not return. And when his father made him go to the shrink . . .

He could see it now; his intelligent, professorial father, worried, that look of loving concern on his face. Pure sanctimony.

'I believe Clement is ill, Doctor. He has no empathy . . .'

Asshole. The diagnosis, that he suffered from a mild form of psychosis – lack of human empathy, lack of relationships. An intrusion. He was focused, that was all. He had little time for fripperies.

The day his brother Rupert died, Clement was there. In the pub, drinking, watching Rupert eat his lunch, his wife laughing. And then the accident.

Nobody knew that he, Clement, had been driving the car.

It was not deliberate. There was a pheasant, it ran into the road. Clement had swerved, startled. The car had lurched from his control, hit a tree.

Rupert, his brother, was dead. But we all die, Clement thought, we all die some time . . .

He told only his other brother, Marcus. And young Marcus had exploded.

Accused Clement of horrible indifference. Of *madness* . . .

'My company's just taking off. We're buying a diamond mine in South Africa. I can't have the publicity.'

'Sod the company, Clem, you're part of this family. Mum thinks Rupert was drunk. Those girls have lost their parents. Can't you see?'

'Rupert's gone. Nothing can bring him back. You want me to suffer too?' Clement was outraged. 'The police might blame me, Marcus, do you want that? Maybe you do.'

His younger brother stared. 'You're sick, Clem. You're paranoid.'

'You're against me.' Clem remembered his mother's coldness. 'You're all bloody against me. I won't risk what I've worked for.'

'It's just money, Clem. What does that mean compared to family?'

'Everybody puts money first, Marcus. Don't be naïve.'

'You're wrong. You're ill, Clem, let me get you some help.'

Get your hands on my diamonds, more likely. Clem, seething with jealousy and rage, had jumped on a plane. When the deal for the mine was done, he went to the Seychelles.

And never saw his ungrateful family again. A call, now and then. Until he realised the girls were grown up.

And the resentment that had gnawed at his soul all these long years took shape. The girls – Rupert's heirs, Marcus's heirs.

He would show his oh-so-pious relatives the real value of money. And how their precious daughters would put it over so-called 'family values' every time.

Their acquiescence would prove he was right.

And the girls, smothered in money, had always acquiesced. Always proved Clem right. Always given structure, justification to his life.

If the girls rejected his money, they'd be proving him wrong, that day of the car crash, when he didn't tell his parents; proving Marcus right; proving his nightmares about Rupert were true.

His mind could not take that. He was on his way back now, back to England. To blackmail, coerce, physically threaten, if necessary.

Whatever it took to put an end to this.

Chapter Twenty-Seven

Juno awoke the next day feeling very strange. A sort of deathly calm had settled over her. Bai-Ling was gone, the money was finished, and their uncle was on the warpath. Yet she had never felt freer in her life. Getting up, showering, dressing, she felt an amazing sense of control, of empowerment. Perhaps this was her lowest point, but the other girls were right: it was all in her hands now.

That did not stop her heart from being broken.

Sometimes when she first woke up, half asleep, still emerging from subconsciousness, she thought that Jack was still there. Sometimes she rolled over, reached for him. And then the absence hit her, and Juno struggled into dawn knowing again, like it was new, that the bad dream was real.

But today there were no false promises. Her carry-on case was by her bed, already packed and ready to go; her clothes were where she had left them the night before, on her armchair, to save time. She had resisted the temptation to pick her most attractive dress, and gone instead for a sharp Chanel suit in grey and black, with modest court heels by Stephane Kelian, and her reliable string of House Massot pearls.

When in doubt, she thought, always go to Chanel. It was her trademark, her armour. Her suits had been designed to fit her body perfectly, and they always made her feel stylish, elegant, in command. A sensation that was doubly important today.

She tugged on her silk slip, then her fitted T-shirt and suit, tights and shoes. She grabbed the matching silver quilted Chanel bag. Make-up took two minutes; Juno never varied her routine, except for eyeshadow and lipstick. She added a spritz of custom-blended perfume. The whole thing had taken her less than a quarter of an hour. She went into her new, tiny kitchen, fixed herself a black coffee and ate a grapefruit without sweetener; she was weaning herself off sugar, easier to do when your heart was broken. In fact, her tailored suit was starting to gape a little at the waist. The heartbreak diet, she thought ruefully. Sure to be an instant craze.

At seven a.m. sharp there was a honk outside the front door. Juno grabbed her case and slipped into the waiting taxi. At least there would be little traffic at this time, she thought. And she wanted to get to Edinburgh good and early. There was a deal to be done later in the morning, and it was even more important than normal. Achieving something would make the confrontation with Jack that much easier to bear. She didn't think she could face him without respecting herself.

*

The apartment was fabulous, a three-bedroom on the Royal Mile in a period Georgian building; it was in walk-in condition, with an owner who'd loved gadgetry, so that alongside the stellar view and country-house decor there was wi-fi internet access, hidden cinema screens, underfloor heating, and remote controls to work everything from the central vacuum to the floor-to-ceiling blinds in the conservatory. Problem was, there were only eight years left on the lease. The owner had gambling debts; the freeholder couldn't wait to reclaim a key part of the family estate. It was an almost unsaleable deal.

'He'll let it go cheap,' the estate agent practically begged her. 'If you're a serious buyer.'

'Of course he will. It's an eight-year lease.' Juno thought about her contacts in New York; nobody had a client making a movie in Scotland that year. She'd have to be creative. 'I'm not paying even close to the asking price, tell him that. I do want it, but only if the numbers work.' Idly she toyed with the phone in her pocket. The challenge of placing a rental outside of her normal client list was strangely exciting. She was starting to get a feel for it, she decided, this little niche business she was carving out for herself. Something told her this place was a winner. It was just a question of finding the right person.

Business could be like love, in that way.

'I'm going to make a few calls.' Her own voice, decisive, startled her. She actually sounded like she knew what she was doing. 'I'll get back to you.'

'Please do,' said the agent desperately.

Twelve noon. Seven a.m. on the East Coast; nobody would be in the office yet, not even the bond traders. But Juno had a man in mind. David Amesh, the junk bond king, now semi-retired at the grand old age of forty-seven. His wife, a desperate social climber, had been part of Juno's circle when they lived in London. Juno had introduced her to some titles, and the Ameshes had flown Jack and Juno to Mauritius for their major wedding anniversary party.

David had two defining characteristics, Juno remembered. He was proud of a distant Scottish relation in Clan Gordon, number one. And he adored golf, number two.

She dialled Ellen Amesh from memory. Ellen was a keep-fit fanatic, rose at five thirty daily for her swim and callisthenics, then ate a breakfast of wheatgrass and rolled oats and proceeded to dive into the papers. Seven a.m. for her was like noon for most people.

'Ellen? It's Juno Chambers.'

'Juno!' A long-drawn-out yelp of fake delight. Juno blushed; that had pretty much been her own MO during her long years of wanting to be London's premiere hostess. Lord, what a pathetic ambition. 'Juno, dear. Long time no hear from!'

'It has been. How are you?'

'We're just divine, sweetie. And you? I heard you split from dear Jack?'

Ellen's voice was alive with rubbernecking curiosity. She wanted to revel in Juno's misfortune. But hadn't they all been like this, all the wives on the gilded circuit? Poking over the entrails of every failed marriage, every business crash? When your life consisted of rating yourself against somebody else, *Schadenfreude* was everybody's personal favourite spectator sport.

'I did. In fact I'm in Edinburgh today to sign divorce papers,' Juno said. Thankfully, her voice was completely calm. Whatever her private pain, it was much easier to will it away when somebody else wanted to gloat. 'Jack's doing very well, he's quite the restaurateur.'

'And is he seeing anybody?'

Well, she knew how to put the high-heeled boot in.

'Yes. A young girl from a good family. I hope to meet her today,' Juno replied with amazing lightness. 'Jack and I are still on excellent terms. He's helping me with a new business I'm starting.'

'A new business!' This time Ellen's amazement was quite genuine. '*You?* You're working?'

'It's fun, it's something new,' Juno said. 'And of course it's very exclusive. I only bring things to an exceptionally small group of private clients.' She named three film stars and a German margrave.

'What? What are you doing?' Ellen was breathless with excitement. 'You know, I've often said to myself,

Ellen Amesh, you could be another Martha Stewart if you went for it.'

Juno smiled; her ex-friend saw it as a diversion, a little game like Marie Antoinette's sheep, perhaps the latest craze amongst the European wives.

'I find *very* chic properties, really boutique apartments, and rent them out to clients at the absolute top end of the market. They all have historical significance and are world-class. And there's a waiting list, so a year is the longest terms I can give.' Juno sighed. 'Most people, our friends even, simply can't afford them.'

'You think you have something for us?' Ellen asked eagerly.

'Possibly. I wanted to give you first refusal, anyway. It's a golf apartment in the Royal Mile in Edinburgh. Less than two miles from the nearest helipad out to St Andrews, but in the heart of Scottish society. It belongs to the Earl of Pitlochrie and it's been in private hands.'

'Oh my gosh, it sounds divine,' Ellen breathed. 'David would love it. But you know, Juno, I don't know if I can stand those freezing Scottish nights – he's always fighting to drag me into some draughty British castle.'

'But that's the beauty of it. This is ancient; David will adore the window seats and the coats of arms in the wood panelling. Yet the family has done it up very modern.' She ran through the inventory. 'Not even the Queen has this at Balmoral, Ellen.'

'Oooh.'

'But I should warn you. It's very expensive, probably too expensive for you.'

'How much do they want?'

I want, Juno thought. 'Ninety-six thousand. Eight grand a month. Year lease – non-negotiable.'

'Ninety-six thousand dollars?'

'Afraid not. Pounds.' Juno squared her shoulders, feeling the adrenalin pumping. 'But I really only offered it to you as a courtesy. Because I know David's taste. The Johnsons are next on the list, so if it's not for you, I understand.'

The Johnsons. Cynthia and Dwight, the Ameshes' rivals on the Eurotrash party rounds. She was the daughter of a newspaper proprietor, and he was in waste management. Cynthia infuriated David by claiming she was a Cameron.

'No, no. I want it. Definitely.' Ellen lowered her voice. 'It would be a fantastic anniversary gift for him, wouldn't it?'

'It sure would. So original. You know, he loves you because only you know him well enough to give him something truly personal like this.'

Wow, Juno thought. Listen to me, I'm a natural.

Not that it was *total* bullshit. David Amesh would love the apartment, and he would think it a thoughtful gift. They both knew the undercurrent in Juno's compliment: Ellen was David's age, and so she had to compete to keep him every year. And the soulmate card was her ace, played against any hard-bodied little mistress that he might have stacked in a rental in Hoboken.

'He will absolutely love it. Juno, I want it. Don't call the Johnsons. Fax it over to me, I'll wire the money.'

'That's terrific, Ellen.' Juno allowed herself a well-placed note of envy. 'I had no idea you could drop the whole ninety-six thousand up front.'

'It's nothing. David's a dream, gives me such a wonderful allowance,' Ellen said proudly. 'Fax the lease, Juno.'

Juno hung up, then called the agent.

'I'm not giving you ninety-six thousand. You can have seventy-eight.'

'That's less than a thousand a month,' he said, outraged.

'Yes, but it's guaranteed for the full eight years. No voids, no fuss. Seventy-eight.'

'No deal.'

'In cash,' Juno said. 'Wire-transferred this afternoon. You have to take the offer to your client, Donald. That's the law.'

As she expected, he called her back within three minutes.

'Done. But we want the money today.'

'Then get the papers to my solicitor,' Juno said.

She clicked her phone shut and sat down, elated. She'd just spent half an hour, bought a flat and rented it out for a profit of eight grand – with seven free years left on the lease. Every penny she made after that was pure, gorgeous profit.

It was an incredible feeling. Better than the afterglow of the best damn dinner party she'd ever had.

She looked at her watch. One thirty. Time to eat something, a small salad perhaps. With Scottish salmon. She wasn't hungry, but it would be no good to have her stomach rumbling this afternoon. The buzz from her deal began to fade away, and thoughts of Clement, Bai-Ling, the girls, her reality, all returned. But they meant nothing compared to what she was about to go through.

Sod it, Juno thought. I may hate this. I *do* hate this. But I don't hate myself. I'm going to survive it.

The offices of Stone, Pilkie & Fisher were exactly as Juno had imagined they'd be: low-key, but quiet and confident. They were located in a grey stone building in the Old Town, and the tartan curtains and thick pile carpet exuded a certain air of moneyed calm. Now she was here, Juno thought, it was a bit like going to the dentist: painful but necessary. The hysteria of her grief had begun to subside. Of course, that was easy to say when Jack hadn't even got there yet.

She sat in the waiting room, composed. They were late. Juno decided she would wait twenty minutes, as an apology to her ex-husband for the way she'd treated him, and then she would leave. She was not going to be pushed around. Not any more.

'Mrs Darling?'

William Pilkie, the senior partner, was Jack's solicitor. He was in his fifties, a serious-looking man, grey-haired and jowly, in a crumpled tweed suit, wearing a vintage watch and good shoes. Juno had no doubt he was preparing to fillet her like Jack working on a salmon.

'It's Ms Chambers,' Juno replied coolly. 'I have been using my maiden name since Jack left.'

'Ms Chambers. Terribly sorry to keep you waiting. My client apologises. His meeting ran late . . .'

'William!'

The door opened and a young woman walked through. She was moderately attractive, with a button nose, bright eyes and a rounded face, but extremely well groomed. Juno ran a practised eye over the sharply cut bob, the A-line woollen skirt, the immaculate cream silk shirt with little pearl buttons at the cuffs, and the discreet diamond earrings. Her feet were snugly encased in chestnut leather Armani boots. Juno knew immediately that this was Mona McAllen.

Wreathed in smiles, she came over and air-kissed the old man on both cheeks, deliberately ignoring Juno.

'Good to see you again. How are you?'

'I'm very well.' A little stiffly, he drew back and gestured towards Juno. 'Mona, this is Mrs – this is Ms Juno Chambers, Jack's soon-to-be ex-wife.'

'Oh, right,' said Mona with a bright fake smile. 'I'm Mona. Jack's girlfriend.' The tones were softly Scottish, with that clipped, upper-class accent Jack had never had. Juno stole a glance at the woman's left hand; yes, she was wearing a signet ring on the little finger of her left hand. Family crest. Jack had reverted to type, had gone for a blue-blooded girl. Just one ten years younger, and a little prettier, than Juno. 'How do you do?'

Mona extended one manicured hand and shook Juno's without enthusiasm. Then she slid into an armchair and crossed one slender leg over the other, allowing the sexy boots to dangle. Juno noticed now that she was well built, slim-waisted but with large breasts. Automatically she pressed a hand to her own chest, more conscious than ever of her small cup size.

'It's very good of you to hurry this along. Some exes put all kinds of roadblocks in the way. Jack and I are looking to get married as soon as possible.' She gave Juno a confidential little smile. 'I want to get working on those babies, you know?'

'We all want to move on, I'm sure.' Juno stiffened her back. There was a cruel light to Mona's eyes that she hated, and she determined instantly that the younger woman would not see her suffer.

'My client,' William Pilkie interrupted, 'has been delayed because his meeting is running late. It's with his bankers and extremely important – he asks for your patience, Mrs Darling, and he apologises profusely.'

Juno couldn't be annoyed if Jack was being so polite.

'That's fine,' she said. 'How long will he be?'

Mona gave a little laugh. 'Oh, isn't that Jack all around? Always making excuses. Of course his money thing with the banks is important, but what he doesn't say is that he was late to *that* because we – well, you know.' She flipped her sharply cut bob and bared white teeth. 'He's so exhausting! He really wipes me out.'

There was a rap on the door. Mr Pilkie, blushing slightly, leaped to open it. And there was Jack, wearing a killer dark suit, panting.

'I ran all the way from Princes Street.' He turned to Juno. 'I'm so sorry. Really important meeting. You're kind to wait.'

'No problem. Let's get to it, though,' Juno answered. 'I need to get back to London.'

Jack stared. 'Mona! What are you doing here?'

She pouted. 'Darling, this is about us, of course I should be here. I can fit this in between the gym and my appointment at Sassoon.'

Jack turned to Pilkie, and Juno noted the frown in his eyes.

'We thought you wouldn't mind . . . Miss McAllen asked us . . .'

'I'm just so glad this is being resolved amicably,' Mona said, with a sly glance at Juno. 'I wanted to be here for it.'

'Mona was just telling me that you couldn't drag yourself away this morning, and that's why you were late to the bank,' Juno remarked.

'What?' He turned to Mona. 'Why did you say that? You know my car had a puncture.'

'I want to be here,' Mona said, a little steel in the sweet tones.

Jack looked at Juno, who shrugged. She didn't know what to say.

'You know, Mona, I think we had better do this on our own. Juno and I were married, and this is our business really. I'll see you this evening,' Jack said.

It was a simple sentence, but absolutely final. Juno recognised that tone; when Jack was like that, you didn't argue with him.

'Oh, very well.' Mona unfolded her long legs, and flung her arms around Jack, kissing him ostentatiously on the nose. 'See you tonight then, sweetheart. Good to meet you, Juno, and thanks again for being so understanding. This will really help push our relationship forward.'

She bounced out of the door, waving at Jack with just the tips of her fingers, like an American cheerleader.

'Shall we get to business?' William Pilkie asked weakly.

'In a moment.' Jack looked over at Juno. 'I'd like a few moments alone with my wife.'

'Of course.' The older man couldn't wait to get out of there. He exited the room, closing the door quietly behind him.

'Juno. I want to apologise.'

'Your solicitor did that for you.'

'Not about being late. About Mona. She shouldn't have come here. I'm sorry.'

Juno looked him right in the face. 'She wanted to rub it in, Jack. It's human nature; she's jealous. Don't go too hard on her.'

He leaned back against the old tartan chair, a strange look on his face.

'That's not the Juno I know. Time was you'd have had her for breakfast.'

'We all change.'

'Will you tell me a little about what you've been up to?'

She challenged him. 'Why do you care?'

'I do care,' he said softly. 'Always did. And like you said, it's human nature. I'm curious.'

Juno didn't want him to leave this room feeling pity for her. She sat straight, proud in her Chanel suit. 'Fine. I've started a business, niche high-end rentals. I find places on short leases, buy them at a discount, and re-rent to businessmen, actors and so on. People who want the best and will pay for it.'

'Fascinating.' He sounded like he meant it. 'I've never heard of anything like that before. What made you get into it?'

Bai-Ling, Juno thought, but she answered, 'It was just a surge of inspiration.' She decided to tell him most of the truth. 'And I needed something to do, because of that small falling-out with my Uncle Clement.'

Jack's eyes opened, as remembrance illuminated his face. 'Of course. You've offended your uncle. That's pretty serious, isn't it?'

'I'm not going to get into the details,' Juno answered. 'But he offended us – me and Athena, and the cousins. We've jointly decided not to take any more of his money. And that means making our own way.' She managed a smile. 'Luckily I'm not bad at what I do. It's early days but I have a line of credit at the bank, an office – that's the number you rang. I may even hire a secretary. I think I'm going to be rather successful.' Damn, that felt good to say. 'And there's enough left to afford a very small house in town, so I'm happy enough.'

'Well.' Jack breathed out. 'I'd say I don't believe you, except that you're clearly serious. That's bloody wonderful, Juno. Congratulations.'

'Congratulations? I'm giving up half a million a year and goodness knows how much in inheritance.'

'Yes, but this is *yours*.' Jack leaned forward, looked her right in the face; it took her breath away. 'You've made a wonderful start. Can I ask you – do you feel better without the money?'

'No question.'

'When we split up—'

'We didn't split up. You walked out.'

He sat back, eyes dark. 'Only to stop you from throwing me out. And you know it would have happened.'

Juno sighed, defeated. 'Yes, I was thinking about it.'

'When I left, I left because of all that money. Your money – *his* money. And only when I wasn't coming to you for backing was I free. I started the restaurant with an ordinary bank loan, just by myself. And it came right. It will for you, too.'

Juno grinned. 'You're not saying the money was cursed?'

'Dependence is cursed,' Jack said, deadly serious.

'Maybe. Anyway, let's get on with this.'

'Juno.' He reached forward, grabbed her hand. The touch of his skin on hers was electric; she tried, but could not prevent the jolt of desire racing through her; shivers of energy ran across her belly and breasts, tightened her nipples. 'I want you to know I'm proud of you.'

'And I'm proud of you. In case I didn't say it.' She tried, weakly, to pull back her hand; he still held on to it. Oh God, she thought despairingly; there it was, the longing, refusing to be contained, and tears welling up in her eyes. Juno blinked, but there was no helping it. Jack saw.

He let go of her hand at once. 'What's the matter?'

Sod it, Juno thought. She wasn't to blame. It was not undignified to feel some grief.

'Jack. I'm only going to say this once. It's hard on me, all this. So please let's just get it done. You're welcome to whatever you want from our marriage.'

'Why is it hard on you?'

'Why do you think?' she asked angrily, lifting her head, not caring any more if he saw her red eyes. 'I still love you. And seeing your pretty young lass boasting about you getting married is painful.'

'*Marriage?* We've only been going out for a few months.'

Juno dabbed at her eyes. 'Really?'

'You say you still love me.' Jack grabbed her hand again. 'You didn't, you know. Didn't love me before. Wouldn't sleep with me, hardly ever. Looked down on me.'

'Maybe that's true. But I was blinded by the money.' Juno stuck up for herself, even as she dabbed the tears away with a white cotton handkerchief. 'But maybe it wasn't all me, Jack. You could have stood on your own two feet, you could have got the business going without me. After all, you did in the end. Is it wrong for a woman to want a man who's making his own money?'

He sat back. 'Perhaps not, Ju. Perhaps I was too hard on you.'

There was a rap on the door. Juno, horrified, wiped her face as quickly as she could, trying to put herself back together. The solicitor opened the door, carrying two sets of papers.

'Are we ready? Ms Chambers, these are for you . . .'

'Bugger off, William, there's a good chap,' said Jack loudly.

Pilkie lifted his head, saw Juno crying, and hastily retreated.

'Let's not sign papers today.'

'No, let's.' Juno gulped down air, calming herself forcefully. 'I don't want it dragging on.'

'Juno. Let me put it this way. You sign whatever you want. I'm not signing a goddamn thing.'

'What are you saying?'

'I can't get you out of my head. It was difficult to see you the other week. Why I was cold. Mona's a nice girl, all right, pretty and . . . nice,' he said limply.

'Suitable?'

'Suitable,' Jack admitted. 'I think I caught the snob buzz off you. Trying to get you back by finding a laird's daughter. But it wasn't the same. Look, Juno. Give me a few days. I need to see Mona, sort things with her.'

'All right.' Juno stood up. He hadn't asked her back. Not properly. But she had confessed she still loved him, and that was about all she could do right now. 'Jack, think about it. But if you still want a divorce, I need to know in a few days. You can send the papers, I'll countersign them. No more face-to-faces.'

'Fair enough. Juno . . .'

'That's all,' she said. 'Talk to you later.'

And without waiting another second, she barrelled out of the door, marching past the bewildered Mr Pilkie and out into the safety of the street.

She walked half a mile, very fast, before halting to grab a taxi.

'Airport, please.' The cabbie swung into the traffic,

chatting blithely about the weather. Thank God, Juno thought, hardly able to think straight. I have to get home to the girls.

Happiness raced through her. She wasn't divorced. Jack still cared for her. But when he got back, when he faced the scheming little Mona? Curvy Mona, younger and better-looking than Juno?

But not smarter, her brain whispered quietly. And Jack needed a strong woman. He wasn't made to be weak, or for weakness.

It wasn't perfect. He hadn't fallen into her arms. But for now, it was enough. Juno had hope again.

Chapter Twenty-Eight

The sounds were soft and rich. The clink of champagne flutes, knocked together. The whisper of the harpist she'd hired from the London Philharmonic. The popping of corks, the murmur of waitresses offering caviar and blinis or tiny parcels of dim sum. And of course, the gentle hum of all-female conversation.

Athena looked round her club and pinched herself. The palette of creams, browns and greys worked wonderfully; it was businesslike and female all at the same time. The furniture married comfortable, squashy sofas in pretty chinoiserie patterns with sleek modern desks equipped with the latest computers and AV technology. To the left, the spa room, with its massage chairs, was already fully occupied. Cleverly designed hidden lighting, presently dimmed for warmth, created spots and pools all around the room; the grand structure of the former cinema offered tons of space.

'Impressive,' said a fat woman beside her. 'Gotta admit, you did this up nicely.'

'Thank you.' Athena took a tiny sip of her rosé Dom

Perignon; she couldn't afford to get tipsy. 'And you are . . .'

Then it hit her.

'. . . saying that as a representative of the local council, which is all the more flattering,' Athena rescued herself.

Ms Maxime Chilcott was unrecognisable. The size was still there, but she was actually wearing a dress – *Ann Taylor*, Athena thought, plus size – and it fitted her quite well. The jacket added a little shape and hid the worst of her enormous bottom. And Maxime had washed her hair and was wearing it cut to the shoulders. It had been dyed chestnut. The moustache was gone, and if Athena wasn't mistaken, Maxime had put on some tinted moisturiser.

She looked, if not good, at least female. Athena blinked.

'May I say you look . . . well?'

'Hmm. Yes.' Maxime still barked it out as though it were a fact, not small talk. 'I walk half an hour to work. Lost eight pounds.'

'Great. Keep it up.'

'After you left the office, you got me thinking.' Athena could see it cost the older woman a lot to admit this, so she kept quiet. 'Maybe you can be a feminist, and it's all right to look . . . neat.'

Neat was clearly as far as Maxime would go.

'Come with me,' Athena said. She grabbed Maxime firmly by the elbow and pushed her into a well-lit corner where two women in smart suits were chatting and nibbling at her organic olives and feta cubes.

'Maxime, this is Baroness Norris – the junior minister for local government. She's looking for a chief researcher. Lady Norris, Maxime Chilcott is the chief executive here. Very talented woman. And this is Professor Helena Alphege, the art historian. She reviews for the *Standard*.'

'How do you do,' Paula Norris said. 'Athena told us you had the vision for this place.'

Maxime's pudgy face split into a broad smile, and Athena melted away. A waitress offered her caviar; she accepted a blini, it tasted good.

The whole damn party was good.

Athena breathed in, a deep sigh of pure contentment. The Bluestocking Club was everything she'd hoped for. Yes, the decor was very good, targeted right at the heart of the female movers and shakers. But none of that mattered. The internet tables, the massage chairs – they were very nice, but rich women like these could get them anywhere. What actually mattered about the Bluestocking was right in front of her, in Karl Lagerfeld shoes and Vera Wang dresses.

The women. There they were, talking animatedly to each other, and not about childcare or husbands. She had aimed for the perfect mix. There was Sue Pritchard talking shop with Meg Mortimer, the junior culture minister, and Indira Knight, the director. Across the room she saw Persephone Ratcliffe, senior bond trader at Goldman Sachs, getting her back rubbed. The property developer Kathy Conran was talking to Lucy Field, who was the England women's centre forward. Mobile phones were out, numbers were being added; wherever she looked, business cards were changing hands.

And at the front of the club, where her newly hired manager, Kirsten Fowler, poached from the Groucho, was sitting at a walnut table taking credit cards to secure membership, there was already a queue twenty women long.

The Bluestocking. A way to network. A way to beat the boys at their own game. Her subscription rolls were going to be full.

Overwhelmed with emotion, she cast her mind back to that day at Oxford, in the chilly hall, watching a panel of senior arseholes giving *her* professorship to Mike Cross, because he knew how to take part in the university's social life.

Thank God. Thank them. If Athena wanted to pursue her studies, it would be privately, for the love of learning and as a pursuit of leisure. From now on she was going to run this club. A year, she thought triumphantly, to make the Bluestocking a legend in London. And after that, what? Bluestocking New York? Bluestocking Washington? The possibilities danced in front of her. Something just for women. Something that would do good, redress the balance – and make her rich.

Uncle Clem, Athena thought, would absolutely hate it.

She glanced at her watch. The party was in full swing. She had to be the last to leave. But by nine they would all be gone. Freddie was picking her up, taking her home for a late supper. Athena found she was counting the minutes.

'How did it go?'

Athena climbed into the passenger seat of his battered BMW.

'Went fine. Go, go!'

Freddie grinned and pulled into the traffic, just in time to get out of the way of a double-decker.

'You better hope there wasn't a camera on you.'

'Who cares? I'll just pay the fine.' He glanced over at her. 'Wow, you look amazing in that dress.'

It was a clinging number from Krizia, long-sleeved and high-necked, but cut to pour itself over every curve.

'Thanks.' She stole a look at Freddie, while his rough hands spun the wheel. He was wearing slacks and a T-shirt tonight, which did absolutely nothing to hide his soldier's muscular chest. His dark hair needed a cut; it curled down towards the nape of his neck. She had an urge to play with it, to wrap the lock around her finger, lift it aside, and start licking and kissing his neck . . .

'When do I get to take you to bed?'

'What?'

'You heard me.' He kept his eyes on the road, but his

voice was thick with desire. 'I've played it straight with you, Athena. I've waited weeks. Come on. I want you. You don't have any excuses left; you're not living with your sister and your cousins any more.'

She wanted him too.

They turned the corner, and Freddie pulled into Park Street, found his building and stashed the car. Athena was grateful to be able to busy herself with getting out, wrapping her coat around herself and waiting for Freddie to fish out his keys. But the reprieve was temporary; as she walked up the stairs, she knew she was going to have to give him an answer.

Freddie pushed open the door to his flat. A one-bedroom, furnished in the old, chaotic way Athena was used to: seagrass matting on the floors, dark-wood antique furniture, a faded chintz couch, dark green velvet curtains. But it was spotlessly clean; military training, she realised at once.

The old oak table in the kitchen diner was set for two: plates, knives and forks, a beeswax candle in a Georgian silver candlestick. Freddie's attempt at sophistication.

'I ordered in,' he said, shrugging. 'Never could cook.'

'Nor me.'

'Oh dear.' That grin again. 'Mother won't approve. Not much good with a needle and thread either, I suppose.'

Athena hit him.

'There's steak, spinach and stewed apple for pudding. And a bottle of claret.'

'Sounds perfect.'

'Good, because it's bloody nine o'clock and I'm ready to eat my boots if I don't get something down.'

Athena got on with uncorking the wine while Freddie removed their dishes from his oven; they were just warm, not overdone. She poured him a glass of wine, took one herself. He lit the candle; amazing how good the flickering light made her feel. Athena watched Freddie attack his steak with gusto, devouring one mouthful after another. She took a good long gulp of the wine this time, then ate some of her own meal; the blood and juices tasted wonderful in her mouth. She felt herself relaxing, alive with relief and pleasure. When she was with Freddie, everything else just melted away.

'So. Looks like you've got a success on your hands,' he commented. 'All those women driving away from your club. Lots of expensive cars. Did they join up?'

'They did.' Athena half wanted to pinch herself. All those big names, all that money in the corporate account. Most of her debts had disappeared tonight.

'I had rather a good day too. Got planning permission to convert the stables in the second paddock to houses. We'll hive them off from the main grounds with a large wall. It's going to raise about nine hundred thousand for the estate.'

'Nine hundred thousand!' Athena was shocked. 'Freddie, that's huge.'

'Yeah, well.' He shrugged modestly, but she could see

he was delighted. 'It's not bad. Dad was pretty pleased.'

'I had no idea you were dealing in such big sums of money.'

'Don't get too excited. It all goes to Chris, remember. Although I will get some commission. Twenty thou on this deal.'

'You should have more.'

'Maybe.' He shrugged. 'It's family.'

'That doesn't always make it right. What did your brother say?'

'He was too out of it. Got wasted last night on something, spent the day in bed with a hangover, Dad says.' Freddie shook his head. 'He's an idiot.' He looked over the table at her. 'Let's skip pudding now and go to bed.'

Athena jumped back.

'What, you didn't think I was serious? I meant it.' His eyes were dark with predatory intent. 'I want you. What are you afraid of?'

An excellent question. Athena didn't know. What was she afraid of? It wasn't like she'd never had a lover. At Oxford there had been four, forgettable boyfriends. She hadn't cared much then. With Freddie, it was completely different; she was shrinking, reluctant.

'I don't know.' Honest answer.

'Because you think I won't respect you in the morning?'

It sounded ridiculous, but it hit home. 'Yes,' Athena

said, tossing her hair defiantly. 'That's pretty much it.'

'In the morning, if you remember, we're driving to Northamptonshire to meet my parents. Not exactly giving you a tenner for a cab home, am I?' Freddie was starting to get angry. 'Come on, Athena. I never wait this long for any woman. I must really like you. Or be a fool.'

'You're – you're different.'

Athena pushed her chair back, and stood up; Freddie jumped to his feet and came around towards her.

'I feel differently about you. I do. I suppose I think it might . . . might end.'

'And you don't want it to?' Freddie lowered his voice, put one strong hand on her shoulder. 'Tell me everything. Everything.'

'I started dating you really as cover. I wasn't interested. You made me get interested, fast. And now, when I'm with you, I don't want it to be over. I know it's dumb.'

'It is. I date a lot of girls.' His gaze held hers. 'Dated, I should say. They're attracted for various reasons. Some think I'm getting the estate. Some want to be Lady Wentworth. I get quite a few debs who think like that. And there are others who get turned on by a man in uniform.'

Athena mumbled that she didn't blame them, but Freddie wasn't smiling.

'Do you know how many I've brought home to meet the family? One.'

Athena hated her instantly.

'Camilla Davenport. I dated her for eighteen months. Never once did I feel for her what I feel for you. Now tell me straight out. I'm not in the mood for games. Do you want me?'

She nodded, dry-mouthed and mute.

'Want to get married, Athena?'

Athena blinked.

'You're kidding.'

'I'm not.'

'But we've only been going out for a few weeks. I have no money now, no fortune. My parents are penniless . . .'

'I couldn't give a monkey's,' Freddie said. 'We'll make it together. Or not. Whatever.' He shook his head. 'I can't believe you're worrying about me. I'm wild about you, Athena.'

She smiled. 'Are you really serious?'

'I am. Look, let's do this properly.' Freddie dropped to one knee. It wasn't the most graceful movement; Athena had a vision of him leaning forward to set up a sniper rifle. But he took her hand and kissed it. 'Will you do me the honour of becoming my wife?'

'Yes,' Athena said joyfully. 'Oh God, yes.'

'Thank God for that.' He jumped up, and in a single movement peeled off his black T-shirt; Athena was staring at a thickly muscled chest, covered in black hair, broad shoulders, strong, hard biceps. 'Let's hope you don't go for the wiry, poetic types.'

She felt her knees almost buckle with lust. He saw it written in her face, and reached forward, strong left arm around her slim waist; his right hand splayed its fingers firmly over her flat belly, feeling the warmth, the rush of blood pooling in her groin.

Athena gasped.

'Hot,' he murmured, 'literally. And now, my beauty, you're going to pay for keeping me waiting.'

And he scooped her up into his arms as though she weighed nothing, flung her over his shoulder, and carried her into the bedroom.

The offices of Artemis Studios were quite bland, Venus thought, for a place where dreams came true.

She sat across the desk from Eleanor Marshall. The most powerful woman in Hollywood. Rumour had it she'd flown into London specially for this.

'You know we want the movie.'

'Yes. Wide release,' Venus said flatly.

'Not a chance.' Eleanor leaned forward, her golden hair shot with silver streaks; wedding ring on her hand, she seemed to Venus happy and completely self-confident. It made her nervous trying to mess with Eleanor. 'The movie's great, but the production values just aren't high enough. For wide, you'd need to start over and reshoot. My experience? You lose the freshness.'

'Disney offered me wide,' Venus pointed out.

'Yes, but here's the killer.' Eleanor picked up a copy of a contract and slid it across the desk. 'We market this, you make two more movies for us. Low budget.'

'What's a low budget?'

Eleanor shrugged. 'Ten million dollars.'

'Either a percentage of the gross – real gross – or a million a movie,' Venus said.

'Three hundred a movie. We don't know what your first film's gonna do.'

'Tell you what.' Venus smiled disarmingly. 'Three hundred, unless my movie makes you twenty million dollars in gross box office receipts. Then a million five. *Per film.*'

Eleanor threw up her hands. 'Done.'

Venus breathed in. 'Send me the amended contract.'

She got to her feet, hoping she could walk steadily out of the door. This was amazing, one of the best moments of her life. And she wanted to get out of here, call Diana, her cousins, share it with the girls. Screw Uncle Clem. Who bloody needed him?

Of course she had believed in herself, believed in the movie. But it was different when you actually signed the deal and it all came true.

'Would you like to go have lunch, celebrate? This is a wonderful movie,' Eleanor said. 'For a first-timer, it's truly impressive. I don't think it'll make twenty million, but it's not going to be long for you, I can see that.'

'Thanks. But no,' Venus told her. 'Some other time.'

'You already have plans?'

Venus smiled slightly. 'Yes, ma'am. I'm going to have lunch with Hans Tersch.'

The Bluebird was crowded but Venus hardly noticed. She walked up to the hostess, prepared to wait.

'He's already here.' The girl smiled at her. 'Let me show you to the table.'

Tersch was sitting in a corner, screened away from the public; Venus felt her heart start to thump. Oh hell. Her palms were sweating. She wanted to check her make-up, but there was no time. Last time she'd seen Hans, she had been dressed perfectly, beautifully, at Juno's garden party for Bai-Ling; this time, Venus Chambers was wearing a brisk, businesslike trouser suit, her generous breasts hidden under a silk poloneck and well-cut L. K. Bennett jacket. Instead of towering heels with two-inch spikes, she wore practical, elegant chocolate leather boots; instead of loose blond hair and scarlet lipstick, she had a slick ponytail and neutral Bobbi Brown blusher, with nothing on her mouth but a slick of clear gloss. She wore a gold Cartier tank watch and carried a Coach briefcase. She imagined she'd look like an investment banker.

'Your guest is here, sir.'

'Thank you,' he said. The hostess melted away, and Tersch got to his feet. He wore a blue pinstriped shirt, no tie, under a very dark navy suit. Right next to him, Venus felt instantly how big he was, the sheer physical size of him; she blushed, disturbed, and was glad of her solid layers of clothing; Hans could not see the signs that she was turned on.

'Good to see you,' she said, as firmly as she could.

He tilted his head, slightly amused, and indicated that she should sit down. Venus did so immediately, then cursed herself. Tersch was not her boss. She was no longer an actress desperately hoping for favours. You're a producer, girl, Venus told herself. Act like it.

'I saw the print,' he said.

She blushed a little deeper. 'It was supposed to be secret.'

'Very little in this business stays secret from me.' He looked her over, his green eyes sweeping across her body assessingly. 'If I want a print, I get it.'

'And?' Venus couldn't help it; she ached for his approval.

Tersch nodded. 'For a first effort, not bad.'

She sat bolt upright. 'Not bad? My movie is *brilliant*.'

'No. It's quite good. You should make a decent profit on it.' He smiled slightly. 'This is not an insult. I meet thirty producers every week, rich brats who buy lousy scripts and print off a business card. You, on the other hand, have made a releaseable movie with a strong story and a good star.'

'She is good, isn't she?' Venus felt she was on more solid ground. 'You almost crushed her.'

Hans shrugged. 'She was a tigress when I started the affair. I had no idea she would grow attached.'

'You use women,' Venus hissed, lowering her voice.

'No. I *enjoy* women. And I know how to bring them great pleasure.' Hans mercilessly held Venus's eyes, as her stomach did a slow churn of desire. He grinned, and she bit down hard on her cheek to prevent herself gasping with longing. 'As you remember, I see.'

'You're such a bastard. Don't you know you broke Lilly's heart?'

'She was young and high.' He shook his head. 'Too young, possibly. Yes, I learned something about women. It was, however, your fault.'

Venus blinked. 'What?'

'Your fault. I acted wrongly, out of a desire for revenge. On women; on actresses. You must shoulder some blame.'

'You're kidding.' Venus lowered her voice and leaned in to him. 'I slept with you, you turned me inside out . . . it was amazing. And then the next day, you spat in my face. Making me audition for the older woman's part, not even giving it to me. You used me, Hans Tersch.'

'I used you? Amusing. You and I were good together. Very good. I wanted to see you. But when I woke up, you had simply left the house. I paid you the compliment, Venus, of not treating you like a hooker. You were auditioned for the only part I'd ever had in mind.' His tone was calm. 'If you thought it was for the lead, you were mistaken; you should recall that you never asked. And I didn't hire you because you weren't the best actress. You see, you failed that audition. You are angry because you think that fucking me was your audition. And angry because I had a little more respect for you than that.' He paused. 'So tell me, *Fräulein*, who was using who?'

Venus sat back, stunned. She had never thought of it like that, never seen it like that. And suddenly it all came hard on her, in a rush, and she was overwhelmed with a deep sense of shame. She felt her skin blush beetroot red to the tips of her ears.

'You walked out. And you did not call me. I was a little tired of being seen by hungry actresses as a walking ticket to stardom.' He leaned back. 'So it was easy to amuse myself with little Lilly, when she reached for me. And I knew it would unsettle you.'

Venus took a drink of mineral water to cover herself. A waiter approached; Tersch dismissed him with a wave of his hand.

'I – I never thought of it like that.' She was dying of embarrassment; she wanted nothing more than to run away. 'Hans. I'm sorry.'

'Don't worry,' he said evenly, and the hunter's gaze was back. 'You are going to make it up to me.'

Venus shifted on her seat. She wanted him again, instantly, badly. But not like before. She couldn't bear to be a one-night stand. For a second, her heart was full of pity for Lilly Bruin. This was Lilly's worst fear, and Venus was going to make it come true. She needed to be more than Hans Tersch's lay of the moment. She needed to be his woman.

'What did you think of the directing—'

'Don't try and talk shop with me.' He cut her off. 'I have waited for this. We'll eat something, then I'll take you to my house, and I'm going to have you. For hours. I'm going to put you through your paces.'

'No,' Venus said, dry-mouthed. 'I've got no intention of jumping into bed with you again, Hans.'

'So you want what? To marry me?'

She smiled. 'Only if you prove yourself good enough.'

He looked at her, startled. 'You are an amazing female. No woman has ever defied me like this. You did wreck one of my movies. By rights, I should destroy you.' He grinned. 'But I have thought about you too.'

'You'll have to earn the right to a serious relationship with me.' Venus lifted her head proudly. 'I'm an independent woman, Hans. I signed a two-movie deal today, guarantee of three hundred a film, maybe more. For Artemis. I'm a real producer now.'

He stared at her, not sure if she was for real.

'Very well, Venus Chambers. Will you go out with me?'

Venus picked up her glass of wine merrily, and took a sip.

'I'll think about it,' she said.

And she really wasn't sure. Either way, it felt incredibly good to have the choice.

*

'So let me walk you through it, Mrs Freedman. Do have a seat.'

Betty-Lou lowered her ample butt into the carved armchair Diana had set up by her computer. She tapped a few buttons, and the screen sprang into life; a clever little movie, a computer simulation, began to scroll across the screen.

'Your look is going to be antique, as requested, but strictly in the American vernacular.' Diana leaned across her client. 'Everything here will complement the pre-war age of the building, but I'm taking advantage of your high ceilings and natural light to go further. Your apartment will be truly antique – but not in the way so many society ladies do it, importing Louis Quatorze chairs and Chippendale sideboards. It's very tired to try to recreate a Rothschild drawing room in Manhattan. No. Your place will be unique – Victorian American. We're going for the days when Harlem was still farmland, and New York had gas lights and horse-drawn carriages.'

'Oooh,' Betty-Lou said, thrilled. 'When you were talking I didn't much care for it, but now I see. Ooh, yes. That looks divine . . .'

'Authentic paint colours, contemporary to the period. Wallpaper as well. And the mirrors, furnishings, Persian rugs, are all as you might find in a Victorian American home. Complete with portraits of Presidents Lincoln, Grant, and Teddy Roosevelt. Who was a New Yorker.'

Diana was proud of the look; it was so authentic. 'But you must tell your husband that he's not to worry. Underneath your elegant skin I have built in every modern appliance and comfort. Full underfloor heating, central vac, security systems, central air, remote-control flat-screen TVs, everything. They are completely concealed.'

Betty-Lou clapped her fat hands. 'I love it! I do. Love it.'

'If you want me to proceed on this basis, I need approval. And the fee, of course.' Diana slid a contract under Betty-Lou's nose; the woman signed it at once.

'You aren't doing this for anybody else, are you?' she pleaded.

'No, ma'am. All my designs are unique,' Diana reassured her.

'Then I'll wire the cash today.' Betty-Lou smiled triumphantly. 'My friends are going to adore it!'

There was a knock on the office door.

'Probably the post. Excuse me.'

'That's fine, I was just leaving.' Betty-Lou hoisted herself up and grabbed her handbag. 'Got a light lunch with a friend.'

Somehow Diana doubted it was going to be all that light, but she smiled pleasantly. 'Have fun, Mrs Freedman, and see you in New York.'

She showed her client to the door, and opened it for her.

And gasped.

It wasn't the postman standing outside. It was Karl Roden.

'Ohmigod,' Betty-Lou squealed. 'Karl, Karl Roden! How divine to see you!'

Diana bit back a smile; Karl looked over Betty's red head, his eyes desperately signalling to her for help.

'Karl, you remember Betty-Lou Freedman,' she said. 'Bobby Freedman, her husband, works for Texaco in Dallas. You met at that business convention there.'

'Well of course I remember *that*,' Roden said, and Diana loved the smile in his voice. But he was kind, not mocking the older woman, taking her hand as warmly as a politician. 'I want to congratulate you on working with Diana Chambers. She's invaluable to me.'

'I know, she's adorable. We must get together some-time!' Betty-Lou trilled. 'Well, I'll let you get to your appointment. It's good to know my designer is in such demand!'

Betty-Lou swayed off to her car, where her chauffeur was waiting, and Karl Roden shut the door.

'Thank you for that.'

'You're welcome.' Diana smiled; Betty-Lou had saved her from an awkward moment. She was ready now, not blushing, properly composed. 'Why have you come?'

'You know why. I have to go back to New York.'

Diana shrugged, as nonchalantly as she could. 'I

already agreed to go out with you. You're in Europe often enough.'

'Diana. I want more. Seeing you like this is good, but I want more, a lot more. It's my nature.' He reached for her, pulled her to him, pressing himself on her, her lips taken in a strong kiss; she responded instantly, the heat welling in her. 'I want you to move in with me.'

'Not a chance. Your live-in girlfriend? I'm a bit old for that,' Diana said.

Karl frowned. 'I can't move to London, honey. Ninety per cent of my business is still domestic. Come live with me. I can't get enough of you. Let's stop dancing around what your cousins think, what society thinks. You do your own thing.'

'I do,' Diana said proudly.

'And I know you like me.' He put his lips to her neck, nuzzling it, teasing her, his teeth on her earlobes. 'Even if you tried not to.'

'I do,' she answered, turning in to him, kissing him. 'I do like you. And I like my new job, too. Particularly since as of next week, it's taking me to New York.'

'But Betty-Lou's a Texan.'

'Her apartment is in Manhattan.' Diana beamed. 'Best place in the world for a designer to work. I plan to rent somewhere, build a client list, build a reputation. And maybe let you take me out to dinner. Now and then.'

'I won't date you in secret, Di, because you have some fucked-up complex about your uncle.'

'You won't have to.' Diana smiled softly. 'Believe me. I could not care less what Uncle Clem is doing. He doesn't get to control us any more.'

Chapter Twenty-Nine

The jet dipped. Clement leaned back in his seat, not bothering with a seatbelt. None of his staff said a word. They knew better. The caviar, the fruit and the lapsang souchong served in bone-china cups had all been cleared away; his chauffeur would be waiting, the limousine fully stocked, the London house in Mayfair prepared.

The plane juddered slightly as the wheels made smooth contact with the tarmac. Nothing rattled or shook. Clement employed the finest pilots in the world, ex-US Special Forces. Unless there was a serious storm, his jets landed like a down feather floating on to a bed.

'Welcome to London, sir. Passport control is waiting on the tarmac, as is the buggy to drive you to the limousine. Your cases will follow later. We hope you had a pleasant journey, Mr Chambers.'

Pleasant? No. Oh, the cashmere blankets and good-looking young stewards had been fine. Everything perfectly acceptable. But he expected that. It was the rest of it, the anticipation, the heartburn, that had wrecked it for Clement.

But he was here now. And it was time to lay down the law. He wondered how the girls had been, waiting for him to come. Conniving witches, the four of them. Ungrateful brats. So what if he had played a few games to amuse himself in his decline? So what if he had dealt roughly with a whore? Bai-Ling had been well paid for the times she'd shared his bed. More money for that two-bit trick than she'd ever seen in her life.

His mind wandered from his nieces and on to the girl for a second. Her hard, whorish survivor's edge, her petty cunning, had interested him, at least momentarily. But not to the extent of indulging her rebellion. When dismissed, she had to go quietly. She thought she had a keen weapon, and it was true; he was not about to be embarrassed. The breaking of the fake engagement had been announced quietly, in all the right papers. Bai-Ling thought that was an end of it, that she could move in society now, established as his ex-fiancée, with some of his money to launch her career. He would see her on the arm of some multi-millionaire in Nice, floating through the gossip columns and celebrity magazines.

No way. No one disrespected Clement Chambers and got away with it. Bai-Ling would be taken out, and in such a way that her contacts never broke their silence. First his men would find out exactly whom she'd been talking to. And then . . .

There were a million ways to do it. Clement could not care less. A yachting accident, a car crash, an overdose.

Every one utterly plausible. He had men at Interpol who would just go through the motions in any investigation.

His life had taught him one lesson.

Everybody was for sale.

Everybody.

He stood up and walked to the plane door; three of his favourite young air stewards were there to assist him down. As the door hissed open, Clement turned to Angela Kirschner, his new senior assistant, ex-secretary to the Chancellor of Germany, fifty years old, discreet, efficient and ruthless.

'Get hold of my nieces. They have left the house in Notting Hill and tried to scatter. Track them down. Ensure they are all at the Mayfair offices of my lawyers at four p.m.'

'Yes, sir.' Frau Kirschner did not ask how it was to be done. It would simply be done.

'And tell the lawyers to cancel every other appointment for today. Starting now, they are to expel every other client from the office. I do not want so much as a messenger boy to have admittance. The firm is for the exclusive use of me and my family.'

'Yes, sir. Absolutely.'

Clement walked down the metal steps on the arm of the handsomest of his cabin crew. The warm, specially designed airport buggy was waiting for him at the foot of the steps; his staff saluted as he descended, as if he was the King of England.

The steward smiled flirtatiously, but Clement was in no mood. He allowed himself to be assisted into the buggy. Time to go to the house, sleep a little. He wanted to be absolutely fresh when he met the girls. Not for the first time, he cursed the age and slowness of his body.

His mind, however, was still razor sharp. And Clement Chambers was not about to be outfoxed by a bunch of spoiled bitches.

Athena looked out of the window at the rolling English countryside. Man, she felt better as soon as she got out of London. Was it that, or was it . . .

She glanced across at Freddie, his eyes on the road, humming merrily to himself. Engaged! She couldn't wait to tell the girls. But his parents, her parents must come first. Since he'd actually proposed, they'd changed their plans; cancelled Farnsworth, and now Freddie was barrelling down the M25 towards the A21, Sussex, and home.

Marcus and Emily were going to get the shock of their lives.

Her phone went off.

'Don't answer it,' Freddie said.

'Might as well. I can't do much with you while you're driving.' Her display said 'Private Number'. Which was most of the Bluestocking's new membership, her banker, and her suppliers. Athena punched the button.

'Listen to me, Ms Chambers. This is Frau Kirschner,' a

voice said, crisply and arrogantly. 'I work for Clement Chambers.'

Athena rolled her eyes. 'Sorry to hear it.'

'Your uncle demands you meet him at four o'clock in the offices of White and Martin in Mayfair. You know the address, I believe.'

Of course she knew it. That firm administered the trust. Athena bristled at the rudeness of the woman, ordering her around as though she were dirt.

'He can demand all he likes. I can't see him, I'm afraid. Tell him I'm visiting my parents.'

'He said you would say something of the kind.' Frau Kirschner's voice was cold with menace. 'He says to tell you to be there – or he will have your parents evicted. He has bought the company which owns Boswell House. I take it that means something to you.'

Athena paled and hung up.

Freddie looked sharply at her. 'What's the matter?'

'We have to get back to London,' was all Athena said.

'Be there. Four o'clock.'

Juno tried to be polite. Her uncle, after all, had given her millions of pounds. Yes, he was an arsehole. But she didn't yet feel the need to humiliate him in front of his staff. He was cut off from the family, and that was punishment enough.

'*Gnädige Frau*,' Juno said carefully, 'my uncle doesn't seem to understand that there has been a final family breach. He cannot order me anywhere. I have work to do this afternoon.' And Jack wanted to see her for dinner, she didn't add. He'd flown back from Scotland – without Mona.

'No. It is you who do not understand, Mrs Darling. I have spoken already to your sister. Clement wants you to know that your parents will be evicted if you do not come. You do not want that.'

Juno blinked. 'Evicted? My father Marcus is his brother.'

There was no change in Frau Kirschner's tone.

'Be there at four o'clock. I tell him yes?'

A strange feeling welled up in Juno's heart: rage, sheer rage.

'Tell him yes,' she said.

Diana was packing when the call came. Not much; she would buy what she needed in Manhattan. Just a few favourite dresses and a long silk coat . . .

'Diana Chambers,' she said gaily. 'And make it quick, I'm off to the airport.'

'You're not going anywhere, Ms Chambers,' said a woman rudely. 'You have an appointment with your uncle.'

Diana listened to the woman issue her ultimatum, and laughed.

'Your boss has *nothing* to do with me, Mrs Kirschner. With all due respect to yourself, please tell him to get lost.'

'You will come,' Frau Kirschner insisted, 'or your sister Venus will suffer.'

Diana froze. The woman didn't sound like she was joking. 'Suffer, how do you mean suffer?'

'Do you want to find out?'

Diana felt sick.

'Don't do anything stupid,' she replied. 'I'll be there.'

Venus was sitting in her new flat off the King's Road, idly flicking through scripts and trying to focus. Her unruly, frustrated body was on fire. Hans had let her go, finally, but not before hauling her close for a deep kiss, letting her feel his body, his strength, impressing on her all the memories of the first time he'd bedded her.

Her concentration was shot to pieces.

She smiled. A small revenge, but one he'd obviously enjoyed very much . . .

Three hundred thousand dollars. A hundred and fifty grand. Not half a mil, but all her own, and all the sweeter.

She shook herself, trying to snap out of it. Venus was determined that her first major studio movie would make Eleanor Marshall's reputation – again.

Start from the beginning, she lectured herself. Find a great script . . .

Her phone rang.

'Venus Chambers?' a voice asked.

'I am.'

'Stop whatever you are doing,' the voice ordered flatly. 'You are to drive to central London. This is your Uncle Clement's personal assistant. You're summoned to a meeting—'

'I'm sorry. I have nothing to say to my uncle,' Venus replied, hanging up.

Her phone rang again.

'A business proposition, Ms Chambers. Your uncle has the power to ensure your first film never reaches the cinemas. He wants you in his solicitor's offices at four p.m.'

'My uncle can go fuck himself,' Venus said. 'Be sure and tell him that from me, miss.'

'Your cousins and your sister will be there. They apparently understand the danger you do not. They want to see you at the meeting.' The woman's tone was firm. 'It is extremely important, Miss Chambers. I do hope you come.'

'If the girls are there, then I'll come. But I'm going to call them first.' Venus was filled with contempt. 'Now pass on that message to my uncle. I mean every word.'

She hung up again. But she knew she would be there. Like Bai-Ling, it was not an encounter the girls could skip.

Clement sat in his lawyer's offices, behind the senior partner's desk. Why the hell not? They were really his offices, paid for out of his fees.

'Mr Chambers.' Hyman White, the senior partner, an accomplished QC, entered the room. Knocking first, of course. Clement permitted no disrespect. 'Your nieces are here to see you, sir.'

Clement looked up. 'Show them in.'

He held the door open, that flunky, and then the four girls walked in. How they must hate that he had brought them together. Again. It was just like Christmas . . .

Juno led the way. Athena, Venus and Diana followed behind her. Without a word, they sat as one in the four chairs that were provided.

'Go, Hyman.' Clement dismissed him. 'See to it that we're not disturbed.'

Clement surveyed them. The so-called fabulous Chambers girls. Fabulous only because of *his* money.

Marcus's girls. Rupert's girls. The products of those bland little marriages, his brothers with their small, conventional lives. He had never married. For years, the girls, growing up in England, had bothered him like an ulcer; an open wound. His bloody brothers. No guts. No glory. But the ability not to shoot blanks.

They both had families. Successors. And he had nothing. Clement had looked on the four pretty women, and gnawed on them, deep in his soul. What his brothers had, he could never have. Not all of your money, Marcus had told him. Not all of your money can buy family.

Well. He would see about that.

He had bought them. Rupert and Hester were dead, and Marcus and Emily, although hating him, would not stand in the way of their daughters' prospects. So, all innocently, Clement had established the trust. How easy, how simple it had been to bring them into his orbit. A little money, a little greed, and they were jumping, just like everybody else; blind to their parents' discomfort and the way they needled each other. And they became lazy, and indolent, and dependent.

He'd enjoyed the idea of Bai-Ling. Messing with the girls when they got a little too comfortable. Showing his holier-than-thou brother just how his precious family would leap to rip itself apart.

That they had defied him – all of them – enraged him. His puppet bride – she would be taken care of. But the refusal of the girls, Rupert's girls, Marcus's girls, to obey him . . .

That was bitter. That was the failure of twenty years' grooming. They were turning on him, turning on his generosity. And preferring the tiny amounts they could make on their own to the luxurious flow of his money.

They were even spurning his inheritance. Clement burned, he burned deeply. It was his brothers' rejection, all over again. And this meeting, right now, was the key point. He was sick. And he wanted to be absolutely certain that he could control the girls, in death, as he had controlled them in life.

They were important. They bore his name. They were

designated as his heirs. He had decided to take them from his brothers, his smug, self-righteous brothers.

They could not say no.

If they did, he would lose. The ultimate, longest fight. The one he had waged with his own brothers. The girls were *his* family now. Even as the rage crystallised in his chest, Clement Chambers fought to control himself. He was at his best when challenged. He would make his nieces fall into line.

'You came.' Clement was calm. 'I knew you would.'

'Uncle Clem.' Juno spoke up. 'We aren't here because of your threats.'

'Juno.' He made his voice impassive, with a great effort. 'I have sustained you, and your sister and cousins, for over fifteen years. At the very least you owe me the courtesy of listening.'

The girls glanced at each other, and Clement saw the hesitation. Good. He had wrong-footed them. Juno was looking at him suspiciously, but then she had always been a clever girl. More so than her sister, who was the academic. Juno, he thought, had the real hard shell. In his house, she had always taken the lead.

Juno nodded. 'Very well.'

The other three followed suit. He bit back a smile. How easy it was to get them to fall into their patterns.

'Perhaps I've been hasty.' Clement spoke softly, in the voice that was reedy with age, the one they all knew so well. 'You've had a shock. We all have. I'm guilty,' he added, watching the surprise cross their pretty faces. 'I felt so betrayed by Bai-Ling that anger caused me to explode.'

'And is that why you threatened my parents?' Athena asked, icy cold.

'I never threatened anyone.' The girls, enraged, started to rebuke him, but Clement held up one gnarled hand. 'Hear me out. I understand my staff have been throwing their weight around. When I told them to get you here, any way they could, they took that literally, I'm afraid. I never sanctioned any threats against members of my family. The people responsible will be fired.'

Venus looked at her sister and cousins.

'We don't want anybody to lose their jobs. But Uncle Clem, I'm afraid I don't believe you.'

'And nor do I,' Diana added clearly. 'The woman who called me this morning was passing on your orders, Uncle Clem. I don't believe she made it up herself.'

He shifted on his seat. 'Girls, I'm not the first old man with money who's been taken advantage of. Perhaps I was foolish, I trusted too much. I allowed my bodily lusts to rule my head. Yes, I am guilty of that. Do you want to cast me out for ever for it?'

Diana started to reply, but Juno held up one cool hand.

'I want you to be my heirs, girls.' Now for the kill. 'Forget Bai-Ling. Forget this year. It's history. It's past.'

He smiled at them, a mesmerising smile, and a little of his young charisma came back. 'We must move forward, as a family. Now, this year you have all proved that you are able businesswomen. It's quite a range of talent, isn't it?' He let his rheumy eyes rest on each girl individually, singling her out. Back in the Seychelles, they had jostled for that honour.

'Juno. A property mogul, a bottom-fisher in a unique market. You've made your own business model. Most impressive.'

Juno returned his gaze, as solemn as a statue.

'Athena. The Bluestocking Club. You're making a loss, but not for long, I expect. It's an impressive client list.'

Marcus's younger girl insolently studied her finger-nails; he filed the insult away, for future vengeance, and went on as though nothing had happened. 'Venus Chambers, film producer. A pick of the future. We have a stake in several studios, Venus. Did you know that? And Diana. Corporate design for hotels and very rich men. You might remodel Chambers offices around the globe; it would keep you and a team of a hundred staff busy for a year.'

Comfortable, now, with their silence, Clement steepled his fingers.

'This year has been a test. A test of your strength. And your loyalty. I am here today to tell you you passed. You are no longer going to be my heirs.' He paused for dramatic effect. 'You are going to be my *partners*. As of

527

today, I propose to sign over to all of you a five per cent interest in the group. You will all be vice-presidents.'

The Chambers girls looked at each other. Five per cent? That was about eighty million dollars apiece.

Clement preened. He saw the greed, saw the ambition in their eyes. Yes! They were back under the thumb.

'There are conditions,' he said easily. 'Of course.'

'What conditions?' Diana asked slowly.

'Well, that the business comes before family obligations. You see, girls, I always told your fathers it did.'

'Fathers?' Diana enunciated the plural. 'You spoke to Daddy?'

Clement smiled, a lazy, triumphant smile.

'Eighty-eight million dollars of your own, Diana, in exchange for a slice of reality. I hate sentimentality. Your father and mother were passengers in my car the day they died.'

Venus stumbled towards her sister, clutched her. Her eyes filled instantly with tears.

'Oh, don't be melodramatic,' he said with casual contempt. 'I didn't kill them deliberately. It was an accident. It just suited me not to have it publicised.'

There was a stunned silence.

'You didn't tell us,' Diana whispered. 'We thought Daddy was drunk.'

'We grew up thinking he got drunk that day,' Venus repeated numbly.

Clement shrugged. 'He didn't. And I don't think he'd complain about the way I have looked after his daughters. I'm offering you now the better part of a hundred million.'

'The conditions,' Athena said slowly.

Of course. They wanted to bargain.

'You will split up. You will leave England. You will all be posted in different areas of the globe. The boyfriends will have to go – I demand complete loyalty. Of course, after I'm dead you can do as you choose.'

'And that's your offer?' Diana said. And to his fury, she started to laugh. 'Oh, Uncle Clem. You're sick. And you're a total idiot. None of us is interested.'

Clement sputtered. 'You think you can defy me?'

'It's not a matter of think,' Venus said. She was furious, suddenly. This man – this *monster*! – had killed her parents. 'The other girls are too kind to you. You need your arse kicked. You're a racist, and a sexist, and I'm embarrassed to be related to you. If you want to get back into this family, you'll need to prove yourself. Do you get that, Clement? You have a long way to go to come back.'

'Let's see,' Juno said. She held up her hand and ticked the items off. 'Make Bai-Ling a payment. Donate half your worth to charity. Apologise to Dad and Mum.'

He stared at them, goggle-eyed.

'You are not serious? I am worth six billion dollars. I am one of the richest men in the world. Under the will you are my heiresses, but that can change, at any time.'

'Change it now,' Diana said, recovering herself. 'We don't need your money.'

'That is not all.' He raised his voice. 'You think you can develop businesses? I can crush you all like insects, every one of you. I can buy the bank that holds Athena's loan, just to call it in. I can evict her and Juno's parents. I can destroy your film, Venus: it would take a single phone call and no cinema would exhibit it. And Diana? I can have you portrayed as a cheap whore in the press of every capital in the world. Try getting commissions then.' His eyes darkened. 'Six billion buys a lot of power, girls. Ask yourselves if you want to be looking over your shoulders for the rest of your lives. Bai-Ling will, and it won't save her. Give her a payment? And you call *me* mad.'

Juno stood. 'I've heard enough. Let's leave.'

'We gave him a chance,' Diana said. 'He can't be helped.'

They stood as one, and Juno instinctively reached out her hand to Venus, who took Athena's, and she linked to Diana; his four nieces, not hating each other – *loving* each other, he realised with total shock.

'Uncle Clem.' Juno, the eldest, formerly his favourite, spoke loudest. 'You *have* provided for us for years. We used you for money, and I'm truly sorry for that. Maybe one day we can start again as a family. But you have to learn you cannot control us. Not one of us will ever take your money again. Change your will; we're not your puppets.'

'You are!' he screamed. The holier-than-thou stuff about family hurt, it made his head ache, it brought up bad thoughts . . . 'Get out! Get out!'

Athena reached into her jacket pocket. To his horror, she brought out a digital dictaphone. She touched it, and his voice came pounding back at him.

'We leave here, and this goes to the police and every major paper in Britain. Sorry, Uncle Clem, but I don't trust you. You're right, we shouldn't have to look over our shoulders.'

He staggered to his feet, wanting to hurt her, now, before she defied him, before she did anything . . .

The rush of blood was sudden, his heart pounding, and suddenly it was hard to breathe, and the pain was there, stabbing him . . .

Terror filled him. He staggered forward, looking at them, looking at them to triumph, to hate him. But Juno ran forward, the cousins behind her, and caught him, and he was in her arms, the darkness rushing up . . .

'Uncle Clem. I forgive you,' she said, and kissed him on his withered forehead. In the background he could hear Venus screaming, 'Help!'

'We forgive you,' Diana said, sobbing, and Athena reached out, and stroked his cheek with infinite tenderness, and for one clear, godly moment he was sorry, so sorry . . .

And then the darkness came, and that was all he knew.

Epilogue

It was a magnificent funeral.

Juno employed all her powers of persuasion. The burial of Clement Chambers became one of the social events of the year. Behind the genuinely grieving Marcus, and the four nieces, sat the better half of London society. There were enough dukes and marquises for a minor royal wedding, accompanied by titans of industry, senior politicians, and hundreds of thrusting socialites, all dressed in the most elegant raven-hued skirt suits, with brooches of jet and black pearls.

Clement would have loved it. Small crowds lined the route of the funeral procession as his cortège was driven through the City of London; below the glittering glass fronts of the towering offices where his fortune had been made and traded, his ebony coffin, embossed with gold, was drawn by six milk-white stallions, plumes of black feathers nodding in the wind. The society photographers were out in force, both at the church and along Clement's final journey. He was buried in the undercroft of All Hallows by the Tower, the oldest church in the City of

London, after Juno made a colossal donation. The send-off was dignified and inexpressibly chic.

The four Chambers nieces, of course, in their stylish funeral dresses, looked amazingly beautiful. Bai-Ling flew back to London at once on hearing the news; there was a silent pact between herself and the girls. Not a word was said, and as the grieving fiancée, she led the mourners, impossibly gorgeous in a long coal-black velvet dress with a matching coat. She was decorous, and occasionally touched an antique lace handkerchief to her eyes. After the ceremony, the girls briskly shook her hand. She stepped directly into a limousine, and left for the airport.

Clement Chambers never had time to change his will. It named the four Chambers girls as heiresses of the estate, with Juno inheriting the greater portion.

Venus wanted to give it all away, but Juno forbade her.

'Money's just money,' she said. 'It was only cursed when it controlled us.'

They found Bai-Ling Wuhuputri was not mentioned in the will, and settled ten million dollars upon her. She immediately ceased dating a Greek shipping magnate twenty years her senior and started to invest in Floridian apartment buildings.

Venus put her money in mutual funds and lives off the interest; she is producing movies and seems unconcerned about finance.

Diana stopped being a designer. It seemed pointless with her level of wealth. She married Karl Roden and works full-time on charity, which she likes even more than redoing all his properties.

Juno is still rediscovering her marriage with Jack. They have moved back in, her wedding ring is back on and they each complain the other is a workaholic.

Athena, Lady Frederick Wentworth, had a glittering society wedding. With her husband's help she purchased an enormous estate in Derbyshire, which he runs while she works at the Bluestocking. Her parents are still living at Boswell, thanks to their daughters.

They are all very happy. The Chambers girls are known to be a tight-knit family.

Now you can buy any of these other bestselling books by **Louise Bagshawe** from your bookshop or *direct from the publisher*.

FREE P&P AND UK DELIVERY
(Overseas and Ireland £3.50 per book)

Glamour	£6.99
Sparkles	£7.99
Tuesday's Child	£7.99
Monday's Child	£7.99
The Devil You Know	£7.99
When She Was Bad . . .	£7.99
A Kept Woman	£7.99
Venus Envy	£7.99
Tall Poppies	£7.99
The Movie	£7.99
Career Girls	£7.99

TO ORDER SIMPLY CALL THIS NUMBER

01235 400 414

or visit our website: www.headline.co.uk

Prices and availability subject to change without notice.